*Look what people are saying
about this talented author...*

"Both the physical and wartime action
between the comrades ramp up the excitement
in this Uniformly Hot! tale."
—*RT Book Reviews* on *Coming Up for Air*

"A quick pace and easy chemistry
make for an engaging read,
starring a couple readers will root for."
—*RT Book Reviews* on *No Going Back*

"Sexy characters that you
just can't help but fall in love with!"
—*Night Owl Reviews* on *Devil in Dress Blues*

"The romance is intense and sure to please."
—*RT Book Reviews* on *Hot-Blooded*

"Wonderful, sexy characters and an exciting,
innovative story make this a winner!
4 1/2 Stars, Top Pick"
—*RT Book Reviews* on *Flyboy*

Dear Reader,

I've always been fascinated by stories about coal miners. Maybe it's because my great-grandfather lost his dad and his four brothers in a coal-mining disaster. Or maybe it's because I'm constantly amazed by the coal miner's indomitable spirit, courage and resilience. And—I'll admit it—there's something incredibly sexy about a guy who's not afraid to get dirty.

Like my heroine, I'm a little claustrophobic and afraid of the dark, so I'm truly in awe of the men and women who willingly descend hundreds of feet below the earth's surface every day, away from the sunlight, in order to support their families. When I decided to write a story about a coal miner, I knew he had to have that same strength and heroic spirit.

Cole MacKinnon is a true hero, willing to put his job, his reputation and his heart on the line for what he believes in. And he believes in Lacey Delaney, the brilliant design engineer who is determined to push him to his breaking point. She's spent most of her life trying to conquer her own fears, but it's not until she meets Cole that she realizes some of the best things happen in the dark….

I hope you enjoy Cole and Lacey's story!

Happy reading,

Karen Foley

Karen Foley

A KISS IN THE DARK

&

FLYBOY

H HARLEQUIN®
entertain, enrich, inspire™

ISBN-13: 978-0-373-79725-7

A KISS IN THE DARK

Copyright © 2012 by Harlequin Books S.A.

The publisher acknowledges the
copyright holder of the individual works
as follows:

A KISS IN THE DARK
Copyright © 2012 by Karen Foley

FLYBOY
Copyright © 2007 by Karen Foley

Recycling programs
for this product may
not exist in your area.

CONTENTS

ABOUT THE AUTHOR

Karen Foley is an incurable romantic. When she's not working for the Department of Defense, she's writing sexy romances with strong heroes and happy endings. She lives in Massachusetts with her husband and two daughters, an overgrown puppy and two very spoiled cats. Karen enjoys hearing from her readers. You can find out more about her by visiting www.karenefoley.com.

Books by Karen Foley

To get the inside scoop on Harlequin Blaze and its talented writers, be sure to check out blazeauthors.com.

All backlist available in ebook. Don't miss any of our special offers. Write to us at the following address for information on our newest releases.

Harlequin Reader Service
U.S.: 3010 Walden Ave., P.O. Box 1325, Buffalo, NY 14269
Canadian: P.O. Box 609, Fort Erie, Ont. L2A 5X3

A KISS IN THE DARK

This book is dedicated to my amazing mother.

1

MORE THAN ANYTHING, Lacey Delaney hated the dark—of being alone in the dark. She wouldn't admit it to anyone, but at twenty-seven years old, she still slept with a bedside light on. It didn't always keep the nightmares at bay, but at least when she woke up, panicked and gasping for breath, she wasn't engulfed in utter blackness. Even now, sitting in the relative safety of her car, she had only to close her eyes to envision her father buried alive in a coal mining disaster so horrific that his body had never been recovered.

Maybe her friend, Julia, was right and she should just find herself a man to keep her so pleasurably occupied at night that she'd be too sated and tired to dream. Unfortunately, both her job as a design engineer for StarPoint Technologies and her overprotective mother kept her too busy to meet many eligible men. Katherine Delaney gave a whole new meaning to the term *helicopter parent.* She didn't just hover; she flew fully armed, ready to obliterate any obstacles in Lacey's path, or to extract her from any danger.

Now here she was…alone, broken down in the middle of nowhere, with darkness pressing in on all sides. If her mother could see her now, she'd have a complete fit. The thought made Lacey smile. Her mother hadn't wanted Lacey to travel to Kentucky; had urged her to give the assignment to somebody else. Of course, the more her mother insisted that Lacey stay home, the more determined she was to go. Sometimes it felt as if the entire course of her life had been dictated by her mother's belief that something would happen to Lacey if she wasn't there to protect her.

Lacey understood the genesis of her mother's anxiety. She'd been just eight years old when her father was killed, and her mother lived in fear that something terrible would happen to Lacey, too. That worry hadn't diminished as Lacey grew older; if anything, it had ballooned into an irrational need to cocoon her against all dangers, real or perceived. And for a long time, Lacey had allowed it. But what had once seemed like parental concern for her welfare now felt like micromanagement of her life. More and more, Lacey found herself resenting her mother's intrusive habits.

She loved her mom, but she wanted to be free, to experience life, and all its pitfalls, on her own terms. She wanted to be taken seriously, and not viewed as someone who needed to be taken care of. Unfortunately, her small stature seemed to bring out a protective instinct in those she worked with, and Lacey was getting a little tired of insisting that she could do things on her own. So when StarPoint Technologies had offered the opportunity to field-test STAR, the new Subterranean Advanced Receiver unit that would become the latest technology in NASA's arsenal of global positioning systems, Lacey had jumped at it.

Her boss had been skeptical, since Lacey's experience was limited to the design lab. She had never before ventured into the field. But Lacey knew if she wanted to be respected as an engineer and a scientist, she needed to be familiar with all aspects of the job, including fieldwork. She just hadn't been prepared for how remote this particular field assignment would be.

The parking lot of the diner, where a short time ago she'd halfheartedly picked at a plate of meatloaf, was completely dark except for one light pole near the entrance. She'd been unable to pick up a signal on her cell phone, and was grateful that the owner of the diner had at least called for a tow truck before he'd snapped off the lights and locked the door, assuring her she'd be fine until Sully—the tow truck driver, she presumed—arrived.

Sighing, she sat behind the wheel of her rental car and left the door open for whatever small breeze might happen by. God, it was hot. Of course, New England could get sticky in the summer as well, but it was only early June and already Kentucky sweltered with heat.

Resting her head against the seat back, Lacey listened to the night bugs in the surrounding trees and watched the tiny blinking lights of the seemingly hundreds of fireflies. Generally, the heat didn't bother her, but tonight was different. Tonight she would have to return to the pathetic little motel she had checked into earlier that evening, knowing she wouldn't sleep a wink. She wasn't a snob by nature, but the only other patrons she had seen were several itinerant coal miners who had been well on their way to getting completely drunk. Knowing a slim length of chain was all that prevented one of them from entering her room would ensure she slept with her clothes on. And to top it off, the room would be about a million degrees since the air-conditioning didn't work.

Her small carry-on bag sat on the passenger seat beside her, and now she dug through the contents, pulling out an emergency pair of panties and bra—courtesy of her mom, just in case the airline lost her luggage—and an eReader as she hunted for the bottled water she had stashed there earlier. Blowing a strand of hair from her face, she took a long swallow of the water and decided it would only be for one night. Tomorrow, she would meet with Sheriff Hathaway, her point of contact while she was in Black Stone Gap, and ask him to recommend somewhere to stay other than the seedy Blackwater Inn. If there *was* any other place, she thought glumly. The motel should have been named the *Back*water Inn, because it was literally in the middle of nowhere. Her own frantic hunt through the phone book she'd found in the bedside table hadn't turned up any other hotels or motels in the area.

She reminded herself again that she wasn't here on vacation. Where she slept didn't matter. She had a job to do, and a dingy motel room wasn't going to deter her. StarPoint Technologies was under contract to NASA to develop a GPS unit that would operate underground, capable of sending and receiving signals through hundreds of feet of rock. Lacey had spent the past three years of her life designing and developing the unit, affectionately dubbed STAR.

Now that the development phase was complete, all that was required before they could turn the unit over to NASA was the final testing. For Lacey, this meant a chance not only to prove herself as a field scientist, but also to get out on her own. She could do whatever she wanted, within limits.

But Lacey was tired of limits.

She'd do her job, but she also intended to have some fun on this trip. Her friend Julia was right; allowing her mother to have so much influence over her life was unhealthy, no matter how good her intentions might be. This was an opportunity to spread her wings a bit and explore her own capabilities.

She'd spend three days with the local search-and-rescue team, demonstrating the use of handheld GPS units designed by her firm, and then one week at the local coal mines, testing STAR. But she'd also have some free time in which to sightsee. She'd spent part of the flight from Boston to Roanoke consulting her tourist book, considering the things she might do while she was in Kentucky. An evening pub crawl with free samples of Kentucky's finest bourbon sounded fun, but so did zip-lining over a forest canopy. Of course, how much free time she had depended on how smoothly the field tests went.

The opportunity to utilize the local coal mines to test STAR had been too good to pass up. Not only would the coal mines that riddled the area around Black Stone Gap provide a perfect test environment, but Lacey owed it to her father to ensure the unit worked deep inside the tunnels, where it could do the most good. If she could prevent even one miner from suffering the same fate as her father, she would be satisfied.

It seemed only minutes had passed when headlights swung toward her through the parking lot. Lifting her head, she peered at a large, beefy tow truck as it turned into the lot where she was stranded. It approached from the side and parked facing her door. The headlights bathed her in a blinding glare as she sat up and shielded her eyes.

She couldn't see who was in the driver's seat, but felt their scrutiny as if it were a palpable thing. She suddenly knew how a deer felt when caught in a car's headlights. Here she was, alone and vulnerable and out in the middle of nowhere, and she could only imagine who watched her from the cab of that tow truck. Lacey had completed a self-defense course in college and she had no doubt that she could take care of herself, but when she heard the opening and closing of the driver's door, it galvanized her into action. Better to be safe than sorry. Swiftly, she pulled her own car door shut and punched the lock down. A figure stepped into the light, silhouetted for a moment in the brightness.

Lacey's breath caught.

His body was lean and powerful, with broad, sloping

shoulders and narrow hips. It was a body that turned a woman's thoughts instantly to sex. The light behind him shadowed his features, but she knew with a certainty they would be as arresting as his body.

He came closer, and as Lacey sat immobile, he leaned down to peer in at her. Her mouth fell open as she stared wordlessly into the bluest eyes she had ever seen. They weren't just your average blue, either. Even in the dim light she could see they were an opulent shade of blue-green that reminded her of tropical waters and warm, secluded beaches.

"Ma'am?" His voice carried low and clear through the car window, and she could see the concern in his eyes. "Are you okay?"

She recognized his voice as the man she had spoken to on the telephone earlier. She would have preferred to roll her window down to talk with him, but with the engine off, the power windows were useless. If she wanted to communicate, she would have to either shout through the glass, or open the door. Already, the air inside the car was suffocatingly hot. She studied him for a moment, and then drawing in a deep breath, pushed her door open but made no move to get out.

He stepped into the opening, bracing one hand on the roof and the other arm along the top of the door frame. He grinned down at her, a lazy this-must-be-my-lucky-night kind of grin. His teeth were white in the darkness of his face. He wore a faded black T-shirt that clung to his muscled torso, and from her vantage point below him, Lacey could see the impressive bulge of his biceps as he leaned into the car.

"You called for a tow truck?" Deep indents flashed in his lean cheeks. His voice was lazy and warm.

Lacey didn't know what was wrong with her. She couldn't seem to find her voice. "Um, yes." She gulped. "I did. My car doesn't seem to want to start."

She wasn't prepared when he suddenly crouched down

beside her. Now he was eye level with her and she could see he had close-cropped, dark hair. Balancing on the balls of his feet, he edged forward and reached toward her legs.

"Mind if I take a peek?" he asked.

A surge of heat coursed through Lacey that had nothing to do with the outside temperature. For one wild, crazy second she was sure he was going to flip back the skirt of her little sundress and, heaven help her, she was going to let him.

But his hand went with unerring skill to the hood release located just under the dash, and only when she heard the popping of the catch did she realize she had been holding her breath. He rose to his feet in one fluid movement and rounded the front of her car to raise the hood, pulling a slim flashlight out of a back pocket.

Lacey sagged back against the seat. If she'd had a fan, it would have been working overtime to try and cool her suddenly flushed skin. He was, without a doubt, the most sinful-looking man she had ever seen, and she thought it had as much to do with the way he looked *at* her as it did with the way he looked.

She struggled to get a grip on her rioting thoughts. What was she thinking? A tow truck driver? She could almost see Julia doing a victory dance. Despite his amazing eyes, he was probably not much better than the leering, beer-swigging coal miners at the Blackwater Inn.

But an image of that leanly muscled physique came back to her, and she knew instinctively she was wrong. He wasn't at all like those men. He was the sort who would take his time with a woman, ensuring her pleasure before reaching his own. He would be assertive, playful and maybe even a little kinky. For one wild instant, her imagination surged. Images of a secluded mountain cabin and fur-strewn floors lingered in her mind. She envisioned him clearly, his tautly muscled body moving softly over her own in the darkness, murmuring husky words of encouragement against her throat, her lips...

He came back around to her door and bent down, interrupting her wayward thoughts. "Ma'am, do you mind if I try to start her up?"

"Oh, of course not!" Unable to meet his eyes, Lacey scooted out of the car to stand out of his way.

She watched as he folded his long frame into the driver's seat and turned the key. Still nothing. He tried again, and then sat back for a moment, considering. Looking up at her, he gave her a lopsided grin.

"Looks like you're going to need my services, after all," he drawled.

Lacey's pulse reacted immediately. *If he only knew.*

Sensing those tropical water eyes on her, Lacey glanced at him. His expression held a heat that made her breath catch, and she knew in that instant that he was interested in her. Then he looked away, his features shuttered.

"Do—do you know what's wrong with the engine?" she asked, clearing her throat against the sudden restriction she felt there.

"Why don't I show you?"

Climbing out of the car, he indicated she should precede him, and her nerves jumped when he placed a hand at the small of her back to guide her. Just that light touch of his fingers seemed to burn through the thin fabric of her cotton dress. A tiny shiver rippled through her. She felt strange, all fluttery and anxious, and her heartbeat pulsed loudly in her ears. She felt shivery, yet flushed with heat. And all because this man had touched her.

He leaned over her engine compartment and flicked his flashlight into its dark interior. He spoke, and she listened to the warm, rich tones of his voice even as she admired the fit of his jeans across his backside. She envisioned those leanly muscled orbs cupped in the palms of her hands.

The next moment she was appalled. What was wrong with her? She was acting like a moonstruck teenager. It wasn't as if she'd never been this close to a gorgeous guy before. She'd had relationships. Okay, so she hadn't been intimate with anyone on any level in several years, and she was probably more than a little sexually frustrated. But between her job and her mother's nearly constant vigilance, she hadn't had an opportunity to develop any relationships, meaningful or otherwise. But here she was, with nobody to tell her what she could or couldn't do. While she didn't think she'd reached the point where she would jump the first attractive stranger she encountered, it was a wonderful feeling to know that she *could,* provided the stranger was also willing.

With a start, she realized the stranger had stopped talking and was watching her, resting one hip against the frame of the car, arms crossed casually over his chest as he waited for her to return to earth.

"Sorry," she mumbled. "You were saying?"

He grinned then, slowly, as if he knew exactly what she had been thinking. "I was saying that it looks like you have an abrasion in the insulation of the wiring harness."

"Oh." Lacey looked at him blankly. "What does that mean?"

The indents in those lean cheeks deepened. "Well, when the wiring isn't seated right, there's too much friction and an abrasion can occur, resulting in a hot spot." He eased himself away from the car and took a step toward Lacey. "When that happens," he said slowly, his voice languid and dark, "the wiring can overheat, melting everything right back to the driveshaft."

Lacey blinked. Her cheeks grew warm. "Really." She slid her gaze away from the sudden heat in those translucent eyes. "A hot spot, huh?"

"Mm-hmm. You're definitely going to need my services."

Turning away, Lacey pressed a palm against her chest and forced herself to breathe normally. "Okay, then. It's a rental car, so whatever's wrong with it, they can fix it. I'll call the rental agency and let them know where they can collect it." She drew in a steadying breath before turning back to face him. "Should I pay you now, or let the rental agency pay you when they come to get the car?"

He shrugged. "Let them pay for it. Here, I'll give you a business card."

She watched as he strode over to the tow truck and began rummaging around inside the cab. He swore softly. "I know they're in here somewhere. Aha!" He came back and handed her a small card. "Give this number to the rental agency."

Lacey glanced at the card. There was the business name, *Sully's Towing Service,* but not his first name. Pushing down her disappointment, she looked back up at him. "Thanks. If you'll wait just a moment, I'll get my things out of the car."

She popped the trunk release and was hauling her presentation materials and the case that contained STAR out, when he leaned in through the driver's door and across the seat. She paused for a moment, peeking around the trunk to admire his ass. When he finally straightened, she realized he was holding her lingerie and carry-on bag in one hand, and her little pocketbook in the other.

"You don't want to forget these."

The delicate satin panties looked ridiculously fragile in his large hand, and she had a sudden image of him sliding them slowly down over her hips. Her eyes flew to his. Those mesmerizing dimples were back again as he handed her belongings to her.

Taking the items wordlessly from him, she struggled to lift the heavy case out of the trunk when he reached in and took it easily from her hands. Then, lifting her presentation case in his other hand, he strode over to the tow truck and tossed them both into the cargo area behind the seats.

"What are you doing?"

He gave her a smile that sent her heart lurching. "I'm taking you home."

Her voice, when she finally found it, came out as no more than a squeak. "You're what?"

"Well, I wouldn't feel right leaving you in a deserted parking lot," he said, running a hand over his crop of short hair and managing to look endearingly concerned. "So unless somebody's already on their way to pick you up, I'll run you wherever you need to go." He gave her a questioning look.

Logically, Lacey knew that what he said made sense. He couldn't leave her here, without a way to get back to the motel. But his words still caused her imagination to surge.

"No," she finally managed. "There's nobody coming to get me. I'm only here for a few days."

"Ah," he said meaningfully. "Well then, why don't you hop into the cab and I'll hook the car up."

Hesitating only briefly, Lacey did as he suggested, sliding past him as he held the door open and taking his proffered hand to hitch herself up onto the bench seat. His skin was warm, his fingers strong and sure as they closed over her own.

She watched him as he came around to the driver's side and pulled himself up behind the wheel. Mere inches away from her, in the confined space of the cab his presence was overwhelming, the sheer maleness of him assailing her senses.

Suddenly, he turned toward her on the bench seat, one arm sliding along the seat back behind her shoulders as he craned to peer through the rear window and align the truck up with her car. Lacey's nostrils flared. *She could smell him.* A clean scent of male sweat and soap. She realized she had only to turn her face and her lips would brush along the smooth bulge of his biceps where they rested on the back of the seat.

Rigid, Lacey clutched her overnight bag with both hands and forced herself to look straight ahead, but found herself staring at his thighs. They were lean and well-muscled beneath the close-fitting blue jeans. She swallowed. His hand on the steering wheel was strong, with long, tapered fingers and neat, clean nails. She noted he wore no rings and felt an unreasonable sense of relief. Sliding a sideways glance at him as he maneuvered the tow truck into position, she couldn't help but wonder what he was thinking about her.

COLE MACKINNON COULD scarcely believe his good fortune as he jumped down from the cab and began the process of hitching the car to the tow truck. He'd been back in Black Stone Gap for less than two days and had stopped by Sully's garage that night on a whim. They'd been kicking back with a cold beer when the call had come in. Sully, his longtime buddy, had been on another line so Cole had automatically picked up the second phone when it began to ring off the hook. He'd helped Sully out before so it was no big deal when he'd offered to tow this one in. He actually enjoyed playing the Good Samaritan. But when the headlights of the truck had first swung over the car, he'd been nearly speechless at the sight of the woman who reclined in the driver's seat.

She was pale and slim, with bare arms and legs, and ginger hair that fell as soft and straight as summer rain to skim her smooth shoulders. In the stifling heat of the Kentucky night, she looked as cool and refreshing as a tall glass of mint tea. When he'd reached under the dash to release the hood, he'd had to fight the urge to skate his palm along the silken length of her leg, fiercely reminding himself that he was there to help her. He had absolutely no intentions of seducing her. No way, not a one.

None.

He finished fastening the coupling on the hitch. As he straightened, he glanced through the rear window of the tow truck in time to see her scoop that silky hair up in both hands and pile it on top of her head, exposing the sweet, vulnerable curve of her neck.

Damn.

He stood transfixed, all his good intentions vanishing, scattering like so many fireflies into the heat of the night.

2

SHE WAS UNEASY. Cole glanced over at her as he eased the truck into gear and slowly maneuvered it out of the parking lot and onto the dark main road. Hell, she should be. If she'd even an inkling of the thoughts that were racing through his head, she'd be a whole lot more nervous. She tried to act casual, but he didn't miss how she stole furtive glances at him, and continually smoothed her fingers over the skirt of her dress.

Everything about her, from her accent to her little designer purse, shouted Northerner. He was betting from somewhere in the Northeast. Which meant she was probably as frigid as a New York winter. She'd no doubt be shocked if she knew of the lustful imaginings he'd just had of her. She'd probably never had a fantasy in her entire life. His eyes slid to the overnight bag that rested on the seat between them. And he remembered what had been spilling out of that bag only moments before.

Scraps of satin and lace.

He felt a smile twitch the corners of his mouth. Okay, so perhaps she did harbor a fantasy or two. He'd give a lot to know what they were. Then do his damnedest to make them all come true.

He'd returned to Black Stone Gap just two days earlier, having been gone for more than five years. Not even Sully knew his real reason for coming back. He'd told his friend that he was looking for work in the coal mines, knowing the word would spread quickly in the small community. A good mining engineer was worth his weight in gold.

But what he hadn't told Sully was that he didn't really need the work; he was undercover for the Department of Labor, investigating an alarming spike in the number of accidents in Black River Mine No. 2, the biggest and most active coal mine in the region. He hadn't wanted to come back; he'd been happy enough in Norfolk, working as a structural engineer for the state of Virginia. Until the night he'd received a call from a friend and former instructor at Virginia Tech.

Cole had studied mining engineering under Stu Zollweg, and had later participated as part of an inspection team led by Zollweg to identify safety issues in several West Virginia mines. He'd found the fieldwork both challenging and satisfying. After obtaining his Master's degree, he'd returned to Black Stone Gap and been hired as an engineer in the Black River Mines. But less than six months into the job, he'd lost a good friend in a tunnel collapse. He'd been consumed with guilt and anger; he should have known about the weak tunnel structure. He should have been able to avert the accident.

Instead of sticking around to help uncover what had gone wrong, he'd bolted. He'd moved to Norfolk the day after his friend's funeral and had gotten a job as a structural engineer, helping to build highway tunnels and bridges.

When Stu Zollweg had called out of the blue, Cole couldn't have been more surprised. But the offer he made was even more surprising. Stu worked part-time for the Department of Labor as a mine safety inspector. The Bureau of Mines had sent safety inspectors into the Black River Mines on several occasions, but had failed to uncover any significant safety infractions. So they couldn't understand why the accident rate in the Black River Mines was higher than other mines in the country. Now the feds wanted someone to go into those mines undercover and find out why the accident rate was climbing. Stu had recommended Cole for the job.

If he could gain access to the tunnels, he could provide evidence of what he had long suspected—that the mines were operating in direct violation of Federal safety codes. He just needed to prove it.

The air-conditioning in the cab was strong enough to softly stir the fabric of her dress, and even by the dim dashboard lights he could see goose bumps raised along her slim arms.

"Cold?" he asked. "I can turn down the air if you'd like."

"No, thanks. It feels good."

She started to say something more when the radio unit on the dash emitted a sudden, loud squawk and a disembodied, static voice filled the cab of the truck.

"Mac, you there? Over."

Cole lifted a handheld mouthpiece from its cradle and pressed a button, speaking into the instrument. "Yeah, I'm here. I'm giving the client a lift home, and then I'll bring the truck and car in. Over."

"Do me a favor, Mac," came the reply. "Can you bring the truck back first? I just got a call that Stu Barlow's boy wrecked his truck out on the gap road and forced another car into the ravine. The kid's fine, but his vehicle's blocking the road. Bobby just headed over there with the other wrecker, so I'll take yours and meet him there. Over."

"Got it. See you in two. Over and out." Cole replaced the mouthpiece and gave his passenger an apologetic smile. "Looks like I need to bring the truck back to Sully first, then I'll give you that lift to wherever it is you're staying." When she didn't immediately answer, he gave her a quick glance. "That is, if it's okay with you."

Her attention had sharpened on him. "You're not Sully?"

Cole grinned. "No, ma'am." Keeping one eye on the dark road, he extended a hand toward her. "Name's Cole Mac-Kinnon."

After a moment, she took his hand. Her fingers were slender and cool. "I'm Lacey Delaney."

Cole thought the name suited her. Soft. Feminine. It conjured up images of delicate lingerie, like the stuff she had in that bag. He slanted her a smile. "Nice to meet you, ma'am." She made no move to withdraw her hand, and Cole's grin broadened as he saw the turnoff to Sully's garage come into view. "Uh, ma'am?" She gave him a questioning look and he dropped his gaze pointedly to their clasped hands. "I'll have to shift in another minute, but in order to do that I'll need—"

She snatched her fingers from his.

LACEY HAD BEEN so busy mooning at the man, she hadn't even realized she was hanging on to his hand. Worse, he was completely aware of her reaction to him. She cleared her throat uncomfortably as the truck turned into a gravel parking lot. There was a large, multibay garage at the far end and she could see lights on in the small office there. A sign over it read Sully's Garage—24 Hour Towing. At the other end of the building were two blue taxicabs, and a smaller sign that read Tara's Taxi Service.

As Cole maneuvered the rental car into a nearby space, the door to the office opened and a huge bear of a man emerged. Sully, she presumed. He had a head of unruly dark hair and half of his face was obscured by a beard and moustache.

Cole glanced over at Lacey. "Wait here where it's cool. I'll unhitch the car first, and then get your things out of the back. No need for you to stand around in this heat."

Without waiting for an answer, he opened his door and jumped down. Lacey watched as the other man approached him. She couldn't hear their words, but she didn't miss when Cole jerked his thumb in the direction of the truck. The bearded man turned his head toward her and Lacey barely resisted the urge to slide down lower in her seat. Sully grinned and said something, and slapped Cole on the back. Lacey heard him laughing as he strode back toward the office.

What had Cole said to him? And why did she suddenly feel like a cheap pickup? But when Cole turned and came alongside the truck to unhitch her car, she could see he wasn't smiling. His face wore an expression of such annoyance that Lacey felt an unexpected rush of gratitude toward him. Clearly he wasn't pleased with whatever conclusion Sully had drawn of his decision to drive her back to the motel.

But when he opened her door, his features were schooled into a mask of politeness. He extended a hand to help her down, and Lacey fumbled for a moment, trying to grasp both her overnight bag and purse. He reached in wordlessly and took the bag from her. As Lacey swung her legs around, her skirt scooted halfway up her thighs, but with one hand firmly clutched around her purse and the other warmly encased in Cole's, she had no chance to tug it down. She heard him suck in his breath, and when she glanced at his face, she saw the heat was back in those translucent eyes.

"C'mon," he muttered. "Let's get out of here before Sully decides to come back out."

She waited as he reached into the back and withdrew her presentation case and STAR, hefting them both in a single grip. "Is he your boss?"

Cole gave a bark of surprised laughter. "Sully? No, he's just a friend. I help him out once in a while, that's all. He's a good guy, but he doesn't have much in the way of manners. Trust me when I say you're better off not getting an introduction. It still amazes me that he actually managed to find himself a wife." He nodded his head toward the opposite side of the parking lot. "This way."

Lacey waited while Cole stowed her gear in an oversize toolbox secured in the bed of a large, black pickup truck. There was no lighting in this area of the lot, and with his dark jeans and T-shirt, the surrounding gloom all but swallowed him up. Lacey hung back, standing just outside the ring of darkness.

She considered herself to be an intelligent woman, but taking a ride from a complete stranger had to be the height of stupidity. It had seemed a perfectly reasonable solution when they were in the tow truck with her rental car hitched to the back. After all, she had been the customer, securing the services of a professional. But discovering he wasn't even affiliated with the towing company, and then accepting a ride in his personal truck seemed somehow…well, personal. Intimate.

"Hey." His voice was quiet, interrupting her thoughts. He had taken a step toward her and now stood watching her. "Having second thoughts?"

The man was perceptive. "No, of course not."

He laughed softly and stepped closer. "Liar."

Lacey barely resisted the urge to step backward as he advanced. His knowing look, combined with a smile that could only be called predatory, should have had her running full-tilt in the opposite direction. Instead, it caused a bolt of awareness to surge through her, rooting her where she stood.

"Why would I be having second thoughts? You don't look like an ax murderer, but if you are, I have witnesses who've seen you with me." She indicated with a nod of her head to where Sully was climbing into the cab of the tow truck. Her voice was light. "You'd never get away with it."

Cole's dimples flashed as he gave her a wolfish grin. "Rest assured, when it comes to pretty women, hurting them is the last thing I have in mind."

Lacey felt her pulse quicken. What, exactly, did he have in mind for her? And how would he react if she indicated, by word or gesture, that she might be a willing participant? The sudden images that swamped her imagination were so vivid and so strong that heat flooded her face, making her grateful for the dim light.

Cole's glance moved beyond Lacey. "If you *are* having second thoughts, now's your chance to say so. Once Sully's gone, it's just you and me."

Lacey turned and watched in silence as the tow truck slowly made its way across the parking lot. She saw Sully raise a hand in brief salute, and then the taillights vanished as the vehicle swung out of the parking lot and onto the main road. Drawing a fortifying breath, she turned back to face Cole with a bright smile. "I guess you have your answer."

He considered her silently for a moment, his expression inscrutable, before stepping back to open the driver's door of the pickup truck. "I guess I do."

He extended a hand toward Lacey, and once more she found her fingers wrapped in the warm strength of his own as he helped her up into the cab. Lacey scooted across the bench seat only to be halted midway by the sight of an enormous animal sprawled on the far side. Its tongue lolled wetly from an open mouth bracketed by long, loose jowls as it regarded her drowsily, and a long tail thumped in greeting against the seat. Her mouth fell open in wordless surprise.

"That's Copper," said Cole, sliding in behind the wheel. "He has a tendency to slobber, so you might not want to get too close." He grinned. "I think he has a thing for redheads."

Lacey recoiled as the dog shook its head, flinging long ropes of saliva against the back of the seat. "Oh, my," she said, laughing in spite of herself, "you weren't kidding. He really does slobber!"

"Sorry," Cole said, sounding anything but apologetic as Lacey drew closer to him in an effort to avoid being splattered. "Once we get going, he'll hang his head out the window, so you'll be safe."

At least from the dog, thought Lacey. With Copper taking up more than his fair share of the seat, it was nearly impossible to maintain a respectable distance from Cole. She could feel the heat that radiated from his lean body, even as he reached over and flipped on the air-conditioning and a blast of lukewarm air billowed her skirt up over her thighs. Lacey pushed it back down and placed her purse over her knees in an effort to keep the fabric firmly where it belonged.

"Here," said Cole, "let me adjust those vents."

He extended one arm across her knees and flipped the louvers upward. His shoulder pressed against hers and his arm brushed against her breast as he pulled back. It was purely accidental, but Lacey was helpless to prevent a swift intake of breath at the intimate contact. If Cole noticed her reaction, he gave no sign, but Lacey thought he reversed with slightly more force than necessary, the tires churning up loose gravel before he changed gears and headed out of the parking lot.

As Cole had predicted, Copper heaved himself to his feet and happily thrust his head out of the open window, his long ears streaming behind him. His hindquarters were dangerously close to Lacey's face, and when his tail started to knock steadily against her chest, she gave a soft exclamation of surprise and gingerly swatted at the offending length.

Cole laughed, the sound sliding over Lacey's senses like warm honey. "That dog," he said ruefully, "has no sense of personal space."

Neither, apparently, did Cole as he leaned suddenly across Lacey's body and with one hand pushed gently but firmly on the dog's rear, forcing it into a sitting position. "There," he said, and his glance slid over Lacey as she pressed herself against the seat. "You okay?"

Lacey met his gaze. Even in the darkened cab, there was no mistaking the expression of taut awareness on his face. In that instant, Lacey knew he wanted her.

The knowledge thrilled her.

Terrified her.

Caused her heart to slam against her rib cage so that she was sure he would hear its betraying rhythm. "I'm fine," she finally managed, hating the way her voice sounded breathless, even to her own ears.

"Where are you staying?" he asked. "Mozelle or Cumberland?"

Lacey looked at him blankly. "Are those hotels? Because I checked and—"

Cole laughed softly again. "No, ma'am, those are towns. The closest ones with decent hotels, at any rate. Unless you're staying with friends here in the Gap?"

Lacey peered at him suspiciously. "Just how close are those two towns?"

Cole shrugged. "Well, they're in opposite directions from here, but I'd guess they're both about an hour away."

Lacey gaped at him. "You'd be willing to drive me all that way?"

He turned to her then, surprise evident on his face. "Yeah. Why wouldn't I?"

Lacey stared at him for a long moment before dragging her gaze away. Of course he was willing to drive her that far. He probably thought he'd be well rewarded for his efforts. After all, she'd done nothing but ogle him since she'd first laid eyes on him. For a moment, Lacey battled with herself, torn between doubt and anticipation, because a part of her wanted him to want her. But she didn't want him to think she was an easy conquest.

His lips tightened before he returned his attention to the road. "I see. You think I'll want some sort of payment in return for the lift."

"No—" Lacey began, ready to deny what she had, in fact, been thinking.

But Cole held up one hand, forestalling any further words. "It's okay," he said. "Because you know what?" He slanted her one long, meaningful look. "You're right. I'd be lying if I said the thought hadn't crossed my mind." He gave a low, self-deprecating laugh. "Hell, it's been the single thing on my mind since I first saw you."

Lacey's breath hitched. His husky confession caused a liquid heat to slip along the underside of her skin, and her pulse began a heavy, languorous thudding. She focused on the dark road, watching as the truck swallowed up the pavement, unable to think of an appropriate response.

"However," he continued easily, "I don't need to use coercion or guilt to get a woman to sleep with me. It's either completely mutual, or it doesn't happen. So you can relax, okay?"

Relax? Was he kidding? Lacey thought she might spontaneously combust. Of course he didn't need to use coercion—he was the kind of guy women fantasized about. Not only gorgeous, but considerate, too. In that moment, she made up her mind. Her friend Julia was right; she'd denied herself for way too long, always putting the needs of others before her own, always conscious of what her mother might think. But out here, there was just her and this man. She was only going to be in Black Stone Gap for ten days. Why shouldn't she do as she pleased? Lord knew when she'd have another opportunity.

She glanced over at Cole. "I'm actually staying here in Black Stone Gap," she ventured, "so you won't need to drive me too far." *To collect your reward.*

He tilted her a questioning look. "Oh, yeah? Where?"

"The Blackwater Inn."

"What?" He bit the word out, his face incredulous.

"There were no other hotels," she said defensively. "The Blackwater Inn is a little grungy, but otherwise it's fine."

He gave a snort of disgust. "Yeah, if you're an itinerant coal miner or a horny barfly."

Lacey looked at him in dismay, recalling the men she'd seen at the motel earlier that night. "I did try to make other arrangements, but there wasn't anything else even close."

Cole ran a hand over his hair. "Hell," he muttered. "If anyone sees you, every guy who's staying there'll be panting at your door. I'll walk you to your room. Once you're inside with the door locked, you should be okay." He shook his head again. "The Blackwater Inn?"

When they pulled into the motel several minutes later, Lacey saw that the bar across the street was doing a brisk business. The parking lot was completely full and the overflow had spilled into the motel's lot. As Cole parked the truck, the door of the bar opened and a man and woman lurched outside, briefly illuminated by the shaft of light from inside the establishment.

Hanging on to each other, they made their way across the darkened street. As they approached the Blackwater Inn, they stopped to exchange a deep kiss. They swayed, stumbled, and then laughingly broke apart to stagger over to one of the guestroom doors. Lacey watched as the woman fitted a key into the lock. The man was groping her from behind. He bent his head and nuzzled her neck even as one hand snaked around to fondle a breast. The woman laughed again and they all but fell through the open door. Lacey caught a glimpse of the two coming together for a passionate embrace before the man kicked the door closed with one booted foot.

Lacey found she couldn't look over at Cole. The raw sexuality she had just witnessed too closely mirrored the fantasy she had briefly entertained about him.

"C'mon," he muttered. "Let's get you to your room."

Opening his door, he slid out and stood back to wait for her. Copper drew his head in from the passenger window and flopped down on the seat once more, staring at them with an expression that stated clearly he was accustomed to being left in the truck. Cole retrieved her gear from his lockbox and indicated she should precede him.

"I'm in the back," she said, aware of his eyes on her as she led him around to the rear of the building. A group of men had pulled several of the plastic patio chairs around a small table on the walkway and were playing cards. Beer cans littered the grass and cigarette smoke hung heavy on the humid air. They paused when they saw Lacey, and the nearest one leered appreciatively at her from over the rim of a beer can.

"Evenin' boys."

Cole's voice was cordial but cool as he hefted Lacey's presentation case over one shoulder and took her elbow with his free hand, propelling her along. Lacey cast a wary look at the men, noting the sullen, almost defiant manner in which they watched her. Despite Cole's casual attitude, she sensed he was on full alert, every muscle in his lean body tightly coiled. He was staring at the men, his eyes challenging them to say something, anything. Two of the men mumbled a greeting and one by one they lowered their eyes beneath Cole's unwavering glare.

"I'm in here," Lacey said when they reached her door. Would he expect her to invite him in? Or would he simply say goodbye? She glanced up at him. He was so close that one small step back would bring her smack up against that tautly muscled chest. He was crowding her, his larger physique shielding her from the nearby men.

"Get your key out and open the door." His voice was low in her ear, brooking no argument.

Turning the knob, she pushed the door open, startled when he hustled her inside and closed it behind them. In the sudden and complete darkness of the room, her chest constricted and she couldn't control her suddenly rapid pulse or the perspiration that popped out along her hairline. She closed her eyes and dragged in several deep breaths, telling herself there was nothing to be afraid of. She heard Cole set her cases down on the floor. When he flipped on the overhead light, she blinked and exhaled in relief, and then sank down on the edge of the bed. Cole opened the door an inch or so and examined the broken deadbolt, testing it. Then he fingered the dangling chain.

"This lock is broken." He slanted her a questioning look. "Did you realize that?"

Lacey swallowed, momentarily unable to form a response. She thought she'd gotten a good look at him in the truck. She'd thought him gorgeous then, but by the glaring light of the overhead fixture she realized she had been wrong. The man wasn't just gorgeous.

He was magnificent.

His face was a masterpiece of lean, chiseled features paired with a sensuous mouth. For an instant, Lacey imagined feasting on those lips with her own. His blue eyes were fringed with thick, dark lashes and his short hair was a deep, rich brown. His skin was bronzed by the sun and his arms were an incredible mix of bulging muscles and lean sinews. Her hands would probably be incapable of spanning those impressive biceps. When he wasn't smiling, like now, he had a decidedly dangerous aura. In the confines of the room, he seemed inordinately large. Lacey should have been nervous, but she wasn't. She'd been an apt self-defense pupil, and if things began to turn sour, she was more than capable of defending herself.

"Yes." She nodded. "I notified the front desk, but apparently there aren't any other rooms available."

Cole closed the door with a click and took several steps into the room. His gaze swept over the gaudy bedspread and stained carpeting, missing nothing. "It's hot as hell in here."

He was right. Fine beads of moisture had gathered on Lacey's skin and her sundress clung damply to her. In the confined room, the heat was suffocating. "It's just for one night. I'll find something else in the morning."

Cole looked doubtfully at her as he fiddled with the thermostat. "I doubt you'll survive a night in this furnace." He flicked the wall thermometer in disgust. "Looks like the air-conditioning is on the blink." He moved to the window and Lacey watched with renewed interest when the muscles in his arms and shoulders bunched with effort as he tried unsuccessfully to raise the sash. After a moment, he stepped back. "Unbelievable. I think they've permanently nailed it shut."

He turned to look down at her, his expression inscrutable. Lacey smoothed her skirt down over her knees and tried not to think about the fact that she was alone in a motel room with an absolutely mouthwatering man. Any fantasy she might have harbored about him had been completely dashed the moment he stepped through the door. He was obviously disgusted by the seediness of the room, and the temperature alone was enough to wilt any blossoming desire. She steeled herself for his departure, unwilling to examine why she felt so depressed at the prospect of his leaving.

She'd been ready to take the plunge with this guy, to step out of her comfort zone and do something thrilling and naughty. The realization that she'd be spending the night alone in this tawdry motel room was a complete letdown. But she could at least accept the inevitable with good grace. There was no way she would let him see her disappointment.

"Well." She pushed to her feet and stood by the door, her hand on the latch. Outside, she could hear raised voices as an argument broke out among the men playing cards. She forced a brisk, businesslike tone to her voice, but found she couldn't meet his eyes. "Thank you so much for your help. I really appreciate everything you've done for me."

There was silence, and when Lacey finally looked up, it was to find Cole standing with his hands braced on his hips, watching her with a bemused expression. He dominated the small room. Lacey's eyes traveled slowly up the length of his body, noting how the black T-shirt emphasized the taut flatness of his stomach and the muscled planes of his chest. There was a light sheen of sweat on the strong column of his throat and she imagined tracing her tongue along that slick skin.

"You don't actually think I'm going to leave you here, do you?" he asked.

Now it was her turn to look bemused, even as her pulse quickened. "What do you mean?"

Her eyes widened when he turned and scooped her discarded pantsuit from the back of a chair where she had tossed it. He folded it neatly in half, dropped it into her open suitcase and flipped the case shut.

"There's really only one thing to do." His mouth curved in a rueful grin. "I'm taking you home with me."

3

LACEY WAS CERTAIN he had to be kidding, but there was nothing humorous in his manner as he zipped her case shut, hefted it neatly in one hand, and stepped toward the door.

"Wait a minute." Lacey threw up a hand to forestall him. "You can't be serious."

"Yeah, you're probably right." Cole's voice was low. "You're definitely better off staying here. I'm sure those men out there will be more than happy to take care of you tonight." He stabbed a finger toward the commotion outside. "From the sound of things, they're well on their way to getting completely messed up. If I leave you here, how long do you think it'll take for them to decide you're fair game? Hmm? Do you really think you're safe in this room?"

Lacey was silent. He had verbalized what she had been thinking. But to go home with Cole? Did she dare? Because she'd be lying to herself if she believed nothing would happen between them. Even now, the tension in the room was almost palpable.

"Look," he said, interrupting her thoughts. "I know what you're thinking." Reaching into his back pocket, he produced a slim wallet, flipped it open and extended it toward her. "Here's my I.D. If you want to take a look and then call somebody to let them know who you're with, go ahead."

Glancing at him, Lacey took the proffered wallet and looked down at the I.D. beneath the plastic protector. It was a Virginia driver's license with a Norfolk address. The photograph had captured the incredible blueness of his eyes. She tried not to stare.

"You're not even from around here," she said, handing him the wallet. "Were you planning on driving back to Norfolk? That's what—five hundred miles from here?"

Cole pocketed the wallet, frustration evident in his expression. "I grew up here in the Gap, but I moved to Norfolk after I got out of school. My family has a place not too far from here, and everyone in town knows who I am. You're safer with me than you are here."

Lacey didn't know about that. Her intentions where Cole was concerned could be classified as anything but *safe*.

He looked expectantly at her. "Okay? Are we good? Now can we please get the hell out of here before we both suffocate?"

He was right. The heat in the room was oppressive. Still, Lacey hesitated. Once she committed to going with him, there would be no turning back.

Seeing her misgivings, Cole sighed, put the suitcase down and spread his hands out in a supplicating gesture. "Look, you're going to have to trust me on this one, okay? I promise, you're absolutely safe with me. I'm staying just a couple of miles from here and there's a separate guest suite so you'll be completely private." He gave a small snort of laughter and muttered an expletive beneath his breath. "I'll even go spend the night at Sully's if it'll make you feel better. But there is no way in hell you're staying here tonight, okay?"

Lacey had the distinct impression that if she refused to go with him, he'd throw her over one broad shoulder and haul her bodily out of the room. She knew instinctively he wouldn't hurt her, would even put himself in harm's way to protect her. It was herself she didn't trust. Just the thought of being alone with this man for an entire night caused her body to react in a way she was unfamiliar with. Her knees felt shaky when she looked at him. There was a fluttering sensation in the pit of her stomach. She'd never been so acutely aware of her own body before.

"Okay," she said, before she could change her mind. "I'll stay at your place, but just for tonight."

"Good." There was no mistaking the satisfaction in his voice.

Lacey followed him outside, unwilling to look at the men as they passed, aware they had ceased arguing the moment she and Cole had emerged from the room. But when one of the men abruptly stood up, shoving the flimsy chair back and nearly upsetting the makeshift card table, Lacey understood why Cole had deliberately positioned himself between her and them.

"Hey, baby," the man crooned, "why you want to go with him, eh?"

"Yeah, stay wi' us," slurred a second man. "We'll show you a good time…a *real* good time."

Lacey edged closer to Cole's protective bulk.

"Don't worry," he said in a low voice, "they're not coming near you."

Lacey looked at the men and knew it was true. While they might muster enough courage to throw comments at hers and Cole's retreating backs, they didn't have the guts to confront the hard-eyed man who propelled her along with one hand at the base of her spine.

Copper lay panting on the seat where they had left him, and now he thumped his tail lazily in greeting. After stowing her gear in the back, Cole started the truck and swung out onto the road. The dog made no move to clamber to its feet and hang its head out the window, as if the heat had finally sapped what remained of his energy. Instead, he gave a jaw-splitting yawn and dropped his head onto Lacey's thighs with a contented huff of breath.

Lacey snatched her hands from her lap and looked down in consternation at the animal. "Well, he certainly isn't shy," she remarked with a laugh. Her hands hovered uncertainly over the dog. "Will he mind if I pet him?"

Cole gave a laugh that was half groan, and eyed the dog with something like envy. "Are you kidding? He thinks he just died and went to heaven."

Smiling in spite of herself, she tentatively stroked the animal's head and ran her fingers over his long ears. "He's so soft," she murmured. "What kind of dog is he?"

"He's a bloodhound."

"Like the kind you see in movies, tracking escaped criminals?"

Cole laughed. "Yeah, except Copper's never had that particular honor. He's retired now, but when he was younger he had no problem tracking down kids and hikers who'd gone missing in the hills around here."

"Really!" Lacey was impressed, and gave Copper a generous scratching behind his ears to show it. "What a good boy. I hope you got an extra treat and a nice, long tummy rub for that."

Cole laughed, a warm sound that caused Lacey to smile back at him. "What's so funny?"

He hesitated, then impaled her with the full heat of his aquamarine eyes. They locked gazes briefly before he returned his attention to the road. "I was just thinking," he murmured, "what an incentive that would be for the local search-and-rescue team. Coming from you, that is."

"What would be?"

Cole slanted her a swift glance. "An extra treat and a tummy rub. Their success rate for rescues would be about a million percent."

Lacey's breath hitched. She stared at his profile, unable to rid her mind of the images his words evoked. Images of her hands stroking over the taut hardness of his stomach, and lower.

She cleared her throat. "Do you happen to know the team?"

"Yeah. But forget about getting an introduction." His mouth tilted in a small smile. "They'd eat you alive."

Lacey laughed softly. They could try.

"So," Cole said, changing the subject, "where are you from and what brings you to Black Stone Gap?"

Lacey couldn't keep the amusement out of her voice. She was born in West Virginia, less than three hundred miles from Black Stone Gap, but she and her mother had moved to New England after her father's death.

"I'm from New Hampshire," she answered, "and part of the reason I'm here is to work with the Black Mountain Search and Rescue Team."

There was a momentary stunned silence, and then Cole laughed ruefully. "You're kidding, right?"

"Nope."

"Don't tell me—you're here to demonstrate the GPS units."

"Right. But how did you know that?"

Cole looked at her. "Sully mentioned something about it earlier tonight. Bringing the rescue team into the twenty-first century is big news around here. Their equipment is all but obsolete, and I understand they're pretty excited about the new devices. But I thought the company was sending a man." His gaze skimmed briefly over her, missing nothing. "And, sweetheart, you're a far cry from that."

Lacey felt herself go warm beneath his regard. "There was initially some talk about sending one of our sales reps out to demonstrate the GPS units, but I volunteered." She sensed his curiosity. "I'm here on other business, in addition to showing the rescue team the benefits of the handheld units."

"I see." There was a pause. "Does Cyrus know about this?"

"Who?"

"Forget it. If he did, he'd never have allowed you to stay at the Blackwater Inn. He'd have insisted on putting you up at his place."

"Oh, you mean Sheriff Hathaway. I was planning to talk with him in the morning and see if he could recommend somewhere else to stay."

Cole gave a short laugh and his voice was like rough sandpaper. "There is no other place to stay, unless you don't mind driving an hour or so each way. Even Cyrus lives a good ten miles outside of Black Stone Gap."

Lacey digested this in silence. She didn't want to stay an hour away, didn't want to traverse the winding mountain roads each day. She'd stay with Cole tonight, but even if they ended up in bed together, she couldn't assume that he'd want her living with him for the entire time she was in Black Stone Gap. That would just be awkward.

Cole swung off the main route, and they made their way up a steeply winding road, pressed close on both sides by dark forest. Twice, the headlights of the truck reflected the glowing eyes of some woodland creature before it darted into the dense underbrush.

Suddenly, they emerged into a clearing and Cole drew the pickup truck alongside a large log cabin. Lacey had envisioned him in a mountain cabin with fur-strewn floors, but even her imagination couldn't have created this charming structure, perched on the mountain crest and bathed in moonlight.

She peered through the windshield, taking in the sweeping porch that surrounded the house, the soaring stone chimney and dramatic windows. It may have been constructed of logs, but the architecture was pure elegance.

"This is your home?" Lacey couldn't keep the surprise out of her voice.

"Well, it's more like the family retreat. I share ownership with my siblings." He opened his door and looked over at her. "Don't worry—they're not here now. We sort of take turns coming out here. C'mon in and make yourself comfortable."

Before she could respond, Lacey's cell phone rang. By the time she fished it out of her bag, the ringing had stopped. "Wow," she commented, reading the signal bar, "you get really good reception up here."

"One of the many benefits to living on top of a mountain." He smiled. "I'll wait outside for you."

Lacey scrolled through her missed calls and saw that her mother had tried calling her eleven times. She sighed. The last thing she wanted to do was to talk to her right now, but she knew her mother would fret until she called. She answered on the first ring.

"Lacey? Is everything okay?"

"Everything is great, Mom. Really."

"I've been trying to call you for hours. Why haven't you answered?" Her mother's tone was reproachful.

"The cell phone reception is terrible, Mom. But I made it here safely and I'll be meeting with Sheriff Hathaway in the morning. Please don't worry about me. I'm *fine*."

"Give me the name of your hotel so I can reach you on their phone."

Lacey hesitated. There was no way she could tell her mother the truth about where she was staying. "It's called the Blackwater Inn, in Black Stone Gap. But I'll hardly be there, Mom. Why don't we just agree that I'll call you each evening?"

"But what if I need to reach you? I need to be able to reach you, Lacey."

She suppressed a frustrated sigh. "Then by all means try my cell phone, but I can't guarantee that you'll always be able to get through, or that I'll answer." She glanced out the window to where Cole sat on the bottom step of his porch, scratching Copper behind his ears. "Look, I have to go. I'll call you tomorrow, okay? Good night, I love you!"

She closed the phone, pushing down the guilt she invariably felt after talking with her mother. Then, just in case her mom decided they hadn't finished their conversation, she turned the cell phone off. Sliding out of the truck, she walked toward Cole, watching as he stood and gathered up her cases. Copper stretched lazily before plodding his way up the steps to the porch.

"Did you grow up here?" Lacey asked. "I mean, in this house?"

Cole snorted. "Not likely. My folks had a ramshackle house at the bottom of the hill, on the main road. My younger brother owns a timber-frame company. After Dad retired, we pitched in and had this place built for him and my mom."

"Are your parents…?"

"Passed away, yeah. They had a few good years here, though."

He spoke matter-of-factly, but Lacey thought she detected a note of regret in his voice. "You said you don't live here year-round." She turned to stare at him in bemusement. "Why not?"

Cole gave a shrug as he preceded her up the steps. "I couldn't wait to get out of Black Stone Gap. I found work in Virginia, and I didn't look back."

Lacey followed him onto the wide porch, waiting while he opened the door. "So what brings you back now? Are you on vacation?"

"Actually, I came back because I got laid off from my job over in Norfolk, but was fortunate enough to find work here in the Gap."

Something in his voice caused Lacey to glance sharply at him, but his expression was carefully blank. She didn't know Cole at all, but she guessed it must be difficult for him to admit that he had been laid off.

"What kind of work?" she asked, but she suspected that she already knew.

"I got a job at the Black River coal mine."

Lacey shouldn't have been surprised, since the coal mines were probably the largest employer in the region, but she hadn't envisioned him as a miner. Although, she acknowledged reluctantly, beggars couldn't always be choosers. He probably knew people who worked in the mines; may even have asked them to pull a few strings in order to get him a job. But she couldn't stop her imagination from conjuring up images of Cole, buried beneath hundreds of feet of earth. She shivered.

Leaning forward, he thrust the door open, leaned in to flip on a light switch, and then stood back to allow her to enter.

Lacey stepped past, unable to prevent herself from brushing against him in the confines of the door frame. She glanced up at him, and with the interior light slanting across his face, his eyes glowed with an intensity that caused a primal awareness to surge through her.

As she stepped inside she had a general impression of soaring ceilings crisscrossed with massive beams, a stone fireplace that dominated one wall, and casually comfortable furnishings strewn with throw pillows and the odd quilt. The coffee table still bore the remnants of his morning coffee, and newspapers, books and paperwork littered the end tables. The natural wood of the floor and walls lent a warm, golden glow to the entire room and Lacey gave a soft exclamation of pleasure.

"Wow," she said. "This is nice."

"Thanks." Striding to the coffee table, he began gathering up the loose papers and stuffing them into a folder. He glanced at her as he shoved the entire packet into a leather attaché case. "It's probably a little rougher than you're accustomed to, but it's comfortable."

"Why would you say that?" she asked, genuinely surprised by his comment.

Cole looked embarrassed. "I don't know," he admitted. "I guess I just picture you in one of those expensive old brownstones in the city."

Lacey made a noncommittal sound, neither denying nor confirming his words. She didn't want him to know the truth; that she still lived with her mother. After her father died— she made a mental correction—*after the state declared her father dead,* she and her mom had moved to New Hampshire and bought a small house near the coast. Right after college, Lacey had moved into an apartment with two other girls, and she'd loved the freedom. But her mother would frequently drop in unannounced, and then spend hours redecorating the small space, cleaning, or cooking enough food to keep them fed for a week.

At first, her visits had been welcome, but it wasn't long before Lacey's roommates began to view them as intrusive. When Lacey had tried to talk to her mother about it, to insist that she really was okay on her own, her mother would become emotional, leaving Lacey racked with guilt for even suggesting that she not visit so often. Eventually, Lacey had acknowledged that living on her own wasn't working, and she had moved back home.

But now here she was, alone with a guy whom she found incredibly sexy, with nothing to prevent her from doing whatever she wanted. Knowing that he found her attractive, too, gave her added courage. The fact that he was a coal miner was a little disconcerting, but it wasn't as if she was going to marry the guy, right? After what had happened to her father, and what she'd seen her mother go through following his death, she'd made a promise to herself never to get involved with a miner.

She reminded herself again that she was only here for a few days. She would deliver the handheld GPS units to the search-and-rescue team, and then work with the owner of the local mines to test STAR. And then she would return to New England. End of story. So whatever developed between her and Cole would be limited to the time she was here.

She allowed her gaze to drift over him, taking in the wide shoulders and lean hips. With her overnight bag and laptop slung over one shoulder, his T-shirt was pulled taut across a chest that was unmistakably muscular.

"I like your house." She gave him a meaningful look. "And everything in it."

The response was instantaneous as the heat smoldering in his eyes flared to life. A muscle worked in one lean cheek as he took a step toward her. His eyes raked her features.

Lacey stopped breathing. He was going to touch her. This was it. The moment when she would either cross the line or step back.

He stopped just short of her and his gaze held hers for a long moment. He was close enough that she could see the amazing striation of blues and greens in his irises, see the individual stubble of whiskers that shadowed his lean jaw and the small scar that bisected his upper lip and made her ache to trace her fingertip across it. His mouth fascinated her. It was a hedonistic mouth, capable of doing wicked things.

She stared at it, mesmerized. As if time itself had slowed, he bent his head fractionally toward hers. Lacey's eyes drifted closed and her lips parted slightly in anticipation.

"I'll show you to your room."

The words were like a dash of cold water, and her eyes flew open. He had stepped abruptly away from her and was now striding across the room.

Lacey almost sagged in disappointment. She had been so certain he was going to kiss her; couldn't believe she had misread him so completely. With a small huff of laughter, she turned to follow Cole.

He made his way up a wide, open staircase to a loft area that overlooked the living room. There was a cozy sitting area complete with armchair, floor lamp and television. Cole pushed open an adjoining door to a darkened bedroom. She stood in the doorway and watched as he set her gear down, moved to a bedside table and switched on a small lamp, bathing the room in a soft glow. A large bed dominated the room. The vaulted ceiling was angled overhead, and through two enormous skylights, Lacey could see the stars against the velvet backdrop of the night sky.

Cole turned to look at her, and there was a taut awareness about him that was almost palpable. She hovered in the doorway, unwilling to be deceived by what she was now certain was her own cranked up libido.

"Thanks," she said, forcing herself to smile. "It's perfect, and just like you said—completely private."

"Yeah, well, the bathroom's next door and you should find everything you need. Help yourself to whatever's there."

"Okay, thanks." Lacey stood back to let him pass, but he continued to stand there, watching her.

COLE KNEW HE should leave. He should go back downstairs and leave her alone, but man, oh, man, all he could think about was this woman in his bathroom. Standing naked in his shower with water sluicing down that gorgeous body.

It had taken every vestige of willpower and restraint he had not to kiss her earlier. He knew she had wanted him to, had seen the spark of heat in her eyes that said she would welcome the feel of his lips against hers. She had all but invited him free rein to that sweet, tempting mouth. He knew the attraction that smoldered between them wasn't just in his imagination. He could practically feel her need and everything in him longed to satisfy it, but he had promised that she would be safe with him.

But there was no denying the fact he wanted her. Wanted her with a fierce urgency he couldn't recall feeling for another woman in a long time. It was with extreme difficulty that he managed to get a grip on his rampant imagination.

"How about something cold to drink? A beer, maybe?"

To his relief, she smiled. "That sounds great. But do you have anything nonalcoholic? I have to get up early tomorrow morning."

"No problem. How about some lemonade?"

"Sounds good."

He indicated she should precede him back down the stairs, and he could have sworn that was a look of longing and regret she flicked between him and the bed before she turned away. With an inward groan, Cole followed her.

In the kitchen, he watched her covertly as he mixed up a pitcher of lemonade and poured two glasses, taking a long swallow from his own. She was standing and looking at a display of framed photos on the nearby wall.

"Is this your father, here?" She indicated a photo of him standing next to an older man, dangling a pair of freshly caught trout from a fishing line.

"Yeah."

She slanted him a sidelong look and a quick smile. "I can see where you get your good looks."

Cole laughed softly. *Oh, baby, flattery will get you everything.* He came around the corner of the island to hand her a chilled glass of lemonade. "Thanks."

She took the proffered glass and turned back to the collage of photos. She sipped at the drink, and as Cole watched, a bead of condensation slid slowly down the length of the glass, hung suspended for a brief instant, and then plopped wetly onto the fragile line of her collarbone. She made no move to wipe it away, but continued to study the photos. Mesmerized, Cole followed the droplet's path down over the smooth plane of her upper chest until it slid slowly from sight beneath the edge of her sundress.

"Are these your siblings?"

Cole dragged his gaze upward. "Huh?"

"It looks like you come from a large family."

Cole leaned over her shoulder to inspect the picture she was pointing to. Damn, she even smelled delicious. He tried not to inhale as he peered at the photograph. "Yeah, that's me with my brothers and sisters, taken a few years ago."

"There are so many of you!" She gave an amazed laugh. "That must have been fun, growing up in such a big family."

"Fun? I don't know if that's the word I would've necessarily chosen. *Interesting,* maybe. *Chaotic,* definitely."

He didn't want to talk about himself or his upbringing. What would a woman like her know about the hardships of living in a small coal-mining town, with barely enough money to scrape by? Or that he and his six siblings had pretty much raised themselves while their mother worked double shifts at a hospital nearly an hour from Black Stone Gap? Nope. Definitely not stimulating conversation. And not nearly as exciting as standing directly behind her.

He couldn't help himself. He bent his head fractionally and allowed himself to breathe deeply. There was the clean fragrance of her hair and the subtle scent of a light perfume. Beneath that was the delicate fragrance that was hers alone. The combination was intoxicating.

She turned her head and he heard her suck her breath in sharply, as if she was suddenly aware of just how close he was. He knew he should back off, but was momentarily transfixed by the small pulse that beat frantically along the side of her neck. Just that tiny disturbance beneath her smooth skin completely distracted him. Made him ditch every good intention he had of maintaining a respectable distance.

She turned slowly, and his eyes skimmed over her face. God, she was pretty. Gray-green eyes, clear skin combined with a faint dusting of freckles across the bridge of her nose, and a pair of lips so pink and lush he ached to caress them with his own. This time, he knew he wouldn't resist.

She was staring at him with a mixture of cautious awareness, as if she were half-afraid he might kiss her and more afraid that he wouldn't. Slowly, he reached out and took the glass of lemonade from her, leaning over to place it on the countertop without ever taking his eyes from hers. He told himself to go slowly. Be ready to back off if she gave the slightest indication this wasn't her game.

He slid his hands beneath her hair and gently massaged the soft skin behind her ears with his fingertips. His thumbs smoothed over her cheekbones.

Lacey's breath hitched audibly, and as he watched, her eyelashes fluttered and then closed, and her breath escaped on a soft sigh of pleasure. He felt his own desire kick up a notch. She swayed slightly, a barely perceptible movement toward him, and with a groan, Cole bent his head and covered her mouth with his own.

She tasted every bit as good as he knew she would. Her lips were unbelievably soft, and when she made a small, incoherent sound in the back of her throat and pressed closer to him, he nearly groaned aloud in satisfaction. He deepened the kiss. He buried his fingers in the silken mass of her hair and tipped her face up to more thoroughly explore the sweet recesses of her mouth.

Her breasts thrust softly against his chest and her hands had crept up to rest against his rib cage. His senses were filled with the taste, smell and feel of her. He was intoxicated by it. And so completely aroused that he knew she must be aware of it.

With supreme effort, he dragged his mouth from hers and stared down at her. Her face was flushed. And right now her eyes were definitely green and glazed with pleasure.

"Damn." His voice was husky, filled with awe. He traced his thumb over her swollen, damp lips. "Lady, if that's what your kisses are like, then we'd better stop right now because anything more is going to kill me."

To his utter amazement, she turned her head and followed his finger, taking it moistly into her mouth and biting down gently on the pad with her white teeth.

Sweet mercy.

The sensation was like a bolt of hot liquid shooting straight down to his groin, where he was already straining against the denim fabric.

His hand cupped her cheek, and she covered it with her own, her skin cool and soft. She raised luminous eyes to his. "What if I don't want to stop?"

He ceased breathing. Damn near ceased existing except to try and formulate some coherent response to that statement.

She didn't want to stop.

The heat that was already coursing through him turned molten.

"Then, baby," he whispered, dipping his head to taste the corner of her mouth, "I'm going to die a happy man."

4

WHATEVER LACEY EXPECTED, it wasn't to be swept completely up into those rugged arms. She gave a little cry of surprise and instinctively clutched him around the neck as he strode from the kitchen and through the living room to a separate wing beneath the loft.

"I want you so badly," he growled low in her ear, "but I don't want our first time to be on the kitchen counter."

Our first time. He spoke as though there was absolutely no question about there being a second time, and even a third. And maybe, if she was very lucky, it would be on the counter. Lacey shivered with anticipation.

He shouldered a door open and they were in a bedroom, dark but for an enormous wall of windows that allowed the moonlit sky to illuminate the room. Cole set her on her feet beside a low, wide bed, but didn't release her. He slid his hands up over the bare skin of her arms to her shoulders and drew her into his warmth.

"Lacey." His voice was low, husky. He threaded his fingers through her hair, cradling her scalp and tilting her face up to receive his kiss.

The intensity of his lips on hers seared through her, fanning the flames of her desire until she moaned softly and wound her arms around his neck, pressing wantonly against his hard frame. His tongue tangled with hers and she welcomed it, drew his head down and slanted her mouth against his to allow him better access. His own mouth was hot and sweet and tasted faintly of lemonade. She was being consumed, lost in a kiss so molten she felt she might actually melt. And all she could think was that she wanted more.

Lacey dragged her lips from his, gasping. Even in the indistinct light, he looked like he was going to devour her. And didn't that sound good? She searched his eyes, seeing her own need reflected there. She knew it was crazy, this overwhelming urge she had to be in his arms, to be crushed against that solid chest and surrounded by his heat and strength.

This man had the ability to send her pulse rate off the charts with no more than a heated glance. She didn't want to wait another minute to discover just what he could do when he *really* put his mind to it.

Silently, without taking her eyes from his, Lacey grasped a handful of his T-shirt in each hand and slowly began to tug it free from the waistband of his jeans. She pushed the fabric up and slid her palms over the lean, muscled contours of his waist. God, he was hard everywhere. There wasn't an ounce of extra flesh to be had, at least from what she could feel. His skin was like hot silk.

"You're incredible," she breathed, and she wasn't exaggerating.

She pushed the fabric up higher until she could feel the hard thrust of his pecs. She smoothed her palms over his muscles until her fingertips encountered the small nubs of his nipples. She heard him suck in his breath, felt his body tighten beneath her questing hands. Barely pausing, she continued to slide the material upward, and he helped her by raising his arms and dragging the shirt over his head.

Oh. My. God.

Lacey gaped at the man standing before her. Moonlight slanted in through the window behind him, gilding his body in silver. He was astonishingly beautiful. Breathtaking. All rigid muscles and lean contours, from the hard thrust of his powerful shoulders down to the sculpted ridges of his stomach.

Lacey's mouth went dry and a liquid heat pooled at her core. Even her overly active imagination could never have created the perfection that was Cole MacKinnon. And she hadn't even seen the rest of him, which she was definitely going to have to do something about.

"Okay." Cole's voice was warm and husky in the darkness. "My turn."

Lacey's insides turned to jelly at the implicit promise in his softly spoken words. She stood in boneless anticipation as he reached out and drew her slowly forward, until an inhale of breath was all that prevented the tips of her breasts from brushing against his chest. He cupped the nape of her neck and tipped her head to the side to allow him unrestricted access to the sensitive skin of her throat. His lips trailed a path along her jaw as his other hand swept down her back, smoothing over the arch of her spine and taking her zipper with it.

Then he was sliding the fabric from her shoulders, easing it down over her arms until it settled around her waist. Lacey shivered, despite the warmth of the evening. He stepped back slightly and switched on a small bedside lamp. She could feel the heat of Cole's gaze like a lick of flame along her flesh.

Holding her gaze, he took her hands in his own and intertwined their fingers as he slowly drew her arms away from her body. Only when they were stretched outward did he allow his stare to drift downward. The hot, raw masculine desire she saw in his eyes was unmistakable, and the sweep of his gaze across her body was like a physical caress. Her nipples tightened and her skin warmed beneath his intimate regard.

"You're perfect," he said on a husky note, and with her fingers still tangled warmly in his, drew her hands up until they encircled his neck. He dipped his head briefly to capture her lips with his own, caressing them.

Lacey closed her eyes, giving herself up to his expertise. His body began a slow, rhythmic swaying against hers as he slid his hands down the length of her arms. Hardly aware of doing so, she pressed closer and then gasped softly into his mouth as he deftly unhooked the back of her bra and eased the straps down.

"I want to see you," he rasped. "All of you."

Setting her slightly away from him, he lowered her arms until the bra slid from her body to the carpet. He made a low growling sound of approval and filled his hands with her breasts. He cupped them, lifted them and squeezed them gently until the nipples thrust upward, practically begging for more. Lacey felt weak, and when Cole dipped his head and swirled his tongue around one engorged peak, she thought she would collapse from sheer pleasure.

"Ohmigod," she gasped, uncertain whether it was the sensation of his mouth, hot and wet, against her sensitive flesh or the sight of his dark head against her breast that caused every rational part of her brain to completely shut down.

She clutched at his head, running her fingers over the rough velvet of his hair and urging him silently to continue. He rolled one nipple between his teeth and then drew sharply on it, his hands sliding down over her hips and back up again, this time beneath the fabric of her sundress. He cupped her bottom as he suckled her, his fingers scant inches from that part of her that was pulsating and damp with need.

Lacey arched her back, wanting to be closer still. She slid her hands over the muscled contours of his arms and up over his shoulders, reveling in his hardness and his heat.

Releasing her breast, he captured her face between his hands and claimed her mouth in a kiss that was completely off the charts. It was a no-holds-barred kind of kiss that was all-consuming and said without words how desirable he found her. She made no protest when he reached down and pushed the sundress from her hips to pool on the floor. Without breaking the kiss, he slid his hands into the back of her panties and cupped the soft mounds of her cheeks, squeezing gently while he fitted himself against her hips. Through the material of her panties and his jeans, his arousal was unmistakable.

"Tell me what you like," he demanded hoarsely, pulling back and searching her face. "I want to make this right, to make it good…"

Lacey laughed unevenly. Was he kidding? Five minutes of his mouth against hers was better than anything she'd ever experienced. From here on, anything else he did was just an added bonus.

"Okay, then," she whispered. "Why don't you start where you are and, um, work your way down?"

"Sweetheart, nothing has ever sounded so good," Cole assured her, and eased her back until her legs came up against the edge of the bed.

With a soft murmur of assent, Lacey lay back across the coverlet and drew him down with her, but he scooped her up and hefted her more fully into the center of the bed, settling himself alongside her. True to his word, he started at her ear, circling it with his tongue, his warm breath sending shivers of anticipation through Lacey. He kissed her briefly, intensely, his tongue sweeping against hers before he began to work his way down her body. He filled his palms with her breasts, kneading them and rolling the distended tips between his fingers before laving each one with his tongue.

Lacey drew her breath in sharply at the exquisite sensation

and arched upward against his questing mouth, her hands exploring the ridges and valleys of his back and shoulders. Too soon, he released her breasts and trailed his lips across her stomach, sliding his hands beneath her.

When he reached the edge of her panties, he kissed the delicate skin just above the fabric and looked up at her. Lacey's breath was coming unevenly. It was almost embarrassing how intensely aroused she was. She wanted nothing more than for him to settle himself on top of her so she could rotate her hips against his hardness.

"Open your legs," he whispered, and cupped her knee with one hand, urging her legs apart.

His soft command was so sexy that Lacey was helpless to prevent her legs from falling open. He bent his head and kissed her through the silky fabric of her panties. The heat of his mouth on her was almost her undoing and her hips jerked in response. "Oh, please, please…"

"Soon, baby, soon," he murmured and reared up to kneel between her splayed thighs. And just like she had imagined, he began to slide her panties slowly down over her hips. She lifted her bottom to help him, raising one leg so he could tug them off completely, and then she was lying there with absolutely nothing to shield her from his molten gaze.

"You're so damned gorgeous," he whispered hoarsely, and cupped her lightly with one hand. "And hot. So hot."

Watching him as he looked at her through half-closed eyes was an incredible turn-on. His expression made Lacey feel as if she was the sexiest woman on earth. She was practically purring.

He bent forward, and Lacey wrapped her arms around him, seeking his mouth and drawing on his tongue. God, he tasted so good. But as wonderful as he felt beneath her hands, she wanted more. She reached between them and began to work at his belt, frustrated when it wouldn't release for her.

He laughed softly, the warm sound curling along her senses. "Easy, sweetheart. We have all night." But he obliged her by pushing her hands aside and releasing both his belt and the button on his jeans in a few deft movements.

"Finally," Lacey panted, and scarcely believing her own boldness, she reached down and cupped him through the denim, watching his eyes darken with desire. He was large, that much she could tell. Leaning forward, she slid his zipper down and began to ease the fabric over his lean hips. "My turn," she whispered. "Now I want to see *you*. All of you."

Cole sat up and swiftly removed his boots and socks. With an urgency that was almost comical, he shoved his jeans down over his knees and kicked his legs free.

He was wearing a pair of black boxer briefs. They were snug and hugged the taut curves of his backside. His thighs were lean and corded with muscle. He could have been a cover model for men's underwear. And when he turned toward her once more, Lacey saw the impressive bulge that strained against the fabric.

Reaching out, she slipped her fingers into the waistband of the briefs and tugged him closer. With a laugh that was half groan, he tumbled onto her, scooping her into his arms at the last minute and rolling across the bed so that they ended up, breathless and laughing, with Lacey half-sprawled across his chest, their legs intertwined.

With her hair hanging like a curtain around their faces, they stared at each other for a wordless moment, until Cole slid one hand to the back of her head and drew her down for his kiss. Their tongues tangled and his other hand cupped and kneaded her bottom.

Lacey moaned softly into his mouth, feeling his hardness pressed against her. She gasped when he dipped his hand between her thighs and stroked her intimately with his finger.

"God, you're so wet," he groaned, and his kiss deepened, his tongue spearing into her mouth even as he caressed her damp, swollen flesh. Lacey's legs straddled his, and she arched her back to grant him better access.

"Cole," she gasped, "I want you inside me."

"Say that again," he growled.

"I want you."

He laughed huskily. "Oh, yeah. I love hearing you say that." He stroked his lips across hers again. "But you said my name. I want to hear you say my name again."

"Cole," she breathed.

In one smooth, fluid movement he flipped her onto her back and then he was over her, kissing her mouth, her jaw, her throat, and working his way lower.

"Wait," she panted when he reached the apex of her thighs and cupped her with his hand, sliding one finger into her while he stroked and teased her breasts with his other hand. An orgasm teetered just out of reach and she knew that if he put his mouth on her sensitized flesh, she would explode. And she didn't want this to end too soon. "Cole, stop."

He glanced up at her, a wicked grin tilting his luscious mouth. "Is there a problem?"

He inserted a second finger and Lacey's hips bucked. "Oh, God, Cole, you have to stop." She gasped when he stroked his thumb over her, a shudder of pleasure racking her body. "Please."

Cole withdrew his hand, but made no move to scoot back up the length of her body. "Well, jeez," he said huskily, "that's a shame, considering I was just getting to know you so well." He smoothed his hands over her hips and then beneath them, raising her up slightly. "Maybe this will change your mind…"

Before Lacey could form a coherent thought, he lowered his head and her entire existence was reduced to this one man and the unbelievable, overwhelming sensation of his mouth on her. And when he flicked his hot, velvet tongue against her, she gave a strangled cry and thrust her hips upward, convulsing in an orgasm so powerful she thought she might actually die.

Only when she stopped shivering did Cole raise himself over her. She wound her arms around his neck and kissed him, tasting her own delicate essence on his lips. He groaned softly against her mouth.

"Oh, man," he rasped with a soft laugh, "that was amazing. Truly, unbelievably amazing."

Lacey had to agree with him.

"I've never felt anything quite so—so powerful before," she admitted, stretching languidly beneath him. "I'd almost forgotten how good this could be."

Cole cocked his head and gave her a quizzical look. "What do you mean?"

Lacey looped her arms around his neck and pressed a kiss against his mouth. "Let's just say it's been a while since I've done this. But I'm glad that you're the one who ended my dry spell."

Cole gave her a tender smile that did odd things to her equilibrium. "Well, I'm glad, too. Can I ask just how long it's been?"

"A couple of years."

Cole drew away slightly, his face registering surprise. "Are you serious? Are the guys up north blind?"

Lacey laughed. "Thanks, but it's by choice. My job is pretty demanding and I don't have a lot of free time."

It was a partial truth, at least.

"I get it, but a couple of *years?*"

"You'll have to help me make up for lost time," she said, and moved suggestively beneath him.

"Oh, yeah? Well, I'm all for that."

Lacey liquefied under his tender expression and the implicit promise in his words. She could feel the hard thrust of him against her hips and, reaching down, tugged at his briefs. "Maybe you want to start by taking these off."

He helped her, sliding them off and kicking them free. And there he was, rising thick and heavy against the tautness of his abdomen. Lacey's mouth went dry.

Unable to prevent herself, Lacey wrapped her fingers around him. He jerked reflexively in her hand. He was hot. And hard. And as smooth as satin beneath her fingertips. She slid her hand down the length of him and felt a surge of feminine pride when he sucked his breath in sharply and buried his face against her neck. Lacey continued to stroke him, tentatively at first and then with growing confidence as he groaned softly and bent his head to her breast, capturing a nipple in his mouth and drawing deeply on it.

And there it was again. The slow, throbbing ache that made her long to wrap her legs around him and bring him completely inside her.

"Cole," she whispered against his hair.

He raised his head from her breast and his eyes were startlingly blue. "Yeah?"

"I want you. Now."

"I almost forgot." He slanted her a crooked grin and then leaned over to open a drawer in the bedside table and drew forth a small foil package.

A condom! God, she hadn't even thought about protection.

She watched as he expertly covered himself, then positioned himself above her. Reaching down, he lifted one of her legs and laid it across his hip, opening her for him. He stroked a finger along her damp cleft and Lacey gasped at the exquisite sensation. But when she felt the fullness of his erection pressing against her, a liquid heat gathered at her core and she lifted her hips in invitation. His breathing was ragged as he gazed down at her and, in one smooth movement, surged forward and buried himself inside her.

Lacey groaned as he filled her and clutched at his shoulders. He captured her mouth with his, sweeping his tongue against hers as he began to move, his hands cupping her buttocks and lifting her to better meet the bone-melting thrusts of his hips. Lacey arched against him and raised both legs to wrap them around his lean hips.

"That's it," he rasped huskily against her mouth.

Lacey had never felt anything so all-consuming. She was being swept upward in a vortex of sensations, clinging with mindless abandon to this amazing man who seemed to understand what it was she needed before she did. He was as attuned to her body as if it were an extension of his own, as if he was somehow hardwired into her. He thrust again, slowly, moving his body sensuously against hers, and she barely suppressed a huff of laughter as she realized he *was* hardwired into her. And she was about to experience a total system overload.

"Ohmigod," she breathed raggedly, as pulsating pressure built once more and threatened to undo her. "Cole…"

He smoothed the damp tendrils of her hair back from her face. "I'm here," he breathed huskily. "I'm right here with you, baby." He ground his hips against hers, thrusting deeper, until he filled her completely.

"Oh, oh," Lacey gasped, and Cole caught her small, frantic cries with his mouth, spearing his tongue against hers as he moved faster, deeper. Reaching a hand between their bodies, he stroked a finger over her, and the simple contact was enough to push her completely over the edge.

Lacey climaxed in a blinding white-hot rush of pleasure, even as Cole gave a harsh cry and she felt him stiffen and then shudder inside her. As she drifted slowly back to reality, she stroked her hands over his back, slick with sweat, and reveled in the feel of his body, heavy and replete against hers.

Cole kissed her, slowly and languorously, but made no move to withdraw from the warmth of her body.

"Hey," he murmured, "you okay?"

Lacey gazed at him and nodded mutely. She couldn't have articulated what she felt at that moment if her life depended on it. Her body still shuddered with small aftershocks. In the indistinct light, his eyes were filled with a tenderness that made her chest constrict.

Rolling away from her, he quickly cleaned up and then returned to the bed, pulling her against his chest and drawing the sheet over them. His hand stroked a lazy pattern over her arm.

"I have a feeling that neither of us is going to get much sleep tonight," he murmured against her hair.

His voice held infinite promise, and outside the night sky was still brilliant with stars. And for tonight, at least, it was enough. She wouldn't think about tomorrow, or all the tomorrows after that.

5

COLE HAD BEEN AWAKE for hours. He bent his arms behind his head, careful not to disturb the woman who lay curled against him like a contented kitten, one hand resting over his heart. Her hair spilled over his shoulder like a skein of pale red-gold silk and her skin was almost translucent against the suntanned brown of his own. One slim leg was thrown across his thighs, and she was pressed against him from his neck all the way down to his ankles.

He groaned softly and tried not to think of how incredibly soft her skin felt, or how good she smelled, or how he had only to turn his hips slightly to gain access to the sweetest, most intimate part of her.

It was almost six-thirty, but he was reluctant to wake her. Reluctant to end a night filled with some of the most amazing moments of his life. He didn't typically go in for one-night stands, and on the rare occasion that he did, he acted in true insensitive-jerk style and made sure he was gone long before the sun rose. He'd never spent a full night with a woman he'd only just met. And he'd never brought a strange woman back to his place.

Until now.

His gaze drifted over Lacey, lingering on the soft fullness of her lips, watching the rhythmic rise and fall of her chest in utter fascination. Her breasts were small, the nipples pale and pink, but they fit perfectly in the palms of his hands.

He closed his eyes and groaned inwardly, knowing he was in real danger here. She aroused every protective male instinct he had. Hell, she just plain aroused him. They hadn't slept more than an hour all night. And in between the mind-blowing sex, they'd talked and nestled together until their bodies recovered and clamored for yet more. She hadn't been kidding when she'd said she was making up for lost time. Yeah, it was definitely a night he was going to remember for the rest of his life.

But right now, all he could think about was how she would react when she woke up in his bed, still wrapped around him. Would she be warm and welcoming, or self-conscious and uncomfortable, wanting only to be gone from his life? He'd been there, done that, and even if *he* had been the one wanting to be gone, it wasn't exactly a fun-fest for either party.

As if on cue, she murmured something incoherent, her eyelashes fluttered, and then he was gazing down into the luminous gray-green of her eyes. Sleepy and bemused, she stared up at him for a moment, and then smiled.

"I'm still dreaming."

"Not unless I'm having the same dream, baby," Cole said softly, and stroked a hand over her hair.

She continued to stare up at him, and the sleepy confusion was slowly replaced with an expression of dawning awareness as she came fully awake.

"What time is it?" She sat up, withdrawing her limbs from his body and curling them inward, dragging the sheet over her nakedness.

So that's how it was going to be. Damn.

"It's barely six-thirty," he answered.

He couldn't help himself. He cupped the nape of her neck and drew her head down, intent on sampling her mouth. She gave him a chaste, closemouthed kiss before pulling away.

"I should take a quick shower and then get going," she said apologetically.

Cole pushed down his own disappointment and opted instead for a light tone. Maybe she was just being typically female, uncomfortable at being seen with bed-head and no cosmetics. Although, hell, he'd never seen a woman look as desirable as she did first thing in the morning.

"Well, as long as you're taking a shower," he said huskily, "can I offer to scrub your back?"

She cast him a swift glance and Cole could have sworn she was considering it. Her gaze slid over him, and he was helpless to prevent the instant reaction of his body. But if she was tempted, she did a great job resisting. She dragged the sheet around her and stood up.

"Thanks, but I really am going to be quick. I have some calls to make, and I'm sure you have things you need to do."

What would she say if he told her the only thing he wanted to do—needed to do—was her?

"Yeah. Okay. Take a shower, and I'll make some coffee. Then I'll run you over to the sheriff's office."

"Thanks." As if on impulse, she leaned down and pressed a swift kiss against his mouth. "And thanks, too, for last night. It was great."

Her words had a ring of finality, and Cole watched as she walked across the room, the sheet trailing behind her. He heard the bathroom door shut, and then there was the unmistakable sound of the lock clicking into place.

Yep. That had gone real well. He flung himself back against the pillows and threw an arm across his eyes.

She was so gone from his life.

But what did it really matter, anyway? He would only be in Black Stone Gap long enough to obtain the evidence he needed to prove the coal mines were operating illegally, and then he'd return to his home on Virginia Beach, just outside of Norfolk. He'd agreed to go undercover for the

Feds, but he hadn't counted on how hard it would be to lie to his friends and family about why he'd returned. If anyone knew his real reasons for wanting to work in the mines, they'd despise him. The local coal mines were the biggest employer in the region, and if they shut down, hundreds of people would lose their jobs. But that was preferable to losing their lives, wasn't it?

Even if he'd been inclined to pursue some kind of relationship with Lacey, it wasn't like she lived locally. Christ, she was from Boston. He could just picture where she lived, in one of those elegant old brownstones on a cobbled backstreet of the city, where the rents went for about a zillion bucks a month and the number of piano bars per capita was exceeded only by the number of young investment brokers.

He snorted. It was no wonder she was anxious to leave. Hell, she'd been slumming last night. No doubt she and her girlfriends would have a good laugh over martinis about how she once did it redneck-style.

But then he recalled her confession that she hadn't been with anyone in a long time, and he knew instinctively he was wrong. This was a woman who apparently didn't share much of herself with others. He suspected she was more than a little self-conscious by her passionate response to him last night. She'd probably never had a one-night stand in her whole life.

All things considered, he was beginning to feel a little better about the situation. He'd almost forgotten that she was from New England, home of the original Puritan. But hell, he wished she wouldn't feel embarrassment over the things they'd done. Because if he had anything to say about it, they'd be doing a whole lot more of those things.

WHEN LACEY CAME out of the bathroom, she smelled the tantalizing aroma of bacon cooking, and heard Cole whistling softly in tune to the radio as he prepared breakfast.

"Smells good!" she called as she scooted down the hallway and up the stairs, wearing nothing but a towel.

"Hey, we don't dress up for breakfast around here," he shouted after her. "Come as you are!"

Lacey smiled, but didn't answer. She could easily envision what would happen if she came to the table wearing only a towel. Not that those images weren't appealing, but Lacey knew she had to get away while she still could; Cole Mac-Kinnon was too irresistible. If she wasn't careful, she could easily be tempted to scrap her work and spend all her time with him, instead. She blushed every time she thought about the previous night. Which was, like, every second since she had woken up plastered against his hard body.

Had that really been her doing those things with a virtual stranger? The entire night was like some surreal fantasy, as if some alien sex goddess had temporarily taken control of her body. That uninhibited, wanton creature surely hadn't been her. And while she didn't regret a single second of the previous night, neither did she want Cole to become a distraction to her real purpose for being in Kentucky. This was her first field assignment and she didn't want to screw it up. She needed to stay focused.

In the guest bedroom, she retrieved her cell phone, turned it on, and saw she had several text messages from her mother, mostly chiding her for turning her phone off. There was another message from her office, and she punched in the number as she changed. Her friend Julia, who worked in the customer service department, answered on the first ring.

"Good morning, StarPoint Technologies. How may I direct your call?"

"Julia, it's me…Lacey."

"Lacey, where are you? I tried calling you last night and you didn't answer."

"I know. I had my phone on avoidance mode. Sorry."

Julia made a sympathetic noise. "Your mom? I understand. As long as you made it there safely, no worries. But please give her a call today or she'll start calling the office, and you know how Sam hates that."

Sam Caldwell was their boss, and although he understood that Lacey had her hands full with her mother, there were limits to his patience.

"I'll call her. Yes, I made it here safely, but…" Her voice trailed off as she wondered just how much she should share with her friend.

"But what?" Julia asked. "Spit it out, Delaney, or I'll start imagining the worst."

Lacey sat down on the edge of the bed. "I met a guy last night and stayed at his place."

"*What?* Oh, come on. You're pulling my leg."

"No, I'm not kidding." Lacey quickly told Julia about the previous night, leaving out only the most intimate details. On the other end of the phone, Julia made little gasping noises, as if she couldn't quite believe what Lacey was telling her.

"When I said you should cut loose and live a little, I didn't exactly mean with the first guy you meet!" Julia said, once Lacey had finished. "Oh, man…your mother is going to kill me! I know she thinks I'm a bad influence on you."

"She can't know, and you can't tell her. I gave her the number of the motel where I initially checked in, but I don't plan on going back there. If she calls the office, just tell her that I can't be reached because of the poor reception in this area, but you'll get a message to me through Sheriff Hathaway. That will calm her down a little. I hope."

"Don't you think you should just tell your mom that it's your life? I mean, c'mon. You're twenty-seven, old enough to do what you want."

Lacey sighed. "You're right. I'll talk with her when I get home. I promise."

They talked for a few minutes longer, and although Lacey would have liked to speak with Sam, he was in a meeting and unavailable. After she hung up, Lacey donned underwear and bra, pulled on a pair of jeans and was just shoving her arms into a pale green top when a voice from the doorway startled her.

"I brought you up a cup of coffee."

Lacey whirled, her fingers pausing over the buttons of her blouse. Cole leaned negligently against the door frame, wearing a pair of jeans and a crisp white T-shirt that only served to emphasize the sun-browned hue of his skin and the startling blue of his eyes. With the morning light slanting through the skylights, she could see the faint shadow of whiskers on his lean jaw. He looked altogether edible.

"I'm almost ready," she said, swiftly fastening the last buttons.

"Hey." He came to stand directly in front of her. "Are you okay?"

She smiled brightly at him. "Of course. Why wouldn't I be?"

He looked at her with a mixture of tenderness and resignation that caused her chest to constrict. "I'm getting the distinct impression that you're either avoiding me, or keeping me at arms' length. What happened between last night and this morning? I mean, did I miss something?"

He made no move to touch her, just stood cradling a mug of hot coffee between his hands as he watched her. She tucked a damp tendril of hair behind her ear and bit her lip to stop herself from blurting the truth. What had happened between last night and this morning was phenomenal, and it scared the hell out of her. She wasn't prepared for her own emotional response to him.

She cleared her throat. "Last night was amazing." She raised her eyes and met his gaze fully, letting him see the truth in her words. "Really amazing. But for obvious reasons, it can't ever be more than what it was. You know…a one-night stand."

"Oh, yeah?" His gaze was intense, the heat in his eyes causing a now familiar flutter in her midsection. He took a step closer and pressed the mug of coffee into her hands, wrapping his own hands around hers so that she was encased in heat. "What if I told you that I want to see you again? No matter what?"

Lacey stared at him and her stomach did an odd flip-flop at the expression of fierce determination on his face. She couldn't breathe. Couldn't speak. Couldn't form a single coherent thought.

He stepped away from her, raked a hand over his hair and swore softly. "Christ, I'm losing my mind." He turned abruptly back to her, his hands raised as if to stop her from speaking. "Listen, I know you're here on business, but I'd really like to spend some time with you. Okay? Even if it's only for a day or so. After that…well, maybe we can work something out."

"Do you think that's a good idea? I mean, we hardly know each other."

To her surprise, he laughed, a rich sound that slid along her senses like a warm caress. "My point exactly." He grasped her gently by the shoulders and pulled her toward him. "We've been as physically intimate as two people can be, yet we hardly know each other. There isn't an inch of your body that I'm not familiar with, and I'm not going to lie and tell you that I wouldn't love to have a repeat of last night." He gave a self-deprecating laugh. "Hell, I live in hopeful anticipation of just such an event."

Lacey's body reacted instantly beneath his heated regard, warming and growing pliant, until she found herself swaying fractionally toward him.

"But it's not enough, Lacey." He stroked a thumb across her cheek. "I'd like more."

"I really like you." She smiled ruefully. "Obviously. But I don't have time for a relationship, you know? Especially not a long-distance one."

"No, I *don't* know." He tipped her face up, forcing her to meet his gaze. "But I do know one thing, and that is we're good together. Better than good. Let's start with that."

He wanted to see her again. Even if it was only for the short time she was going to be in Black Stone Gap. She desperately wanted to see him again, too. That was the problem. Even after just one night, he'd managed to get under her skin.

"I'm leaving in just a few days," she hedged. "And I'll be working most of the time. I don't know how much free time I'll have."

"Okay, so we'll make adjustments based on your schedule. But you need to eat dinner, right? And who better to show you around the area than me?" He dipped his head to stare directly into her eyes. "Will you at least consider it?"

Looking into his blue eyes, Lacey found her resistance slipping. She nodded. "Okay."

"Okay. Great." He gave her a lopsided grin. "When you've finished getting dressed, come downstairs and have some breakfast."

After he left, she shoved her belongings into her overnight bag and slipped on a pair of soft leather flats. She swiftly ran a brush through her hair and then carefully applied a light coat of mascara and lip gloss before examining herself critically in the full-length mirror. Deciding that she looked presentable, she gathered up her bags and made her way downstairs. Dropping her suitcase and overnight bag near the door, she entered into the kitchen. Cole was just scooping some crispy bacon onto a plate, and Lacey's mouth began to water when she spied the omelet and sliced fruit on the table.

Cole looked up and his gaze turned hungry as he watched her. "You look great."

Selecting a wedge of melon from the plate, Lacey smiled at him. "Thanks," she said, and took a bite of the juicy fruit.

Cole's eyes fastened on her mouth. "In fact, you look good enough to eat."

Her mind was immediately swamped with vivid memories of the previous night. She pushed them unwillingly aside. "You've just gone too long without food," she teased. "You're a guy—at this point, anything probably looks good enough to eat."

He grinned unrepentantly and held a chair out for her. "In that case, we'd better eat quickly and satisfy my appetite, or I'll start looking around for something else to do it."

Lacey sat down in the chair he held out for her. His words both thrilled and alarmed her, and a part of her was tempted to sweep the breakfast aside and offer herself up instead. She'd had relationships before, but she couldn't recall any guy who'd made her feel as sexy as Cole did. If her job here in Kentucky wasn't so important, she could easily envision herself and Cole holed up in his bedroom for the next month.

They ate in silence, but Lacey was acutely aware of Cole's eyes on her. He was a difficult man to ignore, and she wondered if she would have the resolve to leave him when her time in Kentucky ended. She wondered if she even wanted to.

6

As Cole drove Lacey to the sheriff's office, she couldn't help but be amazed at the beauty of the surrounding landscape. Lush green mountains sheltered deep valleys, where tiny towns nestled alongside winding rivers. She had spent the first eight years of her life not far from Black Stone Gap, but she had few memories of those days, aside from her father's death.

"I didn't expect Kentucky to be so unspoiled," she finally admitted, turning her gaze from the window to the man beside her.

Cole glanced over at her, one dark eyebrow raised. "What were you expecting?"

"I know this is a coal-mining region, so…I don't know. I guess I was expecting to see strip-mined hillsides and some kind of processing plants spewing black smog." She saw the amusement that curved his lips, before he gave her a tolerant look. "Okay," she admitted ruefully, "so I was wrong. You don't have to look at me like that."

Cole grinned. "Sorry. You're not entirely wrong. Most of the mining is done belowground, so you don't see it. But sometimes it's a battle to keep the rivers and streams clean of the runoff."

"You must know a lot about mining, having grown up here. I mean, even your name says it all."

Cole smiled as he negotiated a sharp turn on the steep road. "Yep. My old man was a coal miner. When he was young, he was injured in a mining accident and my mother was the nurse who cared for him in the hospital. They got married and I was born. They named me Cole for obvious reasons."

Lacey gave him a wan smile. *His father had been a miner.* Now Cole also worked in the mines. "What a romantic story."

He shrugged. "Yeah, well, I wouldn't call their life romantic, but my mom never complained. Mining is in our blood."

"Were you a coal miner before you got laid off?"

"I got my degree in mining engineering, but I only worked in the coal mines for about six months, right after I graduated. I left mining about five years ago and went to work for the State of Virginia as a structural engineer."

"Until you got laid off," Lacey clarified.

"Right."

"Do you think you'll stay here? Or will you try to get back to Virginia?"

He was silent for a long moment, as if struggling with a response. "This is just temporary," he finally said. "My goal is to return to Virginia as soon as I can."

The news should have made her feel relieved, but all she could think was that he would spend time in the coal mines. It didn't matter if he was an engineer; he could still die in those tunnels.

"Well, I hope that works out for you," Lacey said, meaning it sincerely. She fixed her attention on the passing landscape, telling herself that as an engineer, he would naturally take precautions and pay close attention to the conditions inside the mines. Nothing would happen to him, and she wouldn't let her imagination conjure up any horrific images of all the things that could go wrong. She refused to let her fears control her life, the way her mother's fears controlled hers.

They turned down a dirt road near a sign that read Rod and Gun Club. Lacey gave Cole a questioning look. "Where are we going?"

"This is where the rescue team meets, since the sheriff's office isn't much more than a broom closet in the town hall." His gave her a reassuring smile. "I'll get you settled with the team, and then come back when you're finished."

"You don't need to do that," she said quickly. "I'll ask Sheriff Hathaway to give me a ride back when we're through."

They hadn't talked about where she would stay after today, but when she'd tried to carry her suitcase out of Cole's house that morning, he'd set it firmly back inside, telling her they would figure it out later.

"Here we are," he said, ignoring her comment.

They pulled alongside several other pickup trucks beside a low, sprawling structure. It looked to Lacey to be a recreation center of sorts, with picnic tables and barbecue grills scattered beneath tall trees. Beyond the picnic area, she could make out a shooting range. But it wasn't this that caused her words to fade.

The entire area was swarming with men. There were about fifteen of them, and at first glance, they looked remarkably similar, each of them wearing blue jeans, black baseball caps, and bright orange T-shirts with the words *Black Mountain Search and Rescue* emblazoned across the back. For a moment, Lacey wondered if they'd stumbled across some crime scene investigation in progress. There was an assortment of electronic equipment, ropes and climbing gear strewn across the grass, and the men were painstakingly examining and packing each piece.

"They must have just returned from a call," Cole commented as he thrust the truck into Park and turned off the engine.

Lacey glanced at her watch. It was barely nine o'clock. As they climbed out of the cab, one of the men looked up, spoke briefly with the others, and walked over to greet them. He was too young to be Sheriff Hathaway. In fact, he looked to be about Cole's age, and was just as good-looking in his own right, with chocolate-brown eyes and a shock of tawny hair.

"Cole," he said with a grin. "Good to see you, man." He thrust a hand out to Cole, who shook it warmly. "I heard you were back in town. What brings you out here?"

"Carr, I'd like you to meet Lacey Delaney. She's come from Boston to demonstrate the GPS units." He took Lacey's elbow in one hand and drew her forward. "Lacey, this is Carr Hamilton. He heads up the search-and-rescue team."

Carr's eyebrows shot up briefly in surprise before he swiftly composed his features, but Lacey didn't miss the sharply questioning look he gave Cole. "Ma'am." He inclined his head toward Lacey and extended a hand in greeting. "How'd you manage to hook up with Cole?"

Lacey wondered at his choice of words, but was spared from having to answer by Cole.

"I came across her broken down in Mel's parking lot last night. She was staying at the Blackwater Inn, but they're having problems with their air-conditioning, so I persuaded her to spend the night with me." He turned away to retrieve Lacey's presentation materials from the bed of his truck, but not before she saw a telltale dimple flash briefly in one lean cheek.

She bit the inside of her cheek. Not "stay at my place," but "spend the night with me." There was no way anyone could miss the blatant message in those words. He'd just stamped her with his own seal of ownership as surely as if he'd said, "Hands off—she's mine."

To his credit, Carr's expression never wavered from one of polite interest. "Well, you couldn't have been in better hands."

Lacey's face turned warm at the unintended double meaning. "I agree," she murmured in acknowledgment, and didn't dare look at Cole as he set her equipment down on the grass beside the truck.

Unaware of her discomfort, Carr continued blithely on. "Cole used to be part of the rescue team. He was the best damn tracker we ever had. It was a real loss to the team—and the community—when he left." He turned to Cole and stared at him directly, as if challenging him to dispute his words.

Beside her, Cole smiled, but Lacey could almost feel the tension in him. But when he spoke, his voice was friendly. "I signed on as the new engineer at the Black River Mines, but I have no interest in rejoining the team," he said. "And I'm sure the entire community drew a collective sigh of relief the day I left Black Stone Gap."

Carr gave him a quizzical look before clapping him on the back. "Absolutely not so. The team would welcome you back, you know that. Nobody ever blamed you for what happened, except yourself."

"Carr." Cole's voice held a soft warning. Lacey risked a curious glance at him. He turned back to his truck and made a show of rearranging the tools he carried in the back.

Carr considered him for a long moment, and then focused his attention on Lacey, making a visible effort to steer the conversation back to less dangerous ground.

"So, you're actually checked into the Blackwater Inn? That place doesn't have a great reputation. You're smart to stay at Cole's place while you're here."

"It's only a temporary situation." She didn't dare look

over at Cole. "I intend to ask Sheriff Hathaway to recommend another place just as soon as I see him."

Carr's eyebrows drew together and his brown eyes turned somber. "Well, that may not be anytime soon. His wife was involved in a car wreck and she's in the hospital."

Cole turned sharply from the truck. "What? When did this happen?"

Carr removed his hat and ran his fingers distractedly through his hair. "Last night. Seems she was run off the road by Stu Barlow's boy on the way home from her weekly bridge game. She suffered a massive heart attack."

"Christ." Cole stared at Lacey. "That was the wreck that Sully was heading out to last night."

Lacey recalled the radio conversation Cole had had with Sully on their way back to the garage. "You're right."

"He didn't mention that it was Dot Hathaway in the other car. I'd have headed out there myself if I'd known."

Carr's face was sympathetic. "You couldn't have done anything. She's in the cardiac care unit over at County Hospital, but I think Cyrus is going to take at least the next week or so off to be with her."

"Will she be okay?"

"Yeah, I think so. She'll need to stay in the hospital for the time being, though."

Cole turned slowly back to Lacey, and although he said nothing, she could read the expression in his eyes clearly enough. He intended to extend his hospitality to her for a while longer. And heaven help her, she was going to accept.

"So," Carr was saying, as Lacey tried to ignore the promise in Cole's eyes, "I'll be taking over for Sheriff Hathaway while you're here, Lacey. If there's anything you need—day or night—just let me know." He winked at her. "Even if it's a place to stay."

"Lacey has a place to stay." Cole's voice was firm.

Carr gave him an amused glance. "Okay. Just trying to be friendly."

The look Cole gave him was more expressive than words would have been, but Carr only laughed before turning back to Lacey. "Why don't you come with me, and I'll introduce you to the rest of the team."

Giving Cole a tolerant look, Lacey followed Carr over to the grassy picnic area, where the men were rolling up lengths of nylon rope and examining the assorted metal clasps and hooks before stowing them in duffel bags.

"Okay, boys, listen up!" Carr clapped his hands together to get their attention. "This is Miss Lacey Delaney, and she's come all the way from New England to outfit us with her GPS units. But before I trust you morons with expensive equipment like that, you're going to need some training. So finish packing up and we'll reconvene in fifteen minutes in the recreation room."

There was some laughter and a few crudely humorous remarks, but the men seemed friendly enough.

"Don't mind them." Carr jerked his head in the direction of the group. "They're a good bunch of guys, just a little rough around the edges. But they're the best damned search-and-rescue team in the state. We're comprised entirely of volunteers, and we specialize in wilderness, swift water, high angle and cave rescues."

"Just get back from a call?" asked Cole, as he joined them.

"Yeah. Two hikers didn't return to the trailhead last night. We found them a couple of hours ago, about a mile north of Hawkins Ridge. One of them had taken a tumble off a pretty steep cliff, and his buddy was stranded on a ledge trying to reach him."

Lacey couldn't prevent her small intake of breath. "Are they okay?"

Carr shrugged. "The first guy is busted up pretty good, but he'll pull through."

She frowned. "How long were you out looking for them?"

"We headed out just before dawn. Didn't take us more than a couple of hours to locate them, though."

"Your men must be exhausted. Would they rather I come back tomorrow?"

Carr laughed in genuine amusement. "Are you kidding? These guys aren't about to miss this training op. But I think I should warn you they'll probably be very slow to catch on. You might need to extend your stay by, oh, a month or so before they finally figure out how to use the GPS units."

Lacey laughed. "Well, let's hope it doesn't take that long." She slid her gaze to Cole. "I'd hate to outstay my welcome."

Cole grinned, but Lacey didn't miss the heat that flared in his eyes. "No chance."

Before she could think to protest, he caught her against him and claimed her lips in a kiss that was swift and hard. Cole set her gently away from him, and Lacey felt herself sway slightly without his support.

"You're dangerous." He moved away to open the driver's door of the truck. "I'll be back to collect you around 4:30."

Lacey nodded and strove for composure. Cole grinned, fully aware of his effect on her, before climbing into the cab and driving away.

Lacey turned back to Carr, prepared for a snide comment or a knowing smile, but he only looked good-naturedly disappointed. "I always thought MacKinnon was a lucky S.O.B., and now I'm sure of it."

"He's incredibly charming," she admitted. "Shall we get started?"

"Sure thing." He scooped up her gear, and as Lacey followed him over to the building, he pointed out the various members of the team. "That one there is Sam, but everyone calls him Skeeter."

Lacey looked over at the tall, rangy man. "Why do they call him that?"

"Because he looks just like a mosquito—you know, a 'skeeter.'"

Lacey gave the man a closer look. When he glanced up at her and grinned, she saw he had the longest, pointiest nose she had ever seen. "Oh!" She barely suppressed the laughter that threatened to bubble forth. "I see now where he gets the name."

Carr chuckled. "That fella there is Poke, and the one over by the table is Harlan. The two boys over by the shooting range are the Armstrong twins, Bill and Bob. We just call them Blob for short."

Lacey had never heard such an odd assortment of names in her entire life, and she was certain she would not be able to keep them all straight. She suspected it was going to be a very long day.

7

Lacey was so intent on her discussion with Carr, she failed to immediately notice Cole's truck when it pulled into the gravel parking lot. It was only when Carr tapped on her arm, interrupting her enthusiastic spiel about the various applications of the GPS units, that she followed his gaze to where the truck was parked. The sight of Cole striding easily across the grass toward her caused her breath to catch.

He smiled as he came closer. "So, how'd it go?"

Lacey could scarcely form a coherent thought. Late-afternoon sunlight slanted through the overhead trees and played across his features as he made his way toward her. A light breeze molded his T-shirt briefly against the smooth muscles beneath and then fluttered it away again. His eyes gleamed with warmth and pleasure, and Lacey found herself wondering if he would kiss her, the way he had when he'd left her that morning. Instead, he stopped just short of her and rested his hands easily on his hips. He made no move to touch her.

She and Carr were standing near the entrance to the Rod and Gun Club, having wrapped up the last segment of the training just minutes earlier. It had taken nearly twice as long as she had estimated to get through the first phase, but it wasn't because the rescue team was slow in comprehending the mechanics of the GPS units. Rather, they were intensely interested in how the units worked and how they might be used to improve their rescue operations. Lacey had found herself bombarded with questions and what-ifs and she'd been pleasantly surprised and flattered by the team's obvious interest. The day had flown by.

Carr was holding her GPS unit in his hands. "It went better than I had hoped, although I still think Lacey might need to extend her visit." He grinned at her and gave her a friendly wink.

"Actually," she said quickly, "the team has done a great job getting the hang of the units. We even went out and did a couple of practical demonstrations. I think, overall, it went really well."

At Carr's request, she'd called Julia and had ordered a unit for each team member and agreed to conduct some field exercises with them. But with Sheriff Hathaway at the hospital, she still had not made firm plans on where she would test STAR. Since Carr was filling in for the sheriff, Lacey hoped to spend some time with him, outlining her requirements.

"I came by around 4:30," Cole was saying, "but you were still pretty well involved." He glanced at his watch. "It's almost six now. Hungry?"

Before she could answer, Carr's pager started to beep. He yanked it from his belt and glanced at the display, and then punched a number into his cell phone. As Lacey listened, she realized he was receiving an emergency call.

He flipped the phone closed and glanced at Lacey. "Looks like I've gotta run. Three kids have gone missing in the hills, and a fourth kid thinks they went down an abandoned mine shaft."

Without waiting for a reply, he ducked into the building and Lacey could hear him barking commands to the team members still inside.

"C'mon," muttered Cole, hefting her presentation materials in one hand, "let's get out of here."

Lacey turned to him. "Shouldn't we stay?"

"Trust me," he said grimly, "the best thing we can do now is keep out of their way."

As if on cue, the doors of the club burst open and Skeeter and Harlan came through at a jog, rescue equipment thrown over their shoulders. The Armstrong twins were right behind them, and then Poke and Carr. Lacey watched as they loaded the gear into several trucks. She couldn't help but be impressed with the efficiency they demonstrated. There was no confusion about what needed to be done. They had everything stowed and ready to go in less than two minutes.

"Hey, Mac," called Carr. "How about coming along? We could use another hand."

Beside her, Cole raised both palms. "No, thanks."

Carr shrugged and then climbed into one of the trucks. He plunked an emergency light onto the roof and waved farewell before following the other vehicles out of the parking lot.

Lacey turned to Cole. He was walking toward his own truck, his steps long and purposeful. She caught up with him and waited while he secured her belongings in the bed of his truck.

"I hope you didn't refuse because of me," she ventured.

He glanced at her. "My refusal had nothing to do with you."

Lacey frowned. "Then why wouldn't you go with them? They're looking for a bunch of *kids,* Cole. I'd think that would be enough for most people to want to get involved."

He sighed and then turned to her, and Lacey saw something in his expression that made her chest constrict.

Regret. Resignation.

"It's not as easy as that, Lacey." He passed a hand over his face. "There are things you don't understand. Things I'd rather not talk about."

Before she could prevent herself, she put a hand on his arm. He angled his head to look at her, and his lips curved in a small smile.

"I don't do mine rescues," he said in explanation. "The last time I got involved in one of those, it was a complete disaster. I swore I'd never do it again."

Lacey knew her face went pale, but she couldn't prevent her thoughts from returning to the day that the rescue efforts for her father had been suspended. Amidst the chaos of emergency crews, the dozens of media personnel and the throngs of townspeople, she hadn't fully understood what was happening. But she would never forget the faces of the rescue workers as they had murmured words of regret and sympathy to her mother while Lacey had clung to her hand, unable to comprehend that her father wouldn't be coming home. Had something like that happened to Cole?

"Carr said they could use an extra hand," she persisted. "Maybe you could just, you know, help them track where the kids went into the shaft, and then leave the actual rescue to the team."

"Trust me," he said, with a laugh that sounded bitter, "they don't want me on the team any more than I want to be on it. Carr was just being polite."

Privately, Lacey disagreed. Carr had sounded pretty sincere to her and she sensed just from being in his company for one day that he wasn't the type of person who said something unless he meant it.

She watched as he shoved her gear into his stow box, not looking at her. "About my staying with you," she began. "Are you sure—"

Cole smiled then, a rueful smile that revealed the indents in his lean cheeks. Lacey felt her stomach do a slow, backward roll.

"I'm absolutely sure. I want you to stay at my place while you're here." He held up his hands. "No strings attached. If something happens between us…well then, it'll be because you want it to happen, okay?" He dipped his head to look into her eyes. "But I can't leave you at the Blackwater Inn. It's not safe. Is that fair enough?"

He was completely sincere. It was there in his eyes and his earnest expression. God, she was weak. She had absolutely no willpower to resist him. Especially not when he looked at her like that.

She was prevented from answering by the sound of a truck engine rumbling closer. Turning, she saw Carr's pickup truck making its way toward them down the gravel road, followed by the other two vehicles that had headed out at the same time.

They watched as the men got out. Carr threw a bundle of gear over his shoulder. "What, still here?" he called with a roguish grin. "I thought for sure you two would be—well, never mind what I thought."

"False alarm?"

"Yeah, we got a call about a mile out that the kids were found. They're fine. Didn't go down a shaft at all. They were just pulling a prank on one of their friends, and about scared the poor kid to death."

Harlan came around from the side of his pickup, hefting a bag that must have weighed a ton as if it were no more than a briefcase. He was a big man of few words, but Lacey sensed that very little escaped his notice. While the members of the rescue team took great enjoyment in teasing Poke and the Armstrong twins, they took no such liberties with Harlan. Lacey admitted to herself she was more than a little intimidated by the man. Now he nodded in her direction and disappeared inside the club to put away the equipment.

"Well," said Lacey, "I'm glad the kids are safe."

Carr grinned. "We all are, trust me." He shoved his hat back on his head. "Listen, we're heading into town for a drink and a bite to eat. Why don't you join us?"

Cole hesitated. "Thanks anyway."

"C'mon, man. Bring the lady out and show her a good time."

"Maybe another time."

Carr turned to Lacey. "You know, you really hooked up with the wrong guy, ma'am. Now if it had been *me,* I wouldn't be such a cheapskate. I'd be wining and dining you—"

"Okay. Fine. We'll join you." Cole gave the other man a friendly glower. "Just don't feed her that line when we all know how *you* treat the ladies."

Carr looked chagrined. "Well, I *would* at least feed her."

Cole looked over at Lacey. "Does that sound okay to you?"

"Sure. Why not? It sounds like fun." She gave Cole a bright smile.

He gave her a tolerant look. "You know," he said several minutes later, when they were in the truck and following Carr out of the parking lot, "we don't have to do this. We could go somewhere else, just the two of us."

"Why? Aren't you and Carr friends?"

Cole shrugged. "We've been good friends since we were kids. He was pretty upset with me when I left Black Stone Gap, and now that I'm back he likes to give me a hard time."

"Well, he speaks highly of you," she said. "I wouldn't mind having dinner with him and the other guys. It really does sound like fun."

Lacey realized she was hungry, and she'd enjoyed spending time with the rescue team. But when they pulled into the congested parking lot of a club called *The Bootlegger,* with country music blaring through the humid air courtesy of exterior-mounted speakers, Lacey realized they weren't just going out for a bite to eat. This place looked like a true boot-scootin', country-Western club. Lacey leaned forward in anticipation. She wondered if she could persuade Cole to teach her how to country dance.

The atmosphere inside the club was loud, smoky and festive. Lacey was surprised and a little dismayed by how crowded it was. Even at this hour, the place was nearly packed.

Country music filled the low-ceilinged room and throngs of people milled around an enormous bar, or crammed tables that ringed a large dance floor. Somebody—one of the Armstrong twins, although she couldn't tell which one—waved them over to an area at the far end of the bar. Cole took her arm and steered her expertly through the crowd.

"This place is insane!" she shouted to him, although her voice was nearly inaudible above the din.

Cole grinned and bent his head to her ear. "This is nothing. Wait until the live band kicks up around nine o'clock. Then you'll know what crazy is."

Cole procured a stool for her at the bar with Carr, Skeeter and the Armstrong twins on either side of her, then took up position directly behind her. Even without looking at him, Lacey was acutely conscious of him standing close to her, his large frame acting as a shield when the other patrons squeezed by. Within minutes, she found herself with a glass of iced tea in her hands as Cole took a long swallow from a bottle of beer.

He leaned down to speak directly into her ear, and Lacey caught the tantalizing scent that was his alone. Her pulse quickened. She had a nearly overwhelming desire to turn her face and trace her lips along the strong line of his jaw. Memories from the preceding night came flooding back, and she was helpless to prevent the warmth that slid along her veins.

"I ordered us a couple of sandwiches," he was saying, oblivious to the effect he was having on her. "We'll stay long enough to eat, then we can get out of here."

Lacey looked up to tell him she wanted to dance first, but something had caught Cole's attention farther down the bar. One moment his expression was warm and relaxed. The next instant, his features were taut and Lacey caught a glimpse of steel in their depths before he quickly averted his gaze.

Curious, she looked to see a man leaning negligently against the far end of the bar. He was well-dressed in a sports jacket and slacks, in striking contrast to the other men in the club, who wore blue jeans and boots. He smiled as he chatted with the bartender. Lacey guessed him to be in his early forties. He had a little bit of a paunch, and his hairline was receding, but she decided he had a nice face. As if sensing her scrutiny, he glanced in her direction and for a moment, their gazes met. He smiled and raised his bottle toward her in a friendly toast, and Lacey found herself smiling back at him.

"Who is that?" she asked Cole.

"My new boss, Buck Rogan," he said curtly, and nodded in the man's direction.

As they watched, the man pushed away from the bar and threaded his way toward them. Beside her, Cole stiffened, but when she glanced at his face his expression seemed cordial enough.

"Evening, ma'am." The man named Buck stood just outside their small circle. Up close, Lacey could see he was older than she'd originally thought, maybe in his early fifties. "Hello, MacKinnon. My foreman tells me he hired you on as our new engineer. Welcome aboard."

Cole nodded. "Thank you, sir. I'm looking forward to working with you."

"Really." The word was laced with mild sarcasm and even a touch of amusement. "I seem to recall you once told me that you'd see me in hell before you ever worked for me again."

To Lacey's surprise, Cole laughed, although it didn't sound genuine to her. "Well, I said a lot of things back then, I guess. I was young, and it was an emotional time." He thrust his hand out to Buck. "I hope we can let bygones be bygones."

Buck's eyes narrowed briefly, as if he also wondered at Cole's sincerity. Finally, he smiled and took Cole's hand, pumping it firmly. "Of course we can. Your daddy was the best foreman that ever worked for me. I heard about your troubles in Virginia and I'm glad that I can help you out, the economy being what it is. I always have room on my payroll for a good engineer."

"Thank you. I appreciate that."

Buck turned to Lacey. "And who is this pretty lady? I don't recall seeing you in town before."

Before Cole could answer, Lacey thrust out her hand. "I'm Lacey Delaney. I'm here from Boston, working with the search-and-rescue team."

Buck clasped her hand warmly. "Buck Rogan. Very pleased to meet you. I recall Sheriff Hathaway did tell me that you would be in town. He also mentioned that you were interested in doing some work in the mines."

Lacey couldn't believe how easy this was working out for her. "Yes, that's right. I work for a GPS company called StarPoint Technologies. I'm here to perform a field test on a prototype GPS unit that we developed for NASA. I was hoping to bring it into the mines and run it through a series of tests."

Cole turned sharply toward her. "*What?* You didn't tell me you needed access to the mines."

"You didn't ask," she replied lightly. "So Mr. Rogan, is that something you would be willing to let me do? If it's a liability issue, I understand, but I'm willing to sign a waiver."

"No." Cole bit the word out.

Both Lacey and Buck looked at him in surprise. His expression was tense, and Lacey sensed that he forced himself to relax and smile. "I only meant that the mines are no place for someone without experience," he explained lamely.

"I'll make sure that Miss Delaney is well taken care of," Buck said smoothly. Reaching inside his jacket, he pulled out a slim card holder and withdrew a business card. "Call my office and we can make the arrangements." He gave Cole a shrewd look. "Why don't you come over to the mine and see me in the morning? We'll have a cup of coffee and chat, and then I'll show you your new office."

A muscle worked in Cole's cheek, and finally he gave a curt nod. "Fine."

"Good." Buck tipped an imaginary hat at Lacey. "Nice meeting you, ma'am, and I'm looking forward to talking with you about your project."

He turned and made his way through the crowd toward the exit, and Lacey turned to Cole. "Considering that man just gave you a job, you could have been a little friendlier to him."

"I was friendly," Cole protested.

Lacey snorted. "Oh, okay."

"Why didn't you tell me you intend to go into the mines?" The words sounded like an accusation, and Lacey bristled.

"I didn't know that I was supposed to," she retorted. "Do you have a problem with that?"

"Damned straight I do."

Lacey was taken aback by his vehemence, but before she could say anything more, Carr interrupted, smoothly stepping between them. Until then, Lacey had forgotten he was even there. As she glanced at the other members of the rescue team, she saw they all looked uncomfortable, and none of them would make eye contact with Cole. What had just happened?

"How about you and I take a whirl around the dance floor?" Carr asked.

"I'd like that," she said hurriedly, grateful for the interruption.

"I'll watch your drink for you," Cole said stiffly.

Lacey gave Carr a brilliant smile as she slid her hand into his and allowed him to pull her out onto the dance floor. Once there, however, she wondered what she'd gotten herself into.

The small dance floor was crowded with couples who were expertly negotiating the steps to a complicated country dance; one that involved twirling and holding hands, and moving your feet in a precise manner that otherwise might have you tripping up your partner and losing your balance.

Carr was doing his best to guide her through the steps, and Lacey was laughing in spite of herself, embarrassed by her own clumsiness as she stumbled along beside him. The other couples gave them a wide berth as she twirled in the wrong direction, away from Carr, and came up hard against the solid chest of another man.

Cole.

He caught her by the upper arms and before she could protest, tucked her against his side. He nodded briefly to Carr, who gave Lacey a rueful smile and shrugged regretfully before he made his way from the dance floor.

"Looked to me like you could use some help." He smiled. "I figured I should step in before somebody got hurt."

The country song came to an end, but before Lacey could protest that she'd rather not dance, after all, another song started and Cole pulled her firmly into his arms. It was a slow ballad, with a man's heart-wrenchingly velvet voice singing about how shameless he was when it came to loving his woman.

Cole intertwined his fingers with hers, curling her hand against his chest as he pulled her close, and his other hand at the small of her back. Lacey resisted for about a second, her body stiff against his. But when he started swaying softly in time to the music, it was all she could do not to melt against him. God, he smelled so incredibly good, and she could feel the warmth from his body through the layers of their clothing. Her free hand rested on his upper arm, and, seemingly of its own free will, crept upward until it encountered the nape of his neck. His short hair felt like rough velvet beneath her fingertips.

He sighed and pulled her fractionally closer. "I'm sorry. I don't want to fight with you."

"Me either," she murmured. Tipping her head back, she looked up at him. "What was that all about, anyway? Why don't you want me in the mines?"

"Let's save it for another time. It's probably nothing anyway, just me being overly cautious."

"Well don't." Lacey's voice came out sharper than she intended, but she was so tired of having people think that she needed protection. She softened her tone and moved closer to his warmth. "I can take care of myself, okay?"

He made a noise that could have been disbelief or assent, but his big hand slid along the curve of her spine, and she found she no longer cared about anything but the feel of his body against hers.

"I thought about this all day," he murmured into her ear. His warm breath feathered against her neck and caused goose bumps to shiver their way down her spine.

"About dancing with me?" Her voice sounded slightly strangled.

He laughed, his voice husky. "Yeah, that, too."

"Maybe you didn't notice, but I'm not much of a dancer."

"The only thing I noticed," he breathed, "is how damned pretty you are and how much I'd like to kiss you."

Lacey's breath caught. She was trapped in the intensity of his stare. His eyes were fathomless; bottomless pools of translucent blue in the dim light of the dance floor, and she thought she finally knew what it meant to drown in somebody's gaze. She didn't resist when he released her hand from where he held it against his chest and instead pulled her fully into the warmth of his body. The dance floor was crowded, but he apparently didn't care. His hands slid over her back and he pressed her against his solid bulk even as his lips nuzzled her neck.

But it wasn't enough.

As they swayed in time to the music, Lacey wound her arms around his neck, reveling in the feel of him beneath her fingers. "Then kiss me," she whispered, surprised by how much she wanted him to kiss her, right here, right now.

Cole pulled back and searched her eyes. He groaned, and swept his mouth across her lips in a kiss that was hotly sweet and much too short. Before she could protest, he stepped back, grabbed her hand in his and began pulling her behind him as he strode off the dance floor. They were outside in the humid darkness of the parking lot before she fully realized what he was doing.

She laughed. "What about our sandwiches?"

"To hell with them. I'll make us something to eat." His look was filled with promise. "Later."

When they reached his truck, instead of handing her up into the cab, he held her against the side of the vehicle, imprisoning her with his own body. "I'm sorry, baby," he growled softly, "but I can't wait another second…"

He cupped her face in his large palms and slanted his lips across hers in a kiss that rocked her all the way down to her toes. She sighed into his mouth and arched against him, all thoughts of maintaining any distance from him completely gone. If she had her way, there would be absolutely nothing between them. Desire curled through her as he deepened the kiss, spearing his tongue against hers and feasting on her lips.

Oh, God. If he didn't stop, she was going to haul him into the truck and beg him to make love to her right then and there. She dragged her mouth from his, breathless.

"Wait," she panted.

He cupped her face and his fingers massaged the tender skin behind her ears. His eyes glowed as he gazed down at her. "What's wrong?" His voice was husky.

Lacey's gaze slid to where several young men made their way across the parking lot toward the club. "We're in a public place."

He dropped his forehead to hers. "See what you do to me? I think I have a blanket or two in the back—I know of a meadow about two minutes from here where the stargazing is phenomenal." His voice was languid and full of promise.

Lacey's body responded instantly, liquid heat pooling at her center. Her breasts ached where they were pressed against his chest. She wondered briefly if it was possible to become addicted to someone's touch. She didn't want to wait to reach a meadow, or even his cabin. She wanted him, and she wanted him now.

"Let's just drive," she whispered, pulling his head down, "and see where we end up." Her eyes fluttered closed, and then his tongue was in her mouth as he flattened her against the side of the truck and devoured her. The kiss was long and deep, and Lacey felt herself turning to mush in his arms.

He tore his mouth from hers. "Let's get out of here."

He handed her into the cab and flipped the radio dial to a soft country station as he maneuvered the truck out of the parking lot and back onto the main road. He glanced over at her. "We'll be at my place in less than ten minutes."

Lacey was only vaguely aware of the dark forest, interspersed with the occasional light from a home, flying past the windows. She knew she should tell him to slow down, but she wanted him to go faster; didn't want to wait a second longer than she had to to feel him inside her.

"Hurry," she murmured, and laid one hand over the hard muscle of his thigh.

COLE LEANED HARDER on the accelerator, and then, thank God, there was the turnoff to the steep incline that led to his cabin. The truck barely skidded to a stop before he leaped out. He told himself to go slowly and not rush things, but when he opened Lacey's door he had to restrain himself from carrying her bodily into the house. She didn't speak as she preceded him inside, but as soon as he closed the door, she moved into his arms and skated her mouth along the line of his jaw.

Cole nearly groaned at the sensation of her moist lips on his skin. She flattened him against the door with the weight of her body, sliding sensuously against him even as she cupped him through the denim of his jeans. He'd been hard since they left the club, but he felt himself grow beneath her fingers. Meanwhile, she dragged her mouth along his jaw, planting soft bites on his throat and chin, before licking at his mouth.

"So good," she muttered. "I want to taste you everywhere."

Cole groaned. *Oh, yeah.*

Bending his head, he covered her mouth in a kiss that he knew was neither gentle nor seductive, but a testimony to the raw need that raged through him. He wanted to consume her, to take her right there and then, without any preliminaries. His hands slid down to cup her rear and pull her against him so that she couldn't help but feel his arousal. She made a purring sound of approval and wound her arms around his neck, pushing her fingers into his hair. He lifted her, gratified when she hitched her legs around his hips and clung to him.

With their mouths still fused together, he carried her across the room and deposited her on the sofa, shoving aside pillows and swiftly lowering himself onto the cushions beside her.

"Can you turn on a light?" She sounded breathless.

Oh, man, a woman who wasn't afraid to be seen. Could things get any better? Reaching over her head, he switched on a small table lamp.

"Better," she said breathlessly. "I want to see you."

With a small groan, he slanted his mouth across hers. Her tongue slipped past his teeth, the texture and taste of her fueling his own rising need. He felt her working the snap on her jeans, and then she was shimmying out of them, pushing them down over her legs until she could kick them free. Then she pulled him on top of her and hooked her heels against the back of his thighs, settling him into the soft cradle of her hips. She rocked against him, rubbing herself along the length of his erection, and Cole had to grit his teeth against the sensation.

Bracing his weight on one arm, he reached down and skated his palm along the length of her leg until he encountered the edge of her panties. When he eased his hand beneath the silky fabric to cup one smooth buttock, Lacey kissed him and drew hungrily on his tongue. Her hands were everywhere, pulling his shirt up, smoothing over his back, gripping his backside and urging him closer.

"Take these off," she gasped against his mouth. "Hurry."

Cole didn't need any further encouragement. Sitting up, he quickly shucked his boots and then stood up to unfasten his belt. He pushed his jeans and his briefs off in one movement, and then dragged his shirt over his head before lowering himself onto the couch beside her and gathering her into his arms. She was soft and supple and welcoming, and when she slid one leg over his, he nearly groaned aloud.

"I want to see you," he muttered. Raising himself on one arm, he unfastened the buttons on her blouse and pushed the fabric aside. Beneath the fragile cups of her bra, her breasts rose and fell quickly. Cole pressed his hand against her skin, feeling the rapid beat of her heart beneath his fingers. He pushed the lacey material aside, releasing one breast. Her nipple strained toward him, and he bent his head to draw it into his mouth. He heard Lacey's indrawn hiss of breath, but was unprepared when she reached down and curled her fingers around his straining erection. He groaned against her breasts, and she responded by stroking his length and then swirling one finger over the blunt head of his penis.

"I want you inside me," she breathed into his ear, and raised a leg across his hips to emphasize her meaning.

Cole lifted his head. Her skin had flushed and her breathing was unsteady. She moistened her lips and squeezed her hand around him, and Cole was a goner.

"A condom," he managed to mutter. "I don't have a condom."

"I'm on the Pill," she said quickly, and when he sharpened his attention on her, she gave him a smile. "I've been on it since college. I'm safe, in all the ways that matter."

"I'm safe, too," he finally said. "So if you're sure…"

"I am." As if to prove her point, she shifted so that he lay nestled between her thighs, his erection flush against her.

With a rough sound of need, he reached down and grasped her buttocks. All he could think about was being inside her—

being part of her. She'd occupied his thoughts every moment of the day. It was like he'd discovered a secret treasure he wanted to keep to himself for as long as possible, while at the same time he wanted to climb to the tallest rooftop and shout it out to the world. She groaned deeply as he pressed, hard and hot, against the most intimate part of her, and then he was pushing himself into her welcoming moistness.

She gasped in pleasure and raised her legs higher, wrapping them around his hips even as she met the thrusts of his tongue against hers with equal fervor. God, she felt incredible, all slick heat and pulsating tightness. He grasped her silken buttocks in his hands and drove himself into her, knowing he wasn't being gentle, but beyond the point where he could restrain himself. She rode him just as fiercely, moving beneath him with equal urgency. Her fingers speared through his hair and she was moaning into his mouth, making small sounds of pleasure.

He dragged his lips from hers and slid one hand between their straining bodies. "I want you to come," he growled softly. "With me inside you."

"You feel so good," she gasped against his neck.

Cole stroked her hard and she cried out, arching her back. He stroked her again and a shudder went through her body. He felt her tightening around him, gripping and squeezing him until, with a harsh cry, he climaxed in a powerful rush of exquisite pleasure, heat surging up from his balls to explode inside her.

Her arms came around him as he collapsed against her, and the only sound in the room was their harsh breathing. Her fingers stroked his hair, and Cole turned his face and pressed a kiss against the juncture of her neck and shoulder, where her skin was damp with exertion. She smelled wonderful and she felt good in his arms. She'd said she was safe in all the ways that mattered, but in that instant, he knew she was wrong.

She was a danger to him in more ways than she realized.

8

COLE OPENED THE fridge and grabbed two bottles of water, tucking them beneath one arm before picking up both plates of sandwiches. "C'mon. It's a gorgeous night. Let's eat outside."

He and Lacey had showered, and while she dressed, he made them both some food. Now he led the way to the porch at the back of the house and settled himself on a swinging settee, indicating that Lacey should sit next to him.

"Here." He handed her a plate and tucked the bottles of water between them. He nodded toward the horizon. "Take a look."

Lacey gazed out over the panorama that lay before them, and Cole saw her eyes widen in awed pleasure. It made him feel ridiculously pleased. The cabin had been carefully situated to take advantage of the sweeping vista of valley and mountains, bathed tonight in the soft glow of moonlight.

"It's beautiful," she breathed.

Cole hadn't taken his gaze from Lacey, and now he let it drift down over her profile, over the smooth forehead and gentle slope of cheek and nose, past the softly parted lips to the chin that bore the slightest trace of a cleft.

"Yeah," he agreed, "it sure is."

She shot him a swift look and then gave him a soft smile of pleasure. "This is nice," she said. "Really nice. I'd forgotten how much I love the mountains."

Cole gave her a warmly quizzical look. "Don't they have mountains in New England?"

"Of course, but not like this, And I live about five minutes from the ocean, so a trip to the mountains means having to drive for at least a couple of hours."

"How do you like being on the coast?"

Lacey took a sip of her water and nodded. "I love it. I'm not sure I could be landlocked. Although this would be very hard to give up."

"Leaving Black Stone Gap was the hardest thing I ever did," he acknowledged. "But I understand why you love living near the water. My place in Virginia is right on the beach and I fall asleep to the sound of the surf."

"Wow. That sounds amazing. My house isn't quite that close to the water."

"I'll bring you to Virginia. We can fall asleep together."

Lacey didn't say anything. Instead, she slipped her arm through his and put her head against his shoulder. But he knew what she was thinking; that once she returned to New England, whatever it was they had would be over.

He brought her hand up to his mouth and pressed a kiss against her palm. *Baby,* he thought, *you have no idea how wrong you are.*

BY THE LIGHT of the bedside lamp, Lacey stared at her own reflection in the overhead skylights. She looked small and alone in the generous bed. She *felt* small and alone. The windows were black, and because she had the bedside light on, she couldn't even see the billions of stars that she knew blanketed the sky.

How had her entire life changed in the space of two days? She'd never before met a man like Cole MacKinnon. She couldn't stop thinking about him. She'd insisted on sleeping in the guestroom despite Cole's objections. Somehow, it had seemed presumptuous of her to assume that Cole would want her to move into his room for the remainder of her stay, and she hadn't given him the opportunity to try and change her mind. To his credit, he'd apparently meant what he said when he'd told her that any relationship they had would be on her terms.

Now she wished she hadn't been so insistent on sleeping alone. Once she got home, she'd be alone every night. But Cole was meeting with Buck Rogan in the morning, and she wanted him to be well rested. Neither of them had gotten any sleep the previous night, and he needed to be sharp and alert.

With a groan, she rolled over and buried her face in her pillow, scrunching the soft mound in her hands. Even now, her body craved his touch. She thought of how she'd left him earlier, standing in the middle of the kitchen, watching her through heated eyes as she practically bolted for the stairs that led to the guestroom. She hadn't given him the chance to pull her into his arms, knowing if he did, she'd be lost. She had no willpower where he was concerned; if he kissed her, she'd be toast.

She flopped onto her back, restless. She didn't know how long she'd been lying awake, thinking about him. About them. Hours, it seemed. Memories of their lovemaking haunted her. God, she'd been so desperate for him. The only thing that had mattered was him, hot and hard inside her. He'd been so powerfully masculine, surging into her, his face taut with desire.

For her.

Her skin felt flushed and overheated. Just thinking about it made her want him again. Thanks to him, she was becoming familiar with the needs of her body, recognizing the slow, throbbing pulse that signaled her desire. Even her breasts ached, her nipples tight and erect.

With a despairing huff of breath, Lacey threw aside the sheet that covered her and swung her legs over the side of the bed. The room suddenly felt overly warm; suffocating. Even the circulating ceiling fan did little to cool her heated flesh. She thought longingly of the swinging bench on the front porch of the cabin. It had to be cooler out there than in here, and the idea of lounging on the cushioned swing with a bottle of chilled water seemed the perfect antidote to her current ailment.

She crept carefully down the stairs, alert to any sign Cole might not be sleeping. Given her current state, she'd probably attack *him*. She retrieved water from the fridge and headed for the porch. As soon as she stepped outside, she drew in a grateful breath. The humidity had dissipated and the temperature was, thankfully, cooler than it had been in her bedroom. She leaned on the railing, drinking in the cool night air as she tried to push away the thoughts of Cole that still threatened to invade her peace.

The night was far from quiet, however. The sound of crickets was everywhere, interspersed with the occasional hoot of a night owl, and the distant scream of something Lacey didn't want to think about. Fireflies dotted the lawn below the deck, their blinking lights like a reflection of the overhead stars. Tilting her head back, Lacey studied them. She had never seen stars like this in the city. They were brilliant, and so abundant it was as if some careless hand had strewn billions of diamonds across the sky.

A masculine voice cleared itself behind her. With a small cry of surprise, she jerked upright and dropped the bottle of water that dangled from her fingers. Cole lounged back on the swinging settee, much as she had imagined herself doing.

Copper lay sprawled at his feet, and now his tail thumped lazily in greeting. Cole wore a pair of boxer briefs and nothing else. His face, however, was cast in shadow and she was unable to discern his expression.

"I didn't realize you were out here," she said. "I couldn't sleep. It must be the heat."

Cole sat up and swung his legs to the porch floor. "I didn't mean to startle you. Come join me."

Lacey hesitated. She couldn't be blamed for keeping him awake if he was already up. She was so tempted.

"Come here," he said gruffly, reading her thoughts. "You just said it was hot up there—stay until you've cooled down."

It *was* much cooler out here than indoors. Surely it wouldn't hurt just to sit with him for a bit. Picking up her bottle of water from where she had dropped it, she crossed the porch and settled on the swing, tucking her bare legs beneath her. Cole's arm rested along the cushion behind her head, and he used one long, muscled leg to push them into a gentle swing.

"So what's up for you tomorrow?"

Lacey fingered her bottled water. "Well, if it's not too much to ask, I need a ride back out to the Rod and Gun Club in the morning. I'm going to run through several more demonstrations of the GPS units with the team."

In the darkness, she heard his small grunt of exasperation. "It's not too much to ask, Lacey. I'm happy to drive you wherever you need to go. You know that."

She slanted him a rueful smile. "Thanks. I appreciate that."

"There's a county fair over in Pikesville this weekend. I could pick you up early and we could head over there." He continued to push the swing gently with his toe. "You might enjoy it."

Lacey hesitated. Images of cotton candy, Ferris wheels, and strolling hand in hand with this man through the arcades was more tempting than she cared to admit. "Aren't you meeting with Buck Rogan in the morning?"

"That's just an informal meeting. I'm not officially on the clock until Monday morning. It's supposed to be a gorgeous day tomorrow. It'd be a shame to spend it working."

The gentle rocking motion of the swing was almost hypnotic. Lacey looked over at Cole; at all that lean, hard muscle gleaming softly in the moonlight. He'd said his meeting with Buck wasn't formal and he wouldn't actually begin working in the mines for a few more days. Acknowledging that it was useless for her to even try to resist him, Lacey uncurled her legs and stretched out until she reclined back against his solid frame. His arms came around her, and Lacey sighed in pleasure, admitting that this was what she had been missing, alone in that bed.

"I don't know," she mused now, teasing him just a little. "I'm not sure I can spare the time. I have a lot of work to do while I'm here."

She thought he would tease her a little in return, maybe even use some physical persuasion to get her to agree to go with him. Instead, he was oddly quiet as he continued to push them with his foot.

"What is it?" she asked, twisting to look at him. "What's wrong?"

"At the club tonight, when I said I didn't want you to go into the mines, I meant it. I don't want you near those tunnels."

"Why?"

Cole hesitated. "Call it intuition. I have a bad vibe about them and I'd feel a lot better if you just stayed away."

Lacey stared at him, wondering where this had come from. "Cole, nothing is going to happen. I'm not afraid to go into the mines, and you shouldn't be afraid to let me go."

"What's so important about this GPS unit that you need to field-test it inside the tunnels? You won't be able to pick up a signal."

"No, that's where you're wrong. You see, it's a proto-type that we designed for NASA. It can operate beneath the earth's surface. The coal mines are the perfect environment to test its functionality. NASA wants us to start full produc-tion right away. This contract is huge for StarPoint Technolo-gies, and could really put the company on the map. My boss is depending on me to get this done."

Untangling himself from her, Cole stood abruptly up, causing Lacey to hang on tight as the swing lurched into unsteady motion. He raked a hand over his hair, seemingly oblivious to the fact he was wearing no more than a pair of boxer briefs.

But Lacey was aware. He was all satiny skin over sculpted muscles that layered their way down his stomach. She could see the faintest trace of dark hair that ran downward from his navel and disappeared beneath the waistband of his box-ers. The briefs hugged his lean hips and molded themselves over the tops of his powerful thighs. They clung lovingly to the impressive bulge of his…

With a half groan, Lacey tore her gaze from where it was riveted, closed her eyes and took a healthy swig of the water, but the chilled liquid did little to cool her overheated senses. Swiping the moisture from her mouth with the back of her hand, she looked helplessly up at him.

"You need to trust me on this," he said. "My best friend died in those tunnels. I won't let you take that risk."

Lacey felt her heart tighten with compassion and some-thing else; a recognition of sorts. Setting the water bottle down, she stood up and slid her arms around Cole's waist. He hugged her fiercely.

"Nothing is going to happen to me, Cole, I promise."

"You don't know that. Devon was an experienced miner who always put safety first. If it could happen to him, it could happen to anyone."

"Listen to me," Lacey said, using the calm, rational tone that she had perfected when talking with her mother. "I understand your concern, I really do. Don't you think that I worry about you working in those mines? But I would never try to talk you out of doing your job. And this is my job, Cole. This means so much to me. If I can demonstrate that STAR is operational, the potential for saving lives is limitless."

"It's more complicated than that."

"How so? You're the engineer—is there something you know about the mines that you're not saying?"

He sharpened his gaze on her. "What? No. I told you, it's just a feeling I have. But I do know that the number of mining accidents has increased over the past few years."

An image of her father lying trapped beneath hundreds of feet of rock flashed through Lacey's imagination. "Is it just one mine, or all the mines in the area?"

Cole rolled his shoulders and turned abruptly to stare out into the darkness. "I don't know. Like I said, I just get a bad feeling about it."

Lacey understood. She dreaded going into those dank tunnels, but her father's death compelled her to do just that. She'd never rest until she'd assured herself that STAR worked as intended. She wouldn't be able to think of her father at peace until she found some way to ensure that another miner didn't die the way he had. So even though Cole might have reservations about her going into the mines, Lacey knew she had no other choice.

"I'll be the first to admit that I'm not crazy about the idea," she confessed. "But I have a job to do. Maybe if you talked to Buck Rogan, he'd agree to let you come with me."

After a moment, he blew out a hard breath. "If this is something you absolutely have to do, I'd prefer that. Would you mind if I came with you?"

Lacey couldn't help it. Her entire body flushed with heat at his words. Her only excuse was that she'd been consumed with thought about him all night, and now here he was, almost naked and too tempting for her to resist. The empty aching sensation that had plagued her earlier became an insistent throbbing and her nipples tightened instantly. She wanted him again.

Badly.

"I'd like for you to come with me," she said suggestively. "Over and over."

"Lacey." The word was no more than a husky whisper that caused a molten thread of desire to lick its way through her body. Bending his head, he kissed her neck, just below her ear. Lacey shivered as his lips teased the delicate skin. When he caught her earlobe between his teeth, she gasped softly.

"I want you." His husky admission caused a tightening in her body and with a helpless exhalation, she sagged against him, tilting her head to allow him better access.

Her small surrender seemed to spark an answering surge of need in him. He made a sound that was half laugh, half groan, and swept her up into his arms. Lacey didn't protest. Instead, she wound her arms around his neck and clung to him, burying her face against his neck. This was, after all, what she had been longing for since she had gone to bed, hours earlier, alone.

He strode swiftly through the house until they reached his bedroom. Lacey was breathless with anticipation by the time he shouldered the door to his room open and deposited her in an unruly heap on top of the bed.

"The light," she urged softly. "Turn on the light."

As he had their first night, Cole turned on the small lamp before dropping onto the bed beside her and gathering her close against his hardness.

"God, I've been dying to do this," he growled. "I couldn't get to sleep for thinking about you. About touching you... tasting you." He laughed ruefully. "If you hadn't shown up on the porch tonight, I probably would have come upstairs and begged you to have mercy on me." His hands were everywhere, sliding over her back and down over the curve of her hips, while he buried his face in her neck and pressed his lips along the sensitive length of her neck. "God. It's like I can't get enough of you."

His words were like an aphrodisiac. Throbbing with need, Lacey twined her legs around his and pressed her hips against him, telling him with her body how much she wanted him.

The man didn't let her down. In one movement, he swept her nightshirt over her head and slid his hands beneath her bottom, lifting her so that she was pressed fully against him.

"Oh, yeah," he breathed, his voice warm in her ear. "You make me crazy for you." Turning his face, he captured her lips in a kiss that was searingly hot. Lacey moaned softly and wound her arms around him, pulling him closer.

This was what she had been longing for; this man in her arms, driving her wild with the things he did to her. She ran her hands down the length of his back, tracing her fingers over all that bare skin and reveling in his hardness. His lips slanted across hers and she welcomed the intrusion of his tongue, wanting to be closer still.

She was hardly aware of him tugging her panties off, and then there was nothing between them. Lacey dragged her mouth from his, her breathing fast and uneven. He pulled back slightly, keeping his weight on his elbows, and dipped his head to capture a nipple between his lips, drawing it into his mouth. She gasped in pleasure and instinctively arched against him, feeling him hot and hard, poised at the juncture of her thighs.

Lacey knew that at the slightest indication from her, he would take her to heaven. But suddenly, she wanted to be the one to take him there; to do things to him that would make him lose control. She pushed at his shoulders and with a bemused smile he rolled away from her. But Lacey didn't give him a chance to question her, covering him swiftly with her own body.

"What? Hey—" He laughed uncertainly, but when Lacey dipped her head and traced the whorl of his ear with her tongue, he groaned and collapsed back against the pillows. She pushed his hands up above his head, and slid her own hands down the undersides of his arms, silently admiring the impressive bulge of his muscles. Her fingers continued downward, and she scooted backward until she straddled his thighs.

Sitting up, she looked down at him. Her breath caught at the sight he made. He was the embodiment of every fantasy she'd ever had. He lay still beneath her, but there was nothing remotely relaxed about him. His entire body was rigid and his eyes glittered as he watched her through half-closed lids.

"Now it's my turn," she whispered. "You see, I couldn't sleep either because I've been wanting to do *this* all night." She leaned forward until her breasts brushed against his chest and she traced her lips across his. He cupped the back of her head and drew her down for a more thorough, satisfying kiss. Lacey had intended to tease him, to maintain control of their love play until he begged her to release him. But when he smoothed his free hand along her flank and then reached between them to touch her intimately, she knew she was lost. He used his hands to splay her thighs even wider where she straddled him. Then there he was, hot and thick, moving into her little bit by little bit, until Lacey made an incoherent sound of need and pushed back, thrusting him fully inside her.

"Oh, man," he groaned. "That almost feels too good."

Lacey silently agreed, and slowly raised herself up until he was nearly free of her body, before pushing down once more, burying him to the hilt. The hot, throbbing sensation increased as she moved on top of him, gripping him tightly. His hands were on her hips, guiding her, and she watched his face go taut with pleasure. When he slid his hands upward to cup and knead her breasts, Lacey closed her eyes in mindless bliss.

"Yes," she breathed.

"Look at me."

The words were soft but insistent. She opened her eyes and stared down at Cole, seeing the raw, masculine desire on his face.

"I want you to look at me when you come," he rasped. His expression had tightened, and seeing his desire mount just served to fuel her own. She knew he was close to losing control, but when he reached down and slid a finger over her swollen clitoris, Lacey was right there with him. With a soft cry, she began to orgasm. She might have closed her eyes but for his soft command.

"Look at me."

And when he reached his own climax, their gazes were locked on one another in raw intimacy, until with a last shudder of pleasure, he smiled into her eyes and tugged her down until she lay replete against his chest.

He pressed his lips against her hair, and his hands stroked soothingly down her body. When she turned her face up to his, he kissed her sweetly and she could see the tenderness of his expression. If they had been characters in a romantic movie, this would be the scene where he'd confess that he'd fallen in love with her.

"Christ," he said ruefully, "maybe now I can get some sleep."

She mentally rolled her eyes, laughing at her own fanciful daydreams. He was only hers for ten short days, and she told herself that she was okay with that. She'd wanted this. Wanted him. They still had another week to be together, and Lacey intended to enjoy every minute of it.

He tucked her closer against his side, and one hand traced lazy patterns on her shoulder and arm. "Are you okay? I don't think you've said more than five words since we came inside."

A reluctant smile tugged at her lips. "The words *yes, yes, oh, yes* don't count?"

He chuckled. "Maybe if you added, 'Please, Cole, make love to me again,' I'd feel better."

Lacey laughed softly and didn't object when he drew her closer. "Cut me some slack. I'm not as comfortable with all of this as you are."

"Comfortable? Hell, lady, I've been in a serious state of *discomfort* since I first met you. All I can think about is you," he murmured into her ear, his breath warm on her cheek.

Lacey understood exactly what he meant, because it was the same for her. Rolling toward him, she rose up on an elbow to look at him. "When I came down here, I fully intended to step out of my comfort zone and live a little, but I never expected you. Or this."

"Any regrets?" he asked softly.

Only that she had to leave, eventually. She traced a fingertip along his jaw. "Not yet."

His mouth tilted in a half smile, but his expression was serious. "I think about that first night a lot. What if I hadn't been hanging out at Sully's? What if I hadn't volunteered to answer your call for a tow?"

"Then we never would have met."

"I'm not so sure," he mused. "Sometimes, things are just meant to be."

Lacey smiled. "I think you're a romantic. It's one of the things I like best about you. You're so honest about your feelings. About everything."

Cole didn't answer. Instead, he pulled her down until she lay with her head on his shoulder, mostly because he couldn't meet her eyes.

COLE WAITED UNTIL Lacey fell asleep before he slipped out of bed and pulled on a pair of loose pajama bottoms. Moving silently into the family room, he pulled out his laptop case and the thick sheath of paperwork that he had brought with him from Norfolk. He sat down and began to thumb through the dozens of accident reports that had been filed by the Black River Mines. Many of them were vehicle accidents that had occurred inside the tunnels, but several involved injuries sustained from falling debris. By the time the accident reports had been filled out and a safety inspection team had been sent in to investigate, the area had been cleaned up and the risks mitigated.

Cole pored through the reports, wondering how Buck Rogan could have addressed each deficiency and corrected it so quickly. Unless the reports had been falsified, there was no way he could have.

Withdrawing a set of blueprints from a document holder, he rolled them out on the coffee table and studied them. They detailed each level of tunnels within the Black River Mines. Cole had put a small mark near where each accident had occurred. Or, he amended silently, where Buck and his foreman *claimed* each accident had occurred.

He traced his finger along the length of one tunnel, to where it abruptly ended deep inside the mountain. Fifty feet of rock and shale separated that main tunnel from an older network of tunnels that had been abandoned years earlier for safety reasons. The tunnels that made up Rogan's Run Mine No. 5 weren't shown on the blueprint. As far as Cole knew, they weren't on any current blueprints. The Bureau of Mine Safety had deemed Rogan's Run Mine No 5 too unstable to mine, despite the rich veins of ore that existed.

What if Buck had found a way to access those tunnels without anyone knowing? He would have to pay the workers a substantial fee in order to guarantee their silence. Cole knew how tempting that could be to a man with a family to support.

If Buck Rogan really was capable of that kind of duplicity, there was no telling what else he could do. Cole glanced back toward the bedroom. He wanted to come clean with Lacey about his real purpose for being in Black Stone Gap, but he couldn't risk that information leaking out and getting back to Buck. But he promised himself one thing: Lacey would never enter those tunnels, not if there was the smallest chance that something could go wrong.

9

LACEY COLLAPSED GRATEFULLY onto the picnic table bench. The heat and humidity of the day had completely sapped her of whatever energy she had left, which, considering how much she'd expended the previous night, wasn't a whole lot.

In the end, she'd agreed to spend the morning with the rescue team, and the afternoon with Cole at the Pikesville County Fair. It was a small event by any standards, but as far as Lacey was concerned, that only added to its country charm.

Cole had been amused by her fascination with the quilt displays. She had lingered so long over one particular quilt that he'd finally offered to buy it for her. Lacey had adamantly refused, and had let it fall back onto the display rack.

He'd just shrugged. "If it would make you happy, then I'd like to get it for you."

She couldn't explain to him that it wasn't so much the quilt itself, although it was beautiful, as the bittersweet memories it evoked. She'd had one almost like it when she was a little girl. She remembered her parents tucking it securely around her at bedtime, and how safe it had made her feel. The quilt had been lost when she and her mother had moved to New Hampshire.

"Thanks anyway," she had told Cole. "It's just that I had one sort of like this when I was a kid." She smiled, embarrassed. "It brought back memories, that's all."

Cole had looked at her quizzically, but hadn't pressed her. And he hadn't bought the quilt. She glanced up at him now from the picnic table, grateful for the overhead canopy that gave some relief from the sun.

"I'll go grab us a couple of cold drinks," he said. "Will you be okay?"

Lacey smiled at him. "I'm fine, just a little tired."

He braced his hands on the picnic table and leaned down to plant a warm, hard kiss against her lips. "That's my fault," he murmured. "But when the options are sleep or make love to you, it's a total no-brainer. I just wasn't thinking about the fact that you'd be exhausted."

Lacey couldn't help it. She reached up and drew him down for another kiss. "Hey," she responded softly, "you don't hear me complaining."

He pulled back, his eyes warm. "I'll go grab those drinks and be right back."

Lacey watched him go, and then stretched out sideways on the bench, lifting her feet up and smoothing the skirt of her sundress down over her legs. She closed her eyes and tipped her head from side to side, stretching her tired muscles.

"Looks like you could use a good massage."

Her eyes flew open, and for a moment she couldn't focus on the tall figure standing in front of her. When she did, she sat upright, shoving her feet back under the table and smoothing her skirt over her knees. It was Buck Rogan.

He extended a hand to her now. "It's a pleasure to see you again, Ms. Delaney."

Lacey accepted his outstretched hand. "Hello, Mr. Rogan."

"Oh, please," he said, laughing as he released her hand.

"Call me Buck. When I hear *Mr. Rogan* I look around for my old man."

"Okay, but only if you call me Lacey."

He chuckled. "Agreed."

He was well dressed in a pair of lightweight chinos and a blazer. Despite the heat, he looked cool and distinguished.

He indicated the bench opposite her. "Do you mind if I sit down for a moment?"

"Of course not," she said. "I was going to give you a call tomorrow to talk about my project."

He frowned, clearly puzzled. "Really? Cole spoke to me about that this morning, and I understood those plans had been scrapped."

Lacey frowned. She knew that Cole had spent the morning in Buck's office, but when he'd come back to the house just before lunch, he'd only said that the meeting had gone well. If he and Buck had discussed her project, he hadn't mentioned it to her.

"I'm sorry, I don't follow. Cole told you that my plans to test the prototype had been scrapped?"

"Yes, ma'am. He didn't say why, but I got the impression that you had found another testing site."

Lacey bit back the denial that sprang to her lips. Her gaze slid away from him and she searched the surrounding crowds for Cole, but there was no sign of him. She had no idea why Cole would have told Buck such a thing when it was blatantly untrue. But she didn't want to expose Cole as a liar to the man who was now his boss. She knew how much he needed this job, and she wouldn't do anything to jeopardize that.

"Hmm," she said instead, pretending to consider his words. "I think I know why he said that, but it was definitely just a misunderstanding." She actually had no idea why he would have said that, and her mind scrambled furiously for an adequate reason for Cole's statement. "He knows that I'm terrified of being underground, and probably thought he was doing me a favor."

That, at least, was a partial truth and for all she knew, Cole might have thought he *was* doing her a favor.

Buck sat down. He put one arm on the picnic table, drummed his fingers and considered her thoughtfully. "I assure you that you would be perfectly safe in my mines. I don't go into them much myself anymore, but I have a foreman who I would trust with my life. You would have nothing to worry about."

"Thank you. I appreciate that."

They spent the next few minutes talking about STAR and what Lacey was looking for in terms of a testing environment. Buck was attentive and cordial.

"Based on the parameters you've described, I think I know exactly which mine would work best for you," he said when she had finished explaining about the field test. "Now that Cole is my lead engineer, I need to take care of his girl."

Cole's girl.

Before she could protest that she wasn't Cole's girl—not really—Buck continued.

"You know what they say…*happy wife, happy life*. Oh, I know you're not married, but I've seen that boy's face when he talks about you. Same way his daddy looked when he talked about Cole's mama."

"You knew Cole's parents?" she asked, curious in spite of herself.

"Shoot, I grew up with Cole's father. When I took over the mines, he was the foreman." His face grew pensive. "Best damned foreman I've ever seen. He had a real way with people, and he couldn't have been prouder of Cole than that first day I hired him as an engineer, straight out of college and still wet behind the ears. A damned shame what happened."

He grew quiet, remembering. Lacey knew she shouldn't ask, but she was dying to know. "What happened?"

"You don't know? Well, I guess it's natural that Cole wouldn't want to talk about it. In fact, it's why he high-tailed it out of here five years ago."

It took all of Lacey's self control not to reach over and shake the man. *What had happened?* She sat patiently and waited.

"Cole left the Gap after a rescue mission went bad." He paused, gauging her reaction. "His friend was trapped in one of the vertical shafts, and Cole had this plan on how he was going to get him out." Buck snorted. "It went so foul it still stinks to this day. Not that anyone ever blamed Cole, mind you."

Lacey stared at him. In her mind, she could see the scene clearly and a shiver went through her.

"The shaft collapsed, and three miners died, including his friend," Buck elaborated, reading the unspoken question in her eyes.

Lacey's chest constricted. She thought of her father and how his death still haunted her, nearly twenty years later. Did Cole have nightmares about his friend? She now understood his reluctance to rejoin the rescue team.

"I'm sure it wasn't Cole's fault," Lacey said. "Mine rescues can be a tricky business. There are no guarantees." She was repeating the very words that she and her mother had been told all those years ago; words she hadn't wanted to believe then, because she'd needed to blame someone for what had happened to her father. But she didn't want Cole to take the blame for what had happened to his friend.

"You're right," Buck said. "Coal mine rescues can be unpredictable, but—" He broke off abruptly and waved a dismissive hand. "That's all in the past, and as far as I'm concerned, Cole's come back to town with a clean slate. I was surprised to see him, though, but I guess the need for redemption can be a powerful thing."

The implication was clear to Lacey—Buck thought that Cole was to blame for his friend's tragic death. Lacey decided that she'd heard enough.

"Well, it's been nice talking with you. I will definitely give you a call tomorrow to set up a time for the testing."

Buck took the hint and rose to his feet. "It was my pleasure, ma'am. Enjoy the rest of your day." He tipped an imaginary hat to her, before he turned and strolled away.

Lacey sank back down onto the bench, her mind whirling. Why had Cole told Buck that she wouldn't be using the Black River mines to test STAR? And why did Buck insinuate that the accident had been Cole's fault? If she didn't know better, she'd think there was some bad blood there, but he'd had nothing but good things to say about Cole's father.

She found that she didn't want to ask any favors of Buck Rogan, but she'd do it in order to test STAR. The prototype represented years of hard work and sacrifice. But it also represented hope. Hope that no other miner would have to die the way her father had died. The way Cole's friend had died. Testing STAR was her single most important mission right now. There was no way she'd go home without accomplishing that.

"Was that Buck Rogan I saw you talking with?"

Lacey dropped her hands away from her eyes and stared up at Cole. He stood by the table holding two glasses of lemonade in his hands and staring after Buck with an expression of concern.

"Yes."

"What did he want?"

Lacey accepted the proffered lemonade and took a long swallow. "Nothing, really," she fibbed. "He was just being friendly. You were gone an awfully long time. What kept you?"

"I ran into someone," he said, and swung his leg over the bench and sat down facing her. "So what did the two of you talk about?"

Lacey put the lemonade down and carefully swiped a fingertip across her lips before looking at him directly. "He was under the impression that I no longer wanted to use the mines as a testing environment for STAR. I told him there had been a misunderstanding, and that I very much wanted to bring STAR into the mines."

For a moment he just stared at her, and then he blew out a hard breath. When he finally spoke, his voice was low.

"I wish you wouldn't do this."

"Look, Cole, I'm sorry to be blunt, but this has nothing to do with you." Lacey didn't know why she suddenly felt the need to defend her decision. "I need to get into the mines to test STAR. You know how important this is to me. It's why I came here. My company is depending on me to do this. I *have* to do it." Aware that people were beginning to look at them, she lowered her voice. "You had no right to interfere."

Cole leaned forward and tried to take her hands in his, but Lacey pulled them away and looked expectantly at him, waiting for his response.

"There are things you don't know," he finally said, his voice rough.

"Then tell me!"

"I can't."

"Oh, for God's sake." Lacey threw up her hands. "You have to give me something. And not just that you have a bad feeling."

Cole set his drink down on the table. He looked around, taking in the fair-goers at the surrounding tables and seemed to come to a decision. "C'mon," he said. "Let's get out of here."

Before she could protest, Lacey found herself hauled to her feet and practically dragged alongside him as he steered her through the crowds.

His features were set in grim lines and a small muscle worked in his lean jaw as they made their way through the congested fairgrounds to where the truck was parked at the back of a field. There was no one else around, and the air was redolent with the scent of freshly cut grass. Once there, he turned to her.

"I can't let you do it, Lacey."

Lacey tugged her arm free of his grasp. "We've been over this already."

"Let me bring you to a mine where safety won't be an issue."

Lacey narrowed her eyes at him. "Where? West Virginia?"

"What does it matter, so long as you have a safe environment in which to perform your tests?"

"But why drive hours, when I could do it right here in Black Stone Gap?"

Cole stared at her and a muscle worked in one lean cheek. "I'm trying to protect you, damn it."

Lacey tamped down her rising annoyance. Maybe she should have felt appreciation, but she'd heard the same message for nearly her entire life from her mother. She didn't want Cole to see her as fragile or needing to be saved.

"This is part of my job, Cole." She gave him an encouraging smile. "I've dedicated the past several years to developing this unit. I want to help make the mines safe for people like you. I want all miners to come home to their families when their shift is over. I'm sure that's what you want, too, isn't it?"

"That's exactly what I want." He opened the door to the truck and indicated she should climb in. "C'mon, let's go home. There's something I want to show you."

Home. He said it so casually, as if they had been together for years and not just days.

"Cole," she said wearily. "Why won't you let me just do my job?"

He searched her face. "This is important, and it has everything to do with your job. Just hear me out on this, okay? I'm being sincere when I say that I only want you to be safe."

Lacey found her irritation evaporating. She trusted him. If he didn't want her to go into the mines, then there had to be a good reason why. She climbed into the cab of the truck, but when Cole would have turned away, she caught his hand.

He looked over at her, his expression questioning.

"What—"

She pressed a fingertip against his mouth, and then put her other hand at the back of his head, drawing him down. She loved the rough velvet of his hair, and speared her fingers through it, reveling in the feel of his scalp. "Kiss me."

Cole stared at her, and even with the sunlight full in his eyes, she saw his pupils dilate. "Lacey…"

She leaned forward and pressed her lips sweetly against his, tasting him ever so lightly with the tip of her tongue. At the same time, she placed his hand on her knee and slid it upward beneath the hem of her sundress. She felt him go still as his warm palm came into contact with the satin edge of her underwear. But when she lifted her hips, he didn't pretend to misunderstand her, and swiftly drew her panties down her legs until she kicked them free.

"What are you doing?" he rasped softly against her mouth, but his hand was firm and warm against her heated flesh.

"Seducing you," she whispered back. "Is it working?"

"Here?" His voice sounded slightly strangled.

In answer, she shifted to give him better access and nearly came off the seat as he stroked her once. She'd never done anything so bold before. This man made her do things that she'd never thought herself capable of.

"No," she murmured against his mouth. "Let's go home."

10

COLE GRIPPED THE steering wheel of the truck and tried to control his growing concern. After they had returned from the fair, they'd spent several long, memorable hours in his bed. Then he'd shown Lacey the blueprints of the mine. He'd explained his suspicions to her without revealing that he was working undercover for the Department of Labor. When she'd asked how he had obtained such detailed plans of the mine, he'd fibbed and told her they were from five years earlier, when he had first worked for Buck as a new engineer.

He'd shown her where each of the accidents had supposedly occurred, and how they all taken place near the old, vacated mines. She'd been skeptical about his theory that Buck was working the closed sections, but had been willing to consider the possibility. In the end, they had agreed that she would meet with Buck and talk about the field test, but she would not utilize any tunnels that Cole considered to be dangerous.

Cole would spend the day at Black River Mine No. 2 with a team of engineers, inspecting the internal support structures of the tunnels. He hoped that as the lead engineer, he would have access to the blueprints for all the Black River mines, including Rogan's Run No. 5, which had been closed for more than fifty years. He was convinced those closed portions, deemed unsafe by any standards, were being secretly but actively worked. He was certain Buck was paying the miners an exorbitant hourly wage in order for them to work those areas and keep their mouths shut.

Now he just needed proof.

But it would take time to gain the trust of the miners, especially since many of them still remembered the horrible rescue effort that had taken the life of his friend five years earlier. No doubt there were those who still associated his name with that disaster, and maybe even blamed him for it.

"Are you sure about this?" he asked now. "I could bring you to any number of mines over in West Virginia. You don't need to meet with Buck Rogan."

Lacey looked over at him and he could see that she wasn't nearly as confident about this as she pretended to be. But she tipped her chin up and gave him a smile.

"It'll be fine," she assured him. "The only thing that has me a little nervous is the fact that I'm showing up unannounced. He's not expecting me until tomorrow."

"Just say that you have a conflict tomorrow. He's not going to tell you to come back some other time. If nothing else, Buck Rogan is a gentleman. You're only going to talk about test parameters and look at the blueprints." He cast her a stern glance. "Under no conditions are you to let him take you into the mines."

Lacey smiled. "I've got it, Cole. Relax. I'm not going into any mines today. I didn't even bring STAR with me, so there would be no point to it anyway, okay? Don't worry about me."

But he did. He knew she was stronger than she appeared, and yet he still worried about her. He didn't want her to meet with Buck Rogan, but he also knew how important testing

I'm sorry for interrupting," he said, speaking directly ‍Buck. "But I need to speak to you." His gaze flicked to ‍‍ey and then back to Buck. "It's, um, urgent."

‍As Lacey watched, Buck's gaze flew to something on his ‍k. Lacey looked, too, but saw only rolls of blueprints. For ‍‍oment, Buck hesitated, as if he would snatch them up. In ‍ next instant, he nodded at the man.

"Excuse us for just a moment," he said to Lacey.

Lacey murmured her assent, but she didn't miss the deep ‍‍ncern and something else in Buck's eyes, before he left ‍ office, leaving the door open a few inches. But Lacey ‍cognized that expression.

Fear.

She listened as the two men moved away from the door, ‍nd then quickly walked over to his desk, her eyes scanning ‍he blueprints that lay scattered across the top. Technical ‍‍rawings were very familiar to her, and blueprints were not ‍much different. Keeping an eye on the door, she thumbed ‍wiftly through the documents, wondering which one Buck ‍ad wanted. Then she found it.

A blueprint of Rogan's Run Mine No. 5, and the date at ‍e bottom was current, from less than a year earlier. He ob‍iously hadn't been prepared for her visit. If he'd known she ‍as going to show up unexpectedly this morning, he never ‍ould have left these documents out in the open. Lacey ‍uickly scanned the blueprint and saw that access to the ‍osed tunnels could be gained through the Black River Mine ‍. 6. Quickly, her heart thudding, she folded the blueprint in ‍f, and then in half again. Walking back to the conference ‍le, she had just shoved the document deep into a zippered ‍ket on her presentation case when the door opened and ‍k came in. He schooled his features into a polite smile, ‍Lacey could see the anxiety etched onto his features.

her GPS unit was to her. He wouldn't stop her, as much as he might want to.

"Okay, fine. You have my cell phone number. I'll be on the other side of the complex, so call me if you need me."

They were emerging from the thick, impenetrable woods that enclosed the road for most of the twenty-minute drive, and turned onto a wide, gravel lane. Tall wire fences lined the perimeter, marked with No Trespassing signs and directions to the mine entrance.

The route wound upward until they entered a large parking lot ringed with work trailers and wooden structures. Cole drew the truck to a stop in front of a large, concrete building and switched off the engine. He turned to face Lacey. "This is Buck's office." He indicated a work trailer on the far side of the parking lot. "I'll be over there. Call me when you're through, and I'll drive you home."

She gave him a grateful look before she slid out of the cab and closed the door to the truck. As she climbed the steps to the office, the door opened and Buck's massive bulk filled the door frame. He exchanged a few words with Lacey but they were too far away for Cole to hear them. Buck stepped back and Lacey brushed past him into the house. Buck raised a hand in greeting to Cole, and he gave a brief nod in return. Buck stood in the doorway for a scant second longer, before he stepped back and closed the door.

Cole checked his cell phone to ensure he would hear any incoming calls, before he thrust the truck into gear and punched the gas pedal down with his foot, gaining no satisfaction from the sound of the tires as they squealed in protest.

LACEY WAITED AS BUCK closed the door and then turned to face her. As always, he wore a well-cut sports jacket over a crisp, white dress shirt. He looked every inch a successful executive.

"I wasn't expecting you until tomorrow. But no matter. Come into my office," he invited, and indicated she should precede him down a short corridor. They passed an older woman sitting at a desk, who Lacey guessed was his secretary. "Patty, could you bring us some coffee, please?"

"Of course, Mr. Rogan."

Buck opened the door to his office, and Lacey saw it was richly appointed with mahogany furniture, including a desk and a large conference table, and a wall of deep filing cabinets. The desk itself was covered with papers and blueprints, and one wall of shelves contained what looked like more rolls of drawings. He had samples of coal and other minerals displayed in glass boxes on one shelf, and framed photos of miners covered two walls. A window at the rear of the office overlooked the entrance to the mine itself, and Lacey could see a group of workers preparing to go down into the tunnels.

"Have a seat," he invited, indicating the conference table. "So what, exactly, are you looking for?"

Lacey opened her presentation case and withdrew the specifications for STAR and spread them out on the surface of the table. "Here are the specs for the unit I'd like to test. If you look here, you'll see the optimum conditions that we need to achieve in order to perform a successful test."

Buck studied the sheets for several moments. "You need to be at least five hundred feet below the surface, and at least one quarter mile into the tunnels."

Lacey nodded. "Yes, that's right."

Moving away from the table, Buck opened a drawer in one of the file cabinets and withdrew several blueprints. When he spread them out on the table, Lacey saw they were similar to the ones that Cole had shown her.

"These blueprints show the Black River Mines No. 2," he

said indicating one set of tunnels. "I think th[...] your needs perfectly."

Before Lacey could respond, there was a li[...] the door, and Patty came in with a small tray [...] muffins. She set them down on the conferenc[...] Lacey.

"Here you are," she said brightly. "Let me k[...] need anything else."

Buck thanked her, and as Lacey prepared her cup of [...] fee, she listened to Buck explain the various attributes o[...] mine, and had to agree that the conditions sounded perfec[...] which to test STAR. She wished now that she hadn't been so quick to promise Cole that she wouldn't go into the mines.

"Does this mine have a good safety record?" she asked.

Buck sharpened his gaze on her. "Why would you[...] that?"

Lacey decided that honesty was the best policy. "N[...] ther died in a mining accident when I was a little[...] helped to design STAR for NASA, but there is a hug[...] mercial potential for the unit, as well. These could be [...] in the mining community to accurately pinpoint the [...] of miners in the event of an accident." She gave hi[...] smile. "I wouldn't want to jeopardize the project b[...] killed during the testing phase."

Buck's face was somber. "I'm sorry for your los[...] lie and tell you that we haven't had our share of [...] over the years, but I can promise you that the N[...] are absolutely safe."

Lacey also knew they were located miles awa[...] gan's Run Mine No. 5, where Cole thought Bu[...] mining illegally. There would be no chance o[...] anything down there that she shouldn't see. At [...] there was another knock on the door, and then[...] open to reveal a man wearing an agitated exp[...]

"You'll have to forgive me, but I need to excuse myself. Perhaps we can continue our conversation at another time?"

Lacey gathered up her specifications and replaced them in her presentation case. "Please, there's nothing to forgive. You weren't even expecting me this morning, so I appreciate the time you were able to spend with me. I'll let you get back to work."

"Thank you. I'll see you out. Can one of my men give you a ride somewhere?"

Lacey followed him back through the office to the front door. "No, thanks. I'm all set."

After he closed the door, she stood for a moment, acutely aware of the pilfered document in her case. What if he returned to his office and realized it was missing? He would know she had stolen it. She made her way quickly across the compound toward Cole's trailer, expecting to hear Buck Rogan coming after her at any second.

Cole opened the door immediately when she knocked. He took one look at her face and dragged her inside the trailer, closing the door quickly behind her.

"What is it?" he asked. "Are you okay?"

"You were right," she said without preamble. "I think he's working inside the closed section of the mines." She unzipped her presentation case and pulled out the folded document. "Here. I found this on his desk. There were other blueprints, too, but I didn't get a good look at all of them."

Cole took the paper from her and unfolded it, before swiftly scanning it. He gave Lacey one astonished look and then quickly refolded it and shoved it into the back of his jeans, pulling his jacket on to conceal it. He glanced through the window toward Buck's office.

"C'mon," he said, taking her elbow. "Buck is leaving. Let's get out of here before he figures out what you've done."

"I'm sorry," she said as she followed him to the truck. "I don't know what made me take it. I should have just left it there, but I thought you would want to see that your suspicions are correct. "

"No, you did the right thing," he assured her, handing her into the cab. "Did Buck say where they were going?"

Lacey shook her head. "No. A man came into the office to talk with him, and I got the sense it was urgent. Buck seemed pretty anxious to get rid of me."

"That was his foreman. There must have been an accident in one of the tunnels." Cole thrust the truck into gear and accelerated out of the compound. Behind them, a group of workers were jogging toward the entrance to the mine. "Yeah, something is definitely up. Listen, I'm going to drop you off at the house, okay?"

"Where are you going?"

"I have something I need to do. There's food in the refrigerator. I may not be back until late, but don't wait up for me."

There was something in his expression—something calculated—that kept Lacey from asking any questions. Reaching over, she covered his hand with her own.

"Be careful."

11

As Cole had predicted, it was late by the time he returned to the cabin, but not so late that Lacey would be in bed. He noted with satisfaction that the porch lights were on, as well as the living room lights. He parked the truck and bent to greet Copper, who bounded down the steps, tail wagging.

Cole had met with two Department of Labor agents in Roanoke, a drive that had taken him nearly three hours each way. But before that, he'd headed over to the entrance of Rogan's Run Mine No. 5, but there had been no telltale activity outside the long abandoned entrance. On a hunch, he'd also driven past the entrance to the Black River Mine No. 6, where the pilfered blueprint indicated there was access to the closed mine. As he'd suspected, there was a flurry of activity at the entrance to the mine, but there hadn't been any rescue crews or ambulances.

He'd returned to his work trailer and had made some discreet inquiries, but his questions had been met with blank stares. Nobody had heard of any accidents occurring that morning. So he'd left word that he needed to take the rest of the day off, and had headed to Roanoke with Lacey's blueprint in his pocket. But the diagram alone wasn't proof that Buck was using the mines, and after a lengthy discussion with the agents, Cole had returned home with instructions to continue with his undercover surveillance.

He found Lacey curled up on the sofa in the living room, reading a book, wrapped in his terry bathrobe. She looked relieved when he crossed the room and dropped a light kiss against her mouth.

"You look tired," she commented as he crossed to a small wet bar and poured two glasses of bourbon. "Where have you been?"

He handed her a glass and lowered himself onto the cushions beside her. "I had to drive out to Roanoke today."

She stared at him. "Roanoke? But that's hours from here. What was so urgent that you needed to go all the way out there?"

"Business," he said, and tipped back his bourbon and drained the glass.

"Want to talk about it?"

Cole shrugged. "I gave the blueprints to the Bureau of Mine Safety, thinking they would be sufficient evidence for them to send a team of safety inspectors into the abandoned mines, but I was wrong. They won't go in without more substantial proof. Having updated blueprints of an abandoned mine isn't an indication that those mines are being worked. In fact, the Bureau was impressed that Buck had the good sense to have the mines properly documented."

"Aren't you afraid that Buck will find out? I don't want you to lose your job over this." She pulled a face. "What if he realizes that I took the blueprint? He won't let me into the mines. Now I'll have to come up with another plan to test STAR."

"Hey," he murmured, and pulled her into his arms. "Everything will work out. I told you I would take you to another mine, and I meant it. Whenever you're finished with the search-and-rescue team, we'll drive over to West Virginia and I'll take you into one of the coal mines there."

She let him hold her for a minute before she pulled away. "What about you? Will Buck be upset that you took off like that today?"

"He probably doesn't even know."

"What if he finds out that you gave the blueprint to the Bureau of Mine Safety?"

"Don't worry about me."

He didn't want to tell her that his job with the Black River Mines was just a cover. Or that until today, he hadn't been able to figure out how Buck could be accessing the mines without anyone knowing. But thanks to Lacey, he finally knew.

Buck had done a good job concealing whatever illegal mining he was doing. The tunnels extended through the mountains for miles. Only someone involved in the scheme could pinpoint the precise location of the illegal activity. He wanted to tell Lacey the truth, but he'd maintain his secret until he had the irrefutable proof he needed.

Despite the warmth of the evening, Lacey leaned into Cole and savored the heat and strength of his body. His fingers absently stroked her upper arm. Lacey thought she could easily spend every night just like this. But she knew that couldn't happen.

Too soon, she would return home and Cole would remain in Black Stone Gap. Despite telling herself it was for the best, she found the thought left her feeling depressed. But she couldn't stay in Kentucky. Even if she had the fortitude to accept what he did for a living, she had her own career to think about back in New England. She loved her job, and she was pretty sure she wouldn't find anything similar in Kentucky.

"So what happens tomorrow?" she asked carefully. "You've just started a new job, and I still need to test STAR. How are you going to drive me to West Virginia if you're working?"

He blew out a hard breath. "I'll take care of it. Why don't we plan on heading out on Wednesday morning?"

"I'm not sure. I'll finish up with Carr and the others tomorrow, and then give my boss a call and see what he wants me to do. He has the final say." She gave a soft laugh, and then groaned and covered her face with her hands. "I still can't believe I stole that blueprint. You should have seen me—I felt like a spy stealing top secret documents. What if he had caught me in the act?"

Cole hugged her briefly. "He didn't. He may still have no idea that the document is missing, and even when he does realize, I doubt he'll suspect you." He hesitated as if debating his next words. "I hope I'm wrong about the closed mines, but I don't think I am. But I want you to know that not all mining operations are corrupt. Your GPS unit could still make a difference."

"I know it will make a difference. What if I told you that I first became involved with StarPoint Technologies because of a miner?"

"I'd say that I'm trying very hard to suppress my jealousy."

"There's no need to be jealous. He died a long time ago."

Cole sobered instantly. "I'm sorry. Tell me about him, and how you got involved in the GPS business."

Lacey swallowed and looked down at her hands, wondering how much to share with him. She hadn't talked about her father to anyone in years. Even her mother never spoke about him, as if the memories were still too painful. But a man like Cole would understand. She took a deep breath.

"My father was killed in a coal mining accident when I was eight years old. His body was never recovered."

There was a shocked silence. "You're kidding."

"I wish I was."

"Which mine was it?"

"The Spruce River mine in West Virginia. They lost eight men in a tunnel collapse. They survived the initial event and at first the owners were optimistic that they could rescue all the men. But after a week, when two more cave-ins occurred, they discontinued the rescue effort and sealed the mine. I can still remember…" She gave herself a mental shake, unwilling to dredge up those old memories. "Anyway, after that, my mom and I moved to New Hampshire and we've been there ever since."

Cole shook his head, his expression one of dismay. "Wow. I can't believe you lost your dad in that accident. I remember studying that disaster in school."

"I still have nightmares sometimes," she confessed. "About him being alive in the pitch-dark, knowing that nobody would be coming to save him."

Cole's arm tightened around her. "That's why you prefer to keep the lights on."

Lacey nodded. "Logically, I know that he couldn't have survived, and that he was already gone when they stopped the rescue efforts, but sometimes at night…I wonder."

"So you devoted your life to developing a tool that would prevent another tragedy."

"Well, maybe not my life," Lacey replied, "but the last five years, anyway. I was really hoping to field-test STAR while I was here in Black Stone Gap. Even though we're developing the unit for NASA, I can't help but think of all the other applications it could be used for."

"I'll make sure you get your unit tested," Cole promised. "It won't be here in Black Stone Gap, but you'll have your test results."

"I feel like my whole life has led to this," she said. "If STAR can save even one miner's life, then all the years of research and lab work will have been worth it." She raised her eyes to his. "Maybe I'll even be able to sleep without the light on."

"Speaking of which, it's been a long day." Without giving her time to object, he stood up and pulled her to her feet. "Time for bed."

The combination of cool sheets and warm, hard Cole sounded like the perfect antidote to the long day she'd spent worrying about him. She wanted nothing more than to feel his arms around her. She followed him to the loft area. Her room was only dimly lit from the hallway until Cole flipped on the small bedside lamp. In the soft light, his expression was inscrutable. Lacey stood by the bed and waited for him to touch her, to pull her close and slide his hands beneath the edge of her bathrobe and over her bare skin.

Instead, he leaned over the bed and held the blankets up. "C'mon," he said. "In you go."

Lacey was too surprised to protest. She didn't even remove the robe. Obediently, she slid beneath the covers and watched as he pulled them over her, tucking them neatly at her sides.

"Aren't you—"

"Try and get some sleep. I'll see you in the morning." He turned toward the door.

"Cole…"

"I'll be downstairs if you need me. Get some rest."

He left. He pulled the door almost completely shut behind him, leaving a crack of light to spill in from the hallway. Lacey lay still for a moment and wondered what had just happened. She had been so sure he was going to make love to her, or at the very least spend the night in the same bed with her, even if it was just to sleep.

With a small sigh, she shifted onto her side and bunched the pillow beneath her cheek and thought about the events of the day. Cole had driven all the way to Roanoke, Virginia and back. Of course he was exhausted. The man hadn't gotten much sleep since he'd met her.

Tomorrow she would wrap up with the search-and-rescue team. They had their GPS units, and although she suspected they knew perfectly well how to use them, she'd agreed to spend one more day with them. On Wednesday, she and Cole would drive to West Virginia to test STAR. Lacey expected she would need two days to conduct the field test. She would stay in the area long enough to do the follow-up analysis, and then she would return home.

Home.

She thought about how, in the space of just a few short days, she'd begun to think of Cole's house as home. He hadn't actually asked her to stay in Kentucky, and she wasn't sure what she would do even if he did. She'd never intended to stay. So why did she feel so let down because Cole had opted to sleep in a different room? And if she couldn't get through one night without him, how in the world was she going to get through all the nights to come?

COLE STOOD IN the doorway of Lacey's bedroom and watched her sleep. Her hair fanned out on the pillow behind her, and she slept with her hands tucked beneath her cheek, like a child.

With a sigh, he looked down at the small glass he held in his hand, and then tossed back the remnants of the bourbon he'd been nursing. He told himself he should just go back downstairs and go to bed.

It had taken all his willpower not to climb into bed with her earlier that night. He'd just wanted to hold her; to reassure both her and himself that she was safe. But he knew from experience there was no such thing as just holding Lacey Delaney. It seemed whenever they touched something flared, hot and urgent. He had no illusions that if he climbed into that bed with her, he'd have to make love to her. He was incapable of keeping his hands off her. But at some point during the past several days, what he felt for Lacey Delaney had changed. Maybe in the beginning it had been about sex, but not anymore. He was falling for her, and falling hard. When she'd told him about her father, he'd been floored. He still had trouble getting his head around the fact that she came from a coal mining family. That her father had died in the tunnels. No wonder she was so determined to test the prototype.

He'd been shocked by the revelation of her background. Given her innate elegance and conservative nature, he'd been certain she came from wealth and privilege. At least, he amended silently, she was conservative outside the bedroom. The things she did to him when they were alone together completely blew his mind. She'd rocked his world in ways he couldn't even comprehend. But she'd also forced him to face some hard truths of his own.

He'd come back to Black Stone Gap for just one reason—to shut down Buck's mining operations. He held Buck personally responsible for the accident that had killed his friend, Drake Wilson, some five years earlier. He wanted answers. He needed to know why Drake had been working a part of the mines that should have been closed. Buck insisted that Drake had gone into the closed area without permission, but Cole had his doubts. And, of course, there was the part he himself had played in Drake's death.

He rubbed a hand across his eyes, recalling the events of that day. Drake had been trapped in a small cavern as a result of a cave-in. Cole had been so certain his plan to drill a vertical shaft alongside the cavern, and then tunnel horizontally to where Drake was trapped, would work. Instead, the drilling had triggered another cave-in, and Drake had been killed.

After the initial investigations were over and Buck had been cleared of any wrongdoing, Cole had left Black Stone Gap. He hadn't planned on coming back until he'd received a phone call from his former professor Stu Zollweg.

But meeting Lacey Delaney had never been part of the plan. As he watched her sleep, she murmured incoherently and then turned onto her stomach and kicked the blanket aside with one leg. At some point, she'd removed his bathrobe and it lay crumpled on the floor. By the light from the bedside lamp he could see her perfect rear, smooth and round beneath a pair of pale blue panties.

"Jesus," he muttered, all thoughts of maintaining his distance completely gone. He turned to leave before he could act on his desire to join her, but was stopped short when he heard his name.

At first he thought he had imagined it. He looked back at the bed. Lacey had raised herself up on one elbow. Now she pushed her hair back from her face and peered sleepily at him.

"Cole?" Her voice was husky.

"Yeah, it's me. I didn't mean to wake you. Go back to sleep."

"I was dreaming. Cole…" She sank back down against the pillows and extended a hand to him. "Come here."

There was no mistaking her meaning, and Cole made a swift rationalization. He was, after all, just a man. No one could blame him for succumbing to such a sweet invitation. And it didn't have to be about sex. He would just hold her. He could do that. Couldn't he?

With a soft groan, he swiftly crossed the room, setting his empty glass down on the bedside table. He stood beside her, suddenly hesitant. She was all smooth, bare skin and tempting softness.

"Lacey..."

"Come here."

He gave a soft, self-deprecating laugh. "I am so toast." He wore a pair of loose pajama bottoms and nothing else, and the thin material tented over his arousal. He slid in beside her, gratified when she wrapped her arms around him and entwined her legs with his own. Her skin was warm and silky against his.

"I'm just going to hold you, okay?" His voice sounded gravelly with the effort it took to keep his rampant desire under control.

"Okay," she agreed breathlessly, skating her lips along his collarbone, "just so long as you're inside me while you're doing that."

"Lacey..." Her name came out on an agonized groan. "I'm trying to do the right thing here, and you're killing me."

She pulled back enough to search his face in the darkness. "Then do the right thing and make love to me." She traced a finger around the whorl of his ear. "I wanted you to earlier. Why did you leave?"

Cole blew out his breath. "Trust me, it wasn't easy. But you need to get some sleep, and I don't want you to think that I'm only interested in sex." Unable to help himself, he splayed his fingers against her back, feeling the thrust of her shoulder blades and the smooth bumps of her spine. She was both supple and soft, her skin like satin beneath his questing hand.

She made a soft murmuring sound of pleasure and arched against him, rubbing herself sensuously against his bare chest. "Mmm. You feel so good." Her hands roamed across his back and traced a random path over bone and muscle until they encountered the fabric of his pants. The elastic waistband stretched easily beneath her questing fingers, and then her hands were inside, smoothing over his buttocks and grasping them, urging him closer. "You feel *really* good."

Cole gave a laugh that sounded more like a groan. "Lacey, sweetheart, I'm not sure—"

"I am." The words were whispered on a husky note, even as she slid one hand over his hip and around to the front, where his erection strained upward. She grasped him lightly, her fingers exploring the thick rise of his flesh. "Please, Cole…"

With a soft groan of defeat, he bent his head and pressed his lips to the tender skin beneath her ear. He slid his hand down her back to the sweet curve of her bottom, and cupped one cheek, kneading gently. "Okay," he whispered, "but only because you insist and it would be rude for me to refuse."

"Spoken like a true Southern gentleman."

"I aim to please."

"Then prove it." Her voice was warm with laughter.

"With pleasure." It became harder to speak as her hand began to stroke him, and his breathing grew more rapid. "Easy, baby. I've got something to prove, remember?"

She gave a soft laugh, and then her hands were pushing his pants down over his hips, freeing his arousal to bump enticingly against her stomach. She gasped when he kicked the fabric free of his legs and rose over her, pushing her gently back against the mattress.

"God, I want you," he rasped. He searched her face, seeing desire and something else reflected in her eyes. Something he didn't dare to identify. Hope flared inside him once more. He hesitated, wondering if he dared risk another rejection. He'd already told her he wanted more than just a temporary relationship. Maybe he'd do better to just take what she was willing to give him and bide his time.

She parted her legs beneath him and arched her hips, rubbing herself against him. He groaned and lowered his head to press searing kisses along her jaw and down the slender length of her throat. "It was all I could do not to come up here after you'd gone to bed. I want you so much, Lacey."

Her arms drew him down closer and she rained soft, moist kisses over his face. "I want you, too."

He lowered his head and nibbled gently at the corner of her mouth, then traced his tongue lightly along its contours. When she murmured her assent, he dipped his head lower and blazed a trail of molten kisses along the column of her neck and lower still to the fragile line of her collarbone.

He slid a finger beneath the slender strap of her bra and drew it down over her shoulder, pulling the lacy cup with it. He lifted his head and watched in utter fascination as her nipple contracted into a tight bud.

Glancing up at her face, he saw she was watching him through heavy-lidded eyes. Her lips were parted and her breath came unevenly. He smiled and then dipped his head, swirling his tongue around the hard nub, reveling in its texture. She gasped when he drew it into his mouth and suckled her. He cupped her other breast through the thin fabric of her bra, pinching the nipple until it stood tightly erect.

She was rolling her hips now, arching restlessly against him, and it was all he could do not to tear her panties from her and claim her; to plunge himself into her slick heat and make her his own. He slid a hand beneath the silky fabric. She was wet. He inserted first one finger into her tight depths, and then another, gratified when she moaned and thrust her hips against his palm.

"Oh, man," he breathed against her breast, "I don't think I can wait…" He reared back and dragged her panties down the length of her legs. "Here, roll over."

"What?" Her voice was thick with pleasure.

"Roll over."

"Okay." She turned onto her stomach and gave him a seductive look. "Like this?"

"Well, actually more like this…" He raised her hips upward and shoved the pillows beneath her. "Yeah, just like that."

He leaned back on his heels to admire her perfect rear in the moonlight, unable to resist smoothing his hands over her buttocks. She lay with her face against the mattress, and her hands curled into the sheets. He loved the way her slender back flared into the womanly curves of her hips, loved the way she responded when he nudged her thighs apart, affording him a clear view of her feminine center.

He stroked her from behind, first with his hand and then with the tip of his engorged shaft, while she clutched at the sheets and writhed against him. When she rose up on her elbows and looked back at him, he thought he'd never seen anything as erotic or beautiful.

"Cole, please…you're making me crazy…"

He grasped her hips and positioned himself, then in one fluid movement, thrust himself home. She cried out in pleasure and pushed herself back against him. Cole bent forward, covering her with his body. He swept her hair away from her neck and caught an earlobe gently between his teeth before he teased the delicate whorl of her ear with his tongue.

She was moaning now, making sexy sounds deep in her throat as she rocked back against him, her body fisted around him. Cole thrust deeply, and reached around to cup her breast and toy with her nipple.

"Oh, God," she gasped. "you feel so good…"

Cole felt himself swell even more at her husky words, and knew he wasn't going to last. Reaching down, he slid his fingers through her damp curls until he found the slick nub of her clitoris. He swirled his finger over it, trying to give her the friction that their position wouldn't allow, gratified when he felt her stiffen beneath him. Her breath came in short, shallow pants. When she cried out and convulsed around him, he gritted his teeth, willing himself not to lose control.

Grasping her hips with both hands, he raised himself up and slowly withdrew before thrusting himself back into her, his eyes fastened on the point where her body gripped him. But the combination of her flesh squeezing him and the erotic sight of himself sliding into her was too much, and with a strangled cry he climaxed, the force causing his back to arch before he collapsed, completely drained.

He rolled onto his side, pulling her with him, until she lay with her back against his chest. She was still breathing unevenly. He smoothed her hair back from her face and planted a warm, lingering kiss against her jaw.

"That was amazing," she breathed. "The sensations…"

"Yeah," Cole admitted huskily, "pretty incredible." And he wasn't just referring to the sex, although it was without doubt the most amazing he'd ever had in his life. He would never tire of coaxing those sweet sounds of pleasure from her.

He pulled her closer against his chest and tucked his knees behind hers so that he was spooning her. She yawned convulsively and then sighed in contentment. He could hear her breathing gradually become deeper and more even as sleep claimed her. He tightened his arms around her, knowing he had to say it.

"I'm falling in love with you, Lacey Delaney." His voice was no more than a whisper.

Beside him, she gave a soft snore.

12

Cole was gone when Lacey woke up the following morning, but she could hear him moving around on the first floor, and smelled fresh coffee brewing. Glancing at the bedside clock, she saw it was already eight o'clock. Throwing back the sheets, she crossed the room to the adjoining bathroom and turned the shower as hot as she could stand it. She stood under the pulsing water, her thoughts going back to the previous night.

He was falling in love with her.

His words had caused her chest to constrict in a way she was unfamiliar with, and a suspicious lump had formed in her throat. She'd wanted to turn in his arms and see the truth of his words in his eyes, but had been immobilized by sudden panic. Instead, she'd closed her eyes and pretended to be asleep.

She couldn't let him know she'd heard him. What would she say? That she was falling in love with him, too? That despite their differences and despite the fact they'd only known each other a short time, she was already coming to depend on his strength and support?

She didn't want to depend on him; didn't want to entrust her heart to someone when they might break it, even if they didn't mean to. There was no way she could let herself fall for someone who worked in the coal mines, no matter how perfect he might be. She'd never stop worrying, and eventually she would come to resent his job. But she knew Cole well enough to realize that he wouldn't give up his job as a mining engineer, not even for her. Buck may fire him, but he'd find another position in another mine. Nope, better to pretend she hadn't heard those softly impassioned words and save what was left of her heart.

She turned her face into the spray of water and let it sluice down her body, recalling the tender passion of their lovemaking. The truth of his words had been there in his touch. In his kiss. In the reverent way in which he'd held her afterward.

The knowledge both thrilled her and terrified her.

Oh, God, what was she going to do? As she turned the shower faucet off and reached for a towel, she realized it was already too late. Because she was falling for him, too.

Downstairs, she expected to find Cole in the kitchen, but he was nowhere in sight. She was pouring herself a mug of coffee when she heard his voice from outside. Moving to a window, she saw him standing on the porch, talking on his cell phone. His voice drifted toward her.

"Give me another week and I can prove he's operating in the closed section of the mines." He paused, listening. "Lacey? I've told her what I suspect is happening, but that's it. She doesn't know my real purpose for being in Black Stone Gap. Don't worry—she won't be a problem. She's on our side. In fact, she's the one who gave me the blueprint." Another long pause. "I said not to worry. I'll take care of her."

Lacey backed away from the window. Who was he talking to? And what did he mean *she doesn't know my real purpose?*

She watched as he shut off his phone and turned to enter the kitchen. His expression registered warm pleasure when he spotted her, but then he frowned when he saw her expression. "What's wrong?"

"Who were you talking to?" she asked.

"A former professor of mine from grad school. Why?"

Lacey swallowed hard. "Because I heard you. What did you mean when you said I was on your side, or that I won't be a problem? What's going on, Cole?"

He smiled at her, but Lacey thought it looked a little strained. "Nothing. At least, nothing you need to worry about. Are you hungry? I thought I'd make breakfast."

Lacey waved a dismissive hand. "I'm not hungry. Tell me what you meant when you said I don't know your real purpose for being here. What does that mean? I thought you were an engineer."

"I am," he said simply.

"Then why—?"

He took a deep breath and braced his hands on the counter, before angling his head to look at her. "I'm working undercover for the Department of Labor."

Lacey frowned. "What?"

"They asked me to help," he explained. "And I agreed." He scrubbed a hand over his face, looking frustrated and tired.

Realization dawned. "You're investigating Buck Rogan. You want to shut him down."

Cole raised his hands in self-defense. "That's up to the Bureau of Mine Safety, and only if I find evidence that he's operating in violation of safety laws. Buck Rogan runs a mining operation that borders on illegal. In fact, I'm pretty sure it is illegal."

"Why didn't you tell me?" she asked. "All this time, I've been thinking you were a mining engineer and you're actually some kind of undercover agent?"

Cole's voice grew terse. "I *am* an engineer. I just also happen to be working this investigation. I couldn't tell you the truth without jeopardizing the entire operation. What difference would it have made, anyway?"

Lacey stared at him in disbelief. "You could have told me. I wouldn't have said anything to anyone."

He made a sound of exasperation. "I told you as much as I was able, except for the part about working undercover. That's why they call it undercover work, Lacey, because nobody is supposed to know about it."

"Buck said that you blame him for your friend's death. Is that why you're so determined to expose him? As revenge?"

Cole stared at her for a moment, and a dark flush shadowed his lean jaw. "If you believe that, then you don't know me at all. But for the record, I do blame Buck for Drake's death. But not as much as I blame myself."

Lacey considered everything he had told her. She was shocked to find out that he was working undercover, and although there was a part of her that resented the fact he hadn't told her, she also understood why he hadn't. What he'd said was true; they were on the same side. He wanted to save lives as much as she did.

"Okay," she finally said. "So what's your plan? How are we going to prove he's operating in the closed sections of the mine? Is there any access to those tunnels?"

Cole looked at her in disbelief. "First of all, there is no *we* in this operation. I won't have you involved. It's enough that you took that blueprint. No, you just spend the day with Carr and the boys, and let me figure this out."

"But I can help you," she insisted. "I could tell Buck that I need access to the mines right away, and that I need an engineer to come with me. He's seen the test parameters, and he knows that would be the truth. Once we're in the mine, we can work our way over to where you think the access to the closed section is."

"Absolutely not. Out of the question, so you can just forget it."

"Why? I can help you with this."

"I won't risk you getting hurt," he clipped. "And that's the end of it, Lacey. If you're not hungry, then I'll drive you over to the Rod and Gun Club."

Lacey compressed her lips and nodded. She knew he was right, but that didn't mean she had to like it.

"Lacey—" His cell phone rang, interrupting his sentence. He glanced at it, his face reflecting sudden tension. "I need to take this call, and then we'll talk, okay?"

She watched as he stepped outside, keeping his voice low enough that she couldn't make out his conversation. He returned less than two minutes later, his expression grim.

"That was Buck," he said. "He wants to see me in his office right away."

A frisson of alarm shot through Lacey. Had he discovered the missing blueprint? Or had he discovered that Cole was working with the federal agents?

"I'll come with you," she said quickly. "I'll explain about the blueprint."

To her surprise, Cole stepped forward and caught her face between his hands. "No, I want you to stay here. It may very well be nothing, but whatever it is, I can handle it."

"But Cole—"

"I'm serious." As if to punctuate his words, he pressed a warm, firm kiss against her mouth. "Stay here, fix yourself something to eat, and I'll be back as soon as I can."

THIRTY MINUTES LATER, Lacey was pacing the kitchen when the sound of a car engine in the driveway alerted her. Peeking out the window, she spotted a taxi, and frowned. Then she saw Sam Caldwell, her boss, climb out of the back and speak to the driver.

Alarm shot through her. What in the world was her boss doing here? She strode through the house and pulled open the front door. Sam was just climbing the steps and his face was set in grim lines. When she opened the door, he looked up and his features sagged in relief.

Sam was in his early forties and had started StarPoint Technologies right out of grad school. Lacey had worked for him while she was in college, and had been thrilled when he'd hired her as a full-time member of his development team. He treated her like a favorite kid sister, and now she felt a pang of guilt that she hadn't called him since she'd arrived in Black Stone Gap.

"Sam, what are you doing here?"

"Jesus, Lacey, thank Christ you're okay."

Stepping back, she opened the door wider and gestured for him to come in. "Of course I'm okay. Why wouldn't I be?"

Sam stepped into the living room, his gaze sweeping around the spacious living room in appreciation. But when he turned to Lacey, she could see he was annoyed. With her.

"You've been down here for five days, and I haven't heard from you once. *Not once,* Lacey. You literally vanished into the wilds of Kentucky with a piece of equipment valued at more than two million dollars, and you ask me why I look upset? *Jesus!*"

Lacey's mouth fell open. Had she really not contacted him since she'd arrived in Kentucky? Her mind flew back over the past several days, and she realized he was right. She'd turned her phone off in order to avoid having to talk with her mother. "I spoke with Julia," she said lamely.

Sam thrust a hand through his hair, making it stick up wildly. "Once. You talked to her once. How do you think

I felt when I called the motel and discovered that you'd checked in, but that you left with a man that first night and hadn't been seen again since? Hmm?"

Lacey felt her face go hot with embarrassment. "My car broke down, and then I met this guy—"

To her astonishment, he grasped her by the upper arms and shook her lightly. "I was ready to call that search-and-rescue team to go look for you! Your mother is frantic, Lacey. She's been calling me incessantly and I couldn't even tell her with any certainty that you were okay. I finally reached Sheriff Hathaway, and he told me he hasn't even met you yet. Do you know what went through my head?"

Lacey shook him free. "Okay, I get it. I'm sorry if I worried you. I should have called, but everything is fine, Sam. You had nothing to worry about."

"I realize that now. I tracked down Carr Hamilton this morning, and he told me that you did a fantastic job demonstrating the handheld GPS units."

Lacey glanced at her watch. It was barely eight-thirty. "You've already seen Carr? When did you get here?"

"Last night. I'm actually staying at the Blackwater Inn, probably in the same room you were originally checked into." Finally, he gave her a crooked smile. "I don't blame you for leaving—that place is a dump."

Sensing that forgiveness was within her reach, Lacey stepped toward him and gave him a brief, hard hug. "I'm so sorry, Sam. I should have called. I turned my phone off because my mother wouldn't stop calling me."

Sam laughed and stepped back. "Trust me, I understand." He looked questioningly around the room. "So where is this guy you've hooked up with? Carr assured me he's decent, and that you were never in any danger. I already knew that, but I'd like to meet him for myself."

"Cole isn't here. He's actually over at the Black River Mines, talking with the owner. But he should be back soon." She paused. "Wait. What do you mean, *you already knew that?*"

Sam sighed. "Cole MacKinnon called me the other day and expressed his concern about testing STAR in the Black River Mines. He thinks they're dangerous, and after talking with him, I'm inclined to agree. I want you to pack up your gear and come home with me."

What? Lacey stared at him, dumbfounded. "Cole actually called you?"

"He did, yesterday. He thought I should know that the Black River Mines are part of a federal investigation, and that he considers those tunnels to be a danger."

"I don't believe this," Lacey murmured in disbelief. It was one thing to ask her to conduct her testing elsewhere, but why did he have to call her boss? "I haven't even begun to field-test STAR. We can't leave yet, Sam. Even if the Black River Mines are off-limits, Cole is going to bring me to one of the mines in West Virginia tomorrow."

Sam shook his head. "That's not necessary. We'll do the testing in New Hampshire, in the caves near Plymouth."

"The Polar Caves?" she asked in disbelief. "Sam, they're not deep enough. They won't give you an accurate reading. I thought we agreed that the coal mines would be perfect."

Sam's face grew serious. "That was before I knew about the accident rate in these mines. Cole is right—it's too risky." He glanced at his watch. "I'll give you ten minutes to grab your things."

As Lacey packed her belongings, her mind worked furiously. Because of Cole, her first field test was a failure. More than that, he'd made her look incompetent. As if she couldn't be trusted to do anything on her own. She still couldn't believe he'd had the audacity to call her boss!

In the next instant, she sat down on the edge of the bed, acknowledging that Cole hadn't made her look incompetent; she'd done that all on her own. She should have maintained communication with her office while she'd been here. But she'd been so determined to do this on her own that she hadn't considered how it would look when she didn't call in each day. The fact that Sam had flown all the way here to make sure she was okay was mortifying. And now he wanted her to return to New England with him, and she couldn't very well refuse.

She sat on the bed for several long moments, trying to control the tight, panicky feeling in her chest at the thought of leaving Cole. It was the same way she felt when she found herself alone in the dark. As if she might suffocate. As if she, too, might die alone in the utter blackness. With effort, she picked up her suitcase and her overnight bag and made her way downstairs to where Sam waited.

"All set?" Sam asked, as she entered the living room.

Lacey nodded. "Yes, I just need to get STAR. Sam, do you think we could stop by the mine before we head out? I don't want to leave without saying goodbye to Cole. He wouldn't understand."

Before Sam could respond, there was the sound of tires crunching on the gravel driveway outside. Lacey looked out the window to see Cole's truck skid to a stop behind the taxicab. He wrenched open the door and jumped out, leaving Copper in the cab. He cast a quick glance at the taxi before he took the steps two at a time. The door burst open and he was there, filling up the space with his energy.

Lacey's glance flew guiltily to her suitcase and presentation cases, lined up neatly by the door. She braced herself.

"Cole—" Whatever words she had been about to say died on her lips as she took in his tight expression.

"Lacey, I'll explain on the way. Grab that thing you call STUD or STAR, or whatever it is. I think you're finally going to get your chance to field-test it."

"What are you talking about?"

She was forced to step back as he shouldered his way into the living room. "I put it in the back closet." He stopped when he saw Sam standing in the middle of the room. Then he looked at her gear lined up neatly beside the door, and went completely still. When he finally turned around to face her, Lacey caught her breath at his expression.

"What's going on?" His voice was dangerously soft.

"Cole, I want you to meet Sam Caldwell, the owner and founder of StarPoint Technologies. My boss."

Sam extended his hand, and Cole shook it. "We talked the other day on the phone," Sam said. "I appreciate your confiding in me about the conditions of the mine. I wouldn't want to jeopardize her safety."

Cole nodded, and then turned to Lacey. Seeing her expression, he gave an apologetic shrug. "I did what I thought was right. You're strong-willed and quite frankly, I wasn't sure I'd be able to say no to you if you insisted on going into the Black River Mines."

"So you called my boss."

"I did what I thought was right. You did tell me that he had the final say." He gave Sam a resigned look. "I just didn't think he'd come down here to bring you back."

Sam glanced at his watch. "We should get going. If we leave now, we'll just get to the airport in time."

Lacey nodded, unable to believe that this was it; that she would be leaving Kentucky. There was so much she wanted to say, but not in front of Sam. Not like this, with Cole looking distracted and off balance. She recalled again how he had looked when he first came through the door, as if he was on a mission.

"What did you mean when you said I was going to get a chance to field-test STAR?" she asked. "Did something happen?"

"It doesn't matter." He gestured toward her bags. "You need to go if you're going to catch your flight."

"Just tell me what's going on, Cole."

He hesitated, then blew out a hard breath. "Three boys went into an abandoned mine. They triggered a cave-in and now they're trapped."

Lacey felt the blood drain from her face. "When did this happen? Are they alive? Can you get them out?"

Cole shook his head. "I don't know. It happened about an hour ago and we believe they're still alive. Look, I should get back." He extended his hand toward Sam. "It was good to meet you."

Without looking at Lacey, he turned and strode swiftly out the door. Lacey followed him, unable to believe he was going to just leave when there was so much they needed to say.

"Cole, wait."

He stopped halfway down the steps and turned to face her. His expression was bleak.

"Did you know that Sam was going to come down here? Did you know I'd be leaving this morning?"

He shrugged. "I didn't know for sure, but I had a hunch he would. I told him that I would take you to West Virginia, but he seemed uncomfortable with the idea. He cares a lot about you, Lacey."

"And what about you? Do you care a lot about me?"

He came back up the steps and caught her face in his hands. He searched her eyes. "You know I do. That's why I called Sam in the first place. I am curious, though. Were you going to leave without saying goodbye?"

She covered his hands with her own. "No, I was going to come by the mines to see you. I hate this, Cole. I'm not ready to leave."

"Then don't. Stay here." His eyes burned into hers.

"I can't. Not after Sam came all this way to get me."

"He came to make sure you're okay, and to protect his investment," Cole said drily. "Tell him you want to take some time off. He'll understand. Stay a little longer."

The words hung in the air between them, and it took all of Lacey's control not to break down and throw herself at him and tell him that of course she would stay. She stared at him, then let her gaze drift beyond him to the rolling mountains that extended for as far as the eye could see. She loved the rugged beauty of the land and the simplicity of life here. She hadn't expected to love the area—or Cole.

She took a step back, acutely conscious of Sam watching them from inside the open door. "I can't. Now's not the right time. I need to go back to New England and perform the field test for STAR."

Cole considered her for a moment, and then looked past her to Sam. He sighed deeply. "Okay. I understand. Look, I need to get back to the mines. I came here to bring you and the prototype to the rescue site. If you're leaving, then I guess using it is out of the question. I'd better get back and help the team. They'll need to figure out where those boys are by using more conventional methods."

"Like what?"

Cole smiled humorlessly. "A good old-fashioned wild-assed guess."

Lacey's eyes widened. "Are you—?"

"Going in? You bet."

"But you said you'd never do another mine rescue," she protested, knowing it was hypocritical for her to care, when even now Sam waited to take her to the airport. But she couldn't think about Cole going into the mine without her heart clenching in terror.

"I'll be fine. You'd better get going."

Lacey drew in a deep breath and ignored the sharp pain that caused her chest to constrict. "I'll call you when I get to Boston. To find out how the rescue went."

"Just tune in to your local news channel. Once you get back to Boston, that is. I'm sure every major network will be carrying the story."

"You think it will take as long as that?" Lacey frowned.

"Rogan's Run No. 5 mine has been abandoned for about fifty years. It'll take most of the day just to pinpoint where the boys are and then determine the best extraction method."

"Of course." Lacey didn't know what else to say. She knew what was involved in a mine rescue, and how quickly it could all go terribly wrong. There was no way she wanted to witness any of that.

"Well, I guess this is it, then," Cole said grimly, watching her.

Lacey blinked furiously, and looked away from him. "Yes. I guess so."

He gripped her by the upper arms. The fierceness of his gaze penetrated her, making her feel as if he could see all the way to her soul. "Take care of yourself."

He pressed a hard kiss against her mouth. Without another word, he turned and strode to his truck. He didn't look at her as he turned the ignition and thrust the vehicle into gear.

Lacey watched with blurred vision until his taillights disappeared down the wooded road. Then she swiped her eyes and turned determinedly away.

13

LACEY SAT IN the back of the blue taxi and watched Black Stone Gap rush past. There was the diner where she'd broken down that first night when Cole had come to her rescue. Her hand tightened on the purse she held on her lap.

"Everything will work out," Sam said quietly beside her. "You'll see. Things happen for a reason."

She nodded. "I know."

"We'll find another test site for STAR."

Lacey suppressed a small laugh. She thought he'd been referring to herself and Cole. Of course he'd been talking about STAR. While Sam might genuinely care for her, his first concern was for his investment.

"You sure you don't want to test STAR right now? The entire community is scrambling to rescue three boys who are trapped in an abandoned mine."

Sam's expression was grim. "I can understand why you want to bring STAR to the rescue site, but the prototype is untried. What if it fails?" He sighed deeply. "I wouldn't want to give anyone false hope."

Lacey stared at him. "But what if it operates exactly the way we designed it to? What if we're able to pinpoint the boys' location and help the rescue team? This is why we developed STAR." She hesitated, her mind working rapidly. "You said that things happen for a reason. What if the reason we're here is because this community needs us? What if we're here to help with the rescue? Imagine how amazing it would be to have the owner and developer of the unit right on-site."

Sam was quiet for several long moments. "I don't know. Cole indicated the mines—and this one in particular—are dangerous."

"But what if we don't need to go into the mines?" Lacey asked in growing enthusiasm. "I've been thinking about this a lot, since Cole was adamant that I not go into the tunnels. We could equip one of the rescue workers with the remote camera and you and I could control the operations from aboveground. It's what I had intended to do anyway."

Sam looked at her. "That might work."

Something broke free in her chest, and she impulsively hugged him. "It will work, I know it will."

She would see Cole again. He had touched her life and her heart in ways she hadn't thought possible. She couldn't leave without letting him know. She leaned forward to speak to the taxi driver.

"Do you know where Rogan's Run No. 5 is?"

"I guess I do. It's only the entire community of Black Stone Gap that's out there right now, trying to rescue those boys. We can be there in about twenty minutes."

Lacey smiled. "Think you can make it in ten?"

The driver grinned. "No problem."

THEY TURNED OFF the main road onto what looked like a logging road. It wound steeply upward into the trees, and the land on either side was roped off with barbed wire and strung with signs that read Private. No Trespassing.

The road ended at a derelict mining facility. A gravel lot butted up against a wall of shale and rock, and punched into the center was the portal to the mine itself. It looked like a gaping black mouth. Lacey could see it had once been sealed off with timbers, which now lay in a dusty heap next to the entrance. A rusted sign with the words *Danger! Stay Out!*, hung askew from one of the discarded boards.

The taxi driver hadn't exaggerated about the entire community being present for the rescue attempt. It seemed there were fifty or more cars and trucks in the weed-choked lot, and dozens of residents milled around outside the entrance to the mine, which had been cordoned off with yellow tape. Two police officers stood on the other side of the tape and kept people from entering the mine itself. Beyond the small crowd, Lacey counted three police cruisers, a fire truck, and two ambulances parked alongside the other cars. She strained unsuccessfully for a glimpse of Cole's pickup truck.

At the entrance to the parking area, they were stopped by a police officer wearing a khaki-and-green uniform. He leaned down to peer in at them. He was an older man, with a seamed face and a graying mustache, but his eyes were shrewd.

"Morning, Tara," he said to the driver, and his gaze swept past her to where Lacey leaned forward in the backseat, desperately searching the crowd for any sign of Cole. "I'm guessing you're here to lend a hand. Right now, there's not much you can do, but they're organizing food and whatnot for the rescue team down at the church. I'm sure they could use an extra hand."

"Actually, Sheriff, we're here to assist with the rescue." Sam leaned forward and extended his hand through the window. "I'm Sam Caldwell from StarPoint Technologies, and this is my lead engineer, Lacey Delaney."

The sheriff turned a sharp eye on Lacey, and a slow smile

transformed his grizzled features. "So you're the gal that Carr and the boys have been telling me about." He thrust a broad, blunt-fingered hand in through the window to Sam, and then Lacey. "I'm Cyrus Hathaway. I'm sorry I wasn't here when you arrived, but I guess you heard about what happened to my wife."

Lacey took his leathery hand in her own. "Yes, I did. I hope she's doing better."

"She'll be home in a week or so. I hope Cole's been taking real good care of you."

Lacey couldn't be certain, but she thought she detected a glimmer of amusement in his eyes. She blushed and released his hand. "Yes, sir, he has. Actually, I need to see Cole. I have a prototype GPS unit with me that I think he'll be able to use in the rescue."

"Oh, yes. Cole told me a little about it. Let's see if it lives up to its potential." He indicated a parking spot near the entrance to the mine. "Tara, drop them off over there. I'll radio Harlan and have him come out to meet them."

"Thank you, Sheriff Hathaway." So it wouldn't be Cole who met her. Lacey pushed down her disappointment. Tara pulled up near the entrance to the mine, and got out to open the trunk for her.

Sam hefted STAR out of the trunk. "Let's hope we're doing the right thing," he said quietly.

"I know we are."

"Ma'am?"

Lacey turned and saw Harlan striding toward them. He wore a hard hat, and his rawboned face was streaked with coal dust. He carried two extra hard hats and safety goggles for her and Sam.

She quickly made introductions. "Where is Cole?"

"I'll bring you over to where the command center has been set up," Harlan replied.

Lacey glanced quickly toward the small crowd of people who were gathered behind the tape. Some of the women were weeping, causing Lacey to wonder if they were the boys' mothers. She had little idea what had happened beyond what Cole had told her, but fervently hoped she could help.

"Here we go," she murmured to Sam as they followed Harlan.

"Is Cole at the command center?" she asked.

"He's already gone in."

"In? As in, *into the mine?*" She hurried after Harlan as he skirted the crowd of people and the rescue vehicles and strode toward a dilapidated building made of concrete and steel that was almost falling down from neglect.

"That mine is a maze of tunnels, and the kid that escaped the cave-in couldn't remember which ones they'd explored. Cole's the best tracker we've got. Besides, he has Carr and the other guys with him. They'll track the boys to where the cave-in occurred, and then we'll figure out how to get 'em out."

Lacey stopped in her tracks as a wave of fear washed over her, making her dizzy. Cole was in those mines. Her imagination conjured up images of dark, twisting tunnels with unstable walls and roofs that might fall and crush him to death without warning.

Sam paused beside her, watching her through concerned eyes.

"Hey." Harlan's voice cut through her lurid imaginings. "Don't you worry about Cole. He knows the dangers and he'll be careful. C'mon."

He thrust the steel door of the building open. Inside, at least a dozen men were closely studying a series of maps that were spread across the surface of a long table, crudely constructed out of wooden sawhorses and sheets of plywood. Cole's dog, Copper, lay under one of the tables, but surged to his feet when he saw Lacey, his tail wagging furiously. Lacey bent to pet him, and then stood up to survey her surroundings. More maps were tacked onto the nearby wall. As they approached, Lacey could see they were topographical maps and a series of blueprints of what might have been the mines.

They looked up as she and Harlan approached. "This is Lacey Delaney and Sam Caldwell," Harlan said in an expressionless tone. "They brought the GPS unit Cole was talking about."

One of the men detached himself from the group and approached Lacey. She recognized him as the man who had interrupted her meeting with Buck on the day she had stolen the blueprint.

"I'm Wendall Riggs. I'm a foreman in the Black River Mines." He gestured to the men behind him. "We all have experience with mine rescues. Cole said he thought you might be able to help us pinpoint where the boys are."

Lacey forced herself to shift gears, to drag her thoughts away from Cole and the danger he might be in, and concentrate instead on how to help him. She indicated the case that Sam still carried. "This is STAR, our Subterranean Advanced Receiver unit. It can pick up and transmit signals through hundreds of feet of rock."

The men continued to stare at her. Finally, one of them gave a snort of disgust. "How's that going to help us?"

Aware of Sam watching her, Lacey grabbed the case out of his hand and hefted it up onto the table. She snapped open the locks and carefully opened the case, gratified when the men gathered for a closer look. She could almost feel their awe at the display of high-tech equipment inside.

She freed a series of metal poles from where they were secured inside the case and swiftly snapped them together until the entire unit stood about seven feet high. Then she attached a small satellite receiver dish to the top. A GPS unit, not unlike the handheld ones she had supplied to the rescue team, snapped onto the pole.

She carefully removed a small black box from where it was secured inside the case, and slipped it into what looked like a tiny harness. She flipped a switch on the back of it and gestured for Harlan to come closer.

"This is the transmitter," she said briskly. "It has a small camera and sound recorder built into it. I can attach it to Harlan's hard hat, or hang it around his neck, like so."

Harlan obediently bent down so she could slip it over his head. A small red light blinked steadily above a tiny lens on the front of the unit.

"This," she continued, indicating the metal case, "is the control center." Built into the case was a small computer monitor and a sturdy headset. She flipped the power on, and a series of lights flashed alongside the monitor. "If I bring my receiver unit outside so that it can relay with the satellite—" Lacey indicated the pole with the satellite dish "—the transmitter will begin sending signals, which are then displayed on the GPS unit, providing the operator with the precise location of the transmitter, including distance from the earth's surface."

Lacey glanced at the faces around her. They were mesmerized. "If Harlan were to wear the transmitter and go into the mines, Sam and I could sit up here and it'd be just like we were with him. By watching this monitor, and wearing these headphones, we can see and hear everything he sees and hears. Additionally, I can track his precise location on the GPS display. Once he reaches the site of the cave-in, I can tell you the precise location. Then you can make the decision about how best to reach that location to get the boys out."

"Christ," breathed Wendall, "it's exactly what we need." He turned to the other men. "Walt and Ed, take Miss Delaney and Mr. Caldwell outside and help them get the equipment set up. Harlan, can you and Poke catch up with Cole and the rest of the team?"

"Of course." His expression didn't change as he drew the transmitter over his head. "I think we should mount the transmitter to my hard hat, though. That way, if I need to crawl, or if I encounter pooled water, I'm less likely to damage it."

Lacey tried to squelch the lurid images she had of Cole, trapped in a narrow tunnel as it filled with torrents of water, struggling to escape. It was just her overactive imagination, she knew, but part of her wondered if she had the strength to watch Cole on the monitor as he made his way through the mines. In the next instant, she knew she had no choice.

Outside the entrance to the mine, volunteers were setting up canopies and tables for the food and water being brought in from town. Several reporters had also arrived and were talking to the police and the bystanders about what was happening.

"We'll set you up over here," Harlan said, indicating a table and chair on a patch of grass away from the mine's entrance and away from the distraction of the rescue personnel and townspeople. "I'll have a canopy brought over so you can sit in the shade."

"Thanks." Lacey set up the receiver and the satellite dish, and hooked everything to the central monitor. Copper flopped down at her feet and put his head on his paws. Sam watched, but let her control the process. It took her several more minutes to key in her location, but she was rewarded when an image of herself seated at the table popped up on the monitor.

"Hey, that's pretty neat," Harlan enthused, bending closer. Immediately, her image filled the small screen and became distorted.

Lacey laughed in spite of herself, and glanced up at the small unit that had been fastened to his helmet, directly beside the headlamp. "I guess the transmitter is working. Here, don't stand so close." She waved Harlan back from where she was sitting, and the image on the monitor shifted into focus again. "Okay, let's just run a few preliminary tests to ensure the unit is working, and then we can get started."

Ten minutes later, when Lacey had verified the equipment was in working order, she turned to Harlan. "We're all set. The battery in your unit is good for twenty-four hours. After that, I'll still be able to track your location on the GPS receiver, but I won't be able to pick up images or recordings."

"Okay. Can I hear you if you want to talk with me?"

Lacey shook her head. "No. It was never designed to be a two-way communication system."

"I'll make a note," Sam said. "Lacey, I want you to start working on that as soon as we get back."

Lacey nodded. She wouldn't tell Sam that she wasn't going back to Boston. She'd made a decision in the past hour. If Cole wanted her to stay, then she would.

"Harlan, wait."

Harlan turned back to her.

"When you find Cole, tell him…tell him I'm not going anywhere. And tell him to be careful."

She was aware of Sam's arched eyebrows, but Harlan grinned then, revealing a row of strong, white teeth. Lacey couldn't recall him ever smiling before, and for a moment she was taken aback at the way it completely transformed his stern features. "Don't you worry, ma'am. We'll bring those boys—and your man—out of there safely."

He spoke with such easy confidence that Lacey almost believed he could do it. She watched as Poke joined him. Their leather belts were saddled with canisters of water and oxygen, and they each carried a small bag of tools on their hip. Together they disappeared into the black maw of the mine's entrance.

14

SAM PULLED A chair up next to Lacey as she sat down at the table and placed the headphones over her ears. She watched the monitor as the small camera on Harlan's hat adjusted to the darkness of the mine, and the image slowly came into focus. Despite sitting outside in the sunshine, with a warm breeze buffeting her skin, she felt chilled by the utter blackness that surrounded the men.

She watched, enthralled, as they filed into a steel-walled elevator. "Ms. Delaney, if you can hear me, this is what we call 'the cage.'" Harlan's voice sounded hollow and disembodied over the speakers. Through the tiny camera mounted on Harlan's hard hat, Lacey watched as Poke clutched the hand chains over his head. The picture on the monitor lurched sideways as the cage began to descend.

"Seems like the power was never shut off in these mines, but it's anyone's guess as to what kind of condition the equipment is in." Harlan tipped his head down and on the small television screen, Lacey looked past the toes of his worn boots to the grated floor he was standing on. Even on the monitor, the black abyss they were descending into made her feel slightly ill. The fact that the picture was in black-and-white only added to the creepiness of the scene.

She glanced at the GPS, noting their rapid rate of descent. Two minutes later, when the cage came to a grinding halt, they had descended nearly five hundred feet beneath the earth's surface.

"How's it going?"

Lacey looked up into Sheriff Hathaway's face. She quickly removed her headphones. "They just reached the bottom of the shaft. Harlan is going to meet up with Cole and the rescue team, and we should be able to see everything they see from up here." She indicated the monitor, which showed Poke exiting the cage, and then Harlan's hand as he closed the grated door of the elevator behind them.

"Well, I'll be damned," the sheriff muttered. "The miracles of modern technology never cease to amaze me." He tapped a finger against the monitor. "You'll be able to watch them the entire time?"

"Well, provided the camera isn't damaged or the batteries don't die."

As Harlan made a complete sweep of the area they stood in, Lacey could see the two men had come out of the cage into a cathedral of chiseled rock. The walls and high ceilings glowed eerily white in the darkness.

"What is that?" Lacey murmured.

"They coat the walls with fire-retardant limestone powder," Sheriff Hathaway answered. He dragged a chair over to the table and sat down, his eyes glued to the monitor.

Lacey could see ancient, truck-sized power generators covered in dust. Rail-car tracks disappeared into dark portals, and a dizzying network of tunnels twisted outward from where they stood.

She put the headphones back on, wishing she could communicate with Harlan. They had already determined that the ancient telephone system installed in the mines was no longer operational.

"See this mark on the wall?" Harlan's headlamp swept over the entrance to one of the tunnels. "That was put there by the rescue team to indicate which way they went. We'll be able to move fast by following these signs."

Lacey peered at the encircled arrow that had been drawn on the wall. But despite Harlan's predictions that it wouldn't take long to catch up with Cole, she spent nearly two hours watching Poke's back as he negotiated the maze of intersecting tunnels, before he gave a whooping shout.

"Ms. Delaney, if you can still hear me, we've found the rest of the team."

Lacey leaned forward, only vaguely aware of the small crowd of people who had gathered around her equipment and watched with equal fascination. In the distance, barely visible on the monitor, she could see a series of bobbing lights. As Harlan drew closer, she realized they were the headlamps of the rescue team.

"Hey, Carr! That you?" Harlan's voice echoed eerily through the headphones as he shouted down the length of the tunnel. "It's Harlan and Poke and Ms. Delaney!"

Lacey heard the amusement in Harlan's voice as he called out to the others, and she smiled. Then there was Cole, sprinting out of the darkness of the tunnel into the light of Harlan's headlamp, his eyes searching the darkness beyond the two men.

Lacey's heart constricted and she felt weak with relief. He was safe. His face was so close to Harlan's that she could see the coal dust streaking his lean features, see the brilliance of his eyes as he glared at the other man.

"Goddammit, I told her not to come into these mines." He looked furious. "Where the hell is she? I swear, if you left her back there—"

"Easy, man. She's right here." Lacey saw Harlan's hand as he reached up and tapped the small transmitter. "She's safe aboveground, watching and listening to every dumb-ass thing you do and say." Harlan laughed aloud as Cole narrowed his eyes, and then looked directly into the camera.

Directly at her.

Lacey's breath caught. She couldn't help herself. She reached out and traced his image with her fingertips, uncaring of who watched. "Tell him what I said," she whispered urgently.

"She said to tell you she wasn't going anywhere," Harlan added, as if he could hear her talking to him. "Oh, yeah, and to be careful."

Right then, as she watched, Cole's face twisted and he swiftly looked away for a moment. When he finally turned back to the camera, he was smiling, but Lacey could have sworn there was a suspicious sheen to his eyes.

"Sweetheart," he said, "I know we have a lot to work out, but we'll get there. I'm going to help get these boys back home, and then you and I are going to figure this thing out, okay?"

Lacey pressed a hand against her mouth to prevent a small sob from escaping, but she couldn't stop the swift flow of tears that his words caused.

"Oh, Christ, this is embarrassing," she heard Harlan mutter. "Very touching, of course, but completely embarrassing."

Lacey gave a snort of laughter, even as she swiped at her damp cheeks, her gaze clinging to Cole's.

Beside her, Sheriff Hathaway chuckled. "He's a good boy, that MacKinnon. Like his daddy. Recognized true love as soon as it looked him in the eye, I guess."

Lacey nodded, sniffling. "Thank goodness he recognized it. I was too blinded by my own prejudices."

"Well, we all got our faults, I suppose. I just wonder how your boss feels about the fact that you're not going back."

He shot her a sharply questioning look. "You *are* staying, aren't you?"

She nodded mutely, still watching the monitor.

Sam gave an exaggerated sigh. "Damn it. I guess I'm going to have start looking for a new design engineer." But he was smiling, and Lacey knew he approved.

"Okay. Lacey, darlin', I'll see you on top." Cole grinned at her in the camera, and then turned away.

Harlan and Poke followed him along the tunnel to where the rest of the rescue team were standing at the intersection of a bisecting tunnel, staring at something. Lacey tensed.

Harlan's headlamp swept into the adjoining tunnel, and Lacey frowned, peering at the image. For a moment, she wasn't certain what she was looking at, then realized the connecting tunnel was illuminated by a series of overhead industrial lights. In the middle of the tunnel was an enormous piece of machinery that even to Lacey's inexperienced eye didn't appear to be a relic from five decades earlier.

"Son of a bitch," she heard Harlan mutter. "You were right, MacKinnon."

"Yep. Looks like somebody has broken through from the Black River Mine No. 6 into Rogan's Run Mine No. 5."

Lacey watched as the rescue team continued to make their way down the tunnel. It was supported along the sides by evenly spaced old timbers. Cole looked at the ceiling, and when Harlan tipped his own head back, she could see a series of bolts embedded in the overhead rock.

"No question about it," Cole said grimly. "Somebody is mining where they have no business mining. These tunnels have been closed for fifty years, but here I see ceiling bolts that look brand-new. Although—" he took several more steps, still staring upward "—it appears he's cut corners here. Even if this mine were in any condition to be worked—which it's not—I count one roof bolt for an area that should have a minimum of three." He angled his gaze at the camera, looking directly at Lacey. His expression was somber. "I'll give you one guess as to who it could be."

Lacey risked a peek at Sheriff Hathaway, whose own expression was darkening with each passing minute as he peered over Lacey's shoulder at the monitor.

He yanked out his radio and pressed the button. "I want Buck Rogan up here just as soon as you can find him. He has some answering to do. And tell Wendall Riggs to get his ass out here." He glanced down at Lacey. "This ain't going to be pretty. MacKinnon suspected this was going on, he just couldn't prove it."

Lacey recalled her own doubtful reaction to Cole's suspicions. She saw Wendall Riggs approach them, and from the expression of weary resignation on his face, she knew Cole was right. Wendall was one of the foremen in the Black River Mines. If anyone knew anything about Buck's illegal mining practices, it would be him.

Sheriff Hathaway gave a long-suffering sigh and pushed himself to his feet. He laid a friendly hand on Lacey's shoulder. "You keep up the good work, and let me know as soon as they find those boys. I got to take care of some unpleasant business."

Lacey watched him go, and then turned back to the monitor, adjusting the volume upward in order not to overhear the sheriff's conversation with Riggs.

"Hey, Ms. Delaney." Harlan's voice was sharp. "We found something up ahead. Looks like a rockfall."

Lacey's heart hitched as Harlan approached what looked to be a dead end. As he got closer, however, she saw it was actually a jumbled pile of rock and debris that effectively sealed off the tunnel and prevented them from going any farther.

"Okay, I think we've found our cave-in."

Lacey tore the headphones off and shouted to Sheriff Hathaway. She was immediately surrounded by a dozen or more people, all of them clamoring for a view of the monitor and demanding to know the precise location of the cave-in. She checked their position on the GPS unit, and swiftly gave the coordinates to Sheriff Hathaway. "If the boys are, in fact, on the other side of that cave-in, they're about 550 feet below the surface."

"Okay, let's see what Carr's team wants to do," the sheriff said, gesturing for silence.

Lacey sat down again and replaced the headphones, wishing fervently that the system was equipped with a two-way speaker.

"Okay, folks," Carr said, "we'll need to drag some timbers over here to shore up the roof, but I think we can get to the boys from this side." Carr was examining the rockfall and the roof above it with a critical eye. "It doesn't look like a major fall—more debris than anything else. I don't see any slabs that've come down. We should be able to get through."

Lacey repeated what Carr had said to the people who were crowded around her chair, and a jubilant cheer went up.

"I want five more men in that mine helping move that rock," shouted Sheriff Hathaway. "I want three stretchers and four paramedics down there with them."

He hadn't even finished talking before men were scrambling to obey. If she'd been impressed with the speed and efficiency of the search-and-rescue team, Lacey was equally impressed by the determination and fearlessness exhibited by these people as they hastened to help.

On the monitor, she watched as the rescue team in the tunnel shored up the exposed portions of the roof, and began methodically removing the rock and debris that blocked the tunnel. It was backbreaking work and the process was agonizingly slow. Sheriff Hathaway sat beside her as she watched the monitor, occasionally stepping away to update the townspeople and the increasing number of reporters on the progress they were making.

Two hours later, Lacey was beginning to wonder if the rockfall might not be more extensive than they originally realized. The team continued to work tirelessly to remove the debris, but even she could see they were beginning to flag.

She was massaging her aching eyes when a loud cheer came through the headphones. Lacey's eyes snapped open and she stared at the monitor, expecting to see they had finally broken through the barrier. Instead, she realized that the reinforcements sent in by Sheriff Hathaway had succeeded in reaching the first teams.

Lacey sighed in relief, and turned to announce the news to those gathered nearby. They smiled and embraced each other, cautiously optimistic. During the past several hours, the townspeople had moved away from the entrance of the mine and had instead congregated around Lacey and Sam, taking turns peering over their shoulders at the small screen. Sympathizing with their hunger for news, Lacey kept up a steady narrative of what was happening down in those dark depths. Now, with nearly a dozen additional men, Carr and his crew set back to work with renewed vigor.

"Lacey, we're through," called Harlan.

At first, Lacey didn't understand. They were through? As in done? But when she peered at the activity on the monitor, she realized they had actually succeeded in breaking through the obstruction.

"They're through!" she cried. Hardly aware of her actions, she leaped to her feet and snatched the headphones off. Wheeling around, she grabbed the portly sheriff in an exuberant hug. "They're through!"

Sheriff Hathaway grinned, and then gently disentangled himself from her arms. "That's fine news. Now let's see if the boys are okay."

Replacing the headphones, Lacey watched as a small opening appeared at the top of the rockfall. Carr and Skeeter worked to enlarge the hole until finally it was wide enough for Carr to poke his head and shoulders through.

"I can see two boys," he called back to the rescue team. "They're not moving."

Lacey bit her lip, and looked over at the sheriff.

"Well, what is it?"

"They can see two of the boys," she said quietly, "but they're not moving."

He leaned back in his chair and blew out a breath. "Okay. They could be knocked out from the rockfall, or unconscious as a result of the air quality. Not much oxygen down there. Guess we'll have to wait and see."

"Do you want to tell the others?"

The sheriff sighed. "Guess I better get them prepared." He heaved himself to his feet, and Lacey watched, her heart in her throat, as he slowly gathered the family members away from the rest of the crowd.

"Ms. Delaney." Harlan's voice echoed through the headphones. "Carr and Cole and the medics are going in to check on the boys. I'll go in so you can see for yourself what's happening."

Mesmerized, Lacey watched as Carr wormed his way into the small hole until only his lower legs and boots were visible. Then he was gone.

Cole and Skeeter carefully picked their way up the incline of loose rubble until they reached the small opening near the top. Cole glanced back at Harlan, and before he vanished through the small opening, he looked directly into the camera and winked. Two of the four paramedics went next, but the hole wasn't large enough to permit the stretchers to go through.

"Okay, we'll have to work on opening this up a little more," Harlan said. He directed his gaze back toward the rockfall, and on the monitor, Lacey saw Cole poke his head back through.

"We found all three boys, and they're all alive," he called down to Harlan. "One of them is trapped beneath the rock, and the other two are injured, but if we can get them out quickly, I think they'll pull through."

Lacey tore the headphones off and leaped up. "They found them and they're all alive!"

She found herself grabbed in an enormous bear hug as those nearby simultaneously cheered and cried. Lacey didn't know the woman embracing her, but she hugged her back with equal enthusiasm.

When she was finally freed, she turned back to the monitor and put the headphones on, unable to contain her foolish grin. They had done it. They had found the boys. Even Sam was being embraced by complete strangers, and he looked as happy as Lacey felt. *Now, please, God, let them all come out quickly and safely.* She wanted Cole back aboveground; wanted to touch him and reassure herself of his safety. But more than anything, she wanted to tell him she had been wrong in thinking she could walk away from him. She knew now she didn't want to live without him.

As if to mock her silent prayer, she heard Harlan swear.

"Goddamn it, MacKinnon! Let's move! It's coming down!"

He turned his head, and Lacey saw the timber posts along the side of the tunnel begin to bow under the tremendous burden of earth. At the same time, she became aware of an odd noise, like a deep groaning. In dismay, she realized it was the walls of the tunnel beginning to creak and pop.

"Oh, my God," she breathed. "The mine is collapsing."

She was hardly aware of the press of people around her as they stared in horrified fascination at the small screen, or that she was gripping Sam's hand so tightly that her knuckles were white. When Harlan tilted his head back and looked up, Lacey saw the steel roofing bolts begin to snap and shoot to the floor with a metallic *ping*. The groaning noise was louder now, and Harlan was shouting at the other men, telling them to run.

"Get out! Get out!" Lacey was only distantly aware of somebody yelling to the team, and then realized it was her.

Harlan started to run toward the pile of rubble and the opening where Cole and the boys were, but then the camera angle altered sharply, as if he had abruptly changed direction, or somebody had grabbed him and spun him around.

She caught a glimpse of the other rescue workers fleeing back down the tunnel. There was a tremendous roaring noise, like a locomotive, and a swift blur of movement on the monitor.

Before Lacey's horrified eyes, the small screen went black, and the headphones grew silent.

15

ROCKS RAINED DOWN on him. Choking dust filled his nostrils and mouth. The pitch-black cave was filled with suffocating silt, but at least the terrible roaring noise of the cave-in had subsided. Dust filled his lungs. He coughed, spat and coughed again.

Beneath him, the boy whose body he protected with his own shifted and groaned. Cautiously, Cole lifted his head. Swirling clouds of dust made visibility nonexistent, but he thought he heard a voice to his left. He'd heard the telltale sounds of the impending collapse and had only precious seconds to warn the others and corral them into the far corner of the small cavern where they'd discovered the boys before the roof had let go.

"You okay, son?" He pushed himself away from the boy, shaking the loose rock and debris from his body. His headlamp was broken, and now he groped in the darkness for the boy, his hands moving swiftly over him, checking for injury.

"I—I'm okay," the boy croaked.

Cole knew the kid had suffered a broken arm and possibly several broken ribs from the previous rockfall, but it seemed this one had at least spared him further injury.

"What's your name?" he asked the boy.

"Devin."

"Okay, Devin, I'm going to leave you here for just a minute while I go and check on your buddies. Can you tell me their names?"

"Jack and Ryan."

Cole patted the child's face. "You'll be fine, okay? You'll still be able to hear me, because we're going to keep on talking. Can you do that?"

"Sure. My arm really hurts."

"I know it does, and you're going to have a real impressive cast once you get out of here." Cole had already moved away from Devin toward the spot where he'd heard the voices. "The girls will love it."

"Ew, gross."

"Not into girls, huh?" Cole groped his way across the rock and rubble that littered the floor, gratified when he touched a denim-clad leg. "That'll change. Who's this?"

"Hey, Cole." It was Skeeter. "I've got one of the boys here with me. He's breathing, but still unconscious from when we found him."

Cole dropped his head and breathed a silent thank-you for their safety. "Okay, what about Carr and the paramedics and the third kid?"

"Dunno."

"I'm over here," called a disembodied voice. "It's Joe Green. I've got the third boy over here."

"I'm coming," Cole called to him.

The dust had begun to subside, and Cole saw Skeeter's headlamp glowing dimly in the darkness. It was as if a thick, black fog had descended over them.

"Hey, Devin, how're you doing over there? Can you still hear me?" Cole called to the first boy.

"Yes, sir."

"Good boy. Stay where you are. I'll be back in a minute."

He patted Skeeter's leg. "Let me borrow your headlamp. I'm going to check out the rockfall and try to locate the others."

They exchanged hard hats, and Cole made his way gingerly over the uneven floor of the cavern. The boys had worked their way through the tunnels until they had come up against a dead end, the result of a previous cave-in. Cole knew that sometimes it took no more than the vibration of a raised voice to cause a rockfall in an area already compromised. In this case, the boys had been lucky that they'd been trapped in a small area between the two cave-ins. They could have been crushed. His headlamp picked out a boot and then a leg, and he realized it was one of the paramedics.

"Joe Green?" he called.

"I'm still here." The voice was close, but it didn't come from the body in front of him.

"I think I found your partner." The man's body was almost completely buried beneath rubble. Working quickly, Cole cleared the debris away and was rewarded when the man rolled to his side and began coughing.

Cole sat back and wiped the sweat from his face. The dust had settled to the point where he could more or less see the entire cavern. Swiftly, he scanned the small chamber, looking for Carr. He could just make out Skeeter and the boy who lay limp in his arms on the far side. Several feet away, Devin had pushed himself to a sitting position and sat huddled, cradling his injured arm.

Joe Green was several feet behind him, still working to free the boy who had been trapped by the first rockfall.

"What's your name, son?" Joe asked.

"Ryan." The boy groaned softly as Joe tried to work his foot free from where it was pinned beneath a slab of shale.

"Where the hell is Carr?" Cole muttered, and then froze. Protruding from the pile of rubble was a man's head, shoulders and arm. He was so completely covered with dust and small rocks that Cole had missed him at first glance. "Skeeter, give me a hand over here."

They scrambled over to where Carr was half-buried under the rocks, finally managing to pull him free. He was unconscious.

"His pulse is thready," Skeeter said. "No telling what kind of internal injuries he might have."

"Okay, let's make him comfortable, and then let's get that boy dug out."

It took them more than an hour before they were able to free Ryan's foot. It was badly broken. They moved him over to join the other two boys. Carr and the injured paramedic lay side by side. Skeeter, Joe and Cole sat with their backs against the cold sable wall, each lost in their own thoughts.

They were all alive, which was a miracle in itself, to Cole's thinking. He fervently hoped Harlan and the rescue team had fared as well on the other side of the rockfall.

"I'm going to see how bad the cave-in was," he told the others, and clambered over to where the opening had been. It didn't take long for him to realize the new rockfall had completely buried the opening to the tunnel. There wasn't the slightest hint of air movement, light or noise where the hole had once been. He had a bad feeling about the fate of Harlan and the others. He didn't believe they could have moved away in time to avoid being crushed beneath the falling torrent of shale and rock. As he surveyed their small cavern, he realized it might very well become a tomb. It could take rescue workers hours, maybe days, to dig through the new rockfall to reach them. He suspected they would run out of oxygen long before then. He thought of Lacey's father, who had died under similar circumstances. The last thing he wanted was for her to endure another tragedy.

"Okay, let's take an inventory of our supplies," he said, picking his way back down into the chamber. "If we're conservative and keep only one headlamp on at a time, and ration our water and oxygen, I think we can make it until a rescue team arrives."

"Can we dig ourselves out?" Skeeter asked.

"I don't think so. We're pretty well buried, and exerting ourselves would only deplete our air and water. I think our best bet is to sit tight and wait for help."

"You don't sound too nervous," observed Joe.

Cole looked at the other men. "I'm not. You see, I happen to know there's a lady up there with a very sophisticated piece of equipment, who can pinpoint our exact location. They'll be down here to pull us out before you know it." He ruffled Devin's hair. "You wait and see. In a few hours, you'll be safe at home."

They fell silent once more.

Hours slipped by, and both Devin and Ryan fell into a fitful sleep. Cole and Skeeter monitored the two injured men and the unconscious boy, and rationed out sips of the water they had with them. The air quality was poor, and Cole knew the sleepiness he felt was a direct result of the dwindling oxygen. Despite what he had said about Lacey and her equipment, inwardly he was scared to death—scared the rescue team he knew was on its way might not reach them in time. He didn't want to think about that; didn't want to think about never seeing Lacey again, of not being able to tell her how much he loved her.

With a deep sigh, he tilted his head back against the wall and closed his eyes. He could see her in his mind's eye, with her ginger hair and luminous eyes, smiling at him. God, he wanted to be with her. He knew she must be terrified, wondering if he was alive or dead. She wasn't as tough as she liked to pretend. She was soft and vulnerable, and completely head over heels in love with him, even if she couldn't admit it.

Which was why he intended to survive.

"Hey, Cole," murmured Skeeter, "you feel that?"

Cole stilled. It was a deep, distant rumble that caused the wall at his back to vibrate.

"Come here, son," he commanded softly, and dragged the nearest boy closer, keeping his eyes on the overhead ceiling. He hunkered over the child, using his body as a shield against this new menace.

A shower of small rocks rained down on them. The vibration increased to a rumble.

"Jesus," Cole whispered, watching the shower of dust and debris continue to fall.

Suddenly, even his headlamp failed to penetrate the thick, choking dust that blossomed around them as overhead the roof exploded inward.

16

DAWN WAS STILL several hours away. The first fingers of light hadn't yet begun to filter over the distant horizon. Lacey could scarcely believe it had been more than forty hours since Cole had first disappeared into the mines. Of course, you'd hardly know it was dark outside with all the floodlights that had been brought to the site.

They had moved the rescue operation to a spot in an open field, directly over the cavern where Cole and the boys were believed to be trapped. Even now, an enormous machine was drilling down through five hundred feet of earth to reach them. If the coordinates on Lacey's equipment were correct, they had penetrated the roof of the cavern more than ten hours ago. Warm air was being pumped through a pipe to keep any survivors comfortable. They were working on enlarging the shaft enough to lift them out.

When they had first broken through to the cavern, they had heard what they believed were the survivors tapping on the pipes. But that had been more than eight hours ago. Sheriff Hathaway had suggested the noise from the drilling might have drowned out attempts at communication. Lacey wanted to believe him, but she couldn't shake the fear that overrode every rational argument presented, and lingered despite the sheriff's assurances. She knew the feeling wouldn't subside until Cole was safe in her arms. Her stomach felt hollow. She was restless with anxiety.

The sheriff had sent an additional dozen men into the mines to determine the extent of this new cave-in, and to determine if Harlan and the others had survived. Bitterly, Lacey wondered how many more men would be sacrificed to the greedy belly of the mines. Even now, law enforcement officials and rescue teams continued to arrive from neighboring communities to help bring the victims out.

"How are you holding up?"

Lacey turned to see Sam and the sheriff standing beside her. The rescue effort was taking its toll on Sam, as well. His face was haggard and his eyes were red-rimmed and weary. She shrugged and tried to smile.

"As well as can be expected, I guess. I just wish—I just wish I knew if he was okay." Her voice broke. She turned swiftly away and pressed her fingers against her eyes, willing herself not to cry. She felt the sheriff's hand, large and comforting, on her shoulder.

"It'll be okay, gal. You're sure about the coordinates for their location, eh?"

Lacey blinked back the tears that threatened to spill, and turned back to the sheriff, smiling. "Yes. It's the only thing I am sure of. I went over those coordinates a dozen times."

"You know if you're wrong…"

"She's not wrong," Sam asserted. "This unit is operating beautifully."

"But if she is…" the sheriff persisted.

"I know. A miscalculation of even a few feet, and we waste precious time by drilling in the wrong spot." She met the sheriff's narrowed gaze. "But I'm not wrong. I trust my equipment, and I trust what I saw in those last seconds before I lost visual contact. Harlan was running away from the cave-in. Whether he was…killed, or if he just lost his hard hat, the GPS indicates the transmitter is just outside the spot where Cole was last seen. I've adjusted the coordinates to take that into account. I'm certain we've got the right spot."

A thirty-inch-diameter drill had arrived from West Virginia before nightfall to drill a shaft wide enough to drop a rescue cage down and pull the victims to the surface. Drilling was expected to last at least twelve hours. Lacey didn't think she could stand the suspense. She'd go crazy.

Her gaze drifted over the people who had gathered to wait. Sheriff Hathaway and the rest of the rescue team had thought of everything. Ambulances waited to bring the victims to the nearest hospitals. Several helicopters stood ready in case the severity of the injuries required the victims to be air-lifted out. The family members of those who were trapped or missing had been notified, and although most of them had gathered at the local school, there were still others who insisted on remaining at the rescue site. The only person who was conspicuously absent was Buck Rogan.

Lacey had recognized Cole's siblings, distinctive because of their blue eyes. Her heart had nearly exploded out of her chest when she caught her first glimpse of his younger brother Garrick. She had been just steps away from flying into his arms before she realized it wasn't Cole. Garrick had been amused. Apparently it wasn't the first time he had been mistaken for his older brother. He had introduced her to his siblings, but Lacey found herself consumed by a sudden shyness. Cole's family had regarded her with cautious politeness, but Lacey could see they were curious as to her relationship with their brother.

"You should go back to Cole's place and try to get some rest," Sam advised her. "I'll be here, and I'll call you if there are any new developments."

Lacey smiled wanly. "I wouldn't be able to sleep, know-ing he's down there. Thanks, but I'll stay."

She sat down at the table where she had set up STAR. The blank monitor stared dully back at her. She picked up the headphones for what seemed like the hundredth time and put them on, but there was only silence. She checked the GPS display, but the blinking light that indicated the location of the transmitter hadn't moved.

"Please, God," she prayed silently, "let Cole and the oth-ers be okay. Let them all be okay."

She removed the headphones and set them aside, and then laid her head down on her forearms. Behind her, the noise of the enormous drill was deafening. She would close her eyes, just for a moment. Maybe, if she was lucky, she would open them to find it had all been no more than a terrible dream.

"LACEY, GAL, WAKE UP!" A hand shook her shoulder.

Lacey raised her head, feeling bemused and bleary-eyed. Her back and neck were stiff from having slept half-sprawled across the table. Her mouth was cottony and her eyes felt swollen.

"What? What is it?" She pushed the hair back from her face, and looked up at Sheriff Hathaway. It was still dark, but Lacey could see the barest shimmer of red-gold on the distant horizon, heralding the arrival of morning.

"How long did I sleep? Why didn't you wake me? What if Cole needs me?"

"Hush, gal. Harlan and the others just came out of the mine on the elevator."

"What? Harlan? Oh, thank goodness." Lacey ran her hands over her face. "Is he okay?"

"He and the others are a little banged up, but otherwise they're fine. They managed to dodge the cave-in, but Harlan lost his hard-hat. That's what the transmitter was attached to, so that's what we've been tracking on the GPS unit."

"Where are they now? Can I speak to Harlan? Maybe he knows something."

"They've been taken to the hospital for a checkup." He indicated the machinery behind them. An enormous crane was positioned directly over the hole that had been drilled overnight. "But I didn't think you'd want to miss this. They're getting ready to lower the cage to bring the boys up."

Lacey leaped to her feet, but was prevented from sprinting forward by Sheriff Hathaway's strong arm.

"Best stay back here. We'll know soon enough how your young man is."

Lacey searched the crowd that surrounded the area. Sam stood with several of the rescue crew, but as if sensing her scrutiny, he turned and met her gaze. He gave her a subtle thumbs-up. She spotted Cole's family standing together, their attention riveted on the hole. Throngs of rescue workers swarmed across the site. Pulsating beams of red, yellow and blue strobe lights from the nearby emergency vehicles flashed across the faces of the crowd, lending an eeriness to the already tense atmosphere. Her eyes narrowed when she spotted Buck Rogan on the edge of the crowd. He was flanked by two sheriff's deputies.

Then, as she watched in utter fascination, the cage slowly rose out of the hole. A small figure was strapped securely inside, and before the cage had completely cleared the hole, eager hands reached for it and pulled it to safety. The crowd erupted into jubilant cheers. Lacey watched, her heart in her throat, as the first of the injured boys was rushed to a waiting ambulance. His mother clung to his stretcher, her face streaming with grateful tears.

It was another twenty minutes before the next boy was lifted out of the hole, and then the next. Lacey's heart beat hard against her ribs as the fourth trip brought up a man. He was so covered in dust she couldn't determine his identity. She surged forward with the rest of the crowd, and this time the sheriff didn't try to stop her.

It was Carr, barely conscious. Lacey had no opportunity to get near him before he was transferred to a stretcher, and then to a waiting ambulance.

The cage was lowered once more into the shaft.

The two paramedics came out next, then Skeeter. Lacey's throat constricted with happiness as he stepped nimbly out of the cage and waved to the cheering crowd.

The cage descended for the last time. It seemed an eternity passed before the hydraulic winch began raising the cage to the earth's surface. Lacey clutched Sheriff Hathaway's arm in a near death-grip. She could hardly breathe. Her chest felt tight with dread and anticipation. The cage slowly rose into view, and Lacey would have recognized the lean, hard body inside anywhere.

She released the sheriff's arm and moved forward through the crowd, pushing past the throngs of rescue workers and reporters, nearly blinded by the glaring lights that had been set up around the perimeter. The cage opened, and Cole stepped out. He was immediately surrounded by emergency personnel and well-wishers, and for a moment, Lacey lost sight of him.

In the next instant, he pushed free of the surrounding crowd. Lacey saw him search the crowd of people. His face was completely black with coal dust, making the brilliance of his eyes all the more startling. His clothes were torn and filthy. But when he finally found her, he grinned, his teeth white against the blackness of his face.

She saw his lips form her name, and then she was running toward him as the crowd parted. He opened his arms, and she flung herself at him, hardly aware of the cheers of approval that roared around them. She was in Cole's arms, crushed against his hard body as he held her fiercely. She could hear him laughing.

"I love you," she said raggedly, choking on tears of happiness. "I couldn't stand that I didn't tell you, and now you have to know. I love you so much."

"I know, baby, I know." His hands buried themselves in her hair as he tipped her face back, and then his lips claimed hers in a kiss that was both fiercely possessive and heart-wrenchingly tender.

"Oh, Cole," she gasped, when he finally lifted his head. "I've been so scared...not knowing if you were okay. Don't ever do that to me again!"

"Sweetheart," he murmured against her lips, "that was nothing compared to the scare I had not knowing if I'd ever see you again."

She stroked a hand along one lean, dusty cheek. "I want to stay here with you. Is your offer still open?"

"Well, I'm going to look like one hell of an idiot if I don't, seeing as how the entire town seems to know that I'm crazy about you." His eyes crinkled in tender amusement. Copper had squirmed his way through the crowd and now he pushed at Cole's legs, demanding his attention. Bending down, Cole gave the dog a hug, and laughed as Copper lapped his face.

Lacey couldn't help it. She began to cry. She thought she'd lost everything, and now it seemed she was being given a second chance. She didn't deserve to be so happy.

"Hey now, don't do that," Cole admonished, and pulled her into his arms.

Lacey laughed through her tears, and pressed the palm of his hand against her cheek. "They're happy tears. I'm happy."

Cole hooked an arm around her shoulders and tucked her against his side. "In a few minutes," he murmured against her temple, as he began to make his way through the crowd to his siblings, "we're going home, and you're going to come into the shower and help me wash this coal dust off, and then I'm going to make you happier still." He slanted a mischievous glance down at her. "Deal?"

Lacey smiled, her heart accelerating at the implicit promise in his voice. "Deal." On the outer perimeter of the crowd, she saw Buck Rogan being led to one of the police cruisers. "What's going to happen to him?"

"There'll be an investigation, and he'll be cited for illegal mining practices and a whole slew of safety violations. They'll close all the Black River mines temporarily until they're up to standards, and then they'll reopen again."

"Will Buck still be the operator?"

"Well, not if I have anything to say about it, but I guess that's up to the Feds. Quite frankly, I just don't care what happens to him."

"Me, either. I have you, and that's all I care about."

She kissed him, uncaring of the cameras and lights and onlookers.

She was home.

Epilogue

One Year Later

COLE PAUSED ON the threshold of the back porch and drank in the scene that greeted him. He wondered if he would ever get used to the fact she was his.

Lacey sat on the swinging bench wearing a nightgown that made her look incredibly sexy. Copper lay contentedly at her feet. She lounged against the cushions and stared up at the stars. As he stepped onto the porch, he kept the package he had for her hidden behind his back.

Lacey looked at him as he walked toward her, and her eyes glowed with pleasure. "There you are." Her eyes narrowed, and she smiled. "What are you hiding?"

Cole grinned and sat down next to her, drawing the package out to lay it gently across her thighs. "I have something for you. An anniversary gift, if you'd like. It's been a year since you first came to Black Stone Gap, and I think the occasion warrants an acknowledgment."

They had traveled from his house in Norfolk to Black Stone Gap just the day before. Since the dramatic deep-mine rescue a year earlier, StarPoint Technologies had been overwhelmed with requests for STAR. With Sam's support,

Lacey had developed a commercial version of the prototype, and equipped it with a two-way communication system. In the end, StarPoint Technologies had opened an office in Norfolk.

She had wanted to work through the summer, but Sam had been adamant that she take at least two weeks of vacation. She and Cole had decided to spend that time in Black Stone Gap. The Black River mines had reopened under new management, and although Buck Rogan hadn't actually served any jail time, he was prohibited from having any involvement in the actual operation of the mines. From now on, he would sit on the board, more a figurehead than anything else.

They had invited Lacey's mother to join them for one of the two weeks but to their surprise, she had declined. It seemed she had met someone through her volunteer work at the hospital, and things were going so well that she didn't want to leave, even for a week.

Now Lacey stared at the pretty package on her lap and her mouth fell open. She turned to Cole with a stricken expression. "I didn't know we were celebrating an anniversary. I didn't get you anything."

Cole laughed gently. "Sweetheart, you've already given me everything I've ever wanted." Leaning forward, he pressed his mouth against hers. It was a slow, restive searching of her lips, and Cole was gratified when she leaned into him and sighed her pleasure.

"Open it," he coaxed.

Lacey pulled back and stared at him. He could see the childish anticipation on her face before she ripped the ribbon free and tore away the bright wrapping.

"Oh…Cole." She lifted the quilt free of the tissue paper and held it up to admire the intricate pattern that had been stitched with such care. "I didn't know…you never said…"

She raised her face to his, and Cole could see her eyes were damp. "It's so beautiful."

Cole kissed her, enjoying her pleasure.

"It's the same quilt from that day we spent at the county fair," she breathed, tracing her fingertips along the stitching. When she looked up at him, her eyes were misty. "You never told me you bought it."

Cole shrugged. "There never seemed to be the right time. But you said the quilt brought back some nice memories of your childhood." He grew serious. "I'm glad that you have some good memories."

Lacey smiled, and shook the quilt open, then covered them both with it as she stretched out and drew Cole down beside her. "I do. I have some very good memories. In fact, I haven't had any nightmares in months. I'm looking forward to sleeping under this quilt every night."

"Speaking of which, it's pretty dark out here tonight. Do you want me to turn on the porch light?"

"No." Lacey slid her arms around his neck and nuzzled him. "I enjoy the dark, especially when you're kissing me."

With a soft groan, Cole slid his hands beneath the hem of her nightgown, smoothing his palms along her thighs until he encountered the silken skin of her buttocks. He raised his head. "You're not wearing any panties," he growled in delight.

She arched against him. "Nope," she agreed wickedly, and unsnapped his jeans. "Maybe we can make some memories of our own under this quilt."

"With pleasure," Cole rasped, and captured her mouth in a soft kiss.

* * * * *

FLYBOY

This book is dedicated to my husband, John, and to our girls, Caitlin and Brenna, for enduring many weeks of benign neglect and never once complaining.

Huge thanks also go to
Lieutenant Commander John "Z-Man" Zrembski
and Bobby Ascolillo, my go-to guys for all things
related to naval flight. You guys are awesome.

And a special thanks to Brenda Chin,
for believing in this book.

1

IF WHAT THEY SAID about reincarnation was true, Sedona Stewart decided she was coming back as a man in her next life.

She snatched her sheet of paper from the copy machine and marched back toward her office, determined to ignore the sounds of merriment coming from the small conference room to her left. Another promotion was being celebrated, the third in as many months, all of them going to her male counterparts.

Despite the fact that she had as much education, experience and time on the payroll as any of them, she had been passed over yet again for the position of senior engineer, and for Bob Lewis of all people. It was like a slap in the face. The guy was a total dork. She'd be damned if she joined them in their good-old-boy ass-slapping and shoulder-punching congratulations.

She threw her paperwork down onto her desk, flung herself into her chair and acknowledged it was time to look for a new job. As an aerospace engineer for the Department of Defense, she'd worked damn hard to earn a promotion. She'd played the game, tried to be one of the boys, in an environment dominated by the opposite sex. She'd taken on additional duties, worked long hours, traveled when nobody else was willing to, sacrificed her personal life for her career, and where had it gotten her? In exactly the same position she'd held for five years now.

She gave a snort of self-disgust. So much for the edicts her father had imposed on her when she was younger. He'd disapproved of any activity, extracurricular or otherwise, that didn't further her chances of being accepted into the best technical college in the country. How many times had he expressed his opinion that women could only expect to get ahead in a man's world by emulating them? A woman who came to work dressed in a manner that distracted men shouldn't be surprised when she bumped her head on a low glass ceiling.

As a teenager, cheerleading hadn't been an option. School dances were prohibited as frivolous and rife with opportunities to go astray. Her father had been unrelenting in his belief that short skirts, makeup and jewelry would only result in an unwanted pregnancy and the end of all her dreams.

His dreams, really.

Her father hadn't had a clue about her dreams. But she hadn't dared oppose him, and in the end, had reluctantly boxed up and gotten rid of her feminine frills and fripperies. She'd even given up her dream of pursuing a career in fine arts, though she hadn't been able to give up her sketchbook. Some people kept a journal, others took photos; Sedona documented life through her drawings and sketches, not that she'd ever share them with anyone. Nope, drawing had become her secret thing, her escape when her overbearing father became too much to handle.

She'd obediently followed his advice and obtained an advanced degree in aerospace engineering. When she'd accepted her current position, the artist in her had secretly thrilled at the beauty and power of the fighter jets the company produced. It seemed impossible for so sleek and elegant a machine to contain so much strength and speed. She'd thrown herself into her job with a determination that surprised even her. It was only now, looking back on those years, that she realized she'd spent so much time trying to be one of the guys, she'd all but forgotten how to be a woman. These days, she didn't even know what it was like to feel feminine.

What would her dad's reaction have been learning that despite all of her hard work and sacrifices, she'd been passed over for promotion yet again? Her shoulders sagged. Her father had been gone now for three years, and while there were times she missed him terribly, she told herself she no longer had to please him. She could do what she wanted without fear of his criticism or censure.

She thought briefly of her two younger sisters, Allison and Ana. Allison was the good girl, who'd opted to stay at home and take care of their mother. She ran a small shop that sold bath and body products, but had never shown any ambition to do more with her life. She was sweet and unassuming, and their father hadn't pushed her to excel. He'd acknowledged the benefits of having one grown child remain at home to help out.

Ana, on the other hand, had violently opposed her father's strict edicts and gone completely in the opposite direction. As an exotic dancer in Las Vegas, she derived great satisfaction in telling Sedona how much money she made doing nothing more than shaking her stuff.

In some ways, Sedona envied Ana. Comfortable in her own skin, Ana had a natural sex appeal that attracted men wherever she went. For as long as Sedona could recall, Ana had been able to charm and manipulate the opposite sex, including their formidable father. He hadn't even argued when, at nineteen, Ana had declared her intent to move to

Las Vegas. He'd just hugged her and gruffly said to call him if she needed him. To Sedona's knowledge, she never had.

While Sedona might never possess the kind of allure or kittenish appeal that Ana had, she told herself it didn't matter. She was an aerospace engineer. She didn't need to exploit her body in order to make a living.

She scrubbed a hand over her eyes. Aerospace engineers were in high demand in private industry. As much as she hated the idea of embarking on a new job search and having to relocate, neither did she want to throw her career away working for an agency that obviously didn't appreciate her talents. Her boss, Joe Clemons, was a good guy and she actually liked working for him. He'd be disappointed if she left, but it didn't seem like a good enough reason to stay.

She wasn't getting any younger, either. She felt about twice her age, which, at twenty-eight, wasn't a good thing. To think, when she'd first taken the position right out of grad school, she'd actually harbored hopes of meeting a guy who would respect her for her intelligence and abilities. Ha. That was such a joke; the guys she worked with were a bunch of uptight misogynists who wouldn't recognize a good woman if they tripped over her. Although, it seemed they had no problem squashing them underfoot as they muscled their way up the career ladder.

She looked around the office where she'd worked for the past five years. Maybe the reason she'd never brought anything personal in, like framed photos or a potted plant, was because on some level she knew she wouldn't be sticking around.

Beside her desk hung a large poster of a jet engine emblazoned with the words *Thrust You Can Trust*. The poster had to have been designed by a guy. Only a man would come up with a motto like that. Even the shape of the engine was phallic, right down to the afterburner with its smooth, curved cap. The poster never usually failed to wring a wry smile out of her. Now it just made her grimace.

She wrenched open a side drawer in her desk and bent over to rummage through the hanging files, looking for a copy of her old résumé. It was way past time to get that baby updated and on the street. Maybe she could teach some engineering courses at one of the local colleges; all those fresh young minds would definitely be an improvement over what she was accustomed to working with.

"Excuse me, Miss Stewart?"

"Yes?" Sedona recognized the voice of the administrative assistant, Linda, but didn't look up.

"Um, there's a gentleman here to see you. An, um, officer gentleman."

Sedona shot upright in her chair so fast she nearly threw her back out. Linda stood in the doorway to Sedona's small office and, despite her round proportions, was completely dwarfed by the man behind her. Linda stared at Sedona in a meaningful way, mouthed the word *wow* and fled, leaving Sedona alone with her visitor.

She gaped at the man standing there. Her gaze slid over him, from his cropped black hair, past the impossibly wide shoulders and slim hips, to the long legs, all encased in a dark-green jumpsuit emblazoned with the American flag on one shoulder and a flight-squadron insignia on the other. For those who thought Antonio Banderas was hot, all Sedona could say was they hadn't seen Lieutenant Angel Torres.

She couldn't find her voice, couldn't think of a single coherent thing to say. There was only one thought that kept buzzing through her head.

He came back.

"You're back," she said, her voice no more than a squeak. Then she wanted to die. Nothing like stating the obvious.

To his credit, he didn't roll his eyes or look at her as if

she'd come from another planet. He stepped into her office and extended a hand across her desk. "Yes, ma'am. I wasn't sure you'd remember me. After all, it's been almost a year since I left."

Remember him? Was he kidding? A day hadn't gone by that Sedona hadn't thought of the navy fighter pilot whose job it was to test-fly the military jets as they rolled off the production line. When he'd been reassigned to an aircraft carrier in the Persian Gulf ten months earlier, she was certain she'd seen the last of him.

Rumor had it he'd been grounded after a combat sortie went bad, but she hoped it wasn't true. She didn't know any details about the incident except that he'd apparently disobeyed a direct order from a superior officer. Lieutenant Torres was a Top Gun graduate, and Sedona knew he possessed more than an average intelligence, so she had to assume he'd had no other choice in disobeying the order. He didn't strike her as the kind of guy who would throw his career in the toilet for pride's sake.

Now here he was, standing larger than life in her office. He looked even better than her memories—and her fantasies—gave him credit for. His Spanish heritage was evident in the blackness of his hair and eyes, the thrust of chiseled cheekbones and his proud nose. He also had a set of dimples you could drive a truck into, although they were barely evident until he smiled. His skin was darker than she remembered, burned to a coppery hue by the Arabian sun. He reminded Sedona of a Bedouin sheikh, desert-hot and just as fierce.

She'd forgotten how seductive his voice was, deep and warm, with just the barest hint of a Spanish accent. Once, during a meeting when he'd given an overview of test-flight parameters, Sedona had sat in the back of the darkened conference room with her eyes closed and let his voice flow over her like warm, dark chocolate. In more private circumstances, she'd bet he could bring her to orgasm using only his voice.

Blushing at her own wayward thoughts, she pushed herself to her feet and clasped his hand and tried to ignore how large and warm it was.

"Lieutenant Torres." *Please, don't let my voice wobble.* God. She was like a teenager, but there was no denying the effect he had on her. Every cell in her body responded to him on a primal level. She drew in a deep, steadying breath and released his hand. "I'm happy to see you made it back safely."

He smiled at her across the mess that was her desk and Sedona felt her pulse react. "Yes, ma'am. But it's lieutenant commander now."

"Oh. Congratulations." Sedona's eyes flew to the broad thrust of his shoulders, noting the gold oak leaves embroidered there. Whatever transgression he'd committed hadn't prevented the navy from promoting him. So why was he here, and not aboard the USS *Abraham Lincoln,* keeping the bad guys at bay?

"Thanks." He shifted his weight. "Listen, I understand several changes have been incorporated into the Coyote engine design since I left, and I was hoping we could set up a time for you to brief me on what impact they have on flight performance."

Sedona pushed down the disappointment that surged through her. Of course he was here on business. What had she thought? That he had come all the way over to her office just to see her again? Guys like Lieutenant Commander Torres were too busy saving the world to think about plain-Jane engineers like herself.

Forget about coming back as a man in her next life. She was coming back as a gorgeous, long-legged, sultry blonde.

She forced a smile. "Of course. Just let me know what time is convenient, and we can go over the drawings."

"How about first thing in the morning?"

Forget about looking for a new job. It was suddenly the last thing she wanted to do. This time, she didn't have to force a smile. "That sounds great. I'll bring the coffee and doughnuts."

He grinned then, revealing the deep indents in either lean cheek. "Thanks, but I'm not much for pastries." He laid one hand over his flat stomach, drawing Sedona's gaze irresistibly to his midsection. "The cockpits on those jets are tight enough as it is."

"Um, okay. Just coffee, then." How was it that those two words, *tight* and *cockpits,* were enough to send her imagination nosediving into the gutter?

He smiled again and Sedona felt her own tummy turn over. God, she had missed seeing his face. The agency she worked for, the Defense Procurement Agency, maintained a government office at Aerospace International, one of the top five aircraft manufacturers in the world. Her agency oversaw the production of the military jets and provided final acceptance on behalf of the customer, in this case, the U.S. Navy. It had been her experience that when the navy sent test pilots to their facility, they were on temporary assignments that rarely exceeded three years.

For the six months Angel had initially worked on their flight line, she had lived in hopeful anticipation of seeing him or talking to him. Their brief encounters had never been anything but professional, but Sedona had harbored an embarrassingly intense crush on Angel Torres from the moment she first saw him. His departure for the Persian Gulf had left a huge void in her otherwise unexciting, predictable world. She'd thought she'd never see him again. And now here he was.

"Great," he was saying, "it's a date. I'll see you in the morning." He turned away, and then paused in the doorway. He angled his head toward her and his dark gaze traveled slowly over her. "It's nice to see you again, Sedona. You look…good."

And then he was gone.

Sedona sat down slowly and drew in a deep breath. She was trembling. But then, Angel Torres had always had that effect on her. In the past, all she'd had to do was see him from a distance and her heart would pound, her knees would literally go weak and she would start to tremble. It was worse than any high-school crush she'd ever had.

He'd called her Sedona. He typically only ever addressed her as "ma'am." He'd called their meeting a date, but that was definitely just an expression.

He'd said she looked good.

Sedona expelled her breath in a whoosh. What did that mean? Good could mean anything. He hadn't said she looked great. Or gorgeous. Just…good.

She glanced down at her khaki slacks and plain white blouse. Nothing overly exciting there. She didn't have a bad shape, but she certainly wasn't under any illusions about her appearance. Her hair was nice, but she usually kept the thick, auburn mass neatly clipped up on the back of her head. She had her mother's green eyes, and while she privately thought they were her best feature, she admittedly did little to enhance them. She was reasonably slender, although her butt was bigger than she would have liked, despite the fact she worked out on a regular basis.

Still, there wasn't anything about her that would make a man like Angel take a second look. He was probably just being nice. All part of the officer-and-a-gentleman protocol.

Sighing, Sedona pushed to her feet. She'd go pull the drawings they would need for their meeting, and reacquaint herself with the details of the engine changes. If she couldn't dazzle Lieutenant Commander Torres with her beauty, at least she could impress him with her brilliance.

The room where they kept the thousands of blueprints and drawings was aptly named the Drawing Room. It comprised row after row of tall cabinets with long, shallow drawers containing specific drawings, cataloged by number. After compiling a list of the ones she would require, Sedona walked among the cabinets until she found the corresponding drawer. It was close to the floor, so she pulled up a low, rolling footstool and sat down on it as she leafed through the contents.

"Hey, looks like that trip to San Diego really paid off, huh?"

Startled, Sedona looked up. There was nobody in sight. She recognized that the voice belonged to Mike Sullivan, one of her fellow engineers, and realized he must have entered the Drawing Room after her.

She groaned inwardly, dreading any confrontation with him. He was nicknamed Hound Dog for his daily practice of strolling through the office to check out what the women were wearing. If that wasn't bad enough, it was common knowledge he sent emails to his male colleagues entitled Hound Dog's Pick of the Day, and identified the woman he considered the hottest that day. While Sedona was pretty sure she'd never been one of Hound Dog's top picks, the complaints she'd lodged against the alleged practice went unheeded.

She was about to stand up and reveal herself when a second voice, belonging to the latest promotee, Bob Lewis, chimed in.

"I'm telling you, man, if I'd known how easy it was to get promoted, I'd have been banging chicks left and right a long time ago."

Sedona blinked. *Excuse me?*

"Yeah, it's a pretty great system. Why do you think we volunteer to do so much business travel?" Mike Sullivan chuckled. "Get laid, get promoted. All you have to do is bring back the proof. Speaking of which, those photos were amazing. I mean, I've gotta hand it to you, not just one babe in your bed, but two! I think you actually put the other members to shame."

Sedona's mouth fell open.

"Well," Bob drawled, "it was all in a day's work, so to speak. You can tell the Membership I was happy to oblige."

"You can tell them yourself," Mike replied. "We're going to have a quick meeting at two o'clock today in the East Wing men's room. You know, to officially celebrate your promotion." There was the sound of a high-five hand slap. "Good job, my man."

Sedona listened to their laughter fade as they left the room. She forced herself to remain seated despite the fact that she wanted to leap up, chase after them and confront them. She could scarcely believe what she had heard. She didn't know what was more shocking, the discovery of a secret club that promoted men based on their sexual exploits, or the fact that dorky Bob Lewis had actually gotten it on with two babes.

She didn't consider herself to be a prude, but this was completely off the charts. It was one thing to have an affair. It was another thing altogether to deliberately use sex as a means of career advancement. Worse, Sedona had been part of the team that had traveled to San Diego with Bob, and she hadn't had a clue about his extracurricular activities. She shuddered. Not that she wanted to. But it drove home the fact that she spent way too much time alone.

Her sister Ana had inherited the sultry good looks and the feminine wiles. Sedona had inherited the brains. Ana viewed guys in terms of their potential as bed partners. Sedona's only interest in the men she worked with was whether they would help or hinder her job performance, and how much competition they might pose for the next promotion.

She'd learned early on that most of her male colleagues didn't take women seriously. They made insinuating remarks and casual suggestions with impunity, and it still amazed her that the women in question didn't slap the bastards with sexual harassment suits. While she suspected her male co-workers considered her something of a bitch, it didn't bother her. They might actively dislike her, but at least they respected her.

She couldn't envision any man enticing her into having a one-night stand. The very thought of being intimate with a complete stranger made her go cold inside. There were just way too many risks involved to even consider the idea.

She took a deep breath. What to do? Go to Human Resources and report them? She snorted. Yeah, right. Like anybody would believe her. She'd be laughed out of the office. With his lank hair, oily skin and seventies-something wardrobe, Bob Lewis was hardly the picture of animal magnetism. And since she had just been passed over for promotion—for the third time—her story would no doubt be viewed as the malicious rantings of a disgruntled employee. Never mind that the reason she'd been passed over was apparently because she wasn't getting any on the road.

She pressed her fingers against her eyelids and tried to think rationally about how to handle the situation. The government had a merit promotion system specifically designed to prevent favoritism or unfair advancement practices, but there was no denying they did, in fact, exist. Sedona understood office politics accounted for many of the recent promotions, but she'd have never guessed they might be based on sexual prowess. It was almost too unreal to be believed.

More important, why would anyone risk their job—their very career—by taking part in such activity? What was the point? It made no sense.

But one thing was certain; there was no way she could continue working for this particular government agency, not after what she'd just heard. She had to find another job, and didn't that just suck? Because Lieutenant Commander Torres had finally returned, and leaving was suddenly the last thing she wanted to do.

Grabbing the drawings she would need for tomorrow's meeting with Angel, she pushed herself to her feet. There was really only one thing to do.

She would find a way to expose the members of the secret club. Once the truth came out, the agency would have to admit they had a real problem and deal with it accordingly. She had no idea how many men were involved, but she was going to put a stop to it.

All she needed was proof.

2

ANGEL GLANCED UP from his paperwork in time to see Sedona Stewart stride out of the Drawing Room and come to a jerky halt in the corridor, as if debating which direction to go. She didn't seem to notice him sitting in the small conference room just across the hallway.

The Drawing Room appeared to be a popular place this morning. He'd gone in and pulled several drawings of the redesigned tail section, and had taken them across the hall to spread them out on the table in the conference room. He'd watched Sedona go in, followed several minutes later by Mike Sullivan and Bob Lewis. The two men had left after a few minutes, but Sedona remained inside. Angel had refocused his attention on the drawings, but to his mild annoyance, found himself waiting for Sedona to reappear.

When she finally did, she was visibly upset. Twin patches of bright color rode high on her cheekbones, and he didn't miss how she fisted her hands at her sides. He was halfway to his feet when she spotted him.

Their eyes locked.

Hers shimmered with anger. They stared at each other for a full minute. Angel knew the instant she became aware of him, as the fury in her eyes clouded and became softer.

The color in her cheeks slowly spread, until her entire neck and face were rosy. She blinked, like a child coming awake after a disturbing dream, and for a moment she looked confused, disoriented.

Angel was already pushing his chair back when she made an incoherent sound of distress, accompanied by a vague gesture of dismissal. Before he could stop her, she turned and fled in the direction of the administration offices, head bent and one hand pressed against her temple.

Curious, he stepped out of the conference room and watched as she hurried down the corridor and stopped outside the Human Resources office. She hesitated, and Angel was certain she was going to turn and walk away. But then she squared her shoulders and he knew if he was closer, he would hear her indrawn breath of resolve. As he watched, she pushed the door open, entered and closed it firmly behind her.

Slowly, Angel turned back to his drawings. Sedona Stewart was considered unflappable. Cool and levelheaded, she approached every issue with a calm, almost Vulcan-like rationality that infuriated her coworkers as much as it amazed them.

So what had caused her uncharacteristic display of emotion? Of course, he reminded himself, she hadn't known he was watching her. Otherwise, he was pretty sure she'd have controlled her expression before she left the Drawing Room.

He lowered himself back into the chair and drummed his fingers on the table, considering. It had to have been some dumb-ass, chauvinistic thing Mike Sullivan had said to her in the few minutes he and Bob Lewis had been in the room with her. Mike had a reputation for being a prick where women were concerned, and Angel could definitely picture the guy saying something completely inappropriate to Sedona, just to see her reaction.

Recalling the distress in her green eyes, the Cuban part of him—that traditional, old-fashioned part that demanded all women be treated with respect—wanted to hunt Mike down and kick his ass. But the military part of him said that would be a poor decision, especially given his own recent misconduct. It would be an excuse for his commanding officer to bust him back down to lieutenant and stick him behind a desk to push paper for the rest of his career.

He took a deep breath and flattened his hands on the surface of the table. He needed to put Sedona out of his thoughts. She was an adult. Whatever shortcomings she might have, he was pretty sure sticking up for herself wasn't one of them. Hadn't he seen her go into the Human Resources office? He smiled wryly. It wasn't Sedona he should be worried about; it was Mike Sullivan.

"What do you mean you can't do anything?" Sedona stared at the woman on the other side of the desk. She'd figured Human Resources would be skeptical, but where else could she turn? "I'm telling you, these guys have been getting promoted based on how many *babes* they bang when they go on business travel."

Gladys Drummond smiled, apparently in sympathy, but Sedona could see it didn't reach the older woman's eyes. Sedona wanted to scream with frustration.

"I'm sure what you overheard was nothing more than a joke. A bad joke, in very bad taste, but a joke nonetheless." The director of Human Resources sat back in her chair and considered Sedona. "I understand how you might be feeling put out about Bob Lewis getting this latest promotion, but I can promise you it had nothing to do with his—his male prowess. All promotions have to be approved by the Promotion Selection Board."

Sedona blew out her breath in frustration. "But they seemed so sure of themselves. This—this 'club' must have influence at higher levels. If they say the promotion goes through, then it does."

Gladys tented her fingers together. "Do you know who the other members are?"

"I have no idea."

"Then we're back where we started, Sedona. You can't make these kinds of accusations without substantial evidence."

Sedona leaned forward eagerly. "I can get evidence. The members are supposed to get together this afternoon for a secret meeting. I could…I could sneak into the room and spy on them. Or…I could record what they say! That would be proof, wouldn't it?"

Gladys smiled, a patently false smile. "I believe there are laws against recording people without their knowledge. Even if it's permissible, it's not something I have the authority to approve. In truth, this whole issue is more or less beyond my purview. I'm only the director of Human Resources."

Sedona shook her head in disbelief. "So you're saying there's nothing you can do?" When the other woman didn't answer, Sedona gave a huff of defeat. "I'm sorry to hear that, I really am. I feel as if you're not leaving me any choice but to resign." She shrugged helplessly. "Consider this my two weeks' notice."

The other woman's eyebrows shot up. "Really, Sedona. Don't you think you're overreacting?"

Was she kidding? "No, quite the opposite. How can I even contemplate working for an agency that condones this kind of behavior?"

Whatever Gladys believed, Sedona knew what she'd overheard hadn't been a joke. It had been all too disgustingly real. She watched as Gladys picked up her PDA and consulted it. After a moment, she scribbled a number down on a piece of paper.

"This is the number for the Defense Criminal Investigative Service. They can put you in touch with an agent who might be able to help you." She handed the paper to Sedona. "I'm sure you'll find this whole thing is just a misunderstanding. I hope you'll reconsider leaving."

Sedona took the slip of paper. Fat chance. As expected, Human Resources didn't believe her, and it was unlikely DCIS would, either. Like HR, they'd probably decide she was just trying to get even with her male coworkers. And they'd be right, to a certain degree. Exposing and putting an end to the Membership would be her last effort to level the gender playing field.

"Thanks," she muttered, and pushed the slip into the pocket of her pants.

Leaving the director's office, she determined she *would* contact DCIS. She'd already declared her intent to resign, and she wasn't going to change her mind about it. Therefore, she had nothing to lose. She strode toward her office to make the phone call. As she passed the Drawing Room, her footsteps faltered, recalling that moment when she'd realized Angel had been sitting in the room directly across the hall.

Watching her.

And for just a moment, she'd been so completely flustered, she'd all but abandoned the idea of exposing the Membership. For one brief, crazy instant, the thought of leaving the agency just when Angel had finally returned seemed too high a price to pay.

Now, as she passed the conference room, her gaze was drawn irresistibly toward the chair where he'd been sitting. She shouldn't have been surprised to find it empty, but there was no denying the disappointment that surged through her. In every way that counted, he was so gone from her life.

3

FROM HER HIDING place in the women's bathroom, located directly beside the East Wing men's room, Sedona peeked through a crack in the door and watched no less than eight men slip covertly into the adjoining lavatory. With the entire East Wing closed for renovations, it was the perfect choice for a clandestine meeting. While she wasn't personally acquainted with all the men, she knew who they were. With the exception of Mike Sullivan, she was shocked by who she saw.

There was Tony Webber, whose intensity and single-minded dedication to the job she'd always found a little intimidating. She'd never have guessed his determination to succeed went this far. Then there was Alberto DeMasi, whom she'd always categorized as the warm, grandfatherly type. Apparently, there were no age restrictions on becoming a member, either. She knew he was a widower, but she cringed just thinking about him hitting on some strange woman in order to get promoted. Kevin Donnelly was middle-aged and divorced, and it was common knowledge he was struggling to raise two teenagers. Was his financial situation so tough that he needed to prostitute himself in order to get ahead?

Sedona pushed down the sympathy that threatened to sap her determination. She couldn't allow personal feelings to interfere. But of all the members she saw, none surprised her more than Ken Larson.

In his mid-thirties, Sedona had first noticed him because of his quirky sense of humor and easy camaraderie with the other engineers. He wasn't good-looking in the traditional sense, but he was friendly and likable, and there had been a time when Sedona had briefly considered dating him. And then Angel had come on board, and suddenly every other man she knew paled in comparison.

Still, she felt a huge sense of betrayal to discover Ken was involved with the Membership. She'd worked with him on several engineering issues and had found him reliable and knowledgeable. He was one of the few guys she actually enjoyed working with. Clearly, she'd given him way more credit than he deserved.

Biting her lip, she stepped back inside the women's bathroom and gently closed the door all the way, careful not to make any noise. She'd made the call to DCIS and had spoken with an Agent Curtis Denton. Despite his gruff voice and clipped manner, he'd taken her allegations seriously. When she had suggested confronting the members while wearing a recording device, he'd approved, with the promise of a full investigation to follow.

She adjusted the small tape player she had tucked into the waistband of her pants, beneath her blouse, to a less conspicuous position. Her finger was on the Record button when the sound of male laughter startled her.

Her fingers slipped on the buttons.

They were starting. Not wanting them to disperse before she had time to confront them, she stepped quickly into the corridor. She paused outside the door to the men's room and drew in a deep, fortifying breath. Then, placing her palm on the door, she gave it a mighty push so that it burst inward, slamming back against the inside wall with a resounding *bam!*

YOUR PARTICIPATION IS REQUESTED!

Dear Reader,

Since you are a lover of romance fiction – we would like to get to know you!

Inside you will find a short Reader's Survey. Sharing your answers with us will help our editorial staff understand who you are and what activities you enjoy.

To thank you for your participation, we would like to send you 2 books and 2 gifts – **ABSOLUTELY FREE!**

Enjoy your gifts with our appreciation,

Pam Powers

SEE INSIDE FOR READER'S SURVEY

For Your Romance Reading Pleasure...

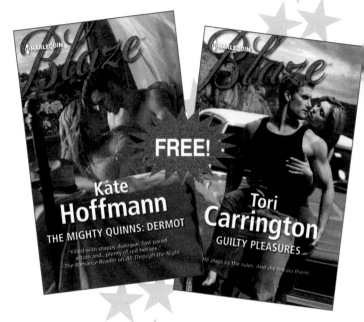

Flyboy

. His gaze swung back to Mike Sullivan with
ke desperation.

now what you've heard," Mike said in a hard
stepped forward, "but I'm going to have to ask
. Now."

urned away from Bob to stare at Mike. "I'm not
where, Hound Dog, until you tell me everything
know about the Membership."

ughed, but it sounded forced. "I have no idea what
king about, Stewart."

eah?" Before they could guess her intent, Sedona
rward and snatched the photos from Ken's hands.
her back on the men, she swiftly flipped through
dozen prints. Oh, God. It was true. There was Bob
sprawled half-naked in an enormous bed with two
ia-blonde bombshells. Who would have guessed the
d so much body hair? Ew.

Mike reached over her shoulder for the photos, Sedona
im a warning glance and turned away again.

h, this is a good one," she said, holding up a photo of
sitting in a hotel-room chair with a scantily clad bru-
on his lap. "It certainly doesn't look like your wife."

ike visibly sagged. "Okay, Stewart, what do you want?"

What do I want?" She thrust the pictures beneath his
e. "I want this to stop! It's not only illegal, it's immoral.
d degrading." She turned to the other men, fixing the cha-
ned Tony and Alberto with a disapproving frown. "I'm
rprised at all of you. I'd expect this kind of juvenile be-
avior from teenagers, not grown men." She gave Alberto
look that she hoped conveyed her deep disappointment.
And certainly not men with small grandchildren."

"Oh, get real, Stewart." One of the men—she recalled his
name was Brad Something-or-Other—stepped forward, his

A group of men, includi
tention from where they'd b
Under any other circumstanc
and horror might have been a
in turquoise-green, was awash
and smelled faintly of disinfect

"Hello, gentlemen," Sedona
terrupting something?"

Mike Sullivan stepped forwar
in here, Stewart? I mean, come on,

Sedona forced herself to smile i
pounding heart. "I heard there was
discuss future advancement opportun
to miss it. Actually, I heard there's a
program that practically guarantees p
nored his gape-mouthed expression an
stop directly in front of Bob Lewis. "It
a program. After all," she murmured, trac
the front of his madly patterned silk tie, "i
for Bob."

She stared directly into Bob's horrified e
flush crept up his neck and suffused his fac

"I—I don't know what you're t-talking ab
mered, his gaze darting to Mike.

"Oh," Sedona crooned, "I think you do. Or
ready forgotten the two babes you banged in Sa

In the mirror behind Bob, she saw Alberto's a
pression as realization slowly dawned. She also no
Larson holding what appeared to be several phot
He looked even more horrified to see her in the mer
than she had been to see him enter. He was trying
the photos covertly into the pocket of his pants, onl
were too large, so he oh-so-casually palmed the picture
tucked his hands behind his back. Poor Bob looked as

expression contemptuous. They had once worked together on an engineering investigation, and she hadn't much liked him then. He was a cocky man, with pale blue eyes and skin that bore evidence of what must have been a horrific case of adolescent acne. Now he shrugged. "So what if we like to indulge in a little extramarital activity? What are you going to do about it? Huh?"

"I could care less what you do on your own time," she snapped at him. "But when this kind of activity is not only condoned by management, but encouraged as a means of getting promoted, then I definitely have a problem with it. Big-time."

"You'll never prove it," Brad taunted. "Anyone can tell you our promotions were based purely on performance."

Sedona snorted and held up the photos. "No kidding."

"So what's your big plan?" Brad took another step forward, his smile mocking, and before Sedona could protest, snatched the photos from her fingers. "Going to report us to Human Resources? Tell the director about our evil club?" He laughed. "Go right ahead. I can hardly wait to see what kind of reaction you get."

Inwardly, Sedona rejoiced. This was what she had been hoping for. The photos be damned. If she could get the men to discuss the club openly, it would all be there on her tape recorder.

"Considering your...inclinations," Brad continued smoothly, "this will actually be something to look forward to."

Sedona frowned and noted the expressions on the other men's faces. They ranged from cautious amusement to outright smugness. "What do you mean by that?" she demanded. Inclinations?

"I mean that you're considered to be something of a man-hater, Stewart."

Sedona's mouth fell open, then snapped shut. The anger and frustration that had been simmering just below the surface finally bubbled over. "Careful," she warned in a falsely sweet tone. "Your insecurities are showing. If I have a limited tolerance for the opposite sex," she continued, turning hard eyes on Ken Larson, "it's no wonder."

She wasn't at all mollified when Ken flushed and turned his gaze downward, clearly embarrassed.

"So tell me, Ken," she asked, "have you been banging babes, too?"

Ken turned a darker shade of red. "No," he mumbled. He raised his gaze to Sedona's and gave her a sheepish grin. "I mean, I haven't been promoted, have I?"

"So why are you doing this?"

Mike Sullivan stepped forward, effectively preventing Ken from answering. "You want to know why, Stewart? I'll tell you why. Because women like you are taking away our job security and our promotional opportunities."

Sedona gave him a bewildered look. "What are you talking about?"

Mike snorted. "It isn't enough to be a good engineer anymore. Hell, being a great engineer isn't even enough. Especially if you have one qualified female thrown into the mix. I'm telling you, it's reverse discrimination at its best. Call this our way of getting what we deserve—in every way that counts."

Sedona stared at him, appalled. "But why degrade yourselves?"

"You call it degrading. We call it proving our worth." Mike's voice was contemptuous. "Do you know how tough the competition is for the higher grades? Being competent and conscientious doesn't cut it anymore. These days, it's about being completely dedicated, about proving you'll do *anything* for the job, no matter what."

"Even if it's something incredibly intimate, or personally repugnant?" Sedona couldn't believe what she was hearing. They were like a bunch of frat boys.

"Especially if it's intimate or repugnant." Mike gestured to the men around him. "Each of these guys deserves to be promoted. But how to determine which one is the right one for the job?" He leaned forward until his face was inches from Sedona's. "By putting it all on the line, baby. No guts, no glory."

Sedona couldn't keep the sarcasm out of her voice. "I can't recall where in the job description it says 'must get laid.'"

"Hey, don't knock it 'til you try it. In fact," Mike said, smirking, "I think you need to get laid in a big way, Stewart."

There was a snort of muffled laughter, and several of the men had to turn away to hide their amusement. Tony and Alberto looked mortified, but Sedona knew the others were getting a huge kick out of her embarrassment.

"Oh, and I suppose you're just the man for the job, huh?" Sedona injected as much scorn as she could into her voice. "Trust me, I wouldn't sleep with you if you were the last man on Earth."

But far from looking wounded, Mike just laughed. "No kidding. Unless I'm mistaken, you wouldn't sleep with any man. Period."

Sedona realized her hands were clenched into fists at her sides, and she forced herself to relax, though every cell in her body wanted to scream her denial at this jerk. "What, exactly, is that supposed to mean?"

"I know that when you go on business travel, you spend every night hiding in your hotel room." He arched an eyebrow at her, as if challenging her to deny it. "Remember when we were in Saint Louis for two weeks? You wouldn't even join the rest of us for dinner, never mind any late-night entertainment. Hell, your idea of excitement is probably finding a mint on your hotel pillow."

Ouch. That hurt, probably because it was no less than the truth.

"Just because I choose not to have affairs," she said tightly, "does not mean I'm incapable of having them."

Mike's eyebrows flew up and he exchanged a knowing look with the man nearest him. "Oh, really? Well, excuse me if I don't believe you. You've been working here for what— five years? And from what I hear, you haven't even had a date, much less an affair."

"So what are you saying, Mike?" Okay, this was it. If she played this right, she would have all the proof she needed to expose them. "Are you saying if I have an affair the next time I go on business travel, I'll get promoted?"

Mike grinned, clearly enjoying her outrage. He turned to the other men. "What do you think, boys? Should we let Stewart join our elite membership?"

"No way," interjected Bob. "She's just trying to screw us. Figuratively speaking, I mean."

"Supposing I agree," Sedona said, ignoring him, "what's my guarantee? I mean, how can you assure me that the next promotion will be mine?"

"Don't you worry about that," Mike soothed. "We have five members who sit on the Promotion Selection Board. All we have to do is give them a name. You just bring back proof of the affair." He smirked. "If you can."

Sedona drew herself up and raked the group of men with what she hoped was a scathing look. "Despite what you think, I'm just as capable of a little on-the-road romance as the rest of you." She looked at Mike. "So, that's it, then? I just bring back some kind of proof? Like a pair of men's underwear?"

Mike laughed. "Oh, no. It's not that easy. Just ask Bob."

Bob mumbled something under his breath.

"What was that?" Sedona took a step closer. "I didn't quite catch that." *On my tape recorder.*

"I said you need to bring back photos." His tone was almost defiant.

"Photos," Sedona repeated. "Photos of what?"

"Sedona…forget it, okay?" It was Ken Larson, stepping forward. His face was still red with embarrassment, but his eyes met hers squarely. "Don't get mixed up in this. It's—it's not worth it."

"Photos of the significant other," Mike continued, interrupting Ken and impaling the other man with a hard stare. "Preferably in a position that leaves no doubt as to the nature of the relationship."

Seeing Mike's censure, Ken ducked his head and retreated to the far wall. Despite her determination to see this operation through, Sedona nearly ran for the door. She'd never been so completely mortified in her entire life. Drawing in a deep breath, she nodded. "Got it. What else?"

Mike laughed. "Okay, then. The picture has to contain something that will clearly indicate the time and location of the event. Like a newspaper and a room key, prominently displayed. You get the idea."

"Fine. The next time I go on business travel, I'll bring back the proof you need. Okay?" Sedona had no intention of bringing back proof of anything. She already had the proof she needed to put an end to this "club."

Ken looked at the other men, and although some of them looked away or down at their feet, Mike nodded his approval. "Okay, it's a deal. Oh, and Sedona?"

She looked at him questioningly.

"The picture can't be staged. You can't get your brother, or your cousin, or your good friend to pose for it, just to fake us out."

"Great. So that's it? Okay, then. I, uh, should probably get back to work," Sedona muttered, suddenly anxious to get out of there. The sordidness of the entire scheme made her feel ill. "I'll let you know when I have what you need."

Without waiting for a reply, she bolted for the door. She walked quickly through the deserted corridors of the East Wing until she reached the main part of the building. Only then did she place her hand over the slight bulge in her waistband, reassuring herself that the small recorder was still there. She had it all on tape.

IN THE PRIVACY of her office, Sedona pulled the tape player from beneath her blouse. She stared in dismay at the small device.

The Record button was off.

Maybe she had inadvertently hit the Power button on her way back to the office. Please, let that be the case. With trembling fingers, she pushed Play. There was nothing but the soft whirring of the tape as it wound from one reel to the next. There was no recorded conversation. There was nothing but silence. She rewound the tape and played it again. Still nothing.

With a groan of self-disgust, she tossed the tape player onto her desk, sank into her chair and buried her face in her hands. She had neglected to hit the Record button. She'd been so busy making sure the tape player was hidden, and then so nervous about confronting the men, that she hadn't even turned the damn thing on.

She had absolutely no proof, not a shred of incriminating evidence against the members. It would be her word against theirs. Worse, she had lowered herself to their level by agreeing to have a sordid affair of her own in order to gain access to their disgusting club. Though she had only been pretending, she felt cheapened and dirty.

She picked up the phone and punched in Agent Denton's number, dreading the inevitable.

"DCIS, Agent Denton."

Reluctantly, Sedona identified herself and let the story tumble out.

"So you see," she concluded, "I have absolutely no evidence. I blew it."

"Not necessarily," Agent Denton replied. "You agreed to join the club, to become a member based on the same conditions imposed upon the others. That's definitely something we can work with."

Sedona floundered in disbelief. "I wasn't serious—I mean, I never... I don't think..."

"Miss Stewart," Denton interrupted. "I'm not suggesting you do anything you're not completely comfortable with. I'm merely saying this could be a way for us to get the evidence we need to really nail these guys."

"Agent Denton," she protested, "I could never do what these guys do. I couldn't live with myself. In fact, I haven't told my supervisor yet, but I submitted my resignation to the Human Resources office earlier today."

There was a brief silence. "I understand. Of course, this doesn't change my intent to conduct a full investigation into your allegations. However, if you should change your mind about assisting us, you have my number."

Sedona replaced the receiver in the cradle, completely drained by the day's events. She scrubbed her hands over her eyes.

She sat there, her mind replaying the scene in the men's bathroom. When somebody knocked on her office door she started guiltily, fearful that someone had discovered her clandestine meeting with the Membership, and was coming to confront her.

The door opened, and she found herself staring at Joe Clemons, the director of Engineering.

Her boss.

Her heart sank as for one instant she envisioned herself being fired before she had the chance to tell her boss she quit. Then her gaze traveled to the man standing just behind Joe.

It was Angel Torres, and from the taut expression on his face and the dangerous glint in his black eyes, she knew the reason for their visit went way beyond the Membership and its dirty little secrets.

She stood up. "Joe, come in. What's going on?"

Joe's face was pinched with concern as he entered her office. He didn't say anything, merely placed a memo on her desk. Sedona couldn't prevent herself from glancing at Angel before she picked it up. He was rigid with suppressed anger. Or frustration. She wasn't sure which, but she could sense the coiled tension in his lean, hard body. He dominated her small office with his presence. He was all dark, simmering power held under tight control.

Sedona shivered.

She forced herself to concentrate on the memo, but it was a moment before the words on the page shifted into focus and became legible. She quickly scanned the page, and her stomach tightened in dread. It was an electronic memo, issued by the Secretary of the Navy, and the words *urgent* and *investigation* leaped off the page at her.

"Oh, my God," she breathed.

Three F/A-44 Coyote fighter jets had crashed into the Pacific Ocean in three separate training incidents over a twenty-four-hour period, resulting in pilot ejections. Two additional jets had experienced problems when their throttle-levers had locked up, but the pilots had been able to activate in-flight emergency shutdown procedures and conduct single-engine landings.

The Secretary of the Navy was demanding an immediate investigation into the crashes, as well as an inspection of all remaining Coyotes. Until the problem was resolved, all jets were grounded.

"What does this mean?" Sedona wasn't sure if she was asking Joe or Angel.

"¡Maldita!" growled Angel. "It means we have one hell of a problem on our hands. There's a war going on, and with our fighter jets grounded, we can't provide the air power our troops need to stay alive." He looked at Joe. "I'd like to fly out to Lemoore as soon as I can. Tomorrow, if possible."

Sedona frowned. Lemoore was the location of a naval air station in California. It was just her luck that he had finally come back, and now he was leaving. Again. Her hopes of seeing him during the remaining two weeks of her employment were dashed.

Joe sighed and ran a hand over his face. "I agree. The Aircraft Mishap Board is scrambling to get their folks out to the three crash sites. The other two jets are en route to a hangar at Lemoore for inspection. We'll have a full team ready to head out there first thing tomorrow."

Sedona held her breath, hardly daring to anticipate his next words.

Joe looked at her. "Sedona, I want you to head up a team to inspect the engines. You'll be gone for a couple of weeks, so take the rest of the afternoon to make whatever personal arrangements you need to. The other divisions are putting together their own teams to analyze the power-level control and the hydraulics systems." He glanced over at Angel. "Lieutenant Commander Torres will conduct flight tests of the grounded jets and put together baseline evaluations. You'll be working together pretty closely, so I'll reserve a block of rooms for the teams at the same hotel. That way, you can spend the evenings going over your findings."

Angel turned his gaze on Sedona, and she felt her breath hitch as she stared into the fathomless darkness of his eyes. For an instant, she wondered what it would be like to have that gaze heated with passion. To have it directed toward her.

"I think that's a good suggestion," he said, and his eyes drifted over Sedona's features.

Was it only her imagination, or did they linger for a moment on her mouth? Nervously, she ran the tip of her tongue over her bottom lip.

"I'll be making my own travel arrangements just as soon as I get back to my office," Angel continued, his eyes still on her. "If it's okay with you, ma'am, I'll reserve us seats next to each other on the plane. It's a long flight from Boston, so we might as well use the time to go over the Coyote incident reports."

Sedona stared back at Angel. Sit with him on the plane? A couple of weeks in the same hotel together? Working closely with him, and perhaps getting together in the evenings? Holy Coyote, there really was a God!

She looked swiftly down at the navy memo and pretended to reread it in order to compose her features and hide the fluttering excitement she was feeling. Excitement she had no right to feel, not in the face of such a blow to the navy flight program.

When, after a brief moment, she glanced back up at Angel, she prayed her expression didn't reveal her feelings. "That, um, sounds fine." She tried to sound cool, but her voice quavered ever so slightly. She cleared her throat. "Just give me a call to let me know what flight we're on. I'll meet you at the airport."

Angel smiled then, his teeth strong and white in his tanned face. Sedona's heart rate kicked up a notch and her stomach did a slow roll.

"Since it looks like we're going to be partners," he said easily, "I'll do you one better. If you give me your address,

I'll pick you up in the morning and give you a lift to the airport."

Sedona knew right then that she had been wrong.

She had thought she could never engage in an affair while on business travel. Up until that moment, she couldn't envision herself having an affair, period. But when Angel Torres looked at her like that, she knew she would gladly toss every one of her old-fashioned ideals and morals out the window for just one night—one amazing, never-to-be-forgotten night—in his arms.

4

TUCKED INTO A window seat of the commercial airliner, Sedona tried not to stare as Angel stowed their carry-on luggage in the overhead compartment. She had never seen him wear anything other than his military flight suit, and the sight of him clad in a black T-shirt and jeans was entirely too appealing. From her vantage point beneath him, it was difficult not to admire the impressive bulge of his biceps as he secured their belongings. Apparently, she wasn't alone in that regard.

A trio of pretty young women sat in the row of seats across from them, and Sedona had heard their collective sigh of longing when Angel made his way down the narrow aisle, ducking his head to avoid contact with the ceiling. His dark good looks, combined with his rugged build, were guaranteed to capture the attention of every female on board. But when he smiled at the three women and inclined his head politely in greeting, Sedona thought they might actually swoon with delight. Even now, she could hear them tittering as they ogled his backside. To his credit, Angel appeared oblivious to the attention he attracted.

Satisfied their gear was safely stowed, he bent down and eased his large frame into the seat next to Sedona. His sheer size dwarfed her. He had managed to secure seats next to the emergency exit, which afforded them a little extra legroom. Even so, the space barely accommodated his long legs, and his knee brushed against hers in the close confines.

He quirked a rueful grin at her. "Well, this is cozy."

When he looked over at her and flashed those incredible dimples, Sedona's brain just about shut down. She pressed tighter against the window to accommodate his wide shoulders. She hadn't counted on being in such proximity with him and was glad she'd taken extra care that morning with her appearance.

Still, she couldn't help but feel completely self-conscious by his nearness. God, the guy even smelled great. An intoxicating blend of clean cotton, soap and something mildly spicy that might have been aftershave, made her want to inhale deeply. She watched as he buckled the seat belt across his lean hips. He had strong hands, with long, tapered fingers and neat nails. And, thankfully, no rings.

One of the airline attendants, a pretty woman with blond hair and large brown eyes, stopped by their seats. Although she smiled politely at Sedona, her eyes barely left Angel.

"I'm required to tell you that you're sitting in an emergency-exit aisle," she said, dimpling down at him. "Do you have any physical…restrictions that might prevent you from opening the emergency door and assisting other passengers in the event of an emergency?"

Angel looked up at her, and his lips curved in the barest hint of a smile. "Uh, no, I don't believe so."

The woman was practically eating him alive with her eyes.

"Well," she purred, "I didn't think that was the case, but regulations require me to ask. Oh!" She lurched forward into Angel's lap, thrusting her breasts into his face in the process, as a passenger squeezed past her in the aisle.

Angel caught her by the upper arms and steadied her as she braced herself against him with both hands on his broad shoulders. Sedona barely contained her indelicate snort of disgust.

"Oh, my," the attendant said, breathless and laughing. "I am so sorry!"

Yeah, right, Sedona thought. Like that wasn't completely planned.

"No problem," Angel assured the woman, and set her firmly back on her feet.

"Well," she said, practically preening in the aisle, "if there's anything you need, just let me know." She indicated her name tag with one pink-tipped finger. "I'm Taffy."

Sedona turned toward the window, rolling her eyes. Angel murmured something vague in response, and she turned back in time to see the woman waggle her fingers at him before sauntering away.

"That was helpful," she muttered darkly, "considering I'm the one sitting next to the emergency door." She turned to Angel. "So just what is it I'm supposed to do in the event of an actual emergency?"

Angel's black eyes danced with devilish amusement as he looked at her, and a lazy smile creased his features. "The only thing you have to do, *mina,*" he drawled, "is get the hell out of my way, and I'll take care of the rest."

Sedona's eyes widened in surprise, and she had a vivid image of him bodily lifting her out of the way before assuming the manly duty of controlling the emergency door. Part of her was taken aback by his sheer cockiness. But another part was secretly thrilled by that same arrogance. He was supremely confident, capable of anything. He made her feel both fragile and safe.

"Hey, Sedona," interrupted a masculine voice. "Looks like we'll be working together."

She dragged her gaze away from Angel and nearly groaned aloud in disbelief. It was Ken Larson, making his way down the aisle. He paused near their seats and smiled almost shyly at Sedona. She stared back at him in utter horror.

"I'm, uh, really looking forward to it," he continued. Was it just her imagination, or did his eyes sweep over her in a proprietary way? "It'll be, you know, a real team-building experience. Who knows? There might even be a promotion in it for some of us." Noticing Angel for the first time, he extended a hand toward the other man. "Aren't you Lieutenant Torres? Good to see you back, sir. I'm Ken Larson. I'll be part of Sedona's team of engineers." He smiled again at Sedona. "Like I said, I'm really looking forward to working with you again. Maybe this time…" He let his words trail off, then laughed self-consciously and shrugged. "Who knows, right?"

He moved past their seats, but his words echoed in Sedona's head. Her heart sank. Ken Larson believed she was interested in joining the Membership. He'd expect her to take advantage of this opportunity to acquire the proof she'd need to claim the next promotion.

She swore silently.

As soon as they reached the hotel, she'd pull him aside and disclaim any interest in joining their club. What he decided to do was his own business, but no way would she have him believing she would sink to the same level.

"You work with that guy?"

Sedona glanced guiltily at Angel. "Yes," she muttered. "We've worked together on investigations before."

There was a momentary silence.

"Oh, yeah? So…you're just coworkers? Nothing more?"

Sedona stared at him in disbelief. "No! I mean, yes! I mean—" She was spluttering in indignation, acutely aware that Angel watched her with amused interest. "We are definitely just coworkers. God." She recalled Ken's expression as he'd swept his gaze over her, and shuddered in revulsion. "Please tell me you didn't think—"

Angel laughed and held up one hand to forestall her. "I'm sorry, it's just that there seemed to be…something between the two of you. I just thought…"

"Well, you thought wrong."

"Fine."

"Fine." Sedona slid him a last sidelong glance before turning to look out the window. This whole trip was fast becoming a nightmare of huge proportions. It was completely unfair that one of the Membership should be part of her team. She needed to set Ken straight immediately, or they'd have a tough time working together. And the last thing she needed was for Angel to believe they were involved in any way.

She sneaked a look at Angel, and then colored hotly. He was watching her, and the expression in his dark eyes was thoughtful.

ANGEL WATCHED AS Sedona wrestled her suitcase, laptop and overnight bag through the doorway of her hotel room and then closed the door firmly behind her. He shook his head slightly in bemusement and turned his attention to his own door, directly next to hers.

The woman was a complete contradiction and damned if he could figure out what was up with her. He'd heard the rumors about her, even down on the flight line. Personally, he wasn't convinced she was some kind of man-hater. She just had a zero-tolerance policy for stupidity. He'd heard she was one of the agency's best engineers. He'd even read a couple of her technical reports and had to agree. Personally, he believed the malicious whispers about her stemmed from the feelings of inadequacy she engendered in her male counterparts.

He'd seen the way she looked at him when she thought he didn't notice. He wasn't conceited, but he recognized female appreciation when he saw it. And Sedona Stewart, despite her acerbic and sometimes mannish manner, had appreciated just about all she could see of him in the scant seconds he had caught her looking.

Normally, that would be all the incentive he'd need to begin a pursuit, but there was something about Sedona that made him hesitate. It had nothing to do with her looks. She was attractive enough, but her cool reserve made him reluctant to explore just how appreciative she might be. He liked his women on the adventurous side, and Sedona didn't strike him as the daring type.

Stepping inside, he closed the door to his room, noting it had a balcony overlooking an interior courtyard where the pool and hot tub were located. He could hear the shouts and cries of several kids as they splashed in the water. Dumping his bags on top of the bed, he opened the sliding-glass doors to let some fresh air into the room, and paused when he noticed movement on the balcony next to his.

He leaned against the doorjamb just inside the room and watched as Sedona moved over to the railing of her balcony. She had shed the navy blazer she'd worn during the flight, and she was barefoot. Her toenails were painted a glossy shade of cherry-red.

She stretched her arms up over her head and loosely linked her fingers together. Then she arched her back and bent sideways at the waist, first to one side, then the other. The movement pulled the fabric of her modest, button-down shirt taut across her breasts. Angel's eyebrows went up. Maybe not so mannish, after all.

Stepping carefully back into the room, he quietly pulled the drapes closed, reluctant to disturb her. But even with the curtains drawn, he couldn't get the image of those brightly painted toes out of his head. Not that he had a foot fetish; they just weren't what he'd expect to see on her. They intrigued him. Made him wonder what other feminine attributes she kept hidden from the rest of the world.

They'd agreed to meet downstairs in the lobby for dinner, but that was still several hours away. If he hurried, he could head over to the hotel gym for a quick workout before he had to meet Sedona. He'd make a few phone calls first, to let his commanding officer and the guys at the naval air station know he'd arrived, and to confirm they'd be at the hangar to begin inspecting the grounded jets first thing in the morning.

It felt good to be back in California. He'd been stationed at Lemoore Naval Air Station early on in his career. He'd done his initial flight training there in an F-14 Tomcat. He hadn't thought anything could be more thrilling than flying that fighter jet, until he'd climbed into the cockpit of a Coyote to conduct test flights on behalf of the navy. Then he'd been deployed aboard the USS *Abraham Lincoln,* an aircraft carrier in the Persian Gulf, and life was just about as perfect as it could get.

During the ten months he'd been aboard the carrier, he'd flown more than sixty sorties from her deck in support of the war against terrorism, and he'd accomplished each one flawlessly. At least, he amended, until that last one. Yep, that one had been the last straw for his commanding officer, who had seen to it Angel was taken out of combat flight.

He tried hard not to be bitter that they'd shipped him to a manufacturing plant on the East Coast to perform test flights. He knew he was lucky they hadn't busted him back down to lieutenant. At least they hadn't completely clipped his wings.

When they'd first assigned him to Aerospace International's facility, nearly eighteen months earlier, it was to be a three-year stint. Angel knew he'd been given the assignment as a sort of reward. Extended shore-based assignments were highly sought after by guys who had spent months at sea. It was an opportunity to attend school, to strengthen family bonds and to recharge.

Angel didn't need any of that.

He'd already graduated from the Navy War College, he had neither wife nor kids, and the only thing that recharged his engines was combat flight. So when he'd been deployed to the navy carrier after just six months of performing test flights, he'd been thrilled. Not that conducting test flights was a bad gig; there was a certain thrill in taking a jet on its maiden voyage into the skies. He just didn't want to do it for the rest of his career.

But according to his commanding officer, after the stunt he'd pulled during his last sortie, that's just what would happen if he didn't straighten up and fly right—literally. So he'd sucked it up and resigned himself to completing his shore assignment, with the knowledge that it would only be for another eighteen months, and then he'd be back aboard a carrier.

Close to thirty minutes later, he finally pushed open the doors of the gym, and stopped dead in his tracks, riveted. The workout room was empty except for one other person.

Angel's brain almost shut down at the sight.

It was a woman, standing with her back to him. Well… sort of. She was bent over at the waist, legs slightly apart as she gently bounced the palms of her hands against the floor. She wore a pair of tight biking-style shorts, and Angel was transfixed by the sight of her perfect rear, displayed to full advantage by her position. It was lusciously heart-shaped, and he wondered rather dazedly how those cheeks would feel in his hands. She wore some kind of sports bra, and above the waistband of her shorts, her skin was smooth and golden. He couldn't see her face, but through the inverted V of her splayed thighs, her breasts bounced enticingly with each move she made.

Every cell in his body urged him to walk up behind her, grasp her hips and press himself against the feminine softness she so blatantly presented to him. Stifling a groan, he held his towel low in front of himself and moved swiftly to the opposite side of the room. He couldn't remember the last time he'd had such an instant physical reaction to a woman, but yep, there it was.

He scanned the equipment in the room and settled on the treadmill. It was the only piece of machinery that faced the wall, away from the temptress. He decided a quick five-mile run would take his mind off his libido and allow him to warm up before he tackled the weights. He had just settled into a nice stride when he realized there was a mirror on the wall beside him, providing him an unobstructed view of the woman. She was on the floor now, legs splayed wide as she bent forward, head down, and grasped her toes.

His eyes narrowed.

Her auburn hair was pulled back in a thick, glossy braid. When she straightened, she raised her arms above her head and stretched her spine before bending low over the other extended leg.

Angel very nearly fell off the treadmill. As it was, he lost his smooth stride and had to grasp the handles of the machine and do a quick two-step to regain his balance.

Goddamn. It couldn't be. Could it? But when she raised herself upward again and twisted in his direction, her eyes met his in the mirror. She froze, arms stretched over her head, her supple breasts thrust forward beneath the stretchy material of her top.

It was Sedona Stewart.

If the expression of horror on her face was anything to go by, she was just as shocked to see him. Angel swiftly recovered his composure and even managed to give her a benignly polite smile, as if he hadn't just been thinking about thrusting into her, while cradling her sweetly curved backside in the palms of his hands.

In the mirror, he saw her blush and was momentarily transfixed. The flush of color spread slowly downward, until it seemed her entire body was rosy. She gave him a brief nod and scrambled to her feet.

Angel stared. He couldn't help it. He wasn't an expert where women were concerned, but he prided himself on having a good eye. But holy mother of God, who would have ever guessed that hidden beneath her conservative business attire was a body like that? It was better suited to pole dancing than sitting behind a desk.

As he watched, she snatched up a towel and a bottle of water she'd left on the floor. Damn. She was going to bolt. She hesitated, her hand on the door, before she looked over at him.

"So…I'll see you at seven o'clock?"

His breath was coming a little unevenly. He told himself it was from his exertions on the treadmill. "Yes, but I hope you're not leaving on my account."

She turned even rosier, if that was possible. "No," she said quickly, and Angel knew she was lying. "I'm—I'm done with my workout. I was just cooling down when you came in. So…I guess I'll see you later."

As if unable to help herself, her eyes slid down the length of his body. Angel tightened beneath that swift scrutiny. Her eyes flew back to his, and his gaze was drawn irresistibly to her mouth when she ran her tongue over her lips. And in the brief instant before she turned away, he knew.

She wanted him.

But before he could say anything more to her, she yanked the door open and was gone.

Angel was hardly aware of the treadmill churning beneath him. His body was operating on autopilot, his long strides easily keeping pace with the machine. But his mind was spinning. He still couldn't comprehend that beneath the all-business exterior Sedona presented to the world was a lush, tantalizingly feminine woman.

Christ, hers was the kind of body men fantasized about. He felt a little dazed, not only by her physical attributes, but his own reaction to them. He was still slightly aroused, and that was just from looking at her.

He gave a huff of disbelieving laughter. Had he really thought she held no appeal for him? He recalled the habit she had of moistening her lips with her tongue. He wondered if she was even aware she did it, or that when she did, it drew one's eye to the ripe fullness of her lips. He wondered how they would feel beneath his own.

He was sweating.

Glancing down at the display on the treadmill, he realized he was already halfway through his five miles. He felt as if he hadn't even expended himself. He was vitalized, charged with a new energy. He recognized it as keen anticipation.

It was the same way he felt when he climbed into the cockpit of his fighter jet to complete a combat mission— the hot, pounding adrenaline of excitement, the sheer rush of going into the unknown. It was the thrill of the hunt, of finding his target and nailing it. Of coming in fast and low, dropping his payload and streaking away before the object ever knew what hit them.

It was how he felt now, thinking about Sedona Stewart.

He wanted her.

Angel wondered if two weeks would be enough time to

entice the prickly, straitlaced Sedona Stewart into his bed, then decided it had to be.

He'd never failed a mission before, and he wasn't about to start now.

5

SEDONA GLANCED AT her watch for what seemed like the hundredth time. It was three minutes past seven and she'd been pacing her hotel room for a quarter of an hour. Should she knock on Angel's door? Wait for him to knock on hers? Stand outside in the corridor and cough discreetly until he heard her?

She wished for the first time in her life that her experience with men went beyond competing with them for promotions. Establishing personal relationships with them had never seemed all that important before.

From the time she'd been a young teenager with an uncanny aptitude for math and sciences, her life had revolved around her education and subsequent career. Even now, she could hear her father's voice. *If you want to succeed in this world, you have to be willing to sacrifice. Your looks may get you the job, but your brains will get you to the top. You have to be tough to make it in a man's world.*

She knew he'd only had her best interests in mind. A successful man, he believed his oldest daughter should demand the same respect—and salary—he had. As a senior vice president of a Fortune 500 company, he'd traveled frequently and worked long hours. When he was home, he ruled with an iron fist, ruthlessly steering his children in the direction he thought they should go.

At fifty-five, he died of a massive heart attack. Her mother had found herself alone, lacking any practical skills beyond child rearing and the ability to plan dinner parties. While there was a sizable life insurance policy, nothing could compensate for the years of loneliness she'd endured.

Sedona was grateful for her career and her ability to support herself, but she had to admit, her ambition to succeed in a man's world had done nothing for her on a personal level. She had few friends, male or female. She'd never had a real boyfriend, at least none to speak of, and never for any length of time. She spent her evenings at home watching reruns of *Sex and the City,* vaguely shocked at the blatant promiscuity and sexual freedom the characters portrayed, and secretly wishing she could be more like them.

She thought about how Angel had looked at her in the fitness room. For just an instant, his expression had been taut and hungry, as if he wanted to eat her alive. A primal awareness had surged through her and a slow, pulsing throb had settled low in her abdomen. It had scared her so much she'd bolted, praying he hadn't seen the naked desire she'd felt for him.

Back in her room, she berated herself for being such a coward. She wanted Angel Torres. She'd fantasized about him more times than she cared to admit. She should have stayed. She should have continued with her stretching exercises; maybe acted coy and asked him to show her how the weight machines worked. She'd been a total wimp, but no more. She was going to change her attitude and go for what she wanted.

As she paced, she caught sight of her reflection in the mirror and stopped to examine herself with a critical eye. Lacking anything overtly feminine in her wardrobe, she had finally settled on a pair of faded jeans topped with a sleeveless blouse in a soft, moss green. She had debated over what to do with her hair, and finally opted to wear it loose around her shoulders, where it gleamed in soft waves of red and gold. She wore no cosmetics, unless a quick slash of tinted, fruity lip balm across her mouth counted.

For her, these concessions were huge, but would they be enough to attract Angel's attention? Hopefully, because if he didn't show at least a tiny bit of interest in her as a woman, she wasn't sure she'd have the courage to go through with her plan.

She was going to sleep with Angel Torres.

Well…she hoped it would be more than just sleeping, actually. A lot more. She remembered again all the hard, lean muscle he possessed, and the ease with which he'd worked the treadmill. Her imagination conjured up sultry images of him directing that strength and stamina into a different kind of workout. The images she carried of him in her mind had even inspired her to fill several pages of her sketchbook.

She'd made up her mind about what to do as she'd fled the fitness room, her heart still beating hard from the jumble of emotions he stirred in her. She was going to have him. It hadn't been as much a conscious decision as a physical imperative.

She'd probably end up getting her soft, stupid heart completely broken, but she was determined to know—just once—what it would be like to be with Angel Torres. To be one with him, connected on a level so intimate her chest constricted thinking about it.

She'd never done anything so reckless in her entire life. She recalled Mike Sullivan's comments about hiding in her hotel room each time she went on business travel. She'd always been so concerned about her reputation that she'd pretty much denied herself any enjoyment. Her father would have said there was a name for women who consorted with their male colleagues after hours. He'd have had no respect for those women, and Sedona reluctantly acknowledged it was one of the reasons she chose to remain alone and aloof.

But her father was gone. There was nobody to criticize her behavior except herself. How much worse would she feel if she let this opportunity slip away? If she was ever going to fulfill her fantasy, now was the perfect time. She was at a point in her life when she had decisions to make, both personally and professionally. Her entire life had been spent setting her own dreams aside in order to please others. Well, now it was time to please herself.

Sedona admitted Angel was out of her league. On a sexometer, he was off the charts. She might be able to keep his interest for the short run, but eventually he'd move on. She was prepared for that. This wasn't about keeping him. It was about taking control of her life and finally doing things to please herself. She had the distinct feeling that having Angel in her bed would please her very much.

But she didn't have much time to accomplish her goal. She had no idea how long the inspection of the grounded jets might take. She'd told her boss she was resigning but hadn't been truthful about why, except that her career wasn't advancing as she'd hoped.

While she had initially given just two weeks' notice, she'd finally agreed to stay with the agency long enough to complete the Coyote inspections, however long that might take. They could be on the West Coast for weeks, or they could get lucky and identify the cause of the mishaps within the first few days. Either way, they couldn't stay at Lemoore Naval Air Station indefinitely, and once they returned to the East Coast, her employment with the agency would be over.

She was never going to be this alone with Angel again. Even if she weren't leaving, he could be recalled to combat duty at any time and she might never see him again. That knowledge added a certain desperation to her feelings; made her bolder and more determined.

A sharp knock on her hotel-room door caused her to jump guiltily. She gave herself one last, appraising look in the mirror, smoothed her blouse down over her hips and opened the door.

Her pulse quickened a beat at the sight of the dark-eyed man who stood waiting for her. Angel wore a white, button-down shirt that emphasized the bronze hue of his skin. His black hair gleamed wetly from a recent shower, and Sedona caught the tangy scent of his soap. He smelled good enough to bite. When he smiled, she wanted to trace the deep indents of his dimples with her fingers, pull his head down and crush her mouth against his.

His eyes swept over her, missing nothing. Sedona was glad she'd decided to leave her hair down when his gaze lingered for a moment on the glossy waves. "Ready to go?"

She ducked her head, half afraid he might see her intent in her eyes, and rummaged through her purse to ensure she had her room key. "I'm ready. What did you have in mind for dinner?"

He shrugged and indicated she should precede him down the hallway toward the elevators. "I usually let the lady choose. What are you in the mood for?"

You.

"I'm not familiar with this area, so I'll let you choose. Although," she added with deliberate nonchalance, "we could always stay in and order room service."

She sensed his sudden attention, but they had reached the bank of elevators where several other hotel guests were

g back proof of her own illicit behavior. But she knew
wouldn't believe her. He'd probably think she was com-
tely nuts. Nobody would believe such a club could exist
today's world of political correctness, and especially not
a government office.

Besides, telling him about the club might very well ruin
y chance she had of getting him to sleep with her. If she
ld him about the Membership, he might think she was com-
ng on to him in an effort to further her own career.

They reached their rental car and Angel opened the passenger door for her. Sedona paused, one hand on the door
frame, and looked up at him.

"Ken Larson has made it pretty clear that when he's on
business travel, he's on the make," she said, trying to con-
vey a sense of what Ken was up to, without mentioning the
Membership. "I try not to associate with him unless the reason is business related. Ken's the kind of guy where if you're
friendly to him, he thinks you want to have sex with him."

Angel's eyes glittered as he stared down at her, looking intently at her mouth. "Oh, yeah? So if what Larson
says is true, and you never go out when you're on business
trips, why'd you agree to have dinner with me tonight?"
He shrugged. "Maybe I'm cut from the same bolt of cloth
as Ken."

"Well," she said archly, her insides churning, "a girl can
always hope."

She slid into the car and waited while Angel came around
to the driver's side and eased behind the wheel. He started
the engine and flipped the air-conditioning on, but made no
move to put the car in gear. Sedona held her breath when he
turned in his seat to face her. His expression was taut. His
entire body seemed coiled with tension.

"Okay, Sedona." His voice was low. "That's about the
third time in the last ten minutes you've made a suggestive
remark to me." One black eyebrow arched in question. "So

already waiting, and he didn't respond to her veiled suggestion. Her heart pounded at her own temerity.

His casual remark about letting the lady choose had
mildly annoyed her. How many women had he been with?
And how many of them had offered themselves for dessert?

As they stepped into the elevator, Sedona was pressed
into the corner by the other occupants. Angel stood beside
her, his large frame protecting her from getting squashed by
those around them. As Sedona determinedly stared at the
illuminated numbers blinking their descent floor by floor,
Angel leaned down and spoke quietly into her ear.

"Would you rather we order in?"

A warm wash of heat suffused her neck and crawled upward, and she risked a glance at him. He watched her with
a careful intensity that made her breath catch. For a moment
she worried about what the others in the elevator might think,
but they stared fixedly at the closed doors, and she doubted
they could hear Angel above the piped-in music.

"Honestly?" she asked softly. "Yes. But it's only our first
night here. There'll be other nights when we can opt to stay
in."

There. Let him make what he wanted out of that. The elevator came to a halt and the doors slid smoothly open. Sedona started only slightly when Angel took her elbow and
steered her past the small groups of people congregated in
the lobby. The heat of his hand on her bare arm caused a
shiver to course through her.

"Cold?" he asked. "We can go back upstairs and get you
a sweater, if you'd like."

"No, I'm not cold," Sedona murmured. "Just the opposite, in fact. But if you'd like to go back upstairs…" She let
the sentence trail off suggestively.

Angel's eyes narrowed and a hint of a dimple appeared in
one cheek as he considered her. "I think you enjoy teasing

me, *mina*. If I weren't so hungry, I might take you up on it."
He laughed as she came to an abrupt halt and stared at him.
"Relax. Now I'm the one who's teasing."

He looked away, his eyes scanning the lobby. Sedona
scowled at him. Dratted man. It had taken a lot of nerve for
her to make that comment, and for one heart-stopping second she had actually believed he was considering her offer.
Apparently, he wasn't hungry enough. For her, at least. She
was definitely going to have to do something about that.

"We can always grab a bite to eat at the hotel restaurant,"
Angel commented, interrupting her thoughts. "Looks like a
pretty popular place."

Across the lobby a dimly lit restaurant and lounge was
segregated by a low wall and a row of potted palm trees.
Strains of music drifted toward them, interspersed with noisy
laughter and loud conversation. It looked like a sports bar,
and Sedona's stomach tightened at the thought of having
dinner in that overtly male setting. It was exactly the type
of place Mike Sullivan and his cronies liked to frequent;
the type of place where single women were easy targets for
their lewd attention.

As if on cue, she heard her voice being called. Moaning
inwardly, she turned to see none other than Ken Larson and
a group of men from the engineering division stroll across
the lobby toward them.

"Hey, Sedona," Ken called, a friendly grin splitting his
features, "you and the lieutenant care to join us for dinner?"

"No!" she said quickly. Then, sensing Angel's curiosity, she hurried to add, "We were actually just heading out
to find someplace a little…quieter." She smiled brightly at
Ken and tried to pretend she didn't want to wipe the knowing look from his face. "But you go ahead, enjoy your meal.
We'll see you later."

"Okay. But speaking of later," Ken continued blithely, ignoring the warning daggers she was throwing at him, "we'll

be in the lounge if you want to join us when y⟨…⟩
He turned to Angel. "We tend to get a little ⟨…⟩
we're on business trips…you know how it goes. ⟨…⟩
a good time. We've been trying to get Sedona ⟨…⟩
loose a little bit and join us, but she's a tough nu⟨…⟩
But, hey—" he leaned forward to give Angel's s⟨…⟩
friendly slap "—maybe you'll have better luck."

"Maybe she's just particular about the compa⟨…⟩
keeps," Angel replied, looking pointedly at his sh⟨…⟩
and then at Ken.

Sedona watched as Ken's eyes narrowed, and his⟨…⟩
tures tightened. He stared at Angel for a full minute be⟨…⟩
he spoke. "Maybe you're right, Lieutenant," he finally s⟨…⟩
his tone cool. "In all the years I've known her, I can't ⟨…⟩
call a single time she's ever agreed to have dinner with o⟨…⟩
of the team." He cocked his head slightly as he considere⟨…⟩
Angel. "So what does that say about you?"

"That I'm one lucky son of a bitch," Angel replied, grin-
ning as he took Sedona by the arm and steered her toward
the exit.

"Yeah, well, I hope you remembered to bring your camera, Sedona," Ken called after their retreating backs. "After
all, I wouldn't want you to miss any of the *sights*."

Sedona knew he was referring to the "proof" she had
promised to bring back to the Membership. It was obvious
Ken didn't expect her to go through with it, and as soon as
an opportunity presented itself, she'd let him know he was
right. There was no way she wanted anything to do with his
nasty little club.

As they pushed through the revolving door and out into
the dry, cloudless heat of early evening, Angel glanced down
at her. "So what was that all about?"

For one instant, Sedona was tempted to tell him about
the Membership and how Ken believed she was going to

tell me now, do you get some kind of cheap thrill from teasing guys? Are you the type who likes to string a guy along with your sultry come-ons, but never comes through with the goods?"

Sedona stared at him in dismay, momentarily at a loss for words. Did he really think that of her? That she was a tease? She felt wild color come into her cheeks as she forced her gaze to deliberately travel over the thrust of broad shoulders, down the arms corded with muscle, to the lean, hard body that dominated the interior of the small car. But when she slowly met his eyes, there was no mistaking the heat she saw there, and it lent her courage to say the things that until now, she'd only ever dreamed about. She drew a deep, unsteady breath.

"I never tease, and I never string guys along." She ran the tip of her tongue nervously across her lips. "And I'm definitely not stringing you along. If you really want *the goods,* then come and get them."

6

ANGEL STARED AT her, stunned. This couldn't really be happening. It was like a miracle or something. Here he'd been trying to figure out how he was going to get her into bed, and she'd practically offered herself to him on a plate. If someone had told him yesterday that Sedona Stewart would put the moves on *him,* he'd never have believed it.

Want her? Was she kidding? For just an instant he let his imagination soar with all the possibilities the coming night held. He had an incredibly sharp image of Sedona, less her clothes, straddling his hips.

He'd surprised himself with the intensity of his desire for her. When she'd opened her hotel-room door to greet him, his eyes had immediately been drawn to the rich abundance of glossy hair that framed her face and fell softly around her shoulders. She didn't wear any perfume, yet he'd caught the clean, light scent of something floral. Her shampoo, he'd guessed, and his eyes had lingered on her hair. He'd wondered briefly how it would feel beneath his hands. Silky? Cool?

Her breasts thrust gently against the soft fabric of her blouse and for the first time he'd noticed how green her eyes were. And when she'd preceded him down the corridor to-

ward the elevators, his attention had been fixed on her luscious backside, encased in a pair of jeans that were worn
nearly threadbare across her buttocks. She wasn't all that tall,
but her long legs and curvy hips lent her an aura of height.

Oh, yeah, he wanted her. But as he stared into her eyes,
he also realized she was the kind of woman a guy could get
serious about. The kind of woman who probably didn't get
involved with someone unless she had long-term plans. She
probably fell in love with every guy she slept with. He had
to make it clear that he wasn't interested in anything permanent or long lasting.

He'd seen plenty of relationships fall apart under the stress
and demands of a military career. Add combat duty and extended overseas deployments, and it was a recipe for marital
disaster. Nope, it took a special woman to commit herself to
a navy man. So while he was perfectly willing to engage in a
fling, he didn't want Sedona to delude herself into thinking
it would be anything more than that. He could be recalled to
combat duty at any time, or be reassigned to another squadron, and there was no way he was going to ask a woman to
wait for him while he was gone. It wouldn't be fair.

But in the meantime…he was already anticipating fitting
himself against her lushness, and was unable to prevent the
tightening of his body in response.

"I know what you're thinking," Sedona said.

Angel arched one eyebrow at her, and couldn't quite suppress a smile. "Oh, I don't think you do, *mina,* or you'd already be halfway back to the safety of your hotel room."

To his surprise, she smiled, a slow, sensual curving of
her lips. "That's where you're wrong. I might be anxious
to get back to my room, but only because I'd be dragging
you with me." She turned slightly toward him in her seat. "I
want you, Angel Torres. So, what do you say? I know you're

hungry. You said so yourself. Shall we forgo dinner and go right for dessert?"

A primal response coursed through Angel, a rush of heat that poured through his veins like liquid fire. But although her words were full of bravado, he could sense her uncertainty. This wasn't something she did frequently, if she'd ever done it at all. His gaze drifted to her mouth, ripe and moist. He wanted so badly to sample those tempting lips, to taste her and find out if she was as delicious as she appeared.

He leaned toward her across the center console as his eyes swept her features. Why had he never before noticed how damn pretty she was? Her skin was smooth and golden beneath a dusting of freckles across her nose and brow, and her lips…Jesus, her lips could tempt a saint.

Hardly aware of doing so, he reached out and slid a hand beneath the cool, silken fall of her hair and drew her forward. Her pupils dilated, turning her eyes almost black, before her breath escaped in a soft rush and her lashes drifted down to shield her eyes from him. Her lips parted, and then he was covering them with his own.

Her mouth was incredibly soft and pliant, and she tasted vaguely of something sweet, as if she'd recently sucked on a piece of candy. But if he'd thought he was going to be the one doing the kissing, he'd thought wrong.

She made a soft, needy sound that inflamed his senses, and then she arched against him, tentatively seeking his tongue with her own. When he responded, she met him eagerly. She wound her arms around his neck. She drew him closer, gently thrust her tongue against his and did some exploring of her own until he groaned aloud and angled her head for better access. She clutched at his shoulders, slid her hands along the back of his neck and speared her fingers through his hair.

Her mouth was hot and sweet, and Angel's entire body

responded to its pull. His hands moved down her back, over her smooth shoulders and the bumps of her spine, to the bare strip of skin revealed where her shirt gaped away from her waistband. His fingertips caressed the exposed flesh, learning its texture and warmth.

She gave a soft gasp and wriggled closer, slanting her mouth across his. She caught his tongue and tugged on it, sucked it until Angel's world was reduced to nothing more than the woman in his arms and the feel of her hot, insistent mouth on his. When he ran one hand along her rib cage and captured her breast, she gasped and arched her back. He caressed the soft mound through her blouse, reveling in the weight of it against his palm. When he rubbed his thumb across the peak, her nipple hardened instantly, thrusting against him until he rolled it between his fingers.

He was only dimly aware of working the buttons on her blouse until the fabric fell away and he encountered the silken flesh beneath. He dragged his mouth from hers and used his lips to sear a path along the elegant arch of her neck to her collarbone. She gripped his head, encouraging this new exploration. Her breath was warm and ragged against his cheek, his neck.

Slipping one hand behind her, he bowed her across his arm and tugged her bra downward until her breasts spilled free. They were round and firm, pale and smooth except for the ruddy nipples. He bent his head and sucked one into his mouth, pressing the hard nub against the roof of his mouth while he cupped and kneaded her other breast.

Vaguely, as if from a great distance, he became aware of a car engine roaring into life somewhere close by, accompanied by the sound of voices. Slowly, the realization of what they were doing in the parking lot of the hotel sunk into his lust-sodden brain.

"Jesus." Angel jerked himself away from her.

She lay half collapsed against the seat, her naked breasts pushed high by the bra that was still bunched beneath them. Her nipples were stiff and rosy and gleamed wetly from where he'd suckled them. Tousled hair fell around her flushed face.

She looked like an erotic fantasy.

Her breathing was as labored as his, but her eyes were still closed, her lips moist and parted as she struggled to draw breath. If Angel didn't know better, he might have thought she was still savoring the taste and feel of him. When she did open her eyes, they were hazy with pleasure. She stared at him with a mixture of wonder and longing, and for the first time in years, Angel felt a frisson of fear.

Almost harshly, he dragged the open edges of her blouse together. "Cover yourself, *mina*." His voice sounded rough, even to his own ears.

Confusion, then embarrassment, replaced the warmth in her eyes, and she struggled to sit up. She bit her lip and turned slightly away from him as she adjusted her clothing.

Angel blew out his breath in frustration and resisted the urge to drag her back toward him. He flung himself into his seat and scrubbed his hands over his face. What the hell had just happened? He'd come so damn close to losing control. Too close. He'd wanted to haul her across the console, tear her jeans off and take her, right there in the freakin' car in the middle of a goddamn parking lot. He still wanted her. He was aching and uncomfortable with need, and it scared the hell out of him.

Sedona wasn't the first woman to come on to him in such a blatant way. In fact, women had been chasing after him or propositioning him since he was in high school. He was, to a certain extent, used to it. The difference was that he was the one who decided whether or not to let the pursuer catch him. He always retained the upper hand, never let his libido rule his better sense. He never let himself lose control. End of story.

Until now.

It was as if an unseen hand had tilted the world ever so slightly on its axis, causing the very laws of nature to redefine themselves. He recalled again those three little words she'd uttered, and the instantaneous surge of reaction they'd elicited.

I want you.

Christ. He'd responded like a horny teenager. How was it that a woman he'd scarcely noticed until a few short hours ago was now the single, white-hot point of focus in his life? He wanted to consume her, to eat her alive.

He raked a hand over his hair. *Madre de Dios.* For several minutes, he'd completely lost control.

What was worse, though, was how much he'd liked it.

7

"LET'S GO GET that bite to eat."

Angel growled the words as he thrust the car into gear and maneuvered out of the parking lot. He drove faster than he should have, but there was no question he handled the car with smooth efficiency.

Sedona risked a peek at him, more unnerved than she cared to admit by the raw hunger and energy that rolled off him in waves. She ran a shaky hand through her hair, still stunned by what had just happened.

The reality of being kissed by Angel was far different than the fantasies she'd indulged in.

Her trembling fingers absently traced the swollen fullness of her lips as she remembered the fierce intensity of Angel's kiss and the all-consuming passion that had both shocked and delighted her.

Any girlish daydreams she'd harbored about him had been completely and utterly destroyed in the scant moments she'd been gripped in his arms. In her feeble imaginings, she'd envisioned Angel as a tender, considerate lover who would woo her with gentle patience and all the gallant consideration of his rank, anticipating her needs and satisfying them with sweet eagerness. Never had she imagined the incredible strength or heat that had accompanied his embrace, sweeping over her like a firestorm, melting her resistance—if she had any—and incinerating her on the spot.

Her breasts ached where he'd touched them; no, where he'd devoured them. Just the memory of his dark head bent over her, tasting her, caused liquid heat to gather at her core. She thrummed with longing.

Neither of them spoke as Angel negotiated the busy local roads and pulled in to the parking lot of a small pub. He was clearly disturbed by their encounter, but Sedona couldn't tell if he was pissed off, disgusted by her behavior or just plain regretted his response to her.

He turned off the engine, but when it seemed he would get out of the car without saying anything to her, Sedona reached over and touched his arm. He stiffened and slowly turned to face her.

Sedona recoiled at the raw flame she saw in his eyes. He waited, not saying anything, but a muscle worked in his lean jaw.

She wet her lips nervously. "I, um—I'm not sorry about what happened back there. So if you're going to apologize to me for your less-than-gentlemanly behavior, forget it. I don't want to hear it."

He smiled then, a predatory smile that caused Sedona's heart to kick into high gear. "I have no intention of apologizing, *mina.*" His eyes raked over her, the intensity of his scrutiny as palpable as if he had touched her. "But before we get completely carried away and do something we both regret, we need to talk."

"Oh." Sedona nibbled her lower lip and stared at him uncertainly. Was she right? *Did* he regret kissing her? If there was even the slightest chance of getting him into her bed, she certainly didn't want to give him any opportunity to talk himself out of it. She could almost hear the arguments he'd present: he had a thing about getting involved with coworkers, or his military career made relationships impossible, or he had too much integrity to screw around with somebody while they were on official business.

She watched him as he gave a self-deprecating laugh and rubbed the back of his neck with one hand. "You blew me away back there. You know that, don't you?"

"I did?" Sedona couldn't keep the pleased surprise out of her voice. She'd been operating on pure instinct, responding to him on a primal level. He'd overwhelmed her senses, reduced her to a quivering mass of greedy nerve endings that clamored for more, and he was saying she'd blown *him* away? Maybe she was better at this sex thing than she realized.

With newfound confidence, she slanted him what she hoped was a come-hither look from beneath her lashes. "Well, consider that the appetizer, flyboy. Just wait until I serve up the entrée."

Angel's surprised laugh gave way to a choking fit as he stared at her in utter disbelief. "You're not serious?"

"Why not?"

Angel made a noise that was part laugh and part groan. "It's just that I'm having a little trouble convincing myself you're for real. One minute, you're this no-nonsense engineer who's all about getting the job done. The next, you're this smokin'-hot babe who practically gets me off in the driver's seat of a car in broad daylight! Pardon me if I'm just a little confused by it all."

Happiness, pure and dizzying, swept through Sedona. She'd done it. She'd made him want her, maybe even as much as she wanted him. All her life, she'd been called the brainy one, the sensible one. Hearing Angel describe her as hot was amazing. She knew she had the advantage and there was no way she was letting it go. She was nothing if not determined.

"Oh, I'm for real," she murmured, and leaned toward him,

not at all deterred when he pulled back, as if afraid she might touch him. "And just so there's no confusion, I'm definitely all about getting the job done."

Angel's eyes drifted to her mouth and lingered there for several long seconds. In the next instant, he seemed to give himself a mental shake. "Oh, no, lady," he growled softly, "we're not doing a repeat performance in this parking lot. We're going to go inside and have something to eat. Then, after we've cooled down, maybe we can talk about this rationally without jumping on each other."

Sedona smiled. She did want to jump him. "Okay," she conceded, "but can't we do fast food or, even better, takeout?"

He chuckled warmly and squeezed her fingers. "We'll save that for another night."

Clearly, there would be no more exchange of delicious intimacies until he'd had his chance to talk. But at least he'd said there would be another night. All was not lost.

She gave him a quick smile. "All right. Something tells me we're going to need sustenance, so let's go eat."

She didn't wait for him, but opened the car door and climbed out, taking a quick opportunity to comb her fingers through her hair and smooth her clothing. The sun was just beginning to sink over the horizon, streaking the skies with brilliant pinks and yellows. Even now, Sedona could feel the heat of the day beginning to subside, with the promise of a cooler night in store.

Inside the pub, Angel steered her past the lounge area, with its noisy crowd of young people, to a booth in a quiet corner. Sedona was scarcely aware of ordering her meal. She was completely focused on the man who sat on the other side of the table.

He perused the menu and after the waitress had taken his order, sat back and surveyed their surroundings as he absently drummed his long fingers against the table. They might have been complete strangers for all the notice he took of her. Sedona sipped her drink and played with the stir stick as she watched him from beneath her lashes. Finally, unable to stand his inattention any longer, she cleared her throat.

"So…you wanted to talk?"

Almost reluctantly, he turned to look at her. He held her gaze for several long moments in which Sedona was unable to discern his thoughts, before turning his attention to the beer he cradled in his palms.

"You must know I find you attractive," he said at last. When he glanced up at her, his eyes were banked with heat. "I guess I've made that pretty obvious."

Sedona swallowed. Why was this beginning to sound like a gentle brush-off? "I'm sorry. I know I came on pretty strong—"

"Let me finish," he admonished, taking the sting out of his words by slanting her a quick grin. "I had absolutely no problem with the way you came on to me. But I think it's only fair to let you know I'm not in the market for a serious relationship."

Sedona almost sagged with relief. "That's great. Neither am I."

He gave her a look that clearly said he didn't believe her.

"Really, I'm not," she insisted. "It's just that—well, it's just that I've had this thing for you for so long now. And here we are, together for a couple of weeks… I just thought…"

"You just thought you could indulge in a little sexfest with the itinerant military guy, and nobody would ever know, is that it?"

"What? No! My God, I can't believe you'd even think that!" Sedona stared at him in horror, despite the fact that was exactly what she'd thought. "I've never done anything like this before in my life."

Angel sighed and pinched the bridge of his nose between his fingers. "Okay, forget I said that. You're right, I don't really believe it, anyway." He leaned back in the booth and considered her. "I must be insane to even question your motives. I mean, what do I care what they are? You've made it clear you're interested in me. You're attractive and single, so why shouldn't I take you up on your offer?"

Sedona gave him a wary smile. "Right."

"So long as we both go into this with our eyes open, with the understanding that it will only last for as long as we're out here, right?"

"Right." Sedona moistened her lips, hope flaring inside her. "I mean, it would be too uncomfortable if we continued to see each other when we got back to the office." She didn't see any reason to tell him that for her, there would be no going back to the office.

"Right."

"So...we're on?"

Angel laughed. "We're on. Jesus, this is just too weird."

Sedona tilted her head to one side. "I don't know, I'd think it's what every guy fantasizes about. I mean, think about it."

"Oh, I have," he said, and let his gaze travel deliberately over her.

Sedona blushed. She could scarcely believe she was really going to do this. She hadn't had a relationship of any kind since she'd been in college, and even that had been more physical than emotional. She'd briefly dated a guy in one of her thermodynamics classes, and while the sex had been good, it hadn't been great. Too many times, Sedona had been left unsatisfied, wanting more. Pragmatic to the core, she'd become pretty adept at satisfying herself. After that, having a guy in her life had seemed, well, superfluous.

As a whole, she found men to be self-absorbed, needy creatures. Thanks, but no thanks. After she graduated and took the government engineering job, she hadn't met anyone who interested her on any level.

But with Angel… Suddenly she couldn't wait to find out what it would be like to have him in her life, even on a temporary basis. He didn't strike her as being egocentric. And she was quite certain that his lovemaking would never leave her frustrated or wanting.

Their food arrived, saving Sedona from having to respond to Angel's words, but as she looked down at her plate, she realized she wasn't the least bit hungry. Her stomach was knotted with nervous anticipation.

"So," she blurted as Angel took a healthy bite of his burger, "I notice you keep calling me *mina*. What does it mean?" She laughed and held up her hand. "I only want to know if it's complimentary. I mean, if it's something like man-hating she-bitch, please don't tell me."

Angel smiled, clearly amused. "No, it doesn't mean that, although I'm not so sure you'll like the true translation." He folded his napkin before he arched her a look that was half challenging, half defensive. "In Cuba, it means mine. Or my little one."

Sedona nearly choked on the iced tea she was sipping. *Mine? As in…his?* She coughed until her eyes watered and Angel half rose to his feet. She held up a hand to forestall him.

"No," she finally gasped. "I'm okay." She took another, careful sip of her drink and wiped the moisture from her eyes. "It just surprised me, that's all."

"I know, it sounds a little territorial and corny, but it's actually a common form of address among Cubans." He shrugged, and Sedona could have sworn that was embarrassment coloring his neck and jaw. "More like a casual endearment."

"Mmm. It's fine." She nodded, as if contemplating his

words; as if she was accustomed to having men call her *little one* every day. But she couldn't bring herself to meet his eyes for fear he'd see her pleasure. Instead, she snatched her napkin up, held it over her mouth and pretended to cough a little more. Anything to hide the silly grin that threatened to spill free.

Mine. His.

The words were more than just music to her ears. They were like a full violin concerto.

"Well," she said, when she could finally speak, "I think it's very…sweet." She gave him a bright smile. "I didn't realize you were Cuban."

He shrugged again. "My parents fled Cuba in the sixties, after the revolution. I was raised in San Diego."

Sedona tilted her head as she considered him. "Not Miami? Don't they have a huge Cuban population there?"

He smiled. "Actually, I was born there. But my father wanted his kids to be raised in a community that was fully American. He said too many Cubans refuse to assimilate, believing they'll eventually return to Cuba. So we moved to San Diego and…assimilated."

"Your mom didn't mind?"

Angel laughed, but Sedona thought it had a slightly bitter edge to it. "My mother still dreams of returning to Cuba. She let my dad move us to San Diego, but refused to speak anything but Spanish in our home." He chuckled wryly. "She'd like nothing better than for me to marry a nice Cuban-American girl and settle down."

"Oh." Sedona looked at her hands. Her pale, WASP hands. "Is that what you want?"

There was silence and after a moment, Sedona looked up to see Angel smiling at her. "Is this a fishing expedition?"

Sedona flushed. "Of course not. I was just making conversation." She knew her voice sounded defensive, but couldn't help it. Yes, dammit, it was a fishing expedition. Just because he didn't have a ring on his finger didn't mean he wasn't committed to somebody.

"Then the answer is no," he said smoothly. "I have no desire to marry."

"Not ever?"

He shrugged. "Not anytime soon. My job isn't exactly conducive to settling down."

Angel's dark eyes locked with hers, and for a brief instant, Sedona thought she saw something in their depths; regret. Then it was gone, carefully shuttered behind his roguish grin and nonchalant shrug. "Maybe someday, when the war is over, or when my flying days are done. Who knows?"

Sedona tried to imagine what it would be like to be married to a guy like Angel. To send him off, not knowing if he'd come home or not, enduring long months without him. It would take a special woman to share his life on those terms, but Sedona was willing to bet she could do it. The guy was incredible, not just amazingly good-looking, but intelligent and funny, too. Not to mention that he kissed like a dream. It'd be hard to go six months without him, but she could do it in a heartbeat. The rewards would be well worth the wait.

Angel took a swallow of beer. "I came close, once, but it didn't work out." He shrugged. "I guess we just weren't meant for each other."

You were meant for me.

For a moment, Sedona thought she might have uttered the words aloud. She glanced at Angel, but he continued to eat his meal with unrestrained gusto.

"C'mon," he urged her. "Eat your salad. The sooner we finish up, the sooner we can get out of here."

She glanced from her spinach salad to the robust burger he'd ordered for himself. She didn't know how he could have an appetite.

"Aren't you nervous?" she finally asked.

He washed down his mouthful of burger with a healthy swig of beer before he spoke. "About us? Hell, yeah, but in a good way. It's when you're not nervous that you need to be worried. You don't want to be too cocksure, because that's when you make mistakes. Crash and burn, baby."

Sedona pushed her salad around with her fork, unable to suppress a smile. "Are we talking about sex, or flying?"

He wiped his mouth and grinned unabashedly. "Is there a difference?"

Sedona raised her eyebrows. "If you're so cautious, then why were you sent back to us? You still had another six months aboard the USS *Abraham Lincoln,* right?"

For the space of a single heartbeat, he looked completely taken aback. Then he shrugged and looked down at his plate and the moment was gone, but not before Sedona saw the quick flash of pain in his eyes. "I took some risks considered unacceptable to the senior brass."

"Oh. That's not how I heard it."

Angel gave her a tolerant smile and pushed his plate slightly away. "And just how did you hear it?"

Sedona flushed, but pressed on. She *did* want to know. "I heard you disobeyed a direct order from a superior officer."

Angel's smile grew wider. Sedona tried not to stare at his dimples, or the perfection of his white teeth. "That's not exactly how it went down," he said, amusement evident in his voice. "Do you want to know what happened?"

"Okay." Her heartbeat picked up a notch. He was actually willing to share his story with her. Was that significant?

Angel sighed. "It was a couple of months ago. I was lead jet in a five-jet formation to fly deep into Iraq and drop several bunker busters on an area where senior members of al-Qaeda were believed to be hiding out." He picked up a saltshaker and turned it over thoughtfully in his hands.

"We'd already nailed our target and were returning to the carrier when we were informed that a second sortie had been deployed to take out another target pretty damn close to where we were."

He glanced up at Sedona. "Intelligence sources on the ground said the target was on the move and would be past the point of engagement in about eight minutes. The second sortie was still fifteen minutes out, and it was unlikely they'd arrive in time."

Sedona stared at him, mesmerized. "What did you do?"

And so he told her that with his remaining ordnance and scarcely enough fuel to make it back to the carrier, he had blown off his wingman and separated from formation, and gone in, low and fast. He'd dropped below the hard deck of ten thousand feet, putting himself into range of enemy surface-to-air missiles. He'd located the target and succeeded in destroying them just seconds before they might have reached a safe zone.

"I made a snap decision that put my wingman in danger when he chose to follow me. In the opinion of my commanding officer," he said ruefully, "that was bad enough, but when I finally reached the USS *Abraham Lincoln,* I did a four-point victory roll across the bow of the carrier." He shrugged. "They saw it as an act of glory-seeking theatrics and shipped me back to the East Coast to cool my heels and contemplate what it means to be a team player."

"Sort of like a military version of a time-out."

Angel gave her a half smile. "Sort of. My commanding officer said he doesn't need any heroes in his jets. He wants team players who put their own safety and the safety of their wingmen first, not hotshot mavericks out to impress the top brass."

Sedona frowned. "But surely he understood the position you were in? Didn't it matter that you'd taken out the target and probably saved countless lives in the process?"

Angel set the saltshaker down with a small thump. "Independent thinking isn't always encouraged in the military. I did what I thought was right, what I was trained to do."

"What you love to do," Sedona finished softly.

"Yes. Exactly." Smiling ruefully, he shrugged. "I have no one to blame but myself. I knew what I was doing."

"So you're okay with being grounded."

"I can accept the consequences, yeah. And just for the record, I haven't been completely grounded. I'm doing test flights." He lifted the glass of beer and contemplated the amber liquid before bringing it to his lips.

"But you miss combat flight."

She'd surprised him again. It was there in the way his gaze snapped up to meet hers. His mouth lifted at the corner. "I do, yes. There's nothing else like it."

"Tell me about it." She leaned forward, eager to hear him describe why he loved to fly, eager to hear him talk about anything he loved.

He set his beer down and his eyes grew distant. "If there is a heaven, I'd say streaking through the skies at Mach speed is the closest I've ever come to it. It's exhilarating and frightening at the same time. It's knowing you have the power of life and death in your control. It's the thrill of avoiding detection, of eluding radar and completing the mission, despite the danger." He laughed and shrugged. "I know, it sounds hokey, but it's the truth."

Sedona stared at him, humbled by the obvious passion in his voice, and jealous, too, knowing she'd never be able to share that part of his life with him.

"It sounds amazing." Sedona sighed, and cupped her chin in her hand. "I've always wanted to fly in a Coyote," she admitted. "It seems so…exciting."

"Oh, it is." He quirked an odd smile at her. "Who knows? Maybe someday you'll get your chance."

Sedona snorted. "I doubt it. I'm not a celebrity, and I'm not a member of the media, and those are the only people who get free rides in a Coyote. Lowly civil servants like me don't rate."

Angel laughed. "I'm not sure I agree with you."

"Well," she said, smiling, "I'm not even sure I'd actually have the courage to do it, given the chance. I'm humbled by guys like you who do it for a living, under the most hostile conditions imaginable." She paused. "Do you think you'll ever return to combat flight?"

"Christ, I hope so." He held up a hand. "Not that I mind being a test pilot. It's just not the same as flying sorties."

"Well, if it's any consolation, I'm glad you're not flying combat missions." She grinned. "After all, we wouldn't be sitting here, making plans…"

His eyes glinted with sudden heat. Reaching into his wallet, he pulled several bills out and tossed them onto the table. "C'mon, let's get out of here."

"You don't have to pay for my meal," she ventured. "I'm on per diem while we're out here."

"Indulge me," he said, and stood up. "You've already preempted me on the whole seduction thing, at least give me this."

Sedona faltered. Was she being too aggressive? She knew there were guys in the office who were put off by her less-than-feminine ways. She sincerely hoped Angel wasn't going to be one of those men who couldn't treat a woman as an equal partner.

"Fine," she conceded, pushing her chair back to stand up, "but I pay tomorrow night."

He put a hand at the small of her back as he guided her out of the restaurant. "Oh, no, *mina*," he said softly into her ear, "you'll pay tonight."

His words both thrilled and infuriated her. Thrilled her with their implicit promise of hedonistic pleasure; infuriated her with the implication that he was paying for her services.

"Listen, flyboy," she said sweetly as they passed the hostess stand and stepped out into the darkness of the parking lot, "you'll get nothing from me if you don't watch your step. Paying for my meal does not instill you with any inalienable rights."

She wasn't prepared when he suddenly pushed her up against the side of the car, and followed with the long, lean heat of his own body against hers. He was pressed against her from thigh to breast, all hard, hot male. He smelled incredibly good.

"First of all, I am no boy." He dipped his head and traced his lips along the side of her throat, causing her to gasp with sensation and silently agree with him. "Second of all—" his voice was low and rough against her skin "—I don't expect anything from you that you're not fully prepared to give of your own free will. *Comprende?* If I gave you that impression, it was completely unintentional. This, however, is not."

He captured her face between his hands and claimed her lips in a kiss that was completely off the charts and seared Sedona all the way down to her toes.

She moaned.

He tasted faintly of the beer he'd been drinking. His mouth slanted hard across hers, forcing her lips apart for the intrusion of his tongue. There was nothing gentle about it; the kiss was designed to inflame and consume.

Sedona welcomed every scorching second.

She slid her hands upward, along his ribs and over his chest and curled one hand around the strong column of his neck. She found the heartbeat at the base of his throat and reveled in the feel of it pulsing strongly against her fingertips.

He feasted on her lips. He wasn't just kissing them, he was plundering. She couldn't think. If she wasn't pinned against the car by his solid, delicious weight, she'd probably slither to the ground in a boneless pile of mush. She could only feel and respond. His thumbs smoothed over her cheekbones and his fingertips soothed the sensitive skin behind her ears as he held her face in his hands.

When she slid her hand between their bodies, he eased back just enough to give her room to explore. His stomach contracted when she touched the hard ridges of flesh beneath the soft fabric of his shirt. Oh, my. The guy was layer after layer of firm muscle. When her fingertips dropped lower and encountered his belt, he stiffened and groaned, deepening his kiss.

Sedona made a soft sound of approval and slid her hand lower to cup the impressive length of him beneath his jeans. Her knees turned to Jell-O. What did he have in there, a heat-seeking missile? Even through the denim, he was hard and hot, and larger than she'd anticipated. When her fingers closed around him, he jerked reflexively. She shifted against him, uncomfortably aware of her own growing need.

He tore his lips from hers and grabbed her hand, dragging it upward. "Stop, *mina,*" he gasped. "You're killing me."

He curled her hand inside his and held it against his chest while he sucked in air. Sedona could feel the uneven thumping of his heart. She dropped her forehead against his shoulder and struggled to control her own erratic breathing. His body was big and warm and hard, and she could feel his erection pressing against her abdomen.

He chuckled softly, but there was no mistaking the rueful resignation in his voice as he gathered her closer. "Oh, man," he groaned, "I am so screwed."

8

SEDONA WAS HARDLY aware of driving back to the hotel. Her thoughts were fully occupied with the man sitting beside her, driving with ruthless speed and efficiency through the darkened streets.

He was impatient.

The realization both thrilled and terrified her. She couldn't stop staring at his hands as he drove, admiring the long, lean fingers and knowing that soon they would be touching her with the same sure confidence. It was still unbelievable to her that Angel found her attractive. Not just attractive, either. *Hot.* It was as if she'd briefly fallen asleep and woken up in some alternate universe where smart, hunky guys fell for everyday, average Janes.

Sedona's thoughts were interrupted when Angel parked the car. She found she couldn't meet his eyes as he took her elbow and steered her across the parking lot to the front entrance. The lobby seemed garishly bright after the intimate darkness of the car. Pulsing music drifted toward them from the hotel lounge.

"Christ, that guy doesn't waste any time," Angel commented.

Through the doorway of the dimly lit lounge, she could see Ken Larson. He was standing close behind a young woman wearing a micromini and a tiny top. As Sedona watched, he bent his head and whispered something that made the girl throw her head back and laugh. At the same time, his hands skimmed down her sides to rest possessively on her hips as he pressed against her backside.

Sedona scowled. "He's probably looking for his next promotion," she muttered darkly.

"Are you saying she's his boss?" Angel's voice was incredulous.

"No, of course not," Sedona assured him, anxious to change the subject. "It was just a bad joke."

As if sensing her reluctance to be seen, Angel pushed her ahead of him toward the bank of elevators, using his bulk to shield her from view. Sedona was grateful for his thoughtfulness, as the last thing she wanted was an encounter with Ken Larson or any of his cronies. As far as Ken knew, she was still on board with trying to gain access to the Membership. She didn't need him jumping to conclusions if he saw her with Angel, and she definitely didn't need him making any comments about the Membership in Angel's presence. If Ken wanted to get promoted by getting busy, it had nothing to do with her.

"Elevator's here."

Angel's voice brought her abruptly out of her thoughts. With his hand lightly cupping her elbow, they stepped into the elevator. They were the only occupants, and during the short ride to the third floor, Sedona was aware of Angel watching her.

"Having second thoughts?" he asked softly.

Her eyes flew to his face. He dominated the tiny compartment with his size and presence. He hadn't touched her during the ride back to the hotel and suddenly, Sedona was unaccountably shy. They were, perhaps, minutes from engaging in the greatest intimacy two people could share, and yet she was conscious they were little more than strangers. Having second thoughts? Only every moment since they'd arrived at the hotel. What if once she got her clothes off, he no longer found her attractive? What if she couldn't please him? What if this whole thing was a huge mistake?

She drew in a fortifying breath. "Not if you aren't."

His eyes darkened perceptibly. "Not a chance, *mina.* But I'm trying really hard not to scare you. I don't trust myself to touch you until we're in your room."

The elevator jerked to a stop and the doors slid open to their floor. Heart pounding, Sedona rummaged for her key as they walked side by side down the hallway. When they reached her room, Angel didn't pause but continued past her to stop outside his own door.

"There's a connecting door between our suites," he said quietly as he eased his key card into his door. "Whenever you're ready, unlock the door from your side. I'll do the same."

"Okay." Her voice sounded breathless. Inserting her key, she pushed open her door and slipped inside. As he'd said, there was a connecting door between their rooms that she hadn't noticed earlier.

Almost immediately, she heard Angel unlocking and opening his side of the door. Once she did the same, there would be nothing to separate them.

She hesitated. Did she really have the guts to go through with this? She flipped on the overhead light in the small bathroom and studied her reflection critically. Her eyes were overly bright, her cheeks flushed. Acutely conscious of the man who waited for her on the other side of the locked door, she brushed her teeth, ran her fingers through her hair and drew in a deep breath. There was nothing more to do. She didn't own any slinky lingerie, and probably wouldn't have the courage to wear it even if she did. She consoled herself with the knowledge that at least her bra and panties were new.

After she'd left work yesterday, she'd gone straight to the mall to buy some last-minute items for her trip, and had gone into Victoria's Secret on a whim. She'd spent a shocking amount of money on underwear, including one silky thong. She hadn't been brave enough to wear it tonight, but at least she wasn't wearing granny undies.

Drawing a deep breath, she stood in front of the connecting door, and with fingers that trembled, slowly flipped the lock open and turned the knob.

ANGEL HEARD THE rasp of the lock in the door. His heart thumped unevenly in his chest. Christ, he was actually nervous. He tried to relax. It was no big deal. She was just a woman, after all, and he'd had more than his share of women. He could handle this. The only reason she'd tested his self-restraint earlier was because he'd been celibate for so long. He never fraternized with female crewmates when he was aboard a carrier, and he'd been at sea for ten long months. It was just his healthy, male hormones reacting to a pretty woman, nothing more.

He'd exchanged his loafers for a pair of flip-flops, and had made sure he had a supply of condoms in the bedside table. In the few minutes before Sedona unlocked the door, he'd located a couple of single-serving bottles of wine in the minibar and put them in a bucket of ice. He'd tuned the bedside radio to a station that played soft music, and dimmed all the lights except for the one in the bathroom, and even then he'd closed the door so only a thin shaft of light fell across the carpet.

He was as ready as he was ever going to be. If seduction was what the lady wanted, he was happy to oblige. They were both adults, after all. Hell, she'd all but said it was just about the sex, so who was he to complain? He was definitely okay with it being about the sex.

But when the door opened and Sedona stepped shyly into the room, his stomach knotted with something that might have been nervous anticipation.

"Oh," she said, tipping her head, listening. "Is that Anita Baker? I love her songs, they're so romantic."

Until that moment, Angel had barely noticed the soft love song playing on the radio. "Well, then, we're off to a good start." He lifted the small wine bottle, questioning. "Care for a glass?"

Sedona came into the room and took the proffered glass, her eyes sliding over the bed and away. Angel wondered if she was imagining the two of them tangled in the bedding, skin sliding over skin. But when she tipped the wineglass back and drained the contents in one long swallow, he was concerned.

"A little false courage?" He took the empty wineglass and set it on the bedside table, smiling as she wiped her mouth with her fingertips and shuddered slightly.

"I wouldn't mind a little more." She reached for Angel's glass, standing full next to hers, but he caught her wrist.

"I think maybe we'll hold off for a bit, *mina*." He tugged her toward him, his thumb sliding over the underside of her wrist where her pulse beat frantically. "I want you conscious and at least partially sober."

She didn't protest when he drew her wrist upward and settled her arm around his neck, and drew her into the circle of his arms with his other hand at her waist. She released her breath on a soft sigh and leaned into him. Her fingers caressed the back of his neck.

"I can't believe we're actually doing this," she murmured, and pressed her lips tentatively against the base of his throat.

"You can still change your mind." As soon as the words were out of his mouth, Angel wanted to retract them. What a dumb-ass thing to say. He absolutely did not want this woman to change her mind. He'd been hard for her since he saw her in the fitness room. He wanted to spend the next eight hours doing decadent things with her. But he didn't want Sedona to be with him if she wasn't absolutely sure it was what she wanted.

"No chance, flyboy," she said, smiling against his throat. "I've spent my entire life doing things to make other people happy. This is one opportunity I am not about to pass up."

Angel breathed a silent thank-you and pulled her fully against him. "Good," he said, his voice husky, and tipped a finger beneath her chin, tilting her face upward. His eyes searched hers, and he watched as the uncertainty that lingered there was slowly replaced with something else, something languorous and heated. She moistened her lips, drawing his attention irresistibly to her mouth.

"I have to kiss you," he confessed, and dipped his head to stroke his lips across the tempting lushness of hers.

Sedona made a soft purring sound of approval and pressed closer. She parted her lips and teased him with slippery, soft strokes of her tongue against his. She caressed the back of his neck even as her other hand crept up to his rib cage and then slid around to the small of his back to draw him closer.

Angel reached down and cupped her buttocks beneath the thin fabric of the threadbare jeans, feeling her heat through the material. He lifted her, fitting himself against the cradle of her hips. She made an incoherent sound in her throat and parted her legs to allow for the intrusion of his thigh between them. She rode him, rubbing herself sinuously against the hard length of his leg even as she deepened their kiss, slanting her mouth across his for better access.

She tasted like wine and sunshine. He pressed his leg harder against her center. Heat surrounded his thigh where she covered him. His cock strained against the confines of his jeans, pulsing with need. From the small, feminine sounds she made, she was as aroused as he was. Time to end the artificial stimulation and move on to the real deal. Angel would have picked her up to deposit her on top of the bed, but she scooted out of his arms before he could get a good hold of her.

"Not so fast," she protested, but her voice was high and breathy, as if she'd just dashed up a flight of stairs. "I have a treat for you."

She caught his hand and led him to an upholstered chair in the corner of the room. She pushed him down into it, but remained standing between his legs, bracketed by his knees. Angel stared up at her.

"I've always wanted to do this," she confessed, wild color rushing into her cheeks.

Before Angel could ask what she meant, her fingers moved to the buttons on her blouse. Slowly, she began to sway her body in time with the sensuous strains of the music, gently rotating her hips so that she bumped against the framework of his legs. Her eyes never left his face.

Angel couldn't move. Couldn't think. Couldn't do anything except stare in utter fascination at the luscious woman who stood in front of him, undulating her body as she slowly began to undress. He swallowed hard and fisted his hands on his thighs.

Sedona unfastened the top two buttons of her blouse and allowed him a tantalizing glimpse of the smooth, golden flesh beneath. She cupped her breasts in her hands and then smoothed her hands down her body and over her hips. She closed her eyes, arched her neck, and slowly slid her hands back up the length of her body until she buried them in the mass of her hair, her lips parting on a sigh of pleasure.

Angel shifted uncomfortably in the soft chair. Sedona must have been aware of his rock-hard erection, but she gave no sign of relenting as she moved slowly to the seductive music. She unfastened the remaining buttons on her blouse and parted the front with devastating leisure. She wore a pale peach bra edged in lace. It was transparent. Angel could clearly see the outline of her nipples through the sheer fabric and right now they were stiff with desire. He groaned and grasped the arms of the upholstered chair, willing himself to stay seated.

Slowly, swaying her hips, Sedona turned her back to him and removed the blouse, letting it slide down the length of her arms until it spilled onto the floor in a puddle of green fabric. He held his breath as she bent her arms behind her back and deftly unhooked the fragile bra. Angel's fingers ached to trace the graceful, indented line of her spine, to smooth his hands over the narrow curve of her waist and gently bite the thrust of her shoulder blades.

He sat, immobile.

Sliding her fingers beneath the straps of the bra, she allowed it to slither from her body. She was bare from the waist up, and Angel thought he'd never seen anything as erotic as the supple line of Sedona's spine, or the feminine flare of her hips encased in the faded denim.

The music changed, became more throbbing and intense. Sedona turned sideways, allowing him a profile view of her perfect breasts. He almost swallowed his tongue when she slid her hands up her taut belly and grasped the distended nipples, rolling them between her fingertips as she threw her head back with a soft moan.

He was halfway to his feet, when she turned fully toward him and pushed him back with a fingertip in the center of his chest. She gave him a mocking shake of her head, but didn't back away. She was so close he could see the nubbed texture of her areolas and the smooth expanse of satiny skin that covered her torso, tempting him to touch, kiss and lick her. He sank back against the cushions, entranced.

Sedona smiled at him, a sultry smile full of sensual promise. She wet her lips and with her hips still rotating in slow motion, unfastened the snap on her jeans and slid the zipper down. Turning her back to him once more, she eased the denim over the roundness of her buttocks and pushed the fabric slowly down the length of her legs, shifting her weight from side to side as she did so.

Angel sucked in his breath, feeling his groin tighten even more. He wondered if he could actually die from wanting. She wore a minuscule pair of peach panties, and though they weren't exactly a thong, they didn't come close to covering the smooth mounds of her cheeks. She bent forward to pull the jeans free from her legs, thrusting her luscious bottom toward him in the process. As in the fitness room, his reaction was instantaneous.

His cock swelled even more, if that was possible, and he ached to bury himself in her delicious flesh. He wanted to consume her, to eat her alive. He couldn't help himself; he grasped her hips and drew her backward, onto his lap.

She squirmed against him, causing him untold agony. "I'm not finished," she protested breathlessly.

"Yes, you are." His voice was a rough growl. "Any more is going to kill me, *mina*. I can't wait. I have to touch you."

He pulled her completely back so that she lay sprawled on top of him, her bare back against his chest, her legs straddling his thighs, her head against his shoulder.

He nuzzled her ear, breathed in the clean fragrance of her hair. Her breathing was rapid and uneven as he trailed his tongue along the side of her neck and gently bit down on her shoulder. "Where did you learn to do that?"

"Wh-what?"

"The striptease, *mina*."

She gave a breathless laugh. "That was my first one. Oh!"

Angel slid his hands up over her arms and then around to her front. He cupped her breasts, kneading and caressing their firmness until Sedona gasped. He plucked at her nipples, rolled them gently between his fingers and then pinched them until she moaned and shifted restlessly on his lap.

He smoothed his hands over the soft flatness of her belly, skimmed them over her hip bones and the silken swatch of her panties, and caressed her thighs. He used his knee to nudge her legs farther apart.

"God, *mina*," he said hoarsely, tracing his tongue around the delicate whorl of her ear, "you feel incredible. You're so responsive, so hot."

Sedona arched her neck to grant him better access, and reached behind her to draw his head down for a deep, open-mouthed kiss, her tongue seeking his with growing urgency.

He slid one hand between her legs and cupped her feminine mound, reveling in the heat that scorched him through the fragile fabric. He rubbed two fingers across her center, gently at first, until she squirmed and her breath shuddered out from between parted lips. She pushed herself helplessly against his hand. Her panties were soaked.

"Oh, my God," she gasped, dragging her mouth from his. "That feels too good. I can't—"

"Shh." He slid his fingers lower until they reached the entrance to her body, shielded by the wet silk. "Let me. I need to touch you…feel you respond to me."

He inserted one fingertip into her as far as the silk would permit. Sedona moaned softly and widened her thighs until they were draped fully across his own. Angel played with her breasts with one hand, and with the other he pushed aside the flimsy barrier and skated a finger over her slick folds, gratified when she sucked in her breath and jerked reflexively.

"That's it," he murmured approvingly. "You're wet for me, *mina*." The movement of her buttocks on top of his straining cock was torture. And when he slid a finger into her drenched heat, it was almost too much for him. He wanted to stand up and bend her over, jerk her panties down and thrust himself into her from behind, again and again. He drew in a deep, controlled breath. He had to slow this down. He didn't want this to end anytime soon. Hell, he didn't want it to end ever. He wanted to take her desperately, but he wanted her primed and ready.

He inserted a second finger into her tightness and used a gentle pulsing motion that soon had her clenching her muscles around him. With his fingers still working, he located the slick rise of her clitoris and pressed his thumb against it. Sedona groaned, a deep sound of sexual pleasure, and arched her breast into his hand.

Angel swept his tongue into her mouth, even as he pumped his fingers slowly and swirled his thumb over the peak of her desire. When he withdrew his fingers, she cried out in disappointment.

"No, *mina*," he soothed her, "I'm not finished. I've barely begun."

He stood up swiftly, sliding out from beneath her and settling her into the upholstered chair. Her head lolled against the seat back as if she didn't have the strength to hold it upright. Angel took a minute to devour the sight she made. She was sprawled gracelessly, her legs still parted, one hand draped over the arm of the chair while the other caressed her breast and toyed with the nipple. When she looked up at him, her eyes were cloudy, glazed with pleasure.

"What are you doing?" Her voice was husky.

"Just this," Angel murmured, and dropped to his knees in front of her. He slid his hands over the smooth plane of her chest until he captured both breasts in his hands. He cupped them briefly and admired the rosy nipples, before moving on to her panties.

Hooking his thumbs beneath the lace-trimmed edge, he dragged them from her body. Sedona closed her eyes and turned her face away, as if embarrassed, but lifted her hips to assist him.

Angel brushed his hands along her inner thighs and pushed her knees apart, and then sat back on his heels to admire her. She was achingly feminine, from the light cluster of damp curls atop her mons, to the lush, pink lips beneath, swollen and glistening with her desire.

"Ah, baby," he groaned, "you're so damn gorgeous down here." He settled himself more comfortably, then drew her knees up until they were draped over his shoulders. Sedona gave a mortified squeak and tried to yank her legs away, but he held them firmly in place. "No, *mina,* don't deny me this."

Then, before she could protest further, he pulled her bottom to the edge of the seat cushion, bent his head and slid his tongue along the length of her cleft.

Christ, she tasted delicious, delicately imbued with the scent of the sea. He was gratified when she whimpered softly and lifted her hips upward, straining toward him. He grasped her buttocks in his hands as he licked her with care and flicked his tongue over the most sensitive of spots. He reveled in her, thrust his tongue into her, slowly and repeatedly until she gripped his head with both hands. He swirled his tongue around the peak of her distended clitoris until she cried out. She was mewling now, soft little cries of delight as she began to rotate her hips and push against his face.

He moved one hand out from beneath her buttocks and slid two fingers into her slick heat, even as he increased the tempo and pressure of his tongue.

"Angel." She sounded desperate.

When she stiffened and her back bowed off the cushions, Angel knew she teetered on the brink. He wanted to see her come apart. He pressed his thumb against her and she gave a long, keening cry of pleasure even as her inner muscles contracted fiercely around his fingers.

Angel didn't give her any time to recover. He bent and scooped her into his arms, taking a moment to brush her lips with his own, letting her taste herself on him. She draped her arms around his neck and stared up at him with eyes that were hazy with wonder.

He tumbled them both onto the mattress. Rolling to his side, he came up on one elbow and looked down into her face, pushing her hair back with his hand.

"Tell me, *mina*," he urged softly. "Tell me what you want."

SEDONA STARED BACK at him, amazed he couldn't read her mind.

You. Inside me.

Despite the mind-blowing orgasm he'd just given her, she ached for him. The bedspread was soft and cool beneath her bare back, in direct contrast to the man who braced himself over her prone body. His face was taut with desire, more erotic than anything she could have imagined, even in the countless sexual fantasies she'd woven around him.

"I'm thinking you have way too many clothes on," she murmured, and tugged the hem of his T-shirt from the waistband of his jeans.

He reared up on his knees and with a swift, impatient movement, dragged the fabric over his head and flung the garment away.

Sedona sucked air into her lungs. From the thrust of his powerful shoulders, down the sculpted, muscular chest, to the six-pack that rode above his belt buckle, Angel Torres was supremely, heart-stoppingly male, and so beautiful Sedona wanted to weep.

Unable to resist, she traced her finger down the deep groove that bisected his torso from collarbone to navel. His skin was smooth and tanned, but she detected a lighter band of skin just below his waistline.

She tried to speak, tried to tell him how infinitely gorgeous she found him, but couldn't find her voice, could only make an incoherent sound of need as she reached greedily for him.

"Easy, *mina*," he gasped, when her fingers hooked into the waistband of his jeans and fumbled with his belt buckle. "Let me."

Sedona's breath hitched as he unfastened the buckle and then popped the button free. His expression was strained as he unzipped his fly and shoved both boxers and jeans down over his thighs.

Her mouth went dry and her brain ceased to function as Angel took her hands and guided them to the biggest, hardest erection she'd ever seen. Not that she'd actually seen that many, but this one topped them all. When her fingers wrapped around him, he inhaled sharply and closed his eyes.

Sedona felt her own desire kick back into full gear as she stroked him. She doubted even the high-tech control stick aboard the Coyote fighter jet, mounted so it was centered between the pilot's legs, was as responsive. The thick veins in his shaft pulsed beneath her fingers, and when she ran the tip of one finger over the engorged head, it came away slick with moisture. He threw his head back and made a deep groaning noise when she cupped his balls and lightly scored them with her fingernails. Then he moved so that he was completely over her, her nipples brushing his chest as he supported himself on his elbows.

"Enough," he rasped into her ear, "or I won't last."

His words thrilled her. She could scarcely believe that she, the pragmatic and boring engineer, had aroused this amazing guy to the point where he strained for self-control. It was a total turn-on.

She pulled him down on top of her and used her feet to push his jeans completely off until they fell to the floor. She ran her feet up and over the backs of his hard legs, feeling his erection bump against her most private spot.

"I want you so badly," she whispered, and pulled Angel's head down for a deep, openmouthed kiss. He braced himself on one hand, dragged his lips from hers and leaned down to take one of her nipples into his mouth. She gasped at the exquisite sensation.

"You're so damn beautiful," he muttered against her skin. Reaching across her body, he opened the drawer of the bedside table and fished out a condom.

Sedona watched as he tore it open with his teeth and then spat the corner away. He sheathed himself with hands that trembled. Did she really have that potent an effect on him? The knowledge was heady. But when he positioned himself at the entrance to her body and began to slide into her, one exquisite inch at a time, she ceased to think.

He was large, and she hadn't had sex in a long time— longer than she'd ever admit to anyone, maybe even herself. He stretched her, filled her, eased himself into her until her buttocks were flush against his hips and there was nothing but the taste, scent and feel of Angel, in her and surrounding her. Her entire world had reduced itself to this one room and the delicious weight of the man who pinned her against the bed.

She heard a desperate mewl of need, and was shocked to realize that it came from her.

"Mina." His voice was rough. "You're so tight… Am I hurting you?"

In answer, Sedona arched against him and drew her feet up until they rested on his firm, taut butt. The movement opened her even more, and when she shifted her hips restlessly beneath him, he moaned and buried his face in her neck.

"I can't—I don't think—" Whatever words he might have said were lost as he gave a helpless groan of surrender and reached beneath her to grasp her cheeks in his hands. "I'm sorry," he rasped hoarsely into her ear, "I don't think I can go gently."

"I don't want gentle," she breathed against his lips, and he plunged into her. The sensation of him filling her was more intense than anything she had ever experienced.

He turned his face and caught her lips in a kiss that nearly undid her. He drew on her tongue even as his pace quickened and he thrust into her with increasing urgency. Sedona felt an answering heat begin to build.

She stroked her hands over the firm mounds of his buttocks, raised her legs higher and wrapped them around his lean waist.

"Oh, yeah," he breathed. "So good…"

He raised himself up and pushed one of her legs to the side, and then reached down and slid a finger over her slick center. Sensation, pure and raw, spiraled through her, causing her to cry out and writhe beneath him.

"Come to me, *mina*," he growled, and punctuated his words with another bone-melting thrust of his hips against hers.

Waves of pleasure coursed through her as he thrust harder, faster, and she could feel the climax beginning to throb in her clitoris. But when he lightly pinched her sex, it was her undoing, and with a choked sob, she convulsed around him as her orgasm tore through her in a blinding rush.

The intensity of her release was enough to push Angel over the edge, as well, and with a hoarse shout, he plunged into her and then stiffened as his big frame shuddered above.

He dropped his head to her shoulder, and Sedona hugged him to her. Their breathing was ragged and she could feel the heavy, uneven thumping of his heart against her chest. She wanted to hold on to this moment forever—bottle it up and savor it.

He turned his face and pressed a kiss against her neck, just at the juncture of her jaw. His breath, warm and sweet, washed over her.

"That was…amazing, *mina*." Carefully, he withdrew from her and discarded the condom, before rolling to his side, pulling her with him and tucking her back against his chest. He dipped his head and bit her shoulder gently before soothing the area with his lips and tongue, causing shivers of sensation to chase across her skin.

Sedona turned just enough so she could angle her head and look at him. His eyes were so dark she couldn't distinguish the pupil from the iris, and one dimple flirted with her as he gave her a lazy, tender smile. He stroked the damp hair back from her face before dropping a kiss onto her lips.

"I think I was wrong, you know," he murmured, pulling her tighter against the hard warmth of his body.

"How so?" God, he was so incredibly yummy. She wanted to look at him endlessly.

"I said there was no difference between flying and sex." His eyes held hers, dark and unfathomable. "But you know what? It's entirely possible that this is better than flying. In fact, I'm pretty sure it's my new favorite thing to do."

Sedona stared at him, stunned. Sex with her was better than streaking through the skies at six hundred miles an hour? Her pulse accelerated until she was certain she was going to die from sheer joy. For her, having sex with Angel Torres was the culmination of a dream come true. But to hear him say that sex with her was more intense, more thrilling, more pleasurable than being in the cockpit of his fighter jet was…well, it was pretty freaking unbelievable.

She didn't protest when he wrapped his muscular arms around her and flung a hard leg over hers, effectively trapping her within the circle of his body. He'd said being with her was better than flying.

For now, at any rate.

Even as his arms tightened around her and he pressed a drowsy kiss against her neck, she wondered how long the joyride would last. Because as a pragmatic engineer, she knew eventually—inevitably—even fighter pilots had to come back down to earth.

9

"GODDAMN. IS THAT guy for real?"

The words were barely more than a wondering whisper, but Sedona looked up from the documents she'd been staring blindly at to follow the other woman's gaze across the room. Angel leaned against the far wall, arms crossed over his chest. The large conference room was filled with members of the inspection team, both civilian and military, as they received the obligatory briefing.

Lieutenant Brian Palmer, the commanding officer responsible for maintaining the fleet of Coyotes, provided a slightly nasal report of the five aviation mishaps, and their own subsequent role in examining the grounded jets. He was a good-looking man in his early thirties, with thinning brown hair and sharp gray eyes that missed nothing. He'd introduced himself to Sedona as soon as she'd entered the conference room, promising full cooperation with her team.

Sedona narrowed her eyes at the maintenance technician sitting beside her. She was pretty enough, if you liked toned, muscular women who exuded raw, physical energy. The kind of woman who could no doubt spend an entire night screwing a guy blind and still wake up in the morning looking gorgeous, and ready for more.

Unlike Sedona, who was exhausted, both physically and mentally, and deliciously tender in places she'd never before imagined.

Just the memory of the previous night brought a lazy smile to her lips. She and Angel had showered together—she remembered the sensual image he'd made as he stood under the sluicing water with his hands behind his head. She'd soaped him with her bare hands—which had led to another heart-pounding interlude of erotic delights.

Later, they'd curled up in bed and flipped through the television channels until she'd made a naughty suggestion to order an adult movie. His eyes had widened in surprise, but he'd laughed and done it. In less than ten minutes, their own moans and sighs had drowned out those of the actors.

It had been nearly 4:00 a.m. when he'd finally escorted her back through the connecting doors and helped her crawl into her own bed, where she'd fallen blissfully asleep—for a whole two hours. She looked as bleary-eyed and worn-out as she felt.

She eyed the wholesome blonde technician with growing dislike. The woman could have been an Olympic contender for the Swedish bust-building team with her supple body and thrusting breasts.

"Hmm…he's a pilot, too," the technician continued in a conspiratorial whisper, unaware of the daggers Sedona was throwing her way. "I hope to God I'm assigned to oversee the maintenance on his jet." She grinned. "It would be a pleasure to give him a lube job."

Shocked, Sedona blinked at her, then scowled and shifted her attention back to Angel. The connecting doors between their rooms had been closed when her alarm had finally gone

off, and she hadn't seen him until she'd arrived in the briefing room of Hangar 29. But he'd only given her a benignly
polite smile of greeting and continued his discussion with
the inspection team's commanding officer, Captain Dawson,
a severe-looking man several years Angel's senior.

Disgruntled, she'd taken a seat and tried to pretend his
apparent disinterest didn't bother her. It was necessary, she
knew, to maintain a professional appearance while they conducted their inspections. Still, she'd half expected to see their
connecting doors open when she woke up that morning. Had
hoped they might share a cup of coffee or several words at
the very least, before they were required to don their mantels
of indifference. She couldn't quite subdue her hurt feelings.

She sneaked another look at Angel. Somebody had
dimmed the lights in the conference room to better view
the overhead slides, but even in the indistinct light, she could
see he was looking at her.

Watching her.

She flushed and looked quickly away. But when several
minutes passed, her attention was unwillingly drawn back
to him. He still watched her and then he slowly dropped one
eyelid in an audacious wink. A wink that told her he, too,
was recalling what they'd shared last night. It was a wink
meant only for her. She blushed, covered her quick smile behind her hand and forced herself to focus on her handouts.

The maintenance technician leaned over to her. "I've gotten his attention," she whispered. "He just winked at me.
Talk about hot. I'll give him something that'll fire his engines." She nudged Sedona with enough force that she almost unseated her.

Sedona cast the woman one long, baleful look, but the
blonde had already turned her attention back to Angel, practically drooling as she stared at him. Dimwit. What was it

like to go through life with that kind of supreme confidence, certain every man who looked your way was instantly attracted to you? Sedona wanted to lean over and tell the other woman that Angel was taken and, oh, by the way, he hadn't been winking at her.

Sedona was only distantly aware that Captain Dawson had stood up to speak. She barely heard him as he talked about the team's responsibility to gather information, establish facts and find root causes. He emphasized teamwork, safety and confidentiality. Sedona had been through the drill before. While she understood the necessity for the brief, she found she was unable to pay close attention.

Thoughts of Angel consumed her, which was not good. There would be time enough for the two of them at the end of the day. Right now, she needed to pull herself together and focus on her job. The navy depended on her expertise to ensure the safety of their grounded jets, which meant now was not the time to let herself become completely distracted. She prided herself on her professionalism and skill. There was no way she would let anything interfere with that.

Her gaze slid back to Angel and lingered on his face as he listened to the captain. His flight suit emphasized his broad shoulders and lean hips, and Sedona wondered what he wore underneath. Maybe those sexy boxer briefs he'd been so eager to get out of last night.

Slowly, she became aware that the conference room was silent and several people had turned to look expectantly at her. She dragged her thoughts back to the present and realized Captain Dawson was showing a slide that identified the various inspection teams. Her name was at the top of one of the teams, and he was staring at her as if waiting for her to say something.

"Um, sorry," she mumbled, her face flaming. "I didn't catch that. Could you repeat the question, please?"

"I asked if you could introduce the members of your team and tell the others precisely what inspection functions you'll be performing."

Captain Dawson's face reminded Sedona of her father's when she'd insisted she wanted to study fine arts rather than engineering.

Disapproving.

Contemptuous.

For a moment, she panicked and couldn't find her voice. Her eyes flew to Angel. A slight frown furrowed his brow as he watched her.

She drew in a deep breath and quickly identified the other engineers who would be working alongside her. "My team will perform hot/cold section evaluation, as well as removal and inspection of engine system components, assessment of QEC kits and external engine components." She refused to look over at Angel. "We'll compare our findings to in-flight test data to identify anomalies or potential performance issues."

"Thank you, Miss Stewart." The commander's voice was dismissive.

Sedona sagged in her seat as Captain Dawson resumed his briefing, but it took several more minutes for her heart to slow down. She'd been caught unaware, not paying attention to her mission here at Lemoore, and all because she'd been too busy mooning over Angel. She really needed to get a grip on herself.

It was nearly an hour later when they followed Lieutenant Palmer out of the room to conduct a quick tour of the enormous hangar where the inspections would be performed.

God, she loved being around the aircraft. She loved the vaulted space inside the hangars, where swallows roosted in the shadows of the high, steel rafters. The rolling hoists and lifts, the enormous, portable tool chests, the oil containers, and the various vats of lubricants all fascinated her. She'd never admit it to anyone, but she even enjoyed the rich, acrid smell of the J-5 jet fuel.

She drifted to the back of the group, calculating how many hours would be required to perform each inspection. There were eighty-two grounded jets that would not be cleared for flight until the inspection teams had completed their work. Realistically, Sedona's team could examine two dozen engines in the two weeks they'd been allotted. This meant they would be required to extend their stay until they'd had an opportunity to inspect all the jets, or until the navy opted to bring in additional teams.

"Hey, you okay?"

Sedona looked up to see Angel fall into step beside her. She recalled her earlier lapse in the conference room and colored hotly.

"Yes, of course. Why wouldn't I be?"

He smiled then, a slow smile that said she didn't fool him with her act of nonchalance. "You were daydreaming back there, *mina*." His voice was so low she had to strain to hear his words. "About what? I wonder."

Sedona refused to look at him. "Not what you're so obviously thinking about," she denied. "I was just going over some of the engine-calibration figures in my head and lost track of what was being discussed."

"Uh-huh." His tone said he didn't believe a word. "Shall I tell you what I was thinking about?"

"No. Please…no."

"I was thinking about you, *mina*. On top of me."

"Oh." She turned even redder as heady images of straddling him swamped her imagination. "How nice."

"You bet."

She refused to look at him. If she did, he might see how desperately she wanted him, and that wouldn't do at all. She couldn't think about that now.

"What's nice?" piped a cheerful voice, and Sedona turned to see the maintenance technician from the conference room striding alongside them. She radiated vitality and sensual energy.

"Nothing," Sedona mumbled.

"Actually," Angel said smoothly, "I was just telling Miss Stewart how fortunate the navy is to have their jets in her capable hands. She comes highly recommended."

"Oh." There was no mistaking the surprise in the other woman's eyes as she raked Sedona with an appraising stare. "Lucky us, I guess." She thrust a hand out toward Angel. "I'm Petty Officer Heilmuller. You can call me Suzy." She gave him a cheeky grin. "I come highly recommended, too."

Yeah, for personal lube jobs.

Angel laughed, obviously amused by the other woman's brassy impudence as much as Sedona was annoyed by it.

"I think you'd both better pay attention to Lieutenant Palmer," Sedona said waspishly.

Anything to get Angel's attention off the other woman. Had he noticed the bosomy fräulein was a dead ringer for the St. Pauli Girl beer icon? Sedona knew her own appearance paled in comparison to Petty Officer Heilmuller's Germanic good looks.

Angel arched a brow, looking amused and seemingly undeterred by her caustic tone. "So this is where your team will be working," he said.

They had entered a section of the hanger near the massive doors that opened directly onto the flight line. Two Coyotes had already been rolled inside the hangar. They stood roped off and ready for inspection.

Sedona was always thrilled by the sight of the sleek aircraft. Standing fifteen feet off the ground, each jet was fifty-six feet long and boasted a wingspan of nearly forty feet. No matter how many times Sedona inspected a Coyote, she couldn't help but be impressed by the strength and beauty of the plane.

The rest of the inspection team had moved to the far side of the nearest jet. Lieutenant Palmer droned on about inspection protocol, about the importance of maintaining a clean work site and keeping unauthorized personnel from entering the space. She barely heard him. Nope, she was all about the aircraft. She just wished the brief and obligatory tour were over so they could get to work. She could hardly wait to get her hands on this baby's engines.

Stepping close to the Coyote, she reached up and ran an admiring hand along the nose. The metal was cool and smooth beneath her fingers. She ducked under the wing and stepped to the rear of the jet to take a peek at the engine afterburners, though she knew their configuration by heart.

"She's a beauty." Angel followed her beneath the wing. He ran a practiced eye over the plane. "There're a lot of frustrated pilots out there waiting for you to give the thumbs-up, Miss Stewart."

Sedona rolled her eyes at him, despite his words causing her imagination to surge. "You're speaking from experience, I presume?"

"What else?" He stepped closer to her, until she could smell the distinct fragrance of his soap and the underlying scent that was his alone. "I can attest to the fact that I am one frustrated pilot, *mina.*"

Sedona grew warm beneath his scrutiny. She pretended to be preoccupied with the long, smooth expanse of the wing, running her fingertip along its beveled edge. "I find that difficult to believe, Lieutenant Commander Torres, considering you completed several, ah, maneuvers just last night."

"That's true." He took a step closer. "However, that was only the maiden voyage. As a test pilot conducting trials, I barely became acquainted with this new asset. I believe additional evaluation is required."

Sedona's breathing quickened at the implicit promise in his eyes and the sultry tone of his voice. She glanced under the belly of the Coyote and saw the inspection group begin to move away from the aircraft toward the open doors of the hangar.

"Additional evaluation?" she echoed faintly. "Just what kind of evaluation would that be?"

"Oh, most definitely a performance evaluation." He grinned, a wicked gleam in his eyes. "You see, while I can provide assurance that all systems are operational, and the handling qualities are superb, there is still some question as to how she'll perform under…extreme conditions."

Whew. Either it was getting hot inside the hangar, or she was starting to spike a fever. She pushed a stray tendril of hair from her damp forehead and moistened her lips, when all she really wanted to do was tear her clothes off and drag Angel to the concrete floor. She'd show him extreme. She might not be overly experienced, but she was nothing if not inventive.

"Extreme conditions," she repeated, breathless. "As in…?"

"As in how high and fast can I push her?" His voice was low and husky, the faint Spanish accent more pronounced. "What kind of thrust can she tolerate without beginning to wobble, or shudder, or, worse, fly apart completely? How hot can her engines run before the inner liner of the combustor melts down?"

Sedona slid a finger inside the prim collar of her shirt, pulling it away from her skin. "Yes, I think I'm beginning to understand, Lieutenant Commander." She swallowed hard.

"But it sounds…dangerous. Are you certain you want to do this?"

He was so close, Sedona could see the individual spikes of his lashes and feel his warm breath against her cheek. He was too close. Too hot. Too completely irresistible.

"Oh, yes, *mina*," he purred, "I'm absolutely certain. The only question remaining is…am I cleared to launch?"

She was a goner.

With a soft sigh of surrender, Sedona leaned forward, her lashes drifted closed and her lips parted for the inevitability of his kiss.

"Sir? Ma'am?"

Sedona's eyes flew open and she leaped back from Angel. Unfocused, she turned abruptly away and then gave a sharp cry of pain as her head connected with the horizontal stabilizer, the small wings that protruded from the tail of the jet. Her eyes smarted with tears and she swiftly bent her head to hide her confusion. How was it that when Angel was near, she lost all ability to concentrate?

A young man peered at them from beneath the underbelly of the Coyote, and his blue eyes twinkled with unmistakable amusement. "Ah, sorry to interrupt, sir. Captain Dawson is asking for you."

Angel passed a hand over his eyes and then nodded his acknowledgment. "Thank you, Ensign." His voice sounded rough. "I'll be right there."

"Yessir." The man touched his fingers to his brow. "Ma'am." Then he was gone.

Sedona listened to the ensign's footsteps fade as he sprinted toward the hangar doors, and then pressed her hands against her cheeks, appalled. She had come so close to kissing Angel, right in the middle of the hangar. Worse, they'd almost had a witness. So much for maintaining a professional distance.

"Sedona."

She drew in a shaky breath and looked at Angel. The amusement and regret in his eyes nearly undid her. "Don't you dare apologize," she warned, hating the way her voice wobbled. "Just don't—don't do it again."

She brushed past him and walked quickly toward the exit. Angel reached her before she'd gone more than a half dozen steps. He captured her arm and swung her around.

"Angel, please," she whispered. "It's bad enough—"

"Are you hurt?"

Before she could protest, he uncinched the clip that kept her hair up, causing the unruly mass to tumble around her shoulders. He drew her forward and gently worked his fingers through the loose waves, probing her scalp where she'd struck it. The sensation was cathartic.

"Mmm." The soothing pressure of his fingers was delicious, making her want to melt against him. Just as quickly, she regained her senses and shoved his hands away, horrified. "Stop that. What are you doing?"

"You banged your head pretty hard back there. Are you sure you didn't hurt yourself?"

"Quite sure. I've been told I have a very hard head." She snatched the clip from his hands and turned away from him. It seemed when Angel was near, the only thing she could think about was him. She couldn't remember feeling like this about any other guy. Ever. He overwhelmed her, made her realize again just how completely out of her league she was.

Angel fell into step beside her as they walked through the hangar. He watched as she scooped her hair up and coiled it neatly before clamping it securely to the back of her head.

"Why do you wear it like that?" he asked. "I prefer your hair down."

"It's easier like this. Besides, I can't wear it down if I'm working near moving parts." She thought of Petty Officer

Heilmuller and her short crop of spiky blond hair. The technician managed to ooze sex appeal despite her olive-drab coverall and steel-toed boots. "Maybe one of these days I'll just get it all cut off and be done with it."

"That would be a shame, *mina,* considering how much I enjoy your hair spilled across my pillow." He gave her a roguish grin.

Sedona's stomach flipped and a peculiar heaviness descended into her pelvic region. She closed her eyes briefly against the images his words conjured. She needed to put some space between herself and Angel before she did something completely unacceptable in a military-aircraft hangar. She pictured Captain Dawson's reaction if he came across her clinging to Angel's neck with her legs wrapped around his waist and her tongue down his throat. She almost smiled. Nope, definitely not the way to get on the captain's good side.

She stepped outside into the brilliant sunshine of a cloudless day. Overhead, two low-altitude Coyotes rocketed through the skies in formation, and Sedona's entire body vibrated to the thunderous roar of their engines. Shielding her eyes, she watched them streak across the heavens until they disappeared on the horizon.

"Looks like they've already begun to conduct test flights," she commented. Lowering her hand, she arched an amused brow at Angel. "You're late, flyboy."

He grinned ruefully. "Actually, I was down on the flight line at 0500 hours." Seeing her look of dismay, he shrugged. "Must be the time difference. I couldn't sleep. I told the flight captain I'd report in later this morning, after the brief."

Sedona stared at him. "You could already be in the air, and yet you chose to come to this? Why?"

He gave her a quick smile. "Why else? Because you're here."

Without waiting for her response, he strode across the tarmac toward the assembled inspection teams, leaving Sedona to gape after him. He had voluntarily subjected himself to the painfully boring brief in order to see her? She blinked, then smiled. Oh, yeah. He'd definitely gone above and beyond the call of duty. She conjured up delicious images of just how she would reward him for his sacrifice.

10

"HEY, STEWART! You staying here all night, or what?"

Sedona hunched her shoulders and ignored Ken Larson. She couldn't leave the engine test cell, located in a concrete building next to the Coyote hangar, until she'd assured herself the tests they'd run that day were accurate.

"You know, it's okay to get out and party at least a little while you're here." His voice was friendly. Persuasive.

With a deliberate, long-suffering sigh, she swiveled in her chair to face him as he leaned against the doorjamb of the dimly lit calibration room. "Not all of us are here to screw around, Ken." *Well, at least not much.* "Some of us actually take our jobs seriously."

So seriously, she hadn't gotten back to her hotel room before ten o'clock for the past three nights, and hadn't seen Angel since that first morning at the briefing.

Undeterred, Ken glanced at his watch. "Yeah, well, it's almost eight o'clock, and all work and no play makes you a very dull girl." He grinned at her. "Why don't you go back to your room, get out of that jumpsuit and let me buy you a drink downstairs."

Sedona arched a brow at him. Was it possible he was hitting on her? She coughed indelicately and turned her back on him to resume her study of the test results. "What's wrong, Ken? Striking out with the babes at the hotel bar? Afraid if you don't get somebody to sleep with you, you'll miss out on the next big promotion?"

She didn't hear him enter the room, didn't know he was close until suddenly, his face was next to hers as he leaned over her shoulder and spoke softly into her ear.

"Actually, Sedona, I was hoping we could come to some kind of…arrangement. After all, you said you wanted to join the club." She stiffened when he took a loose tendril of her hair in his hand and rubbed it slowly between his finger and thumb. His voice was low and silky. "I was thinking we could kill two birds with one stone. We could have a great time together, you know. We could get naked, take a few photos and maybe both get promoted."

As Sedona sat rigid with surprise, he turned his face fractionally and inhaled. "Mmm, you smell good. I wonder if you taste as sweet." His face moved toward hers.

She shot to her feet so fast the chair skittered out from beneath her and Ken took a hasty step back to avoid hitting his chin on her shoulder. Her heart slammed in her chest and her blood pulsed in her ears.

They stared at each other for a long moment until finally, Ken laughed softly and stepped back. "Think about it, Sedona. I haven't had any complaints about my performance, and I wouldn't expect our relationship to continue once we get back to the office." He grinned as he looked her over. "But we sure could have a hell of a time while we're here."

"Somehow," she finally managed to say, "I don't think so. I—I've changed my mind about the whole thing. But thanks for the offer."

He backed away slowly, his grin never wavering. "Well, okay, if that's how you feel about it. But if you change your mind, you just let me know."

"I'll do that." *When hell freezes over.*

She heard him whistling as he made his way down the narrow flight of stairs and out the building. She rubbed a trembling hand across her eyes, and reminded herself that if Ken thought she was up for a little casual sex, she had no one to blame but herself. She'd all but begged the Membership to let her prove she, too, could have meaningless sex with a stranger. He probably thought he was doing her a favor by offering himself up as stud. Just thinking about sex with Ken Larson made her shudder. How was she going to work with the guy for the next week and a half?

They were only into their third day, but it felt more like three weeks. Each day, the routine was the same. Under Sedona's watchful eye, a team of navy technicians pulled the engines from each of the hangared aircraft and brought them into four separate test cells. With four engineers on her team, including herself and Ken Larson, they each tested one engine per day.

Sedona examined the records for each engine prior to the engine teardown. During the disassembly, the team recorded torque values and then inspected each component for damage, wear or erosion. The engine components were also boroscoped for cracking.

Sedona spent the entire day behind a window of tempered glass, seated at a control panel that glowed with a multitude of lights, levers and illuminated displays, while she conducted calibration and performance testing on her engine.

While the work wasn't physically demanding, it was mentally exhausting. Worse, the room reeked of the jet fuel they'd guzzled their way through during the tests. Normally, she didn't mind the smell, but today it made her feel queasy.

She'd run several of the tests more than once, had painstakingly compared her findings to the model specifications and, to her relief, everything she'd tested thus far had come up negative. Long after the other engineers and the team of navy technicians had packed away their tools and returned to their hotel or billets, Sedona remained in the calibration room to pore over the test results for those engines she hadn't personally tested.

She didn't want to miss anything vital. There was no way she'd let Angel fly with a compromised engine. She needed to assure herself they were in perfect condition before she allowed them to be reinstalled on the jets.

If she'd known Ken Larson was going to come back down to check on her, she'd have left long ago. She hated to admit it, but the calibration lab made her nervous after hours. It was dark and isolated, and eerily quiet without the residual noise that came with running the engines.

She tore the sheet of paper from the readout machine and stared blindly at the numbers recorded there. A dark thought occurred to her. Did Ken make the offer out of sympathy because he didn't think she could attract a guy on her own? She might not have a body like Petty Officer Heilmuller, but Angel hadn't had any complaints.

Of course, Angel hadn't sought her out since that first morning in the Coyote hangar, either. She didn't think he was avoiding her, but she couldn't help feeling a little bit hurt that he hadn't made an effort to see her again. It didn't help telling herself he was as busy as she was. In addition to conducting the flight tests, the pilots spent hours briefing the rear admiral and his staff on their findings at the end of each day. Combined with her own long days, she'd be lucky if they managed to connect even one more time during the course of their stay.

The thought was completely depressing.

What if it was true? What if the one night she'd had with Angel was all she was ever going to have? She'd thought it would be enough. Hell, less than a week ago she'd have given her left arm for just one night with him.

Crumpling the paper in her hands, she realized it wasn't enough. She wanted more. Wanted to hear his seductive voice enticing her to do things she'd only ever dreamed about. She wanted to see his face tauten with desire, see the muscles tighten in his jaw, neck and shoulders as he fought to retain control.

She hadn't stopped thinking about him since that night. She tried not to wonder why he hadn't contacted her. Because she was weak, she avoided going back to her room, worried that she might throw open the connecting doors and fling herself at him. Only pride kept her from completely humiliating herself.

However, it hadn't prevented her from pressing her ear to the door each night for some sign of activity. Some indication that he was there, yet apparently not interested enough to turn the knob and invite her in. In his defense, his room had been completely silent each night. It seemed no matter what time she returned, he returned later. It was clear that unless she took some drastic action, the likelihood of engaging Angel in another night of bliss was remote, at best.

Throwing the crumpled paper into the wastebasket, she leaned over the test console to shut the power down. She wasn't going to accomplish much more tonight, anyway. Tomorrow, the technicians would reinstall the engines they'd tested today and roll the aircraft back onto the flight line. Then they would bring four more aircraft in, and the process would start all over again. She'd have at least a few hours in the morning to rerun the printouts. She didn't need to stay in the calibration room any longer.

She drew the door closed behind her and locked it, before making her way down the stairwell. Outside, the night was dark and cool. A partial moon helped to illuminate the walkway that led toward the parking lot. The stars over the desert were breathtaking, and Sedona stood for a moment, admiring them.

She was turning toward the parking lot when she noticed a movement beneath one of the jets in the flight line. Was that an animal of some kind? She'd heard that wild coyotes sometimes wandered onto the base, and she sincerely hoped this wasn't one of them. How far away was it? A hundred yards? If the animal decided it wanted to eat her, could she outrun it?

She was debating whether to slip back into the building or make a dash for her car, when the figure shifted. As she watched, it unfolded and stretched upright, and she sagged with relief when she realized it was a man.

Who was he, and why was he out on the flight line at this time of night? Even as it occurred to her that the man might not be authorized to be there, he turned and began walking toward her. A frisson of fear feathered its way along her neck. Just as she was debating whether or not to run, she recognized the man as Lieutenant Palmer, the maintenance officer in charge of the Coyotes.

"Miss Stewart?" There was no mistaking the surprise in his voice.

Sedona expelled a shaky laugh of relief. "Oh, my God, you scared me. I thought at first you were a coyote. You know, the four-legged kind."

He stepped closer, and Sedona could see he was wearing civilian clothing. It was strange to see him out of uniform.

"I'm sorry." He smiled. "I didn't mean to make you nervous." He gestured toward the aircraft. "I was, uh, just doing my final check of the jets before calling it a night." He peered at her. "What are you still doing here?"

"Oh, I was in the calibration room going over some results on the last engine we tested." She laughed. "I won't do that again. This place totally creeps me out after dark."

"Can I walk you to your car?"

"Thanks, no. I'm fine, now that I know you're not some wild animal or escaped lunatic." She didn't miss how his eyebrows shot up. "That was a joke."

"Well, good night, then."

"Bye." Sedona made her way to the parking lot. Halfway down the walkway, she couldn't resist peeking back over her shoulder, mildly disconcerted to see the lieutenant standing where she'd left him, watching her.

She was still thinking about him as she slid into her rental car and began the drive back to the hotel. Was it normal for a maintenance officer to perform checks on the aircraft so late at night? And if he was on duty, why was he out of uniform? She made a mental note to mention the incident to Angel when she saw him.

If she saw him.

Since that first night with Angel, she'd kept her own side of the connecting doors unlocked and open. She didn't even want to think about why Angel had left his door firmly closed. She hadn't had the nerve to try to open it, and the whole thing was beginning to make her crazy. She needed advice, and she needed it now.

As she drove, she rummaged through her backpack and dug out her cell phone, biting her lip as she punched in her sister's cell-phone number. She didn't know if Ana was working tonight or not, but knew her shift wouldn't start until later. Ana's workday kicked into full gear about the same time Sedona's ended.

"Sedona? Hey, this is unbelievable! I was just thinking about you. Really!"

Sedona couldn't help but smile as she heard Ana's voice. Always cheerful, always upbeat, Ana was the epitome of the free spirit. Sometimes Sedona envied her ability to do as she pleased, without regard for what anyone else thought.

"Hey, sis. I was thinking about you, too."

"So what's up? You never call unless there's a problem."

Was that true? Surely she'd called Ana just to tell her she missed her, or to ask how her life was going. But, try as she might, she couldn't recall the last time she'd done that.

"No, everything is good. I mean, Mom is fine and Allison is fine. I just, um, had something I needed to ask you. You know—" she cringed inwardly "—a girl thing."

There was a momentary, stunned silence. "Oh, my freaking God. You've met someone."

Sedona laughed. "Yeah, something like that."

"You've met a guy? Oh, Sedona, that's great!"

Sedona laughed again, this time at the unabashed relief and sincere joy in Ana's voice. "Yeah, it is pretty great. He's…" She paused. "He's the most amazing guy I've ever met and…Ana?"

"Yes?"

"He's incredible in bed."

There was a shrill squeal of delight. "You slept with him! Oh, my God! This is so unbelievable! Tell me everything!"

Sedona did, leaving nothing out, not even the striptease she'd performed for Angel, or the adult movie they'd watched for all of eight minutes before he'd rolled her beneath him. She told Ana everything she knew about him, including the fact she'd had a serious crush on the guy for over a year.

The only thing she didn't tell Ana was her discovery of the secret club that promoted men based on their sexual activities. Nor could she bring herself to talk about Ken Larson and his repugnant offer to get them both promoted by engaging in an affair.

"Anyway," she said, sighing, "I haven't seen Angel since Wednesday morning, and I'm trying not to freak out about it, but what if he's not interested anymore? What if it really was just a one-nighter?"

"Okay, listen," soothed Ana, "this is what you do. Trust me in this, sweetie. There isn't a guy out there who won't roll over and beg at the sight of a beautiful woman, naked and primed, in his bed."

"I am *not* beautiful," Sedona protested with a self-conscious laugh. "You got the looks and I got the brains, remember?"

Ana snorted. "All I remember is you wanting to do everything in your power to make Dad happy, including being the son he never had."

Sedona frowned. "Is that really what you think?"

"It doesn't matter. It's water long under the bridge, and Dad's probably beaming down at you for fulfilling every dream he ever had."

"But not you," Sedona mused aloud, turning in to the parking lot of the hotel. "You thumbed your nose at him and took off for the West Coast."

Ana laughed. "If you say so, sis. I think you missed a lot of what really happened. You were in college by then, remember."

Sedona sighed as she parked the car and turned off the ignition. She didn't really want to remember. Too many of those memories were colored by resentment and unhappiness. What Ana said was true; it was water under the bridge.

"You're right. So tell me what I should do now. I mean, there's always the possibility Angel is avoiding me. I don't want to set myself up for a big fat rejection."

"Honey," Ana drawled, "what I have in mind is absolutely, one hundred percent rejection-proof."

And as she outlined her simple plan for seduction, Sedona had to agree; it sounded pretty foolproof. Daring? Yes. Audacious? Definitely. Designed to bring a guy to his knees? She certainly hoped so.

Fifteen minutes later, she let herself into her room. Unzipping her navy-issue jumpsuit, she crossed to the connecting doors. With one ear pressed against the panels, she hopped first on one foot and then the other as she pulled her shoes off.

Nothing but silence.

Quickly, without turning on any interior lights, Sedona crept out onto her balcony and peered over the railing at the room next to hers. It was completely dark. Angel had not yet returned to the hotel. Or if he had, he'd left again.

Slipping back into the room, she sprinted to the bathroom for the fastest shower of her life. He could come back at any moment. She had to be ready. She stood under the shower and let the hard spray of water loosen the knots of uncertainty in her neck and shoulders. This would work. She refused to be a victim of her own self-doubts. She was desirable. She was feminine.

Or she could be.

She just had to let herself go. At least, that's what Ana had said. She only hoped she had the courage to do what Ana recommended.

Stepping out of the shower, she wrapped her hair in a towel and scrubbed herself dry before wrapping a second towel around her body. She rubbed her hand over the condensation on the bathroom mirror and leaned forward to examine her face.

Her pupils were huge, drowning out the green irises. She bit some color into her lips and pinched her cheeks, wishing she owned some cosmetics to even out her complexion. She yanked the towel from her hair and scrubbed it vigorously. She rarely used a blow-dryer as it only made her hair frizzy. Better to let it dry naturally into the thick waves that defied styling.

With the towel still wrapped around her body, she crept back to the connecting doors and pressed her ear once more against the panels. Still nothing.

Biting her lip, she tried the knob and her heart leaped when it turned effortlessly beneath her fingers. That had been the one unknown variable in the equation. According to Ana, if the door was unlocked then Angel definitely wanted more action, even if he didn't realize it.

The adjoining room was dark and quiet. As she stepped inside, she caught a subtle whiff of Angel's aftershave and froze, half expecting him to materialize from the shadows. When all remained quiet, she drew a fortifying breath and switched on the bedside lamp. She yanked the brightly flowered bedspread down to the foot of the bed and plumped the pillows invitingly. She tuned the bedside radio to an easy-listening station.

Then she dropped the towel, stretched herself out on Angel's bed and waited.

GOD, HE WAS TIRED. Angel scrubbed a hand over his eyes as he rode the elevator to the third floor of the hotel. He'd conducted two flight tests that day, pushing the aircraft through their paces in a punishing routine guaranteed to root out any performance issues.

The jets had performed flawlessly.

Afterward, he and the other test pilots had completed the reams of paperwork required to document the tests, and had spent several long hours in the admiral's conference room, bringing the senior brass up-to-date. He was completely fried.

The elevator doors slid open and he drew his key card out of his wallet as he walked to his room. He paused briefly outside Sedona's door and checked his watch. It was barely nine o'clock. Had she returned? Or was she still in the calibration room, poring over the test results? He raised his hand to knock, then hesitated. He doubted Sedona would thank him for showing up smelling of jet fuel and sweat. He could really use a shower.

He let his hand fall back to his side.

He'd hoped to hook up with her tonight, either for dinner or something a little more intimate, but had been roped into going to the officers' club for a quick bite with the other pilots, instead. He'd tried to call Sedona on her cell phone, and was frustrated when he hadn't been able to get through to her.

But he'd been unable to stop thinking about her, and when his buddies said they were going to finish the evening at a local strip club, he'd declined and headed back to the hotel. If Sedona returned to her room before ten o'clock, he intended to keep her fully occupied for several hours, at least. But a shower was definitely in order. Reluctantly, he turned away from her door.

Inserting the key card into his own door, he pushed it open and then stopped dead in his tracks, speechless. Lying on top of his bed, looking like every erotic fantasy he'd ever had, was Sedona.

Naked.

Smiling.

Waiting for him.

Every cell in his body snapped to attention.

Her pale golden skin seemed to gleam in the soft light. Her hair tumbled in an enticing mass around her face, and the bedside lamp cast intriguing shadows across the curves and contours of her luscious body.

She lay on her side with her head propped on one hand, and as he watched, she bent her top leg and slid it upward until her knee hid the enticing juncture of her thighs from view. He drank in the graceful dip of her waist, the rounded curve of hip and thigh, and the pale globes of her breasts, full and begging for his touch.

She reached up and twirled a tendril of hair lazily around one finger as her smiled widened. "So, flyboy," she murmured in a sultry voice, "you going to shut the door, or stand there until you draw a crowd?"

With a start, Angel realized he was still standing with the door open, his hand on the knob. Shock, and then pure, unadulterated delight had rendered him momentarily incapable of movement. He stepped into the room, dropped his flight bag onto the floor and let the door close with a click behind him. He didn't take his eyes off Sedona as he flipped the dead bolt and slid the security chain into place. No way would he allow anyone to interrupt this.

"So, flyboy," she crooned, sliding her legs sinuously against each other and allowing him a brief, alluring glimpse of the dark patch of curls between her legs, "how was your day?"

He grinned as his body responded with wholehearted enthusiasm to the visual stimulation she provided. "Much better now," he assured her, and stood at the edge of the bed and looked at her. He didn't dare let himself touch her. He just looked, and as he did so, her body slowly flushed with color.

Sedona released the tendril of hair and artfully ran a hand over the curve of hip and thigh. "I couldn't stop thinking about you," she said in a husky voice. "The more I thought about you, the hornier I got."

O-kay. This was unexpected. His grin faltered for a moment as he tried to decide if she was teasing him. "Really."

"Mmm." She sent him an inviting look from beneath her eyelashes. "I've been waiting for such a long time for you to…come."

Her words sent a bolt of liquid heat straight to his groin. He couldn't help himself. He leaned over her to capture her lips. It had been too long since he'd tasted her. But before he could kiss her, she turned her face to the side and pushed him back with a surprisingly forceful hand against his chest.

"Not so fast," she purred.

He straightened and frowned down at her, his body already pulsing with need. What game was she playing? "Christ, *mina*," he said on a half laugh, "don't torture me, okay?"

In answer, she rolled fully onto her back and bent one arm gracefully over her head. The movement pulled her breasts higher and tautened the slender line of her waist. She skated the fingers of her free hand over her body, finally settling on her breast.

"Why not?" she asked, all innocence. "After all, you've tortured me for the past three days."

Angel swallowed, riveted by the delicate play of her fingers against her nipple. As he watched, it tightened into a small bud. He dragged his attention upward, to her face. She studied him from beneath her lashes, and her breath quickened.

"Oh, yes," she breathed. "Every time I thought of you, it was torture. I thought of you doing this."

Angel's body tightened as she arched her back and cupped both breasts in her hands. She alternately squeezed and pinched them, and her hips shifted restlessly against the sheets.

"Okay, *mina*," he finally rasped. "I think I understand. You're feeling neglected, but if you'll just let me—"

He unzipped his flight suit with lightning speed, and peeled it from his shoulders and arms until it hung around his waist. He yanked his T-shirt over his head and sent it sailing, but when he would have unzipped his flight suit farther, she put out a hand and restrained him.

"Wait."

She twisted around and plumped the pillows up behind her. Then reclined back in a half-sitting position. Her knees fell slightly apart and Angel just about wept when he glimpsed her feminine folds. He wanted so badly to touch her. Taste her. Take her.

"Mina," he groaned, "have mercy."

"I want you to watch," she said breathlessly. "I want you to watch what happens to my body when I think about you."

Slowly, then, with her eyes caressing him, she began to tease her breasts with both hands. Then, as a flush deepened on her neck and face, she slid the palm of one hand down over her abdomen until she cupped herself. "Oh," she said. sighing, "I'm so hot. And wet. And that's just from looking at you."

Angel groaned. Mesmerized, he reached over and hauled the hard-backed chair from the desk closer, until he could sit and watch. His heart thudded hard enough that he was sure she would hear it, and the instant her hand dropped low on her body, he broke out in a fine sweat.

His breathing quickened as she used two fingers to open herself, and he swiftly adjusted his seat for an unobstructed view. She obliged by spreading her legs wider.

"Oh, yes," she breathed, and dipped a finger ever so slightly into herself. It came away glistening, and she touched the moisture to her clitoris. "Oh, that feels good."

Her folds were pale pink and smooth, and Angel longed to touch his tongue to them. He shifted uncomfortably in his seat, helpless to look away. She swirled her finger over the spot where he knew she felt the most intense pleasure, drawing her clitoris from its secret fold until it began to blossom.

Angel stared, transfixed by the changes he witnessed. Her gorgeous sex changed, grew flushed and engorged as her desire increased. The sight of Sedona pleasuring herself was the most erotic thing he'd ever seen. His balls ached, and his cock throbbed painfully within the confines of the jumpsuit. It took every ounce of self-restraint not to free himself and take over what she was doing.

"Please," he groaned, and moved to sit on the edge of the bed near her feet, "I need to touch you."

"No," she gasped, her hips gyrating, "you just need to watch."

She inserted a second finger alongside the first, and her head fell back as she let out a soft moan. Then she slid her free hand down her body until both hands were seductively engaged between her thighs. As she pumped two fingers into herself, she used the other hand to caress and stroke her clitoris, sliding a finger down either side of it until it stood out, flushed and swollen, against her tender flesh.

It took all of Angel's hard-won discipline not to reach out and touch her. He pressed the palm of his hand hard against the base of his swollen cock and willed himself not to come. But when he realized Sedona watched him through half-closed eyes, her mouth moist and parted, he was done.

With a subdued growl, he stood up and stripped the flight suit down his legs, pushing his briefs down with it until his erection sprang free. He reached over and grabbed a condom from the bedside table and, in one deft movement, covered himself.

"I'm sorry, *mina,*" he said huskily, and with his flight suit still bunched around his ankles, he propped himself above her. "You make me crazy, you know that."

Poised at the entrance to her body, he braced himself with his hands on either side of her and stared down at her flushed face. She had stopped touching herself, mercifully, but she still writhed her hips in a manner that made him groan with lust.

"Come into me," she breathed. Her green eyes were cloudy with desire as she gazed up at him. "Let's see how my body reacts when I do more than just think about you, when I join myself with you…"

Her words were like a catalyst, crumbling the last remaining fragments of his self-control. With a ragged sigh of surrender, he buried himself in her tightness. She came immediately, crying out with pleasure as her flesh contracted around his length.

Angel watched her face, enthralled, as she climaxed. His chest tightened. It was incredible to watch. The combination of the visual and the physical stimulation was too much, and with a harsh cry, he exploded in a white-hot rush of pleasure that caused his eyes to roll back in his head and his back to arch.

Long minutes later, when he could breathe again, he rolled to his side, pulling Sedona with him. "Damn," he gasped. "Where did you learn to do that?"

Sedona laughed softly and curled her body against his. "Years of practice. But," she added almost shyly, "this is the first time I've had an audience."

He raised his head and looked down at her, stunned. "You're kidding."

"What? You think I do this for a living?"

"No, that's not what I meant." He blew out his breath and lay back against the pillows. He tightened his arm around her. "I'm just thinking what an incredible turn-on that was." And how goddamn sorry he was for every guy who'd never get the chance to experience it firsthand. Just the thought of any other guy watching Sedona do *that* caused a surge of jealousy so intense it startled him.

Sliding his arm out from beneath Sedona, he swung his legs over the side of the bed and sat up. He discreetly disposed of the condom, surprised to see he still wore his flight boots. The mattress shifted behind him as Sedona came up on her knees and pressed herself against his back. She wound her arms around his neck and planted a moist kiss against his jaw.

"Hey," she murmured in his ear. "You okay?"

"Yeah." He didn't dare look at her, afraid she might see the conflicting emotions churning inside him. Jealousy. Need. And, unbelievably, desire. He bent over and unlaced his boots and kicked them to the floor, then pushed the rest of his clothing off. "I, uh, was going to knock on your door tonight," he finally admitted.

"Oh. I guess I sort of preempted you again, huh? Sorry."

She sounded anything but sorry as she caressed his chest. Could she feel his heart beating hard beneath her fingers? He shivered when she feathered a kiss along the nape of his neck.

"Mmm," she murmured, "you smell good."

Angel arched a brow in disbelief. "I smell like jet fuel. In fact, I was headed into the shower before I knocked on your door."

"Didn't I tell you?" She caught his earlobe gently between her teeth and then swirled her tongue against the sensitive skin. "Jet fuel is my new favorite scent. But a shower sounds…interesting. I could wash your back. Or something."

Her voice was sweetly seductive and Angel almost groaned aloud as he recalled their last shower together. It gave a whole new meaning to the term *oral hygiene*. Just thinking about that intimate exchange, combined with the moist heat of her tongue in his ear, had him growing hard again.

He laughed ruefully and disentangled himself from her arms before standing up to let her see the proof of his need.

"Oh." Her eyes widened when she saw he was ready for her again. She uncurled her legs from beneath her, scooted to the edge of the mattress and grasped his hips, drawing him into the V of her legs. "Oh, my."

But when she would have reached for him, he forestalled her, grabbing both her hands in his and tugging her to her feet. "Oh, no you don't," he growled down at her. "If you touch me, I'm toast, and since I plan on spending the next—" he glanced at his wristwatch "—six hours loving you, long and slow, let's see if you can manage to keep your hands to yourself for a while."

Sedona laughed and fell back onto the bed, throwing her arms outward in a sign of surrender. "I'm all yours, flyboy."

She watched him through heavily lidded eyes, but the uneven rise and fall of her chest let Angel know she wasn't nearly as unaffected as she let on. He eased himself down on one elbow beside her, letting his gaze travel over her.

He traced a finger over her pale hip bone and admired the whorl of her navel. He pressed his palm against her rib cage, just beneath her breast. Her heart beat fast under his fingers. Leaning over her, he pressed a kiss to the spot.

"God," he said, and sighed, his breath tickling her soft flesh, "I want you again. Unbelievable."

Her tummy contracted as she chuckled. "And here I thought you weren't letting me touch you because you didn't like me."

Angel raised his head and looked at her over the enticing mounds of her breasts. "I think we both know that's not the problem," he said hoarsely, and slowly worked his way upward to her mouth.

Man, oh, man, the woman could kiss. The problem had nothing to do with not liking her, he thought as he pulled her closer, and everything to do with liking her way too much.

11

"I CAN'T FIND anything wrong with any of them. They all seem pretty perfect to me." Sedona stood at the edge of the sun-baked flight line and watched as a dozen or more maintenance officers, each clad in a bright-red T-shirt and camouflage pants, prepared to roll two more Coyote jets into the hangar for inspection.

"Oh, yeah," purred Petty Officer Heilmuller beside her. "No argument there, ma'am. They're all prime cuts."

Turning to the other woman, Sedona made a sound of exasperation. "I was talking about the jet engines."

To her amazement, Petty Officer Heilmuller gave her a broad wink. "Sure you were. Ma'am."

Sedona watched the other woman saunter back toward the hangar, idly swinging a long wrench from one hand. It was just her luck the attractive petty officer had been assigned to her inspection team. Although, to her credit, she was an accomplished mechanic, despite her sometimes ribald sense of humor. On top of that, the other woman was right; Sedona couldn't remember the last time she'd been surrounded by so many young, virile, good-looking guys. Not that it mattered to her, of course. Next to Angel Torres, they were merely boys.

Shading her eyes, she peered farther down the flight line to where two pilots were conducting a visual inspection of a pair of Coyotes in preparation for a test flight. She didn't have to see his face to know one of the pilots was Angel. His tall, broad-shouldered physique was difficult to mistake.

She thought again of the previous night, and couldn't stop smiling at the memories of what they'd done together. The guy was beyond amazing. He hadn't walked her back to her own room in the wee hours of the morning as he'd done their first night together. Instead, she'd stayed wrapped around him until the alarm clock on his wristwatch went off at 4:30 a.m. He'd kissed her and left her in his bed while he took a shower. She'd curled up on the edge of the mattress and watched him as he dressed.

"Sleep in this morning," he'd said as he knelt next to the bed and smoothed her hair back from her face. "I'll send a message over to the inspection team that you had a conference call with Joe or something."

"That's okay," she murmured, smiling up at him. His hair gleamed, sleek as a seal's, from his shower and he smelled delicious. His flight suit was open at the throat, revealing the drab olive-colored T-shirt beneath. "If you can get up this early, so can I."

"Okay." He leaned forward and kissed her so sweetly she'd been tempted to pull him back into bed. "I'll try and get back early tonight, okay? Wait for me?"

Wait for him? Was he kidding? She'd been waiting for him her whole life.

"I'll be right here," she'd responded with a smile. "Well, maybe not right here, exactly. But next door."

She longed for the day to be over. She still had the sense that she was part of a surreal dream, and any moment she'd wake up to find herself back in the unexciting, predictable reality of her plain-Jane life. She didn't want to think too much about what it was that Angel saw in her. She wasn't superstitious, but there was a small part of her that prescribed to the theory of self-fulfilling prophecy. If she couldn't understand why Angel was with her, eventually he'd begin to wonder why, as well. She wasn't naive enough to believe their relationship could possibly last, but she wouldn't do anything to jeopardize it, either.

"Hey, Stewart, want to take a walk with me?"

Sedona turned away from watching Angel, to see Ken Larson striding across the tarmac toward her. She shoved her hands into her pockets. "Not particularly."

"I think you might want to reconsider." He was wearing aviator sunglasses with mirrored lenses, and Sedona couldn't read the expression in his blue eyes.

"Why?"

He jerked his head in the direction of the hangar. "They just brought in the two Coyotes that experienced in-flight engine failures. They're over in Hangar 74. The navy investigation team responsible for inspecting the damaged aircraft is going over them with a fine-tooth comb, but I thought it would be a good opportunity to see what kind of damage the engines sustained. Maybe it'll provide clues as to what we should be looking for."

"Are you kidding?" Sedona's excitement level kicked into high gear. "What are we doing standing here? Let's go."

Finally, something that might provide a hint as to why the Coyotes had crashed. Nearly a week of inspections had turned up nothing. All systems were fully operational and showed no signs of damage or malfunction. She had wondered about the jets that had suffered mishaps, but she hadn't hoped to actually see any of them.

"So," Ken said as they followed the road that led along the flight line to Hangar 74, "what'd you do last night? I sort of hoped to see you downstairs in the lounge, but you never showed."

Sedona gave a sidelong look. "Why would I?"

He spread his hands. "Hey, my offer still stands. I mean, think about it. We're friends, right?"

"I guess," Sedona said warily.

"Well, we could be friends with benefits." He swept her body with an appreciative glance. "We could get wild together, take a couple of photos, then give the evidence to the Membership and get promoted, right?"

Sedona stopped walking and stared at him, mortified. "Ken," she began, "I'm flattered by your interest, but I already told you—" She broke off with a laugh. "I'm no longer interested in being part of the Membership. In truth, there's no way I'd *ever* sleep with somebody just to get ahead in my job. So the answer isn't just *no,* it's *hell no.*"

"You know what your problem is, Stewart?" Ken's voice had turned hard and cold. "You think you're better than everyone else. I know your kind. I've had to deal with bitches like you my entire life. If a guy doesn't meet your exacting standards, he's beneath your notice."

What the...? Sedona couldn't keep the astonishment out of her voice. "What is your problem, Larson? That I won't sleep with you?" She stared at him incredulously. "Get over it. I don't sleep with coworkers."

Ken jerked his sunglasses off. His face was flushed and his eyes simmered with anger at whatever old memories still haunted him. Sedona watched as he visibly struggled with his emotions. Finally, he gave a grim parody of a smile.

"Oh, yeah? Well, here's a news flash for you, Stewart." He leaned slightly forward, until his face was so close, Sedona could see the individual pores of his skin. "There's only one way to get a promotion in this place and you'll never see one."

Sedona watched through narrowed eyes as he strode away, telling herself it didn't matter what he thought.

"Because you don't have what it takes, Stewart," he called back over his shoulder, "in business or in bed."

She shook her head in bemusement as she watched him go. Why had she never realized what a jerk Ken was? She'd been so duped by his easygoing, friendly manner that she hadn't seen he was really no better than Mike "Hound Dog" Sullivan. She told herself his insults couldn't truly hurt her. After all, she was heading up the engine inspection team and sharing bed space with the most perfect guy she'd ever known. All things considered, she'd say she definitely had what it took, both in business and in bed.

SEDONA LEANED OVER Senior Chief Hamlin's shoulder for a closer look at the damaged engine. She and Ken had been permitted to come into the hangar to view the jets, but only after they'd promised not to touch anything. While Sedona looked at the first engine, Ken had deliberately moved away from her to look at the second of the two engines. Fine. She didn't want him hanging over her shoulder.

The engines had been removed from the aircraft and hung suspended from two enormous rolling hoists. Portable workbenches positioned around the first of the crippled Coyotes were littered with boxes of parts that had been tagged and labeled. The smell of oil and grease hung heavy on the air, and the metallic clang of tools contrasted with the high-pitched whine of electric drills and pneumatic wrenches.

"Check out the blades on this blisk," Sedona observed, circling the engine to get a better view of the fan blades. The ends were bent and mangled, as if something small and hard had been sucked through at high speed.

"Yes, ma'am," answered the maintenance officer. "We found a loose ball bearing in the HPC module. If the pilot hadn't shut down the engine when he did, it would have blown out the back and we'd probably never know what caused the damage."

"But how—"

The senior chief shrugged. "Ball bearings are an integral part of the engine components, ma'am. There are several dozen of them throughout. Could've been any one of them that came loose."

"Hmm. I suppose it's possible," Sedona conceded, but inwardly she had her doubts. Without exception, the ball bearings were encased within a titanium or Kevlar housing to prevent them from coming loose. Foreign-object damage was a prime cause of engine failure. To have a ball bearing come loose during engine operation could have catastrophic consequences.

"What about the other Coyote? Have her engines been removed yet? Have you determined if the damage is similar?"

The senior chief glanced up at her with an amused smile. "We're working on it, ma'am. At this point, nothing has been determined. After all, the Coyotes only arrived this morning."

Sedona nodded, embarrassed. "Right. Well, I'd be very interested in your findings." She tilted her head, surveying the bent and twisted fan blades with pursed lips. "These Coyotes are originally from Lemoore, right?"

"Yes, ma'am," he replied. "They all launched from that flight line, right out there." He jerked his thumb in the direction of the hangar doors. "All within twenty-four hours of each other. Coincidence?"

Sedona arched a brow at him. "What do you think?"

"I think you'd better check the remaining birds very carefully, that's what I think."

Sedona turned to look at the flight line. Angel was flying one of those jets right now. The thought of him encountering a problem with the engines midair caused her stomach to clench.

"Who oversees the flight tests?" she asked.

"That'd be Captain Dawson, ma'am," the senior chief replied. "He's got an office over at command headquarters, but I think he's been working out of Building 281 while the investigation is going on."

Sedona sighed inwardly. The thought of having to deal with Captain Dawson made her temples throb. He reminded her too much of her father.

"Is there somebody else—a lieutenant or somebody— who coordinates the flight tests? I mean, Captain Dawson has to have someone else doing the bulk of the work for him, right?"

"Yes, ma'am. Lieutenant Palmer oversees the plane captains. There're a dozen or more of them on the flight line. They control the flight plans and perform the final inspections before the jets actually leave the ground."

His words reminded Sedona of the previous night when she had seen Lieutenant Palmer on the flight line. She'd completely forgotten to mention it to Angel.

"Does Lieutenant Palmer also perform inspections?" she asked.

"Sure. He knows more about those jets than most of the plane captains. Hell," the chief continued, "he's spent more time learning how to fly them than anyone I know."

"Lieutenant Palmer is a Coyote pilot?"

"Nah. He went through the training a couple of times, but couldn't get through the final stage of the flight program. Some kind of medical problem is what I heard." The senior chief shrugged. "But man, it takes balls to go through that program once, never mind three times, and still not make the cut."

"Wow, what a shame."

"You bet. I heard he was pretty torn up about it."

"So where would I find one of these plane captains?"

The senior chief nodded toward the flight line. "That might be a couple of them over there. Too far to tell for sure, but one of them looks like Wheeler, and I think the one on the left is Airman Laudano. He's an aviation machinist's mate."

Sedona flashed him a quick smile. "Thanks very much. And you'll let me know what you find on the other engines, right?"

The senior chief saluted. "Yes, ma'am."

Leaving the hangar, she made her way across the tarmac to where the fleet of Coyotes were lined up, dull pewter beneath the blue sky. She noted with approval that the jets had been separated into two groups—those that had been inspected and those that had not.

As she drew closer, she saw three men standing close together, reviewing some kind of paperwork. They each wore a helmet equipped with ear protectors and a microphone. Dark goggles were pushed up onto the top of the helmets, and one man had two bright-orange flight sticks shoved in his back pocket.

"Excuse me," she called. "Airman Laudano?"

The three men lifted their heads. The one nearest her looked like an advertisement for the all-American boy next door. Sedona glanced at his name patch. Ryan Wheeler, aviation machinist's mate. He gave her a shy smile and nodded toward the man next to him, who stepped away from the others, toward her.

God, when did they start enlisting babies? The boy couldn't be more than fourteen. Okay, maybe sixteen.

"I'm Laudano," he said warily, peering at the badge she wore around her neck. "Can I help you?"

He was a handsome kid with dark eyes, but his good looks

were marred by a sullen expression. He wore camouflage combat pants, boots, a brown shirt and a camouflage vest. He kept his hands shoved in his pockets.

"I hope so," Sedona answered. "I'm Sedona Stewart. I'm part of the Coyote inspection team working over in Hangar 29. I oversee the engine inspections."

He shrugged. "So?"

Sedona raised her eyebrows. "So, I want to ask you a few questions."

He started to turn away. "I already filed a report with the Aircraft Mishap Board. I told them everything I know. I got nothing else to say."

"Hey, wait a minute." Sedona fell into step beside him. "You don't even know what I'm going to ask you."

Resentment sparked in his eyes. "I got a good idea. I'm a plane captain. You think because we're the last ones to inspect the jets before they launch, we must somehow be responsible, right?"

Sedona frowned. "No. Of course not. Why would I think that?"

"Because that's what they all think."

Sedona spread her hands. "Well, not me. Look, I'm not here to interrogate you. I'm just trying to get an understanding of the whole process, and wanted to ask what it is plane captains do before a jet launches. You know, what kinds of safety checks you perform."

He stopped and narrowed his eyes at her. "Why?"

Okay, the kid was beginning to irritate her. "Because I happen to have a…good friend test-flying these jets, and it sure as hell would make me feel better to know you and the other guys are doing everything you can to keep him safe."

He stopped, hands braced on his hips, and stared at her, and suddenly he looked weary and resigned, and much older than she'd originally thought.

"Look, it's a tough job. We work long days, sometimes sixteen-hour shifts. We're each assigned our own aircraft, and it's our job to make sure they're safe to fly."

"So you perform inspections?" Sedona prompted.

He squinted up at the sky and then back at her face. "Yeah. We do constant inspections. We check fluid levels, prepare the cockpit for flight and make sure there's no FOD, stuff like that."

"FOD? As in foreign object damage?"

He gave her a look that said he knew she was fishing. "Yes. Exactly like that."

Sedona refused to be intimidated. "So you would notice if a ball bearing, for example, was rolling around inside the engine compartment?"

Airman Laudano compressed his lips. "Yes, ma'am. I would. I'm the final set of eyes for the aircraft. The safety net, so to speak. The plane, the pilot and the mission rest solely on how well I do my job." He practically bit each word out.

"And do you do your job well, Airman?"

He gave her one long, contemptuous look and then turned on his heel and began walking away. "Speak to my XO. Ma'am."

XO? Ah, military-speak for commanding officer.

"I may just do that," she murmured.

As she turned thoughtfully away, she saw two men standing outside the Coyote hangar. Even from a distance, she recognized one of them as Captain Dawson. She squared her shoulders. He might intimidate her, but it wouldn't prevent her from asking about Airman Laudano's competency as a plane captain. Even as she made up her mind to do so, Captain Dawson turned away and entered the hangar. As she walked across the tarmac, Sedona recognized the second man.

"Excuse me, Lieutenant Palmer?"

He turned toward her with a smile. "Miss Stewart. We meet again." The surprise in his voice was unmistakable. "What brings you over to this part of the base? I'd think the engine inspections would keep you busy enough."

Sedona laughed. "Oh, they do. I was actually taking a look at the two compromised Coyotes that just came in."

His smile grew quizzical. "Were they helpful to you?"

"Yes, actually, they were." She hesitated. "I was just curious as to which of your plane captains were responsible for overseeing the jets that crashed or had in-flight problems."

"Miss Stewart," he began, but Sedona cut him off.

"Please, Lieutenant, I'm not jumping to any conclusions. I just thought…" She paused, and then plunged ahead. "I just thought Airman Laudano seemed a little…well, hostile, when I spoke to him."

Lieutenant Palmer's eyebrows shot up. "You spoke to my guys?"

Sedona frowned. "Is there a problem with that?"

"I guess not. It's just that…well, the kid's been under a lot of pressure, there's no question about it." He removed his hat and rubbed the back of his head. "Airman Laudano is one of our best plane captains. Unfortunately, he's dealing with some personal issues. So if he seems a little unfriendly, please try to understand."

"Can I ask what those personal issues are?"

The officer held her gaze. "I'm not at liberty to discuss it."

"Wow. It must be pretty serious, then. What is it? Drugs?"

Lieutenant Palmer frowned, pinched the bridge of his nose, and looked away, not answering.

Sedona gaped at him. "That's it, isn't it? Why is he still working on your flight line?"

"He hasn't been convicted, and his blood tests came back clean." The lieutenant's voice was soft, but had a steely edge.

"His performance since the incident has been exemplary, and when he's not on duty, he's confined to quarters. It's not a problem."

"Not a problem? I can't believe your pilots are willing to have somebody under suspicion of drug possession oversee their aircraft." Hello! When had the navy surrendered its common sense? With guys like Airman Laudano on the flight line, who needed al-Qaeda?

"Look, maybe it's better if you just stay away from my guys, okay? The last I heard, your job was to inspect the engines on the grounded jets, not act like some CSI investigator." Lieutenant Palmer stared with hard eyes over her shoulder toward the flight line, where even now the airman was performing a wing inspection on one of the Coyotes. "Airman Laudano is one of our best plane captains." He shifted his gaze to Sedona. "And just for the record, none of the planes that experienced problems were under his jurisdiction."

He turned to walk away, and Sedona only just prevented herself from grabbing his arm to stop him. "So whose planes were they, Lieutenant?" she called after his retreating back.

Lieutenant Palmer kept walking, but gave her a warning look over his shoulder. "Stay away from my men, Miss Stewart."

She stood for a moment, debating what to do. She couldn't very well demand information from Captain Dawson, but somehow she would find out whose jets were being compromised. She didn't know whether it was sheer coincidence that all the affected jets originated here at Lemoore, or something more ominous, but until she figured out what was going on, there was no way Angel was going up in one of Airman Laudano's jets.

12

ANGEL STOOD BESIDE the Coyote and stared across the tarmac toward the row of buildings and hangars that bordered the flight line. Even from a distance, he recognized the woman who stood on the walkway, hands on her hips, talking with Ken Larson. If the brightness of her hair hadn't given her away, her long-legged, straight-backed stance would have.

"Sir!"

Angel dragged his gaze away from Sedona and Ken and looked at his plane captain, a kid named Wheeler.

"She's ready, sir!" The kid had to shout over the whine of the engines from two nearby Coyotes, fired up and ready to roll.

Angel had just completed his walk-around visual inspection of the jet he was preparing to test-fly when he'd spotted Sedona striding along the flight line with Larson. She'd said they were nothing more than coworkers, but as he watched, they stopped walking and Larson moved closer to her.

What the hell was going on? Their faces were scant inches apart. They were arguing about something. The hostile body language was unmistakable. But when Larson shoved a finger in Sedona's face, Angel saw red. He shoved his flight book at the plane captain.

"This'll just take a minute," he growled, but hadn't gone more than two steps when Wheeler caught his arm.

"Sir?"

"Let go, Wheeler," he commanded, his voice low and tight. It'd take no more than five minutes to sprint across the tarmac that separated him from Sedona. He could almost feel the satisfaction of smashing a fist into the other man's face.

"Sir." Wheeler's tone was urgent, breaking through the haze of anger that clouded his mind. "The jet's ready to go. You'll miss your window."

Angel knew the kid was right. He had a flight test to conduct, and walking over to kick Larson's ass would not only put him behind schedule, it would raise red flags all over the command. The last thing he needed was to attract negative attention from top brass. They'd stick him in a cubicle somewhere and he'd spend the rest of his military career pushing paper. No thanks.

As he watched, Larson turned away from Sedona and continued walking. After a moment, she followed.

Angel spun on his heel toward his jet. "All right, fine," he muttered. "I'll take care of it later. Let's roll."

Whatever was going on between Sedona and Ken Larson would have to wait until he returned to the hotel. But it sure as hell looked to be more than a difference of opinion between coworkers. If Angel didn't know better, he'd think the guy had a thing for her.

Had Sedona lied to him? She'd admitted to traveling with Larson before. Maybe the last time she'd traveled with him he'd been the one she'd performed private strip dances for. Hell, for all he knew, she made a habit of screwing different men each time she went on business travel. He might be nothing more than her latest conquest. Just the thought made his chest tighten and his hands curl into fists.

The only thing he knew for sure was that something was definitely going on between Sedona and Larson, and he would find out what. Frustrated, he jerked his helmet on and fastened it. Right now he needed to concentrate on doing his job.

It took all his discipline to climb into the cockpit, fasten his seat belt and focus on performing his flight-readiness checks. Even so, he found it impossible to put Sedona completely out of his mind.

He loved takeoffs. Craved the dizzying speed of accelerating down the runway until that final instant when his wheels left the ground and he wasn't just airborne—he was flying. But as the earth fell away beneath him and he shot upward through the drifts of clouds, he couldn't fully appreciate the beauty that surrounded him.

Damned if he wouldn't rather be on the ground.

He looked down at the tiny patch of earth that was Lemoore Naval Air Station. Where was Sedona right now? Was she with Larson? Images of the two of them together swamped his imagination. He pictured Sedona clinging to the other man, making needful little noises as he pleasured her. His hands tightened on the throttle and he banked sharply, pushing the aircraft through her paces.

He glanced down at his gauges, noting the numbers on the tiny digital clock rapidly rolling away the microseconds. The entire test flight would take no more than two hours. He'd spend several more hours completing paperwork and briefing the admiral. It was still early afternoon. With luck, he'd be back at the hotel by supper time.

It couldn't be soon enough for him.

IT WAS ALMOST ten o'clock when Angel set his empty beer mug down on the bar and pushed his stool back. He hadn't wanted to go out with the guys again, but having already turned them down the last two times, he couldn't do it a third. He'd used the base facilities to shower and change his clothes, and had gone along to their favorite club, the 4-Play. But he hadn't been able to relax and after an hour or so, gave up the pretense.

"Sorry, but I'm calling it a night," he said, pulling several bills from his wallet and tossing them on the bar. "But you guys hang around. The next one's on me."

"Hey, man, why you leaving? Got a hot babe waiting for you, Diablo?"

Angel glanced at the man next to him, a fighter pilot he'd trained with nearly twelve years ago. Steve Platt, call sign "Splatt," grinned at him.

"Yeah, something like that," he answered, unwilling to share anything about Sedona with them. They'd use it against him, and even if their ribbing was meant good-naturedly, it would only come back to bite him in the ass. He might not know Sedona as well as he'd like to, but he knew her well enough to guess what her reaction would be to a squadron of Coyote fighter pilots knowing she was intimately involved with him. She'd completely freak. Then she'd unload him like yesterday's trash.

"Hey, Diablo! Where you going?"

Angel looked at his friend, Tony Gregory, call sign Tuna. It stood for the The Ugliest Naval Aviator.

His own call sign, Diablo, or devil, was one he'd grown accustomed to, whether he liked it or not. It was a tribute to his Spanish heritage, and a deliberate play on his name. Call signs weren't something you got to choose. You just hoped you got one you could live with, especially since they were often derogatory and cruel approximations of physical limitations or sexual inadequacies.

No one could ever call the navy overly cerebral with the selection of call signs. With his beaky nose and oversize ears, Tuna might be a homely man, but he was an expert pilot, and had been Angel's wingman on several sorties off the deck of the USS *Abraham Lincoln*.

"I have a morning test flight, so I'm bugging out early."

"Man, no wonder the top brass is always on your ass," Splatt commented. "Don't you know this is considered a team-building experience? Don't you want to show them you're not really a lone wolf? That you can follow direction and be a team player? C'mon, man, don't be such an asshole."

"Don't forget," called Tuna, "twelve hours from bottle to throttle!" He lifted his own beer bottle in a mock salute. "That's why we're not on the books until tomorrow afternoon."

He waved away the good-natured protests and ribald comments and worked his way through the crowded bar. Two attractive young women sat at a small table near the door and eyeballed him as he drew closer. When one of them gave him a flirtatious wink and shifted on her bar stool to reveal a slim length of bare leg clad in minuscule shorts, he just smiled at them.

They were young and pretty and obviously looking for some action, but Angel wanted more. With a sense of shock, he realized it was true. Generally speaking, he had no problem with one-night stands. But now he wanted more than just a night of hot sex with a stranger, no matter how beautiful she might be.

He wanted a woman with substance. He wanted an intelligent, self-confident woman who could hold her own in a discussion that involved something besides superficial nonsense. A woman who was self-absorbed and demanding didn't interest him. He wanted a woman who wouldn't exploit her femininity or compromise her identity to get ahead. He wanted a woman who made him laugh. A woman who made him burn.

A woman like Sedona.

He couldn't stop thinking about her. The afternoon briefings had dragged on and on until Angel thought he'd howl with frustration. When they had finally finished for the day, he'd called Sedona's room but she hadn't answered. Where was she? She'd said she'd be back at the hotel by six o'clock.

She'd said she would wait for him, but he hadn't planned on being out this late. While he didn't expect her to just sit around and twiddle her thumbs until he showed up, he couldn't imagine where she might be.

Angel caught a cab the short distance from the bar to the hotel. The vehicle pulled up to the front doors and he paid the driver. Then he glanced at his watch. It was nearly 10:30. Would she still be awake? Did he dare wake her up if she wasn't?

Hell, yes.

He'd thought about nothing else the entire day. He strode through the hotel lobby, ignoring the loud music and voices that drifted toward him from the lounge, which was in full swing at this time of night. As he rode the elevator to the third floor, he blew out his breath. He was nervous, which was completely ridiculous. Of course she'd be there.

He half expected Sedona to be stretched out on his bed, waiting for him, but when he finally entered his room it was dark and quiet. Pushing down his disappointment, he dropped his flight bag onto the bed and flipped on the lights. The connecting door was closed. The message waiting light on the bedside phone was dark. No messages.

Okay. No problem. He'd just open the door and tell her he had to see her. If she was asleep, he'd wake her up. If she was grumpy, he'd make it up to her.

But when he opened the door, it was to find her side of the connecting doors closed. What the hell? Hadn't she said just that morning that she'd keep her door open for him? Frowning, he turned the knob, relieved when the door pushed open beneath his hand. At least she hadn't locked it. That was a good sign, right?

Cautiously he stepped into her room. The bedside light was on, but he knew immediately she wasn't there. The alarm clock radio played softly in the background. A pair of pajama bottoms lay crumpled on the floor beside the bed, and the matching top had been tossed carelessly on top of the blankets. The room still bore the light, floral fragrance that he'd come to associate with Sedona.

The bed looked as if it had recently been occupied. The covers were thrown back and the pillows were stacked on top of each other and pushed against the headboard. A book lay open and facedown on the sheets with an odd-looking, flat-edged pencil next to it.

Curious, he picked it up. It looked like a drawing pencil. He turned the book over and saw it was a hardbound sketchbook. He stared at the drawing on the open page, and his heart skipped a beat.

It was a picture of his face, captured in amazingly lifelike detail. He wore a small smile, and he thought if he touched his fingers to the paper, he might actually feel the indents of his own dimples. In the background of the picture, she'd drawn an F/A-44 Coyote jet, sitting on the deck of an aircraft carrier. The picture was incredibly realistic. From a distance, he might have believed it was a photograph.

Amazed, he flipped through the book. A scrap of paper fluttered out from between the pages and landed on the bed. Picking it up, he saw it was a photo of himself. He recognized it as a clipping from a navy magazine. The Public Affairs office had done a brief story about the pilots who served aboard the USS *Abraham Lincoln,* and accompanied the story with a group photo of the pilots. It wasn't a great picture of him, and the quality was poor.

Replacing the clipping, he realized there were more sketches of him. In one, he stood in the doorway of an aircraft hangar with his head bent, while an unseen breeze rippled the fabric of his flight suit.

The last picture was of him from the waist up, nude. She'd drawn the texture of his skin so that it gleamed, as if he'd just been sluiced with water. He had his arms bent behind his head, and she'd sculpted the muscles of his stomach, chest and arms with unerring accuracy. The image of him looked out of the picture, directly at the artist. His lips were tilted in the slightest of smiles, so that only a hint of his dimples showed. She'd stopped the drawing low on his hips, just shy of actually showing his credentials, but there was no mistaking the barest hint of his pubic hair.

The picture was alluring. Erotic.

There were more than a dozen pictures of him, each crafted with infinite detail and obvious care. He'd guess some of them had been done months ago, maybe even before he'd been deployed aboard the *Lincoln*.

Had she been that aware of him back then? During those six months that he'd first worked with the Defense Procurement Agency, he'd hardly known she existed. The thought was completely humbling, even as alarm bells jangled in his head.

Sedona had obviously harbored a huge crush on him. What were her feelings now? If her most recent drawings of him were any indication, they definitely hadn't waned. Any idiot could tell how she felt about him just by looking at her artwork.

Christ, he needed a drink.

He placed the sketchbook carefully back where he'd found it and returned to his room. Opening the small fridge, he saw it contained soda, a small bottle of wine and a couple nip-size bottles of sweet liqueur. He definitely needed something stronger. He needed a double shot of bourbon.

He headed down to the hotel bar. He'd have one drink, and then go back upstairs and wait for Sedona to return. He crossed the lobby; the music and noise of the lounge area was raucous. In the short time they'd been at the hotel, he hadn't been to the bar, and he stood for a moment just inside the entrance to get his bearings and let his eyes adjust to the dim lighting.

As he wove his way through the small tables, he recognized several of the patrons as members of the inspection team. But it wasn't until he was almost to the bar that he saw her.

Sedona stood at one end of the bar, near the waitress station. She wore a T-shirt and jeans, and her hair was pulled back into a ponytail. She held a drink in one hand, and she was talking to Ken Larson.

At first glance, they looked to be having a friendly conversation, but Angel didn't miss the rigid set of Sedona's shoulders, or how she held her drink carefully between her and Larson, like a barrier. She was smiling, but the expression in her eyes was less than friendly.

Frowning, Angel began weaving his way through the cluster of tables. When he was about twenty feet away he saw Larson take Sedona's drink and set it down on the bar, then grab her by the arm and pull her toward a side exit.

A cocktail waitress carrying a drink-laden tray stepped directly into Angel's path, effectively preventing him from chasing after them. As he waited impatiently for the woman to move, Ken opened the rear-exit door and stepped into a hotel corridor, pulling Sedona behind him.

Angel felt a flare of white-hot jealousy. He pushed his way past the waitress, muttering an apology when she threw him a disgusted look. He'd suspected Larson had a thing for Sedona, but he couldn't understand why she'd gone with him so easily. She hadn't appeared to even object. How could he have misread her so completely? Just the thought of her with another guy ate at his gut.

With a low growl of anger, Angel reached the rear door and threw it forcibly open. He glanced swiftly down the length of the corridor, but there was no sign of them. But when the door shut behind him, muting the sound of the lounge, he thought he heard Sedona's voice. He walked in that direction with long, determined strides.

As he rounded the corner, he saw Larson gripping Sedona by the upper arms. Before he could reach them, Sedona gave Larson a shove backward. The other man staggered once before he regained his balance and then advanced on Sedona. Angel saw red.

"Larson."

Larson's expression of astonishment gave Angel a brief second of satisfaction, but not nearly as much as when he grabbed the bastard and jerked him away from Sedona.

"Angel!" Sedona's voice was low and shocked.

Surprised to see me, baby? I'll bet. He had Larson by the collar of his shirt, and the little puke's eyes were about bugging out of his head. He glanced over at Sedona, who was watching them with a mixture of horror and relief in her green eyes. Then his gaze fell on her arms, where Larson's fingers had left reddish marks on her pale skin.

It was enough to snap the last bit of sanity he still clung to. Without a word, he pushed Larson slightly away and then followed with a hard right to the guy's jaw. Larson staggered and fell heavily against the wall.

"Angel, oh, my God…"

Sedona took a step toward Larson, arms outstretched as if to catch him, as he staggered and tried to regain his balance. With an incoherent sound of fury, he pushed her away.

"Stay away from me," he spat.

"No, Larson," Angel growled, "you stay away from her." Reaching out, he caught Sedona by the arm and propelled her through the corridor toward the elevators.

"Angel," she gasped, jogging to keep up with his long strides, "I can explain."

He glanced sideways at her. Her face twisted as if she might cry.

"Please," she said, her voice trembling, "I can't keep up with you."

Angel stopped and turned to face her. "No, *mina,*" he bit out, "it seems I can't keep up with *you.*" He raked a hand over his hair. "Jesus." He laughed humorlessly. "When I think I came back here hoping you might actually be waiting for me…"

"I did wait for you!"

"Oh, yeah?" Angel stared down at her. "And then what? You just couldn't wait anymore? You had to go down to the bar and snag the first available guy?"

Her eyes widened. "Is that what you think? Did it really look to you like I was interested in Ken Larson?"

Angel recalled the hard shove she'd given the other man, but right now he was still too pissed off to listen to reason. He raised his hands and turned around to continue walking. He didn't want to see her eyes filling up with tears. Didn't want to hear her excuses.

"Forget it, okay? I don't really want to hear it, anyway." But he hadn't taken more than a step when he found his path blocked by Sedona. Her face was blotchy with suppressed emotion, but she was determined. She glared up at him, hands on her hips.

"Too bad, flyboy," she said, and despite the tears in her eyes, her voice no longer wobbled. "You'll stand there and listen to what I have to say, and then if you still want to walk away…well, that'll be your choice."

Angel blew out his breath in resignation. He was behaving like an ass, and he knew it. He'd seen how Sedona had shoved Ken away and knew whatever had transpired, she hadn't been a willing player. But seeing them together had caused something inside him to bend, and then snap. He'd felt a little rabid. Had wanted to tear into someone.

But not Sedona.

"Okay," he conceded grudgingly. "I'm listening."

Sedona blew her breath out. "I was waiting for you. I was in bed…reading. I was thirsty and wanted something cold to drink, but the ice maker on our floor isn't working. I put some clothes on and came down to get a soda."

Okay, so far what she said agreed with everything he'd seen in her room. Except the part about reading. He shrugged. "So you needed a cold drink because you were, what…hot? So hot you had to run down to the bar and see who was available?"

"No, and if that's what you believe then you don't know me." She crossed her arms and hugged herself, looking miserable.

"Then enlighten me." Angel knew his voice sounded hard and cold.

She gave a small huff of laughter, but Angel thought it had a nervous edge to it. "It sounds so…stupid when I try to put it into words."

He gave her an encouraging squeeze. "Try."

She blew out her breath. "It's just that—" She broke off and groaned in frustration. "You're not going to believe me. I can hardly believe it myself."

Angel gave her a tolerant look.

"Okay," she continued, "I'll just say it." She turned solemn eyes to him. "I found out there's a group of guys at the agency who started a club, where promotions are based on having a fling while on business travel."

"What?"

"It's the truth," she insisted. "And initially, I thought I could expose them, put an end to the whole thing, but they think I want to become a member, and I don't. Ken Larson doesn't get that, though, and he's a member so now he thinks that if he and I have a wild fling while we're out here, we'll both get promoted." The words tumbled out while her eyes sought his with something like desperation.

Angel just stared at her.

Finally, dumbfounded, he raked a hand over his head, and turned away, then spun back to her. "Are you serious?"

"Completely." She bit her lip and watched him. "I'm sorry. I didn't think he'd be so persistent, but I guess he really wants that promotion." She smiled weakly.

His brain was spinning. He'd heard some vague rumors on the flight line about an exclusive club of engineers, but hell, he'd figured it was more along the lines of a math club, not a sex club. "Jesus," he breathed, and shook his head. "I can't freaking believe it. A bunch of Poindexters, starting a sex club?"

"I know, it's pretty disgusting."

"So is that why you…wanted to get together with me? Because you want a promotion?"

Her face paled, and the genuine distress he saw in her eyes said he couldn't be further from the truth. "What? *No.* I already told you, I don't want anything to do with the club! I've told Larson I'm not interested, but he won't leave it alone."

Angel closed the distance between them in one step and jerked her into his arms. "I believe you," he said roughly, knowing it was the truth. "When I saw you leave with him, I thought—" He couldn't finish. "Let's just say I thought the worst."

She tipped her face up and gave him a trembling smile. "I only left with him because I thought he'd found out about the two of us, and I was afraid he'd make a scene right there in the bar."

Angel gave her a quizzical look.

"I don't know how the navy feels about their officers engaging in…" She blushed furiously and averted her eyes. "I just didn't want you to get in trouble, so I went outside to try and reason with him."

Angel tightened his arms around her, breathing in the fragrance of her hair. "I don't care who knows about us," he said. "Even Larson. Especially Larson."

Sedona lifted her face to his. "You thought I was involved with him?" She slid her arms around him and pressed herself closer. "How could I even think about anyone else when I have you, my own real-life fantasy, right here?"

"Is that what I am? Your fantasy?" He cupped her face in his hands, smoothing his fingers over her jaw.

"Oh, yeah," she whispered, and lifted her face to his, her spiky, wet lashes drifting down to her cheeks.

With a groan, Angel kissed her, sweeping his tongue past her lips and claiming her with an urgency bred of fierce relief and hunger.

When he finally lifted his head, Sedona's mouth was swollen and damp. "Jesus," he groaned, fitting his hips against hers, he let her feel the effect she had on him. "I want you, Sedona, right now." He rested his forehead against hers. "When I thought you might be getting it on with Larson…"

He didn't finish the sentence, but when he'd thought she was involved with Larson, he'd wanted to kill somebody. When he had seen her leave with him, he'd been consumed by a surge of jealousy and rage, sure. But there'd been more. He'd felt as if someone had ripped his heart out.

"C'mon," Sedona whispered to him, her fingers caressing his back and neck. "Let's go back to my room."

Angel growled softly and crushed her lips with his. "I thought you'd never ask, *mina.*"

He guided her swiftly toward the elevators, unable to rationalize the crushing relief he felt at knowing she hadn't sought out another man. He'd been crazy to think she was capable of it.

After all, he'd seen her sketchbook, and there hadn't been one picture of Larson in it. Nearly every picture had been of him, rendered by a woman who was obviously infatuated with him.

Maybe even in love with him.

13

SEDONA DUCKED INTO her room, knowing she had about two seconds to scoop the incriminating sketchbook off the bed and tuck it safely away before Angel opened the connecting doors between their rooms. She'd have a tough time explaining that to him.

She snatched up the pad and looked around for a quick hiding spot. When she heard Angel turning the knob of the connecting door, she made a beeline for the bathroom, the only place she could think of where he wouldn't follow her.

"I'll be right out," she called, and closed the door, locking it behind her. The bathroom didn't yield any drawers or cupboards in which to stash the sketchbook, so she slid it between the folded towels on the chrome rack next to the shower enclosure.

Glancing into the mirror, she gasped. God, she looked awful. Her hair had come slightly free of the ponytail and hung in disarray around her face, which was pale except for two bright spots of color high on her cheeks. She'd come so close to crying back there when Angel had turned and walked away.

She felt a huge sense of relief at having told him about the Membership. He'd been shocked, but he'd believed her.

She hadn't told him she would be leaving the agency once their inspection of the Coyotes was over, but there would be time for that later. It probably wouldn't even be an issue, since they'd already agreed their relationship wouldn't continue once they returned to the East Coast. For all she knew, he'd breathe a sigh of relief to discover she wouldn't be a potential burden or embarrassment to him. But for now...

She yanked the elastic band out of her hair and combed her fingers through the unruly mass. She hadn't anticipated running into Angel down in the bar, or she'd never have been caught dead in the T-shirt and jeans she now wore. She'd owned both for more years than she cared to admit, and it showed. But her pajamas were still on the bed in the other room.

What was it her sister had told her? The one thing a guy couldn't resist was a naked woman? Pushing aside her inhibitions, she peeled off her clothing and wrapped a towel around her nudity. Then drawing a deep breath, she stepped out of the bathroom.

And stopped dead in her tracks.

She swallowed. Hard.

Angel sprawled indolently on top of her bed, wearing nothing but a pair of loose pajama bottoms and a wicked smile. The light on the bedside table cast intriguing shadows over the dips and angles of his body. He'd pulled the bedspread down to the foot of the bed, and against the pristine white of the cotton sheets, he looked dark and exotic.

He held her sensible cotton pajama top and bottoms in one hand. His grin widened as his dark gaze swept over her, and with one lazy motion, he tossed her pajamas over his shoulder.

"Well," he drawled, "you won't be needing these." He bent one arm beneath his head and patted the mattress with his other hand. "Come here."

Talk about Christmas in July! Seeing him stretched out on her bed, tempting her with all that bare, tanned skin, was like another of her fantasies come true. She put a hand to her hair, suddenly self-conscious.

"I look terrible."

His eyes grew darker, hotter. "You look incredible. I've been dying to get my hands on you all day, *mina*. Don't make me come get you."

He sat up and swung his long legs over the edge of the bed. She noticed how, even in a sitting position, his pajama bottoms tented over his arousal. Her stomach knotted in anticipation and a languorous heat began to build between her legs. She longed to run her hands over all that wonderfully smooth, bronzed skin. His shoulders bunched as he pressed his hands against the mattress and prepared to rise.

Slowly, her face flaming and her heart thudding with expectation, she loosened the towel from where it was knotted over her breasts, but found she couldn't quite release it. She held a corner of it bunched in her hand and let it hang in front of her, partially obscuring her body from his view. Instinct made her clutch it tightly against her breasts, which was crazy. Angel had already seen her. Every bit of her. She had no reason to feel so self-conscious. Especially not when he eyed her the way a kid would eye a free ice-cream cone.

Heat flared in his eyes, and Sedona didn't miss the way his fingers curled into the bedding.

She dropped the towel onto the floor.

He groaned.

Emboldened, she stepped slowly toward him until she stood within arm's reach. "So…here I am, flyboy."

His gaze slid down the length of her body and he swallowed. Hard. "Jesus, *mina*," he rasped. "I'd forgotten…"

She stepped into the opening between his legs and laid her palms on his shoulders, reveling in the satiny heat of his skin. "What did you forget?" Her words were no more than a whisper.

He tipped his head back to look at her, then grasped her hips in his hands and drew her forward until her legs bumped against the edge of the mattress. "How damn hot you are, and how much I want to do this."

His husky confession caused a liquid heat to slip along the underside of her skin, and her pulse began a heavy, sweet thudding. Still watching her face, he slid his hands up over her belly and filled his palms with her breasts. He cupped them, caressed them until she gasped softly. Then he bent his head and drew one breast into his mouth, gently laving the nipple with his tongue.

Sedona's breath caught and she brought her hands up to stroke his cropped hair, enjoying the rough velvet texture.

"Oh, God." She sighed. "That feels too good."

Angel wrapped his big arms completely around her and buried his face between her breasts. He inhaled deeply. "You smell good."

"I missed you today," she admitted, and rubbed her cheek against the top of his head. It was true. She had missed him. When he wasn't around, she missed his easy confidence and his quiet capability. She missed the way his eyes heated when he looked at her. She missed how he made her feel— feminine, and safe.

"Mmm," he mumbled against her sensitized skin. "I missed you, too. I couldn't believe it when you weren't in your room tonight. I'm sorry about what happened, *mina*. Earlier, with Larson. I jumped to conclusions and behaved badly."

Sedona pulled back slightly and looked at him. "I'm glad you showed up when you did." She shivered. "I mean, I could have handled Ken, but I'm glad I didn't have to."

Angel's arms tightened around her. "You don't need to

think about him again. All you need to think about is this."
He ran his hands down over her hips, grasped her buttocks
and squeezed gently. "I love your ass."

Sedona laughed and couldn't resist caressing his jaw with
her fingers, enjoying the texture of shadowed stubble. "The
navy actually lets you fly their jets? Your eyesight is obviously impaired, or you'd see my butt is huge."

He growled playfully and fell backward onto the bed,
dragging her over him with his hands cupping her buttocks.
His eyes gleamed with devilry. "That's crazy. Feel how you
fit perfectly into my hands."

Her breasts were flattened against the broad planes of
his chest, and his erection pressed on her belly. Only the
thin material of his pajama pants separated them. When he
squeezed her bottom, and slid a finger deftly between her
legs and stroked her cleft, desire licked its way through her.
Molten heat pooled at her center, and her breasts ached for
his touch.

She braced herself on her elbows and stared down at his
face, mesmerized by the endless depths of his dark eyes. Her
gaze drifted lower, to the tantalizing fullness of his lower
lip. He smiled, bringing his dimples briefly into play, and
it was all over for her.

"Yeah, we're a perfect fit," she finally breathed in response, her lips scant millimeters from his, "Angel..." She
covered his lips with hers, putting everything she had into
the kiss. She reached down and stroked him through his pajamas, loving the hot, thick feel of him against her hand, loving
how he moaned and thrust himself helplessly into her palm.

"You feel so good." She slid her hand inside the waistband
of his pants and closed her fingers around him. She squeezed
him, then moved her hand up his impressive length to swirl
her thumb over the swollen head.

"Mina," he choked, "stop."

Sedona smiled against his mouth. "Why? Don't you like it?"

He made a noise that was part laugh, part groan. "I'm trying really hard not to lose it right now. But if you keep that up, I'm not going to last."

In one smooth movement, he rolled her beneath him, dragging her hand from him in the process. Sedona gave a small cry of surprise and clutched at his broad shoulders for support.

For a moment, they stared at each other. When Angel finally bent his head to hers, it was to cover her lips in a kiss that was incredibly sweet. Sedona made a small sound of approval and arched against him, rubbing her breasts against the firmness of his chest. At the same time, she pushed his pajama bottoms down over his thighs and used her feet to free him completely from the soft fabric.

Dragging her mouth from his, she scooted herself partway up the mattress, until her head bumped the pillows mounded in front of the headboard. Pushing them beneath her head, she used her hands to urge Angel higher.

He looked down at her, bemused. "What...?"

"Kneel above me," she urged softly, and grasped his hips to show him what she wanted. But it wasn't until he straddled her waist and she pushed herself up onto her elbows, that he finally understood her intent.

"Mina," he said with an astonished laugh, "you don't have to do this."

"Are you kidding?" she asked, eye level now with his amazing erection. "I've been wanting to do this for a long time."

The thick shaft of his penis bobbed lightly as he edged closer. She admired the dark, glistening head and, leaning forward, flicked her tongue experimentally over it. He jerked reflexively.

She smiled. "Mmm, you taste delicious."

Sliding her hands up the back of his hard thighs, she cupped his buttocks, and then slid one hand between his legs to gently caress his balls. She liked that they weren't overly huge, but hung nicely beneath his straining cock.

Angel groaned, and when Sedona glanced up, his handsome face was taut with desire. She closed her fingers around the base of his penis and admired how the thick veins bulged in response. Slowly, she slid her hand upward, even as she bent her head and swirled her tongue over the head.

He arched his back, made a low, growling noise deep in his throat, and buried his hands in her hair. He didn't force her head down as she'd thought he would. He merely used his fingers to caress her scalp and the sensitive skin behind her ears. That, and the sensation of him in her mouth, was incredible. She urged him closer, stroking the underside of his shaft with her tongue and using her lips to create friction.

As her fingers caressed him, she wrapped one hand firmly around the base of his penis and used every instinct she had to love him with her mouth. When he drew close to the edge, she'd pull away and give him time to cool down, softly licking his shaft and then blowing gently on his damp skin. Then she'd take him into her mouth again and use her lips and tongue to torture him, teasing the sensitive area just beneath the head, and easing her fist slowly along his length as she did so.

She knew he was close to losing control when he made a low, harsh noise in his throat and stiffened. Before she could protest, he dragged himself from her.

"I need to— I can't— Christ, *mina*," he half groaned, and collapsed onto the pillows beside her, sucking air into his lungs. "I don't want this to end so soon."

Raising himself on one elbow over her, he grabbed a condom from where he'd left it on the bedside table and expertly covered himself. When he leaned down and kissed her, she wrapped her arms and legs around him so that he pressed against her sex.

It was a kiss that made no concessions. It was fiercely possessive and primal, and Sedona welcomed it, touching her tongue to his and arching against him. She wanted him so badly. She hadn't thought that pleasuring him with her mouth would be a total turn-on for her, as well.

With one surge, he penetrated her fully, burying himself in her. Sedona cried out and grasped his lean buttocks. He pulled his mouth from hers and swirled his tongue along the edge of her ear, causing shivers to chase along her spine.

With each bone-melting thrust of his hips, he murmured husky words into her ear in Spanish. Sedona didn't have to understand them to know they were words of endearment and encouragement.

She met his thrusts with an increasing urgency of her own, reveling in the smooth skin beneath her fingertips, loving the harshness of his breath against her throat. And when he gave a ragged shout of release and stiffened inside her, it was enough to push her over the edge, as well. She keened with pleasure and shuddered with each delicious spasm that rippled through her.

Angel rested his head on her shoulder and she hugged him fiercely, keeping her legs pulled tight around his lean hips. He might be the embodiment of every fantasy she'd ever had, but this was so much more. The reality of being with Angel exceeded all her dreams.

Not only was he heart-stoppingly handsome, but he had the ability to make her laugh. With him she felt sexy and cherished and protected.

A flutter of fear constricted her chest. She couldn't let herself be this happy. Couldn't delude herself that this could last. This wasn't reality, it was just a brief interlude. In real life, guys like Angel Torres did *not* fall for women like her.

This was just some bizarre twist of fate, where she was in the right place at the right time.

In fact, nothing had ever felt so right in her life. Angel's heart still beat heavily against her own, and his breath stirred the hair at her temple. She knew she couldn't keep him. Guys like Angel needed to be free, to spread their wings and fly. Eventually, she'd have to let him go. But for right now, he was completely hers.

She never wanted this moment to end. Her chest felt as if it was expanding. She was going to burst with the emotion that flooded her. Despite her relative lack of experience with the opposite sex, she recognized all the warning signs.

She was falling in love with Angel Torres.

It was almost midnight. Sedona leaned back against Angel's chest and let him squeeze the warm water from the washcloth over her breasts, making rivulets in the sudsy, fragrant froth that covered her and exposing the skin beneath.

"Mmm," she said, sighing, and stroked his thigh with her hand, captivated by the way the black hair flattened against his bronzed skin and then swirled upward again with the lapping of the water. "I can't recall the last time I took a bath. To think, I once considered them a waste of time."

Angel laughed softly against her ear. "That's because baths are definitely meant to be shared."

Sedona looked down at their legs, where Angel's lay along the outside of her thighs.

"Hmm," she said. "Maybe in a bigger tub. This one is a little short."

"That all depends on what it is you want to do." His hands swept upward to cup her breasts and toy with the nipples until they stood rosy and stiff beneath his ministrations. Sedona gasped. His fingers were lean and brown against the pale creaminess of her breasts. The sight was erotic, causing a now-familiar tingling to begin between her legs.

When he rolled her nipples between his fingers, she felt his own response in the rise of flesh that pressed against her backside. Her breathing quickened when he ran one hand down over her belly and pressed it between her thighs to stroke her slick flesh.

"Ohmigod," she panted as she pushed against his hand, "what are you doing to me?"

He chuckled. "What does it look like?"

Sedona moaned. "You're turning me into a sex-crazed lunatic." She shivered when he caught her earlobe in his teeth and tugged gently.

"You say that like it's a bad thing," he murmured.

But Sedona wasn't prepared when he stood up, lifting her with him and sloshing water over the edge of the tub.

"What—"

"I want you again," he said roughly, "but this tub is definitely too short for that."

He stood her on the bath mat, and pulled a towel from the rack. Sedona's knees felt weak when she saw how ready for her he was. The man had no right to be so incredibly gorgeous. She had absolutely no willpower when it came to Angel Torres.

But when he turned to face her, she could only admire the sleekness of his skin and all the hard, muscled contours of his body. For the moment, anyway, he was all hers.

He lay the towel across the tank on the back of the toilet, and a second one over the closed seat. Then he tore open a condom that he'd put on the counter earlier and sheathed himself. Sedona smiled uncertainly.

"What are you doing?"

"Come here."

He drew her forward until she stood facing the toilet. She was helpless to prevent a giggle from escaping. "Sorry, but I'm still not getting it."

"Oh, you will, *mina*," Angel said. He stood close behind her until his erection pressed against the cleft of her buttocks. Keeping one hand on her abdomen, he used his other to bend her forward. "Look in the mirror."

Sedona looked sideways at the mirror that covered the wall over the sink. She gasped at the erotic sight they made. With her hands braced on the tank, her breasts hung down in clear view, and the curve of her bottom glistened wetly from the bathwater.

Angel stood behind her, his penis dark against the pale skin of her butt, his hands grasping her hips. She felt herself grow hot and wet at the sight. Slowly, watching their image in the mirror, Angel stroked a hand over one buttock, all the way down to the back of her knee, even as he cupped and kneaded one breast with his free hand.

Sedona's breathing quickened. Instinctively, she shifted to accommodate him. Angel smiled then, a sexy smile of male appreciation, and slid the head of his penis along her cleft. Sedona pushed back against him, feeling herself swell with desire. She was helpless to look away, even when Angel stroked her with one hand, and gently inserted a finger into her wet center.

"Oh, oh!" Sedona clenched her muscles around his hand, and cried out in protest when he withdrew. But her breath caught when he went down on one knee behind her.

"Bend over a little more, *mina*. That's it."

Sedona braced her elbows on the soft terry cloth and arched her back. She nearly swooned when Angel gently parted her folds with his fingers. But she couldn't prevent her cry of pleasure when his hot, talented tongue swept over her, swirling over her clitoris. The sight was the most incredibly erotic thing Sedona had ever seen. He continued to lick her, and then inserted his finger once more.

Her climax caught her by surprise, and she cried out, convulsing around his finger as her body was rocked by one of the most intense orgasms she had ever experienced. But even as she collapsed weakly forward with her head on her arms, Angel stood up.

"I want you to come again," he said, his voice rough with need.

Bending her forward over his arm, he drew her back to him. Sedona's eyes glazed over when she watched him enter her, one excruciatingly delicious inch at a time. He stretched her, filled her, rubbed against her already sensitized flesh until she was helpless to prevent the small, mewling sounds of need that came from her throat.

Angel threw his head back as he thrust into her, and Sedona thought she'd never seen anything quite as masculine or beautiful as the sight of this man, loving her so fiercely. As if on cue, Angel opened his eyes and captured her gaze.

"Watch me, *mina*," he growled softly. "See what you do to me." His eyes were dark and hot. "I'm going to come, *mina,* can you feel me?"

His words were like a catalyst, and amazingly enough she *could* feel him. He seemed to swell within her, to grow thicker and longer. Her flesh gripped him, stroked him, until she was about to explode. She knew he was on the verge, too.

"Oh, please," she gasped, thrusting back against him, "please, don't stop."

As their eyes locked in the mirror, Sedona could have watched herself as she experienced her third shattering orgasm of the night, but she watched Angel instead. Watched him as he watched her climax again, and the expression on his face was one of pure, unadulterated male satisfaction.

Then, Angel bent forward and pressed a tender kiss between her shoulder blades, before withdrawing. He helped her straighten, and wrapped his arms around her, gazing at her in the mirror.

"You are the most amazing woman I've ever known," he said, his breathing still ragged.

Sedona's heart rate pounded unevenly. "Oh, yeah?" she said with a smile. "You should see what I can do with a bidet."

Angel laughed, the sound sliding over her senses like warm honey. "Here," he murmured. "You're cold. Let's dry you off and get you into something warm."

He reached up and took another towel from the rack. Her sketchbook came down with it, landing with a thunk on the bathroom floor.

Faceup.

Open.

An image of Angel in all his nude, muscular glory stared up at them. The ensuing silence was almost deafening, and for a moment the world itself seemed to stop.

It wasn't until Angel bent to retrieve the book that Sedona was galvanized into action.

"Oh. Wow." She swiftly scooped it, snapped it closed and hugged it defensively against her chest. She laughed self-consciously. "I wonder how that got in here."

She couldn't meet Angel's eyes as he pulled another towel down and tied it around his hips. Maybe he hadn't gotten a good look at it. Maybe he hadn't recognized the drawing as himself.

"Sedona." His voice was quiet. Was that resignation she heard?

She smiled brightly and ignored him as she turned toward the door. "I'll just go put this away somewhere. Housekeeping must have gotten it mixed up with the towels, but geez, all that humidity will ruin the pages."

"Sedona, I already saw the book."

Her heart almost stopped. Heedless of her own nudity, she clutched the sketchbook and turned to face him. "You did?"

His smile was tender, his eyes warm and filled with emotion. "I came in earlier, looking for you. You'd left the book on your bed, and I—" He shrugged. "I looked at it."

"Oh." Sedona took the towel he held out to her, wishing the bathroom floor would suddenly open up and swallow her. Heat flooded her face. She swallowed. "How embarrassing."

"Actually," he said, moving closer and taking the sketchbook from her nerveless fingers, "I find it incredibly flattering." He let the book fall open in his hands, this time to the picture of himself standing in the entrance to the hangar. "These are really good, you know that? I mean, really good. There are military artists who sell their work for thousands and in my opinion, their work isn't nearly as good as yours."

Sedona felt her face get even redder. "They're just okay," she demurred. "I do my best work when I have a photo to work with, like those artists you see at the shopping malls." She shrugged. "But the only photo I have of you…"

"Is the group photo from the USS *Abraham Lincoln*," he finished. "I know. I saw that, too. The photo isn't great. Your drawings are."

She knew he was just trying to make her feel better. She was going to have to explain just why she had a sketchbook filled with pictures of him.

"Angel, I know how this looks, but…" She shrugged and pulled the sketchbook out of his hands and clutched it to her. "Well, c'mon, let's admit it. You're pretty hot. Who wouldn't want to capture you on paper? I never tried to hide that I find you attractive." She raised her eyes to his. "In fact, I've pretty much been attracted to you since the first time I saw you down on the flight line. I won't pretend I wasn't."

Angel stepped close enough that she could smell the fragrance of his skin, still warm and slightly damp from their recent bath. He smiled almost ruefully and reached out to tuck a strand of wet hair behind her ear. "I don't want you to pretend you weren't. To be honest, I discovered something about myself tonight." He gave a self-deprecating laugh. "When I saw you with Larson…well, let's just say I didn't like it. And it made me realize I really want to make a go of this."

Sedona felt her heart stutter. "What do you mean?"

He caught her gently by the elbows and drew her forward until the sketchbook was wedged between their bodies. "I don't know, exactly… I just know I hated seeing you with somebody else, and I don't want this to end when we get back to the East Coast."

"Angel… I don't know what to say."

Except maybe, *hallelujah!* Sedona was stunned. She still had a hard time believing this incredible guy found her interesting and sexy enough to spend a night with. And now he wanted to try to make a relationship out of what essentially began as a one-night stand.

"Don't say anything," he murmured, sliding a hand under her damp hair to cup the nape of her neck and tilt her face up. "Just think about it, okay? Now kiss me."

And Sedona did.

14

"ANGEL, YOU DON'T have to do this."

"C'mon, it'll be fun."

Sedona stood at the foot of the bed and stared at Angel, stretched out on the sheet with his arms bent behind his head, wearing nothing but a towel draped over his hips.

"You don't have to do a beefcake pose. I can take a picture of you fully clothed and…" She blushed. "The rest I can do from memory. I only need a picture of your face."

Angel grinned. "If you're going to be drawing pictures of me without my shirt on, I'd just as soon you get it right."

"Oh!" Sedona gave an astonished laugh. "Are you saying I didn't do you justice?"

"I'm just saying I want to make sure you have all my… parts where they're supposed to be." A dimple teased the corner of his mouth.

"I refuse to take pictures of your *parts*," she said indignantly, but couldn't keep from smiling back at him.

"Take the damn picture, *mina*."

"Okaay." Quickly, before she could change her mind, she held up her small digital camera and centered him in the tiny display screen. "Mmm, that's good. Smile." The

camera flashed, and Sedona peered at the display to see the results. "Actually, that's *really* good."

She sat down on the edge of the mattress and held the camera so Angel could view the picture she'd taken. She was unprepared when he pulled her down beside him and wrested the camera from her fingers.

"Smile," he said cheerfully, and holding the camera at arm's length, took a picture of the two of them, sprawled laughing against the pillows.

"Angel," she protested, making a grab for the camera, "delete that picture right now. I'm not decent!"

"You're fine," he assured her, holding the camera out of reach.

"I'm wearing my *underwear*."

"I've seen bathing suits that reveal more than your bra and panties." He grinned and sat up, pulling her with him. "C'mon, get dressed. I already told you, we have a big day ahead of us."

She watched as he disappeared through the connecting doors to get dressed before she collapsed back onto the mattress, unable to keep the silly grin off her face. He'd stayed the entire night in her room, his long limbs wrapped around her as they'd slept. And the way he'd woken her up… Her smile turned dreamy.

Angel had seen her sketchbook, and he hadn't run screaming for the hills. He'd actually encouraged her. Even let her take his picture so she could capture his likeness more accurately in her drawings. She knew it wasn't done out of vanity, but in an effort to please her. Had he guessed that she was falling for him?

He'd said he wanted to make a go of their relationship, but did he really mean it? It was one thing to profess your feelings during the intimate aftermath of lovemaking, but how would he feel once they returned to the East Coast and the first blush of romance had worn off? Sedona didn't need to guess; he'd pretend to still be interested, and maybe he actually would be. But eventually, he'd see how impossible any relationship between them was.

"Hey, c'mon, you're not even dressed yet."

Startled, Sedona looked up to see Angel leaning against the door frame between their rooms. He'd pulled on a pair of faded blue jeans and a black T-shirt that emphasized his dark good looks. His hands were shoved casually into his front pockets. He hadn't shaved and the dark blur of stubble on his jaw lent him a slightly piratical look.

She shivered.

"Sorry," she said, pushing herself upright. "I'll hurry."

"Okay, I'll pull the car around and meet you out front."

After he left, she rummaged through her dresser, undecided on what to wear. It was Sunday, and the inspection teams were working rotating shifts. Neither Angel nor Sedona had to report for work that day. Angel had said he had a surprise in store for her, and now she tried to guess what it might be.

She grabbed a pair of jeans and a scoop-necked gold T-shirt with a slender ribbon of satin piping at the neck. Casual, but still nice. Not overdressed. She almost gathered her hair back into a clip, but then let it fall loosely around her shoulders. Angel had said he liked it that way.

Satisfied, she took the elevator down to the lobby and stepped outside. Angel stood by the rental car, and his dark eyes gleamed with approval when she came around to the passenger side.

"You look great," he murmured into her ear as he opened her door for her. "Really."

"Thanks." She felt ridiculously pleased by the compliment. "So," she ventured, when they pulled on to the main road, "where're we going?"

He just smiled at her. "You'll see."

Sedona frowned when he drove onto the base, and turned in her seat to stare at him as they made their way down the now-familiar roads that led to the flight line.

"Oh! You tricked me. Unfair!"

"What?" Angel laughed as he looked over at her.

"Here I thought we were going to spend the day doing fun things, and all you want to do is work." She cast him a dark look. "Unless you're planning on doing wicked things to me in the backseat of one of those Coyotes, you can turn around right now."

"Actually, *mina,*" he said as he parked the car next to one of the Coyote hangars, "I was planning to put you in the backseat of one of those Coyotes and take you for a ride."

Sedona stared at him, stunned. *"What?"*

Angel grinned. "You heard me. We're going for a ride."

"But how?" Sedona shook her head, bemused. "I mean, what are you talking about? You can't be serious."

Angel turned in his seat to face her, one arm draped over the steering wheel. "Oh, I'm completely serious." He shrugged. "I know it's something you've wanted to do, so I've been planning this for a few days."

He'd been planning...

To her utter horror, Sedona felt her eyes fill with tears and she blinked furiously, unwilling to let Angel see how much his unexpected gesture meant to her.

"Hey, what's wrong? You did say you've always wanted to ride in a Coyote, right?"

His voice was warm and concerned and Sedona knew if she saw the tenderness in his eyes, she'd lose it completely. She waved him away and turned to look out the window, swiping at her cheeks and laughing self-consciously.

On the opposite side of the flight line, a dozen Coyotes gleamed softly in the morning sun. To her eyes, they were incredibly beautiful, representing all the strength and courage of the U.S. Navy. Like the man sitting next to her. Until this past week, being close to either had only been a dream.

She swallowed hard and turned to give him a wobbly smile. "Yes, I did. It's just—it's just that I can't believe you remembered, and then actually went ahead and planned this."

Angel grinned, clearly relieved. "Hey, it's the least I can do. Besides, it wasn't all that difficult to arrange."

He pushed his door open and climbed out as Sedona stared at him. *The least he could do?* O-kay. Nothing like taking the fun out of it; he made fulfilling one of her dreams sound as mundane as giving her a lift to work.

She pushed down her disappointment in his reaction and tried instead to focus on what he had planned. She was going to take a ride in a Coyote! The prospect terrified her as much as it thrilled her.

He grabbed his flight bag out of the trunk. "You haven't eaten anything this morning, have you?"

"Well, when you told me not to eat breakfast, I thought it was because we were going out to eat. If I'd known..."

"What did you eat?"

She grimaced. "A banana. Was that bad?"

Angel laughed. "Actually, if you had to eat something, that was probably the best choice."

Sedona walked beside him as they made their way to the Coyote hangar. "Why is that? Because of the potassium? Does it help with altitude sickness or something?"

"Nope. It's just that bananas taste pretty much the same coming up as they do going down."

"Oh!" Sedona stared at him, horrified.

"Relax," he said, putting an arm around her shoulders and giving her a brief, hard hug. "I'll go easy on you. Besides, you may not even need the air-sickness bags."

"I think I want to change my mind," she moaned.

"Too late," Angel said cheerfully. "We've already scheduled your preflight brief."

He opened the side door to the hangar and sure enough, there was a Coyote flight crew waiting inside for them. She had to sign some release forms, and then the crew went to work ensuring she had at least a basic understanding of what would happen once she sat down in the rear seat of the Coyote.

One of the grounded jets became a perfunctory classroom as the crew chief escorted her up the ladder and helped settle her into the seat directly behind the pilot.

Sergeant Dwight Nelson was a master mechanic, on loan from the Marine Corps flight program to assist with the investigation. He didn't talk; he barked. His voice was loud and gruff, and combined with his shaved head and Marine Corps tattoos, it made him the epitome of a Hollywood drill sergeant.

"This is a small camera mounted on the back of Diablo's seat." Sergeant Nelson sat perched on the edge of the cockpit with his feet resting on the wing as he prepared her for the flight. He indicated a tiny lens affixed directly in front of her face. "It will record the entire flight and capture every scream, squeal, hurl and blackout you experience, so remember to smile every so often."

Sedona gave him a withering look. "I will not *squeal,* and I certainly will not hurl."

Nelson laughed. "Yeah, right. I've seen marines completely incapacitated by the g-forces this baby pulls. It's no big deal."

Sedona glanced down to where Angel stood at the foot of the ladder, arms crossed as he watched them. He shrugged and grinned at her expression of horror.

"Okay," Nelson continued, "this is your seat belt and it straps you in like this." He deftly pulled several straps across her chest and another one up between her thighs until they buckled near her midriff. "You're sitting on top of live explosives, so whatever you do, *do not* touch this handle, here, unless you want a bonus ride." He pointed to a bright-yellow-and-black-striped handle next to her seat.

Sedona looked quizzically at the lever. "A bonus ride?"

"Yep. That's the free ride you'll get should Diablo decide you need to leave the aircraft during the flight. A free ride aboard your own rocket-propelled ejection seat. Pulling up on this handle will eject you from the aircraft with enough force to compress your spine and cause you to black out." He grinned into her shocked eyes. "I'm sure you won't need to use it."

Sedona made a mental note not to touch the yellow handle under any circumstances. Under Nelson's tutelage, she learned about the physical effects the flight would have on her body, and how to counter the g-forces so she wouldn't pass out. She practiced drawing deep breaths and squeezing her leg muscles to keep her circulation flowing during intense maneuvers.

"You want to tighten those muscles," Nelson explained, "to keep the blood from rushing out of your head to pool in your legs. It's the number-one cause of blackouts."

"Wonderful."

It was several hours later when Angel helped her climb out of the seat and down the ladder.

"Here's a flight suit for you," he smiled, handing her a dark green jumpsuit and a pair of flight boots. "We took the liberty of assigning you a call sign."

Sedona's eyes widened, and she held the suit up by the shoulders to admire the name tag they'd affixed to the front. Sedona "Flygirl" Stewart. Oddly, she felt her chest constrict. Angel had given her a call sign.

"It's perfect," she murmured. And it was. "Do I get to keep the suit after the flight?"

"Well," Angel drawled, "we don't have too many calls for suits in a size small with extra room in the rear and chest."

"Oh!" She smacked him playfully on the arm, then grinned. "I'll just go change."

It wasn't until they were on the flight line and standing next to the actual Coyote that would rocket them into the skies that Sedona felt the first real frisson of fear finger its way along her spine. The Coyote engines were already whining with life, and the flight crew was prepping the aircraft. Standing below the jet, looking up at the blue sky and white clouds reflected on the glass surface of the canopy, she wondered if she really had the nerve to do this.

"C'mon, darling, we have a schedule to keep."

Sergeant Nelson indicated the ladder, and with a sense of foreboding, Sedona climbed up. With Nelson's assistance, she sat down in the snug seat and let him buckle her in. He fitted a helmet onto her head and fastened it beneath her chin, and then rechecked all the safety straps one last time. He was like a mother making sure her child was safely buckled into a car seat. His ministrations made her feel both small and cherished, and she gave him a grateful smile.

As he turned to climb down the ladder, she grasped his arm. "Can you…can you tell me who the plane captain is for this jet?" she asked, hoping her voice didn't betray her fear.

"I did the final inspections myself," Nelson assured her. "Diablo took this jet for a test flight yesterday and it's in perfect condition. You're in good hands."

As long as it wasn't Airman Laudano, she was satisfied. After what Lieutenant Palmer had told her about him, she didn't trust the guy, plain and simple. There was no way she'd voluntarily go up in a jet under his watch. "Right." She gave Nelson a grateful smile. "Well then, I guess that's it."

"Have a good flight, ma'am," he said, and gave her a brief salute before disappearing over the side of the Coyote.

Angel came swiftly up the ladder and before he climbed into the cockpit, he stood looking down at her. "Are you okay?"

He was silhouetted against the backdrop of brilliant blue sky, all wide shoulders and chest. Sedona gave him what she hoped was a confident smile. "Of course. After all, I'm flying with a Top Gun, right?"

"Okay, then." His coffee-dark eyes swept over her, and he smiled, his dimples denting his cheeks. "You look good in there."

Sedona rolled her eyes. "Yeah, right. If my butt was two centimeters wider, I wouldn't be able to fit into this seat."

Angel laughed, a low, rich sound that slid along her senses like melted chocolate. "The seats are supposed to be snug, *mina*. That way, you don't slide around. Nelson showed you where the air-sickness bags are located, right?"

Grimacing, Sedona nodded. "Yes. Please don't do anything that will make me have to use one."

"I'll try. Here's what will happen. We're going up with two other jets. Splatt will be piloting one, and my buddy Tuna will be in the other one. We'll begin by doing some basic maneuvers, and then we'll segue into a mock dogfight." He tapped the side of her helmet. "You'll be able to hear me through your headset. Listen for my instructions, and remember to breathe. You'll be fine."

She drew in a deep breath and smiled. "Okay, then. Let's do this."

Angel grinned and gave her a thumbs-up, before shoving his own helmet down over his head and climbing nimbly into the cockpit. There were several more minutes of tense anticipation for Sedona as he meticulously checked and rechecked his controls, and then she heard his voice in

her ear, the sound so close he might as well have been curled
up around her.

"Okay, Flygirl, here we go. The canopy is coming down.
We'll accelerate to 350 knots, and then go into a vertical
14,000-foot-per-minute climb, and level out at 12,000 feet."

Sedona watched as the glass canopy slowly lowered, near
enough to her head that for a brief instant she was certain
it was going to hit her. She expelled the breath she'd been
holding, and tried to control the nervousness that caused
her heartbeat to pulse hotly in her ears. The canopy closed
with a whoosh and a click. Then it was just her and Angel,
cocooned together in the cockpit of the Coyote.

Glancing out through the glass, she watched as two of
the maintenance crew pulled the blocks from beneath the
wheels. The jet throbbed once as Angel kicked the engines
into gear and they roared into life. Then they were slowly
moving forward, taxiing onto the runway as a crew member guided them.

"And here we go." Angel's voice was calm, assured.

They began to accelerate down the flight line until the
surrounding countryside was nothing more than a blur, and
then *bam!* They weren't just airborne, they were rocketing
straight up into the stratosphere.

Whatever Sedona had expected, it wasn't to be pinned
against her seat back by the sheer force of their upward
momentum. She'd been to Walt Disney World once, had
experienced the g-forces of the Mission to Mars ride, but
nothing could have prepared her for the sense of helpless-
ness she now felt.

Her heart was slamming in her rib cage and her entire
world was reduced to the tiny bubble she sat in, her gaze
locked with desperation onto the back of Angel's seat and
the small bit of his helmet that she could see.

"Okay, now we're leveling out. Give you a chance to enjoy the scenery. How're you doing back there?"

"Good," she squeaked.

And they *had* leveled out. Sedona could actually lift her head enough to peer through the glass at the earth below. It was the loveliest thing she'd ever seen—sweeping carpets of brown, beige and occasional green, and at the very edge of the horizon, shimmering under the sun, she could actually see the ocean. She was just beginning to relax a tiny bit when another Coyote drew alongside them.

"Are they supposed to be that close?" she squealed, her voice sounding frightened, even to her own ears.

"That's Splatt," Angel responded, sounding relaxed and unconcerned. "If you look out the left side of the canopy, you'll see Tuna."

Sedona looked, and sure enough, there was another Coyote on their left flank. As she stared, the pilot gave them a thumbs-up and she could have sworn he grinned.

"Okay, here we go," Angel said. "We'll accelerate into a vertical climb, invert into a 360-degree roll, and then drop out through the bottom. Ready?"

Sedona closed her eyes for a brief second. Damn, the maneuver sounded deadly. "Okay." Her voice was breathless.

"Take a deep breath, squeeze your legs, and…here we go."

Sedona knew a moment of sheer terror as she was pressed back into her seat, and then her head seemed to lift free from her body. Her eyes rolled back in their sockets and blackness fluttered at the edge of her vision.

When she opened her eyes again, the Coyote had leveled out.

"Are you back with me?"

Angel's voice was calm and steady.

"Did I leave?" A vague feeling of nausea settled in the pit of her stomach.

"You blacked out, but just for a moment. It happens, nothing to worry about." Angel's warm assurance filled her ears.

"Oh, God, I'm going to be sick." She grabbed the airsickness bag and to her shame, discovered bananas really *did* taste the same coming back up. She clutched the bag in her hands and tried to concentrate on drawing in deep, cleansing breaths.

"Okay, now?"

She could hear the concern in Angel's voice, and the last thing she wanted was to distract him. She needed him to be one hundred percent focused on his flying.

"Yes," she assured him, trying to sound normal. "I'm good."

"Okay, great," Angel replied, "because now comes the challenging part of the ride. We'll do a mock dogfight with Splatt. First we'll be the chase plane, and then we'll switch and be the ones chased. Ready?"

Sedona closed her eyes and concentrated on her breathing, and tried not to think about the fact she was shooting through the sky like a bullet, completely at the mercy of Angel's piloting skills.

"Three, two, one…fight's on."

The next forty minutes were the most horrific of Sedona's life. At times, they were upside down and Sedona completely lost sight of the horizon. Twice, she experienced tunnel vision, and nausea threatened once more.

Angel pressed the Coyote through a series of maneuvers that made her briefly consider pulling the ejection handle—anything to get her out of this torture chamber and back onto the ground. She gritted her teeth and endured the seemingly endless flight as best she could, but just one thought kept pounding through her head: she was an idiot. A complete and utter idiot.

While she'd truly wanted to ride in a Coyote, the reality was she couldn't handle it. She'd been fooling herself to think she could. The Coyote was sleek and beautiful and powerful, and completely out of her league.

Just like the man who piloted it.

"Okay, Flygirl." His deep, warm voice penetrated her thoughts. "We'll head back home now. A hard brake to slow us down and put us into landing pattern, and then we'll be on the ground."

Sedona fought to maintain consciousness as the braking maneuver exerted yet more g-forces on her already exhausted body. She hardly felt the wheels touch the ground, and closed her eyes with a grateful sigh. Finally, they drew to a stop and a half dozen or more of the maintenance crew immediately converged upon the jet. The canopy opened over her head, and Crew Chief Nelson's smiling face appeared over the edge of the cockpit.

"Welcome back, ma'am." He grinned down at her. "Have a good flight?"

Casting him a baleful look, Sedona reached up with trembling fingers and fumbled with the fastening of her helmet. Nelson brushed her hands aside and with deft movements, removed the helmet and released the safety harness.

"Easy," he said as she pushed herself to a standing position.

Sedona swayed. Her legs wobbled and her head floated about two feet above her shoulders. She flung out an arm to support herself, and the crew chief gripped her firmly by one arm and helped her out of the cockpit and down the ladder.

"Easy does it." He looked sharply at her. "You okay? Maybe you want to go sit down somewhere." Without waiting for a response, he turned to a nearby crew member. "Heilmuller!" he barked. "Accompany Ms. Stewart to the ladies' room, please."

Suppressing a groan, Sedona looked up to see the perky maintenance officer standing to one side as she prepared to help shut down the Coyote.

"Not feeling well?" Heilmuller asked sweetly, her eyes dancing with devilry. "Well, it just goes to show, you really do need the right stuff in order to sit in one of these babies." She extended an arm to Sedona. "I'll walk with you to the hangar. There's a couch in the bathroom where you can lie down for a few minutes and get your land legs back under you."

"No, thanks." Sedona ignored her arm. "I'll be fine, I just need a minute." No way was she going to toss her cookies in front of the sweetly smug petty officer.

"Okay," Heilmuller said, stepping back. "Have it your way."

She turned away, but not before Sedona saw the speculative gleam in her blue eyes. She was only vaguely aware of Angel pulling himself out of the jet and speaking briefly with the crew members. She didn't wait for him, but instead forced herself to walk toward the hangar. Her legs felt like Jell-O, and she was just barely keeping her stomach in check when Angel fell into step beside her.

Sedona cast him one sideways glance. He had his helmet tucked beneath his arm, and his face bore an expression of both satisfaction and pride. Sunlight glinted off his black hair, and she could see her reflection in the mirrored lenses of his aviator sunglasses. His flight suit, with its bulky survival vest, made him seem even bigger, if possible. He looked incredibly handsome. He could have been on the cover of *Life* magazine as the epitome of the all-American hero.

Swallowing hard, she ducked her head and continued walking.

"Hey, hold up a minute." He caught her by the arm and drew her to a halt on the tarmac. "You okay?"

Sedona tipped her head back to look at him. "Yes, thanks. It—it was a great ride. Thrilling. Really." She laughed weakly and held up the air-sickness bag. "I even have a souvenir."

She would have pulled away from him, but he refused to let her go. He yanked his sunglasses off, his dark eyes reflecting both concern and bemusement. "Listen, getting sick isn't uncommon. It's nothing to be ashamed of. Are you sure you're okay?"

"I just—I'm not feeling well."

"That's normal, *mina*. Your body isn't accustomed to the stresses of a flight like that. But you did great."

"Yeah. Sure."

Angel blew out his breath in exasperation. "What the hell is it, Sedona? Were you expecting something less intense? Was it too much for you?" He spread his free hand in a gesture of apology. "I'm sorry. Maybe I got a little carried away. It's just that you seemed to be doing so well back there. I didn't realize you weren't enjoying yourself."

Sedona felt a tightness in her throat and chest. She had to say it and be quick, before she started to cry. "That's just it, don't you see?"

"See what?" He was clearly puzzled.

Sedona spread her arms. "I'm completely out of my element here. I thought I really wanted to go up in that Coyote, and I appreciate you making it happen for me, I really do. But the truth is, I hated it. It *was* too intense. It was more than I could handle."

"Okay," he said, and he smiled at her, a smile that was tender. "So it was a little more extreme than you were prepared for. It's no big deal. It typically takes months of training to be able to do what you just did." He tipped his head down so that he was at eye level with her. "You. Did. Great."

Sedona made a sound of frustration and pulled her arm free. She began walking toward the hangar again, with Angel striding alongside. "I can't do this, Angel."

"What can't you do?"

"Any of it. All of it. Us. *You.*"

"Now hold on just a damn minute." This time there was no escaping his grip as he caught her by the wrist and spun her around. "How is this about us? I thought we were talking about the Coyote ride."

Sedona stared at him, feeling a familiar burning sensation behind her eyes. "We were. But don't you see? Being up there just made me realize what it is you do for a living. Guys like you—you're not normal." She gestured jerkily toward the jet, where Petty Officer Heilmuller's derriere was displayed to full advantage as she leaned deeply into the cockpit of the Coyote to secure the ejection seats. "You're better suited to somebody like *her.*"

"What?" His voice was incredulous and there was no more tenderness in his expression, only bewilderment and the beginning of what might have been anger.

"Don't you understand?" Sedona searched his eyes. "I can't be with a guy who takes the kind of risks you take on a daily basis, Angel. That little jaunt through the clouds scared the hell out of me. Maybe right now you're just doing test flights, but at some point you're going to be recalled to combat duty, and I don't know if I can handle that. Just the thought of you doing that…with the enemy firing at you…"

Sedona turned away abruptly and swiped at her eyes.

When Angel finally spoke, his voice was hard and rough, and his accent more pronounced. "So what are you saying, *mina?* We're through?"

She shrugged, not looking at him. "I think it's for the best, don't you? I think we both knew this was going to happen eventually. I mean, how long do you think you'd be happy with someone like me?" She laughed humorlessly, recalling Mike Sullivan's mocking words when she'd first discovered the existence of the Membership. "After all, my idea of excitement is finding a mint on my hotel pillow."

"Sedona." He placed his helmet on the ground beside them and moved forward to grip both her shoulders in his hands, turning her to face him and searching her eyes with an intensity that left her breathless. "Christ. I don't know what's gotten into you, but if you think you can't make me happy, you're *wrong*. You do make me happy."

"Angel—"

"I'll admit," he rushed on, "when I first saw you in the workout room, my intentions were, well, less than honorable. I figured we could have a good time together while we were here, and then go our separate ways after the inspections were done." His hands tightened on her shoulders. "I swore I wouldn't commit myself to a woman while I was still on active duty. But you know what? I *like* being with you." He chuckled ruefully. "Okay, I *love* being with you. I can't wait until the day's over so I can be with you again. Doesn't that mean anything?"

Sedona's gaze slid from his face and fastened on the zipper of his flight suit. She couldn't meet his eyes, not when his expression was so earnest. "It's just lust, Angel. That and convenience. I mean, look at you. You could have any woman you want. You're only with me right now because I came on to you pretty strong." She wet her lips nervously. "I didn't give you much choice in the matter."

"Oh, come on, Sedona." His voice was full of contempt. "Is that really what you believe? That this—this *thing* we have is nothing more than lust?"

She forced herself to meet his eyes without flinching. "Yes. Because one day you're going to look at me and wonder what the hell it was you ever saw in me. This isn't real, Angel. It's like—like a fairy tale or something. It's better to just end it now, while we're still feeling good about each other."

Angel let his hands drop to his sides and took a step back from her, looking at her as if he had no idea who she was.

"You're wrong," he finally told her. "I think you're an amazing woman. You're beautiful and brilliant, and I think we're good together." He rubbed a hand over his head. "Hell, we're *great* together, and what's more, you know we are."

Sedona shook her head. "It would never work, and you know it. You're like that jet you fly—more than most people can handle and best appreciated from a distance." She shrugged helplessly. "I realize…you and the Coyote are a package deal. It's the price of admission, but you know what? I can't afford it."

She turned away, wanting only to escape before she said or did something really stupid. Like throw herself at him and tell him she was completely, foolishly, head over heels in love with him. He tried to forestall her with a hand on her arm, but she pulled away, refusing to look at him, and continued to walk toward the hangar.

"You know what the problem is, Sedona?" he snarled softly. "You're a coward. You're afraid to take risks, afraid to reach out and grab your dreams with both hands and make them come true. Like that sketchbook of yours, you hide them away and hope nobody finds out about them."

Sedona's step faltered and she stopped for just a moment, but she didn't turn around. Her heart was thudding hot and loud in her ears, but not enough to drown out the painful truth of his words. After a second, she started walking again, determined this time not to stop. Not to listen.

"But you know what, *mina?*" His voice was low and bitter. "Those drawings of me won't keep you warm at night. Go ahead and carry them around with you, but they're not me. They're nothing but a flat caricature of the real thing. Kinda like you."

She made it maybe another dozen steps before she stopped and turned around. Angel was striding away from her, back toward the Coyote and the maintenance crew, and the other two pilots who had landed behind them. His steps were hard and the set of his broad shoulders was rigid with anger.

For an instant, she almost called his name. She wanted to run after him and tell him…what? That she'd just made a huge mistake, and of course she was the right woman for him? A frown hitched between her brows and she chewed her lower lip. Better to let him go now than to see him grow bored and turn away from her later. And he would. Eventually, he'd need more excitement than she'd be able to provide. Guys like Angel Torres didn't live happily ever after with plain-Jane engineers like herself.

She turned away, his words repeating themselves in her head. *You're a coward…a flat caricature of the real thing… afraid to take risks.*

She was going to be sick.

She ran the last few yards to the hangar and barely made it to the ladies' room before she began retching. But there was nothing left in her stomach and after a few minutes she collapsed, weak and gasping, onto the sofa in the small, adjoining room. She swiped at the tears that blurred her vision, and sniffed loudly, staring up at the ceiling.

Her entire body ached. She felt nauseous and dizzy. Her head hurt. But even those physical discomforts didn't match the gnawing ache that had settled in the center of her chest. With a small moan of distress, she curled onto her side.

You're a coward.

The words mocked her, taunted her. Made her want to shrivel up and die of shame.

Angel was right. She *was* a coward, and in more ways than he knew. If she was honest with herself—and the cowardly part of her didn't want to be honest—she'd been a complete wimp for most of her life.

All her life, really. For as far back as she could remember, she'd done things to make others happy. Never once had she stood up and done something to please herself. As a teenager, she'd been too afraid of defying her father to pursue a career in the arts. She'd been too afraid of his censure to purchase those fabulously feminine outfits with the short skirts and matching pumps. And she'd been too afraid of failure to try to make a go of a relationship with Angel.

She'd been too afraid for too long.

For a brief instant, she saw her entire life stretched out before her, filled with all the wrong choices she would make because of her own cowardice. Oh, she'd do okay. She'd have a good career and a nice place to live. But she'd be miserable and unfulfilled. Empty.

Like she felt right now.

With a groan of self-disgust, she swung her legs off the sofa and sat up, scrubbing her hands over her face. Even her decision to leave the agency was based on her own cowardice, because she didn't have the guts to do what was required to expose the Membership.

Well, no more. God, she'd been such a moron.

She might not have the courage to make her relationship with Angel work, but that didn't mean she had to be a coward in every other aspect of her life. It was time she took control, and she knew just where to start.

15

"HEY, STEWART, YOU have a call on line three."

Sedona turned away from the glass window that separated the calibration room from the test cell, where she'd been watching two of the maintenance crew prepare an engine for testing.

"Okay, thanks." She acknowledged the engineering technician with a brief smile and picked up the receiver.

"Miss Stewart?" It was a deep, male voice and for just an instant, her heart leaped, until she realized that, of course, it wasn't Angel. She hadn't seen or heard from him since their ugly confrontation four days earlier.

Her entire body ached with longing for him.

"Yes, this is Stewart."

"Ma'am, this is Senior Chief Hamlin over in Hangar 74. We're conducting an engine teardown, and you asked me to contact you if I found anything…interesting."

Sedona's breath caught. "Yes? What did you find?"

There was a brief pause. "Maybe you'd better come over and check it out for yourself."

"I'm on my way. Who else have you contacted?"

"Captain Dawson came over with a couple of his guys and took a look. He's gone now, but he was pretty pissed. He's called for a full investigation and is sending over a security unit. My guess is they'll cordon off this hangar once they see what I've found. I'd hurry if I were you."

"I'll be right there."

She replaced the receiver and turned to the engineering technician. "I have to go over to Hangar 74. Give Ken Larson a call and ask him to come up and oversee this test." She gave him an apologetic smile. "I'd do it myself, but I'm in a hurry."

He shrugged. "No problem, ma'am. I'll call him right now."

Sedona hurried from the test cell, wincing as she stepped outside into a blinding rainstorm. The sullen clouds, clustered on the horizon all morning, had finally moved directly overhead, drenching the air base with sheeting rain. The dismal weather completely matched her mood.

She hadn't seen Angel during the four days since their confrontation on the flight line. He'd even packed his gear and moved out of his hotel room and into the Bachelor Office Quarters on base. Not that she blamed him. She'd been a complete bitch, taking all her fear and insecurities out on him.

She didn't know how long she would have been able to resist him had he remained in the room next to hers. She'd picked up her cell phone more than a dozen times, intending to apologize and beg his forgiveness—anything to have him back in her life. But each time, she remembered his expression of contempt as he accused her of being a coward. He was right. She'd put the phone away without hitting the send button.

She bent her head, bracing herself against the soaking onslaught of rain. Wind howled across the open space, and through the downpour, Sedona could see the Coyotes sitting on the flight line, their profiles blurred by the spray of water.

Was Angel flying in this weather? She told herself it didn't matter; he'd fly well above the cloud bank and would hardly be affected by the storm.

Shielding her eyes against the stinging rain, she skirted the far side of the building where Ken Larson was overseeing the removal of a Coyote engine. The last thing she wanted was to run into him. He'd demand to know where she was going, and there was no way she wanted him tagging along.

She entered Hangar 74 and paused for a moment to swipe at the rain that still dripped from her hair and down her face. As she did so, the sound of low, angry voices drifted toward her from the other side of a large compressor.

Cautiously, she peered around the edge of the machine. Airman Laudano, his face drawn in harsh lines, had Airman Wheeler shoved up against the wall of the hangar as he spoke in hushed, fierce tones to the other man.

"You say my sister means everything to you. Well, now's the time to prove it. You screw this up and you'll never see her again." He gave Wheeler a brief, hard shake. "You have my promise on that."

He let go of the other man, taking a moment to smooth the fabric of Wheeler's flight suit where he'd had it bunched in his hand. Then he turned and walked away.

As if sensing her scrutiny, Wheeler turned his head and his eyes locked with Sedona's. They stared at each other for a long moment. He was pale except for two patches of color that rode high on his cheekbones. For a moment, Sedona thought he would speak, would say something to explain the bizarre interaction she'd just witnessed. His mouth opened, then closed, and before she could say anything, he turned and followed Laudano toward the rear of the hangar.

She watched him go. Was Wheeler dating Laudano's sister? What had Laudano meant by Wheeler not screwing this up? Had he been referring to Wheeler's relationship with the sister, or something more sinister?

Thoughtful, Sedona turned and made her way to where several maintenance-crew members gathered around a Coyote. One of the engines hung suspended from a lift several feet away. Senior Chief Hamlin bent over the remaining engine, still installed in the jet, while the other technicians strained to peer over his shoulder.

"Hey," she said as she approached the group. She tucked several loose strands of wet hair behind her ears. "I came as fast as I could. What do you have?"

The senior chief backed carefully out of the engine compartment, carrying a small mirror in one hand. "Well, this particular jet was out on the flight line this morning, and was mistakenly put into the queue for flight testing."

"Did one of our pilots take it up?" She glanced out the enormous doors of the hangar to where the jets were parked. Where was Angel right now?

"No, ma'am," Hamlin replied. "We caught the problem in time, but if someone *had* taken this jet up, it could have resulted in a catastrophic engine failure."

Sedona's breath caught. "Why?"

He held out his hand. Lying in his palm were three small, metal balls. "I found these inside the fan module."

Sedona frowned. "You found three ball bearings just rolling around? Wasn't that the cause of damage to the fan blades on the last engine we looked at?"

"Yes, ma'am." Hamlin's voice was grim. "But these weren't just rolling around." He drew her aside and lowered his voice. "These were actually fastened to the back side of the fan blades with adhesive."

Sedona stared at him, bewildered. *"What?"*

"I've seen this before. It's usually done to cause engine damage before the jet leaves the ground. However, in this case the adhesive is of such high quality, I believe the ball bearings would remain in place until the jet was airborne. Eventually, the sheer force of the fan suction would cause the adhesive to fatigue. When that happens, the ball bearings would get sucked through the fan modules and the afterburner, trashing the engine on their way out."

"Enough to cause an in-flight failure," Sedona said softly, her eyes wide.

"Exactly."

Sedona met the senior chief's grim expression. "Sabotage?"

"No question."

"Whoever did this believed this particular jet was going to be flight-tested today."

He nodded. "It would seem so. If we hadn't pulled it from the lineup, the jet would have gone up."

Angel. "Oh, my God," she breathed. "How many jets are in the air right now?"

"We've implemented a no-fly procedure until the remaining jets can be cleared, and the commander is sending a unit out to secure the entire area, but we have four pilots conducting test flights right now."

"And they are…?"

Hamlin shook his head. "I don't have that information." Something on the flight line caught his attention. "There's Captain Dawson now, with Lieutenant Palmer. You might ask them. Looks like they're heading up to the control tower."

Sedona followed his gaze and saw Captain Dawson and Lieutenant Palmer surrounded by several other naval officers, heads bent and black umbrellas tipped against the driving rain as they strode across the tarmac toward the building that housed the control tower for the naval base.

"Do they know?"

"Oh, yeah."

"Okay, thanks." She began to turn away, when a thought struck her. "Senior Chief, do you happen to know what the relationship is between Airman Laudano and Airman Wheeler?"

"Excuse me?" His expression was bewildered.

"Is Airman Wheeler dating Laudano's sister?"

"Oh, yeah." The senior chief gave a brief grin. "Actually, I think Wheeler is engaged to Laudano's sister. Met her when Laudano brought him home for Thanksgiving one year."

"Thanks. I was just curious."

Her mind spun as she turned away, alarm bells jangling in her head. It had certainly sounded like Laudano was blackmailing Wheeler, and she didn't have to guess why. As a plane captain, Laudano had access to the Coyote engines. He could easily have planted those ball bearings.

Maybe Airman Wheeler had discovered what his future brother-in-law was up to, and had threatened to expose him. But even if Wheeler lacked the courage to do the right thing, she didn't. She would go directly to the military police and tell them what she suspected. But first, she had to make sure Angel wasn't up there, flying a jet that Laudano had inspected.

By the time she reached the control tower, she was drenched through to the skin and Captain Dawson and his entourage had already vanished inside. She pressed the buzzer next to the secure entrance, gasping for breath from her dash across the base.

"Yes?"

Sedona blinked up at the security camera mounted above the door and spoke into the small speaker beneath the buzzer. "Um, this is Sedona Stewart. I'm part of the Coyote inspection team, and I need to speak with Captain Dawson or Lieutenant Palmer. Right away."

There was a momentary silence.

"Come on up, Miss Stewart." The door buzzed.

She pushed it open and took the stairs two at a time as they wound upward, until her thighs cramped in protest and she thought her lungs would burst. By the time she reached the top of the stairs, she'd climbed eight flights. She paused in front of another door of dark, smoked glass. She pressed the buzzer and this time the door opened immediately.

The control room was cool and dark, dimly lit by neon blue halogen lights. Sedona struggled to check her ragged breathing as she climbed the last flight of steps. Through the observation windows, the air traffic controllers had unobstructed views of the flight line and the surrounding countryside, only slightly obscured by the sheeting rain that drummed against the glass.

The entire perimeter of the small room was occupied by a vast array of computer displays and digital readouts. Three men, each of them wearing a headset, rolled their chairs between the various monitors, watching the blips on the screens and dictating coordinates and flight instructions into their mouthpieces.

Leaning over them, crowding the small space, were Captain Dawson, Lieutenant Palmer and two other naval officers. They all turned to look at her as she rounded the last step and entered the room.

"Captain Dawson." She paused to catch her breath. "Thank you for seeing me."

"Miss Stewart." His voice betrayed his astonishment as he took in her disheveled appearance. "Is there something I can help you with?"

"Actually, yes." She glanced out the window toward the distant Coyote hangar, where she could still see the senior chief standing next to the sabotaged engine. "I, uh, just came from the Coyote hangar, where I saw evidence of sabotage. I need to know if you have any Coyotes in the air right now."

Captain Dawson considered her for a moment, and Sedona thought he was actually going to tell her what she needed to know. But then his lips compressed in what might have been sympathy, before turning back to the controls. "Thank you for your concern, Miss Stewart, but we have everything in hand."

It was a dismissal. Sedona glanced at Lieutenant Palmer, but he stared resolutely through the windows and refused to meet her eyes.

"I understand, sir," she forced herself to say, "but I have reason to believe the Coyotes scheduled for today's test flights may also be compromised." She stopped just short of demanding to know if Angel was up in one of those jets.

"We've already contacted the authorities, Miss Stewart," Captain Dawson replied. "We have the situation contained."

It seemed she wasn't going to get any information from him, and she rubbed her hand across the back of her neck in an effort to dispel some of her tension. "Okay." She sighed. "Can you at least tell me if Lieutenant Torres is up there? We're…friends. I'm concerned for his safety."

One of the men swiveled in his chair to face her, pulling one side of his headset away from his ear. "Hello, ma'am," he said, extending a hand toward her. "I'm Tim Colletti, the flight commander. In answer to your question, yes, Diablo is up there, but I assure you, there's nothing to worry about. I served with him aboard the *Lincoln,* and he was the best damn stick in the squadron."

"Did somebody go over his jet before it went up? Who was the last person to check it, to touch it before it went up?"

Lieutenant Palmer finally turned to face her. "It wasn't Airman Laudano, if that's what you're thinking. He hasn't been on duty since yesterday, and he didn't oversee any of the jets that went up today." His voice held a note of defiance and more than a little smugness, but Sedona hardly noticed for the relief that flooded her. That Laudano apparently had not been on duty that morning, and hadn't been near Angel's jet, allowed her to breathe easier, if only a little.

"So, who was the plane captain for Lieutenant Torres's jet?" she persisted.

Lieutenant Palmer leaned back in his chair and crossed his arms over his chest, looking at Captain Dawson for approval, before turning his attention back to Sedona.

"It was Airman Wheeler," he finally said. "He performed the final inspections. We already spoke with him. Everything seemed in order."

Sedona nodded. "Okay, then." Thank God.

They were each looking expectantly at her, and she shoved her hands into her pockets and took two steps backward toward the stairs. "I just, you know, wanted to make sure he was okay up there, but it seems like you have everything under control, so I'll just be going."

She felt like an idiot, and knew both Captain Dawson and Lieutenant Palmer would have been in complete agreement with that sentiment, but she no longer cared. Angel was safe and that was all that mattered.

She had just turned away when the sound of Angel's voice on the control-tower radio caused her to stop in her tracks.

"Roadrunner, this is Diablo. I have a problem."

Sedona stood, riveted, as every man in the room converged on the instrument panels.

"This is Roadrunner," replied the flight boss. "Go ahead, Diablo."

"I've lost my left engine. It's blown to hell. I have FOD tearing through the fuselage. I have one good engine, but I'm losing altitude."

"Roger that, Diablo. Start ejection sequence."

Even as Commander Colletti began speaking, Sedona heard Captain Dawson swear softly beneath his breath. He turned to Lieutenant Palmer. "Get those other aircraft back on the ground. *Now.*"

"Yessir." Lieutenant Palmer snatched up a spare headset and began contacting the other pilots, commanding them to return to base.

"Negative on ejection." Angel's voice was eerily calm. "I have civilian population below…attempting to reach open water."

"Jesus," breathed Lieutenant Palmer, looking up at Captain Dawson. "If he's already breaking up, he'll never make it."

Together they watched the tiny green blip on the radar screen that was Angel's jet. Without realizing she did so, Sedona moved closer to stare with horrified fascination at the small dot as it blinked across the monitor. She knew the jet was traveling at hundreds of miles per hour, but it appeared to travel at a snail's pace across the screen.

Sedona felt light-headed. This couldn't be happening. The very scenario she had dreaded was unfolding before her eyes. She saw the perimeter of the land mass faintly outlined on the radar screen, and though Angel was closing the distance to the water, she also saw he was rapidly losing altitude.

"Roadrunner, this is Splatt. I have Diablo covered at five o'clock and it doesn't look good. He's spewing body parts and fuel."

Sedona gasped. *Body parts?*

Commander Colletti yanked his mouthpiece away and met her horrified gaze. "Pieces of the aircraft are breaking away," he explained grimly. He shoved the mouthpiece back into place. "Eject, Diablo. Repeat, eject."

"Negative, sir. I can still make open water."

"Diablo, this is a direct order. *Eject.*"

"Roadrunner, this is Splatt. Diablo still in control of aircraft and accelerating toward open water." An instant later,

"Belay that message, Roadrunner. He's losing control of the jet. Hard yaw to the left…now back to the right. He's overcompensated. Aircraft in a flat spin. Looks like an out-of-control Frisbee. He's shooting flames and throwing debris. The aircraft is over open water."

"Dammit, Diablo, *eject!*"

There was a momentary silence. Every person in the control tower leaned forward. Sedona passed a hand over her eyes, feeling ill. Even if Angel did eject, could he do it in time to avoid serious injury? She'd read numerous accident reports during her years with Aerospace International and she knew how dangerous ejection could be to the pilot. With the aircraft in a spin, Angel could inadvertently eject directly into the water and be killed instantly. Even if he ejected correctly, he could be rendered unconscious and drown before they could rescue him.

"Roadrunner, this is Splatt. Aircraft down over open water. Pilot ejected. Repeat, pilot ejected and in the water."

Sedona didn't wait to hear more. With a muttered curse, she turned on her heel toward the stairs.

"Miss Stewart!" Captain Dawson's voice stopped her in her tracks. "Where are you going?"

She looked up, directly into the captain's eyes, and didn't try to hide the tears of fury that blurred her vision. "I'm going to find the son of a bitch who sabotaged that aircraft."

THE CENTRIFUGAL FORCE was enough to pin Angel to the instrument panel as the aircraft yawed in a corkscrew motion. Full thrust on his one good engine swung the tail around and the aircraft veered in the other direction. The sound of screaming engine and twisting metal filled the cockpit, and the acrid stench of burning jet fuel filled his nostrils.

He slammed the stick left to compensate, but it wasn't enough. The vortex of the falling jet caused his one good engine to flame out, and then he dropped below the canopy of clouds and into the thick soup of the coastal storm.

Through a break in the clouds below him, Angel glimpsed the churning waters of the Pacific as the earth rose to meet him. Using every bit of strength he had to push against the g-forces that held him immobile, he reached back and wrapped his hand around the ejection handle and began the ejection sequence.

Almost immediately, the Coyote's canopy blasted away, sucked upward into the turbulent skies. Angel yanked the handle. He slammed back into his seat as the ejection-seat straps responded. One. Two. The rockets beneath the seat blasted him out of the jet. The stunning impact jarred his teeth and caused his head to snap back. Then he was tumbling, free-falling through the stormy skies.

Instinctively, he reached up and groped for the straps that held him pinned to the seat. He pulled on them sharply, then the seat tumbled away and his chute streamed out. He glanced upward, saw it balloon open and gritted his teeth against the violent snap that stopped his fall and jerked him upward until he was floating, suspended in his harness beneath the open chute. He drifted for scant seconds as rain sluiced over his helmet and into his face, before he plunged into the sea.

Something in his ankle snapped, but before he could think about it, his heavy gear sucked him down and the dark waters of the Pacific closed over his head. Almost immediately, the life preserver that was built into his survival vest inflated around his neck, pressing against his jaw. Using his arms and legs, he fought to propel himself upward. Before he could reach the surface, he was yanked hard to one side as the wind caught his chute, dragging him through the churning waters and twisting him in the straps. He was turning over and over as he struggled desperately to release himself from the tangled line.

He burst through to the surface and sucked in huge gulps of air, heedless of the rain that lashed his face. Reaching up, he fumbled with the release snaps, and fell back into the water as the parachute finally broke free and whipped across the waves like a giant kite.

The sea was rough, with eight-foot chops. Gusts of wind blew blinding spray into his face. At one point, when a large wave buoyed him up, he thought he glimpsed debris from his jet floating a short distance away. His heavy gear threatened to drag him beneath the surface once again. His own harsh breathing filled his ears. His body felt battered, almost too weak to continue treading water, and he became aware of the throbbing pain in his left ankle.

Summoning up his last bit of strength, he twisted and fumbled with fingers that were cold and numb, until he located the inflatable raft attached to his harness. He pulled the cord and the orange raft burst open with a hiss until it bounced beside him on the surface.

Angel hooked an arm over the side, pulled himself into the small opening, ignoring the screaming protest of his injured leg, and collapsed onto his back, exhausted. He flung an arm over his eyes and breathed heavily, letting the undulating waves soothe his body.

He was alive.

Pushing to a sitting position, he braced himself against the side of the raft and bent over to examine his injured leg. Gritting his teeth against the shooting pain, he unlaced his boot and peeled the wet fabric of his flight suit back far enough to assess the damage. It looked to be a compound fracture of his ankle. The skin around the protruding bone was ragged and inflamed, but there was little blood and, if he didn't move too much, the pain was bearable. The bone must have snapped on impact with the water, though he barely recalled feeling it at the time. He eased the fabric back into place and sank back against the edge of the raft.

He was alive.

Despite the loss of the Coyote, and the pain in his ankle, he smiled. He'd managed to push the aircraft, even with the damage she'd sustained, to the safety of the open ocean. When he'd first heard the terrifying *boom* of the engine, seen the warning lights begin to flash, and then felt the aircraft shudder and falter as the foreign object tore through the engine compartment and shredded the turbofans, he'd known he wasn't going to be landing. He just wanted to ensure the inevitable crash didn't take innocent lives. But damn, he regretted the loss of the Coyote.

Where was Sedona right now? Had she heard about the crash? God, he hoped not. It would only confirm her belief that his job was too dangerous.

An image of her floated behind his closed eyes—Sedona smiling, laughing, doing things that completely blew his mind and made him ache to take her. Her words echoed in his head. *"Guys like you—you're not normal...I can't be with a guy who takes the kind of risks you take on a daily basis."*

He lifted his arm from his face and stared into the pewter clouds overhead, letting the rain wash against his skin.

He was alive.

Despite the pain in his leg, and despite the fact he was floating somewhere out in the middle of the goddamn ocean with a monsoon pouring down on him, he felt great. Maybe he'd gambled with his life today, but it had shown him how precious that life was. And way too short to go it alone.

For an instant, when he'd been unsure if the Coyote was going to stay airborne long enough to push her out over the water, when he didn't know if he'd be able to eject safely, one thought had consumed him: if he didn't survive, Sedona would never know he loved her.

He'd already known he was falling for her, and fast. Despite his resolve not to become seriously involved, he hadn't counted on his heart having other plans. He'd told Sedona he wanted a relationship with her, but maybe if he'd told her he loved her she wouldn't have walked away.

He needed to talk to her, convince her to give them a chance. As soon as he got back to Lemoore, he'd tell her how he felt about her. He'd even give up combat flying. Maybe he could get an assignment as a flight instructor, either at Lemoore or Oceana. As an instructor, he could experience the thrill of combat flight every day.

The thought of being grounded long enough to actually establish roots brought him a profound sense of well-being. He and Sedona belonged together, and it was way past time he told her so.

16

SEDONA MADE IT all the way back to the Coyote hangar before Lieutenant Palmer caught up with her. He grabbed her by the arm and dragged her to a stop just outside the hangar.

"Just what the hell do you think you're doing, Ms. Stewart?"

Sedona turned to face him, squinting through the rain that lashed her face and whipped hair into her eyes. "I'm going to find Airman Laudano," she said, wreathing her words with a patently false smile, "and then I'm going to wring the little bastard's neck until he confesses."

"I already told you," Lieutenant Palmer said between gritted teeth, "Laudano didn't inspect those jets."

"I know. You already said Airman Wheeler did. But I can't believe he sabotaged those jets. My money's still on Laudano." She bit the words out and wrenched her arm free of his grasp at the same time.

Casting a baleful glance up at the sky, Lieutenant Palmer grimaced and shoved her ahead of him into the shelter of the hangar. "Let's get the hell out of this rain, then we'll talk."

Inside the hangar, Sedona shook the water from her arms and hands, and used her fingers to wipe the moisture from her face. She turned to look at Lieutenant Palmer, who was squeezing the water out of his hat.

"Okay," she said, impatience edging her voice. "I'm listening."

The lieutenant glanced around as if someone might overhear them. "I didn't want to say anything until I was sure, but…" His voice dropped and he cast an uneasy glance over his shoulder. "I have reason to believe Wheeler *is* the one sabotaging the jets."

Sedona's eyebrows flew up. "*Wheeler?* But—"

"*Shh!*" Lieutenant Palmer gestured furiously for her to keep her voice down. "It's only a suspicion I have."

A frown hitched between Sedona's brows. "Well, have you talked to the investigators about your suspicions? I mean, Christ, Angel's jet is down!"

A tightening in her throat, accompanied by a sudden burning sensation at the back of her eyes, forced her to look away. She had to get a grip on herself or she was going to lose it. She blinked rapidly. The man she loved was somewhere in the waters of the Pacific, and she didn't even know if he was alive. Swallowing hard, she composed her features and turned back to Palmer. "Just when were you planning on sharing this bit of information?"

Palmer shifted uncomfortably, and his eyes slid away from hers. "Soon. Right away. I just wanted to be sure. And I am." He nodded his head, as if to convince himself. "Yeah, I'm pretty sure it's Wheeler."

Sedona recalled the plane captain's wholesome good looks and shy nature. There was no way she could envision him doing anything as treacherous as sabotaging the Coyotes. During the exchange she'd witnessed earlier, it had sure looked like Laudano was threatening Wheeler. Had those threats been related to the Coyotes?

She narrowed her eyes at the lieutenant. "What about Laudano? If he's already on restriction because of some offense, wouldn't it make sense to look at him first? Maybe this is some twisted attempt at revenge. Besides, I heard him threatening Wheeler. Maybe it was to keep him quiet."

"I already told you, he wasn't the last one to inspect the jets. Wheeler was."

Sedona turned away and pinched the bridge of her nose. It made no sense. What possible reason could Wheeler have for wanting to jeopardize the lives of the Coyote pilots? She'd been so certain that if anyone was responsible for sabotaging those jets, it was Laudano.

"I just don't get it," she muttered. "Why would Wheeler do such a thing?" She turned back to Palmer, who watched her closely. "Where is Laudano now?"

"You can't talk to him. He's on restriction and I'm sure the investigation team is prohibiting contact with any of the plane captains until they've had the chance to question them."

Loud voices drifted to Sedona from across the hangar, momentarily distracting her. A team of military police strode through the hangar, barking directions to seal off the Coyotes and quarantine the area.

"Well, it's about time," she said darkly. "I'll just bet those MPs will be interested in hearing your theories about Wheeler." Without waiting for a reply, she moved toward them with long, determined strides.

"No, wait!" Lieutenant Palmer took two swift steps after her and grabbed her upper arm, spinning her around.

"What—?" Sedona tried to wrench free.

"Just *wait,* dammit!" Palmer's eyes looked wild and unfocused. He tightened his grip on her arm. "I have to tell you—"

"Let me go," Sedona said, her voice low and tight. *"Now."* She stared at Palmer, and even with the military police just steps away, a frisson of fear feathered its way up her spine as she watched his eyes. He didn't release her; instead, he began to haul her toward him and Sedona had a vision of him dragging her out of the hangar before she had a chance to speak to the police.

"Hey!" She resisted, twisting her arm in his grasp and straining to pull away from him. "I said let me go!"

"No, wait. Please!"

At the same instant she managed to jerk her arm free, she stepped back, directly onto a patch of oil-slickened floor. Her foot flew out from beneath her and she teetered precariously. With a sharp cry, she grabbed at Lieutenant Palmer's shirtfront. Unbalanced, he cartwheeled his arms and in the next instant they both toppled to the floor. Sedona landed heavily on her backside with the lieutenant on top of her. She shoved at Palmer's shoulders. He groaned and rolled to his back beside her.

"Ma'am?"

Looking up, she saw a burly MP bending over them. He extended a hand and hauled her to her feet.

"Oh, man," she said ruefully, "that hurt."

She rubbed her posterior and looked down at Palmer as he sat up. His shirt was partially pulled out of his waistband and several buttons had popped free where she had grabbed him. He leaned forward and pushed himself to his feet. As he did so, a handful of small metal balls fell out of his breast pocket and skittered madly across the concrete floor, like beads from a broken necklace.

Stopping one with her foot, Sedona bent down and picked it up. "What is this, Lieutenant Palmer? A ball bearing?"

Palmer stared at the small sphere that rested in her palm, before his glance shot to the military police with something like panic. "I—I know what you're thinking, but this isn't what it looks like."

Sedona stared at him in dawning horror. "Did *you* do it? Did you put those ball bearings on the back of the fans?"

His eyes shifted to the military-police officer who stood beside her, and his hand pressed furtively against the pocket of his trousers.

"What do you have in your pocket, Lieutenant?" she asked. "Anything you'd care to show us? Maybe some more ball bearings? Is that what you were doing when I saw you on the flight line that night?"

"I—I don't know what you're talking about," he stammered. His gaze flicked between her and the MPs who now ringed them.

Sedona held out her hand. "Then you won't mind showing us what's in your pocket."

When it seemed he might actually refuse, one of the military police took a step forward. "Sir, please empty your pockets."

Palmer looked desperately around, as if seeking some escape. Seeing none, his shoulders sagged. He reached into his pocket and withdrew what looked like a trial-size tube of toothpaste.

"I never meant to hurt anyone," he muttered.

The MP took the tube and turned it over in his hands. "Industrial-strength adhesive," he murmured, reading the words on the outside of the tube. He looked back at Palmer, his eyes hard. "I'm sorry, sir, but you'll need to come with us and answer a few questions."

"Wait a minute," Sedona interrupted. "I just want to know one thing, Lieutenant Palmer." She stared at him, as if by searching his eyes she might glean some understanding of what would prompt him to commit such a crime. "Why?"

"I think I can answer that for you."

Sedona whirled around. Standing several feet away was Airman Wheeler. His face was grim.

"Please tell me you're not involved in this," Sedona breathed.

He flushed. "No, ma'am, except as a potential scapegoat." He gave Palmer one brief glance, filled with both sympathy and disgust. "I found out Laudano's been buying drugs for this guy." He grimaced. "I even agreed to keep quiet about it since we're almost family, but Laudano got caught bringing some of that crap back onto the base. He refused to implicate the good lieutenant here, but it looks like neither one of them trusted me to keep my mouth shut."

Sedona knew her own mouth was open, but she couldn't help it. "That's what all this is about?" She turned to face Palmer. "Because you have a drug problem, you'd be willing to sabotage the Coyotes and set Wheeler up to take the blame?"

The military police moved to either side of Palmer. He offered no resistance when they drew his arms behind his back and secured them.

"You think it was just about the drugs, Stewart?" His voice was filled with contempt. "Those sons of bitches at Top Gun owe me. They *owe* me! Do you know how many years I spent trying to make the cut? And those bastards kept denying me. Do you know what that does to your psyche? To your self-esteem? To be looked down on by guys like Diablo and Tuna?"

Crew members began to drift over from their workstations to witness the unfolding drama as the police led him away. He twisted to look at her over his shoulder. "I'm a good pilot!" he cried. "I could have been up there with the best if they'd only given me a chance! But they wouldn't, and for that they had to pay! *Someone* had to pay!"

"It's not just about being good enough," Sedona replied. "It's about having the right character." She stood and stared after him, but it wasn't until he had disappeared from sight that she realized she was shaking.

"Ma'am?"

She turned to see Airman Wheeler looking at her with concern. She passed a hand over her eyes. "I'm sorry. I—I have to get out of here. I need to find out about Diablo."

"Yes, ma'am. Is there anything I can do?"

"Yes." She gave him a trembling smile. "Next time, have enough guts to do the right thing."

He looked shamefaced. "Yes, ma'am. I only kept quiet because I didn't want to get Laudano in any more trouble. I'm going to marry his sister, and if she thought—"

"If she loves you, she'll understand. She'll stand by you, no matter what."

"Is that what you'd do? Stand beside your man, no matter what?"

Sedona gave a shaky laugh, feeling tears spring to her eyes. "Yes. If he'll have me. If he's still—"

For the first time, a ghost of a smile touched Wheeler's mouth. "Ma'am, the reason I came here was to tell you they just recovered Diablo. He's on his way to the hospital right now."

SEDONA STOOD BESIDE the hospital bed and watched Angel as he slept. The room was dark except for one dim light over the adjoining-bathroom door, but despite the dimness, she thought she could see faint shadows beneath his closed eyes.

A rescue helicopter had plucked him from the churning sea and transported him back to Lemoore Naval Air Station, where he'd undergone surgery to repair the damage to his shattered ankle. Encased in a cast, his lower leg rested in a padded sling suspended over his bed. They'd had to use screws and pins to hold the fractured bones together, but she'd been assured he would make a full recovery.

It was the middle of the night, but Sedona hadn't been able to leave the hospital. The thought of going back to her empty hotel room was completely depressing. She also had an irrational fear that if she didn't stand watch by his bedside, death might still find a way to take him from her. She wanted to be with Angel—*needed* to be with Angel—and when the nurses on duty had seen her determination, they'd reluctantly allowed her to stay on the condition that she did not wake him.

She dragged a chair close to the bed and she sank onto it. Even now, she could scarcely believe he'd survived.

Reaching out, she took his hand in hers and gently stroked the back of it, admiring the long fingers. She loved his hands, loved how strong and capable they were. Loved how gentle they could be.

She started when his fingers closed around her own and squeezed gently. Jerking her gaze upward, she saw his eyes were open. He watched her with a quiet intensity, as if he half expected her to bolt. But there was no way she was leaving.

"Hey," she said softly, and leaned closer, cupping his hand between hers. "How're you feeling?"

"What are you doing here?" His voice was raspy and low, and the sound of it caressed her like a warm flame. "What time is it?"

"It's just after midnight. Everyone else went home. Splatt and Tuna, Captain Dawson…just about everyone from the Coyote flight line was here earlier. Even Petty Officer Heilmuller." She rolled her eyes and smiled. "She was actually here the longest." Sedona didn't tell Angel the other woman had left less than an hour earlier. She'd seemed determined to be at Angel's side when he regained consciousness, insisting he'd want to see a friendly face. Sedona was certain her own less-than-friendly demeanor had finally driven her away. "I—I couldn't leave." Sedona swallowed and dropped her gaze. "I wanted to be with you."

His fingers squeezed hers, and when she looked up, his eyes were warm. "I'm glad you're here. We need to talk."

Sedona shook her head and laid two fingers across his lips. "No, it's okay. You don't need to say anything. You were right about everything. I'm a complete coward. About us, about my life…about everything." To her horror, tears stung her eyes and blurred her vision. "You're a phenomenal pilot, Angel. Nobody could have done what you did up there today." She swallowed hard. "The navy needs guys like you."

"And what about you, *mina?* Do you need a guy like me?"

"Angel…don't." Her voice broke.

"Come here."

She didn't protest when he pulled her hard across his chest and enclosed her in the warmth of his arms. Her face lay buried against his neck and she breathed in his scent and savored the feel of him against her.

"I love you, Sedona Stewart," he murmured, and she felt him press a lingering kiss against her hair. "I know you're scared by what I do for a living, so I made some decisions."

Sedona felt as if her heart had stopped beating. She lifted her head to gaze down at him, searching his dark eyes. He loved her? He'd made some decisions? She held her breath.

"I'm requesting a transfer to the Top Gun school as an instructor." He smiled at her. "Any combat flight I do will be strictly educational."

"Oh, my God…" His features blurred as the tears that had threatened finally spilled over. She swiped at them with one hand. "Angel, you don't have to do this…"

"Shh. Don't you get it? I *want* to." He ran a hand over her hair. "I'm crazy about you. I want you in my life and besides, it's way past time I settled down." He used his thumbs to wipe the tears from her cheeks, and then cradled her face in his hands, searching her eyes. "That is, if you'll have me, *mina*."

Sedona gave a choked sob. "*Have you?* Are you kidding? I love you so much, Angel Torres." Her voice was husky with emotion. "I think I have since I first saw you. And when I knew you were up there, in that jet… I've never been so afraid in my entire life. I just—I just—"

He frowned. "What?"

She laughed self-consciously. "I just can't believe you really love me. I can't get used to hearing you say it…"

Angel laughed and drew her down. "I love you," he growled, nuzzling her neck. "I love you."

And then his lips slanted across hers, claiming her with a fierceness that told her how much he wanted her. He buried his hands in her hair as he deepened the kiss, sweeping his tongue against hers and drawing a soft moan from her. She had one palm pressed against his chest and could feel the heavy beat of his heart. Her own quickened in response.

After several long moments, she pushed away. She was breathless and slightly dizzy from the intensity of his kiss. She braced herself over him and gazed down into his eyes. They smoldered with heat, and something else. Something that caused her heart to trip unsteadily and then swell within her chest.

She cupped his jaw, shadowed with stubble, and stroked her hand tenderly along his cheek. He smiled, turned his face into her hand and pressed a fervent kiss against her palm.

"Stay with me tonight," he whispered. He shifted his weight to one side of the narrow hospital bed. "Here, there's more than enough room. I know you don't want to go back to the hotel, and I don't want you to, either."

"Angel…" She hesitated. "Of course I want to, but what if I bump your leg? Hurt you? Besides, I'm sure there's some kind of hospital rule against overnight guests."

Angel chuckled and drew her down until she was curled against his side with her head resting on his shoulder. "It's the middle of the night and there are only two nurses on duty. Nobody is going to come in tonight," he murmured against her temple, "and even if they did, I think it's safe to say they wouldn't bother us."

Using her feet, Sedona shucked her shoes and stretched out on the narrow mattress next to Angel, careful not to disturb his injured leg. She could hear the strong, reassuring thump of his heart, feel the hard warmth of his body next to her own, and in that moment was so profoundly grateful for both, she wanted to weep.

"I was in the control tower when your distress call came in," she said quietly, tracing a pattern on his chest with her finger.

"Ah, *mina*…I'm sorry."

"I was so frightened. I was so sure you'd be killed, and I'd never get the chance to tell you how much I love you, or that I didn't mean those awful things I said to you the other day after you took me up in the Coyote." She shivered and burrowed closer. "But as scary as it all was, it wasn't nearly as frightening as the thought of going through the rest of my life without you."

His arm tightened around her. "Don't think about it anymore. It's over and we're both here. Together. That's the important thing."

"They've arrested Lieutenant Palmer in connection with the sabotage. There will be an inquest."

"I know. I spoke briefly with Captain Dawson before they brought me into surgery. After he chewed my ass for not ejecting sooner, that is." He gave a snort of disbelief. "I'd have never guessed Palmer carried so much resentment and anger."

Sedona lifted her head to look at Angel, and used her fingers to smooth the frown between his brows. "I guess you never really know what goes on inside another person's head. Or their heart."

Angel brushed a tendril of hair back from her face. "I guess not. I'll try and make sure you're never in any doubt about what's in my heart." He pressed another kiss against her forehead. "The good news is that it's over. Once all the jets are checked over and cleared, the navy can get them back in the air where they belong. It's over, *mina.*"

"Thank God for that," Sedona breathed fervently. "Your last test flight was too close a call for me." She yawned, suddenly overcome by fatigue.

"Let's get some sleep," Angel said, and tipped her face up for a brief, hard kiss.

"Mmm," she said as she sighed, smiling at him. "I *am* tired, but it's probably nothing compared to how you must feel. You've had quite a day."

Angel shook his head. "As bad as it was, it could have been a lot worse. You won't hear any complaints from me."

"I should probably leave." She burrowed deeper into his warmth. "You need your rest, and I can't help feeling I shouldn't be here."

Angel put a finger under her chin and tipped her face up to look into her eyes. "You're here with me, *mina,* which is exactly where you should be."

As Sedona searched his eyes and saw the tenderness reflected there, she knew he was right. She relaxed against him. He was safe, and they were together. Beyond that, nothing else seemed important. Her arm tightened briefly around him as she let sleep slowly overtake her. She'd made a mistake by shutting him out of her life once; she wouldn't do it again.

17

Sedona sat at her desk and fingered the photos in her hands. There was the photo of Angel in her bed, lounging back against the pillows with nothing more than a towel wrapped around his lean hips. He had one arm bent behind his head as he grinned into the camera. She traced a fingertip over the photo. From his bulging biceps to his taut, washboard stomach, he looked altogether delicious.

The second picture was of the two of them, faces close together as he snapped the picture from arm's length. Her face was flushed and laughing. She looked like a woman in love.

Turning the photos facedown on the desk, she pressed her hands against her eyes. She couldn't do it. There was no way she could use the intimate photos of Angel to expose the Membership and their disgusting practices.

"Hey, you okay?"

Sedona pulled her hands away from her face and looked up. She'd arrived back at her office two days earlier and had contacted Agent Denton at the Defense Criminal Investigative Service. She told him she'd had a change of heart regarding the Membership, and together they'd worked out a plan to fully expose the club and end their sordid promotion tactics. All she had to do now was confront the members.

Sedona was done hiding; this would be the first courageous step she took toward her new life.

She was scared to death.

She looked up at Agent Denton. "I really hope I'm doing the right thing."

Denton was old enough to be her father, but there was nothing remotely fatherly about him. He looked tough and uncompromising, and she wondered just what experiences he'd been through to carve such deep lines into his face.

"No waffling allowed, Miss Stewart. Either you're committed to this, or you're not. You've already turned in your resignation. What do you have to lose?"

Nothing, except my self-respect. She just hoped Angel never discovered how she'd used the photos they'd taken. He hated deception. He'd be furious if he knew. Not that there was any chance of that. He wasn't due back from Lemoore for another three days, and he wouldn't be returning to the flight line at Aerospace International until after his ankle had fully mended. By then, this would be nothing more than a distant memory.

"You're right," she acknowledged, looking at Agent Denton. "I have nothing to lose. So…let's do this thing."

"Agent Bates checked your wire?"

"Yes. She said it's good to go." Sedona touched a hand to her midsection where Agent Bates had used first-aid tape to fasten a hidden recording device against her skin. "Hopefully she's a little smarter than I am, and won't forget to turn the thing on."

A spark of amusement lit Agent Denton's hard eyes. "It's already recording." He checked his watch. "We have five minutes. Ready to go?"

Sedona drew in a deep breath in an effort to calm her nerves. "Yes, ready."

"Okay, now stop second-guessing yourself. You'll be fine. Sullivan expects you to be triumphant, even a little aggressive, so don't be afraid to work it. Throw those photos in his face and demand the promotion they promised you. Right?"

She wiped her damp palms on her skirt. "Right."

"You told Mike Sullivan to get the members together in the F/A-44 conference room?"

Sedona scooped the photos up from the desk. "Yes. It's sort of out of the way, and offers more privacy than the other conference rooms. I—I refused to meet them in the men's bathroom."

Agent Denton checked his watch once more. "You should be on your way. I'll be listening right here, and Agent Bates should already be in position across the hall from the conference room." He compressed his lips in what Sedona guessed was his form of an encouraging smile. "You can do this."

Leaving her office, Sedona walked briskly past Linda, who practically leaped from her chair upon seeing her. "Oh, Sedona, I have a message for you."

Sedona held up her hand to stop the other woman. "Sorry, Linda. I'm late for a meeting. I'll catch you on my way back."

Yeah, right. The only thing she was going to catch was a train home. Ignoring Linda's look of dismay, she continued through the hallways, skirting the manufacturing bays until she reached the conference room where the Membership had agreed to meet.

Sedona paused outside the door to collect herself. She glanced quickly over her shoulder at the door across the hall, but it remained firmly closed. The corridor behind her was empty. Before she could change her mind, she pushed open the conference-room door and stepped inside.

ANGEL TRIED TO curb his impatience. "Did you give her my message?"

It was clear the plump administrative assistant was completely flustered by his presence, but he didn't care. He was anxious to see Sedona, and missing her by mere minutes hadn't improved his disposition.

"I tried to give her your message, sir, but she was in such a hurry."

"Okay." He rubbed a hand over his face. He'd pushed himself hard over the past week, both physically and mentally, to get released from the hospital and complete his statements to the investigators. He'd been overjoyed when the lead investigator finally seemed satisfied with his report and said he was free to go home. He'd managed to catch an early flight out of Lemoore that morning. From Logan Airport, he'd caught a taxi directly to Aerospace International. "Can you tell me where the meeting is? I really need to see her."

The woman looked slightly dazed as she stared up at him. "I'm not sure…sir. There was no meeting scheduled on the calendar. It looked like she was headed to the manufacturing bay."

Angel gave her a quick smile and swung away on his crutches. "Thanks, I know where she's going."

The F/A-44 conference room, located on the far side of the manufacturing bay. Whatever meeting she was attending, he'd just slip into the back of the room and wait for her to finish. It had been three days since he'd seen her and he was going crazy.

Bracing himself on his crutches, he swung silently through the corridors. Since he was officially off duty, and out of consideration for the bulky cast on his foot, he wore a pair of loose cargo pants and a T-shirt. He was grateful he didn't run into anyone he knew.

As he neared the conference room, voices drifted toward him through the partially open door. He was just debating poking his head in to see if Sedona was there, when the sound of his name being spoken froze him where he stood.

"So you're telling me you were getting it on with Lieutenant Commander Torres the entire time we were out at

Lemoore? Well, hell, Stewart, that's all you needed to tell me. Why make me feel like it was a personal rejection?"

What in hell? That was Larson's voice.

"Because if Lieutenant Torres even suspected my true reasons for being with him, it would have been all over. But he didn't suspect a thing, and I have the proof."

Angel recoiled.

"Okay, let's see this 'proof.'"

Angel thought he recognized this new voice. It sounded like Mike "Hound Dog" Sullivan, one of the lead engineers for the Coyote program. Angel didn't know the man well, but he was familiar with Sullivan's reputation.

"Oh," Sedona crooned, "you'll get your proof." Her voice hardened. "Just as soon as I get my guarantee that the next promotion is mine. I mean, that was the deal, right? I screw some guy's brains out while I'm on business travel, bring back proof of the deed, and you guys make sure I get promoted. So I ask again—where's my guarantee?"

Angel heard several male voices as they talked in raised, excited tones. He stood immobile, stunned. He felt like someone had just kicked him in the gut. Hard.

"Okay, Stewart," Sullivan drawled. "Show us the proof, and if it's like you say it is, then sure…the next promotion is yours."

"Well, then, here you go, boys."

There was the sound of paper being slapped down on the surface of the table, and then several long, low whistles.

"I'm impressed, Stewart," Larson said. "You really *were* banging Torres. These photos are…inspiring."

"Yes, I think so, too. Now, about that promotion…"

Angel turned away, sickened. Part of him wanted to shove his way into that conference room and confront Sedona. He wanted to throw the deceitful little witch over his shoulder and carry her to some private place where he could wring the truth out of her lying lips; she belonged to him.

Another part of him wanted to go in there and smash a fist into Larson's face. Anything to wipe off the smug expression he knew he'd find there.

Instead, he turned away. He didn't know if he had the stomach to face Sedona, not when he'd been so certain what they'd shared had been special…magical.

She'd told him about the Membership, but she'd left out the fact that she was campaigning for her own position within the club. To find out she'd used him to satisfy some twisted, sexual prerequisite to advance her career was mind-boggling. He felt defiled.

Without waiting to hear more, he retraced his steps as swiftly as his crutches would allow. He was an idiot, a total idiot to have been so completely duped by her. To think, he'd fallen hook, line and sinker for her sweet, sultry come-ons. He didn't know if he'd ever manage to accept that she'd seduced him in order to get ahead.

He thumped his way along the corridor, remembering how she'd protested his taking the pictures. He'd played right into her hands, thinking he was helping her with her artwork. At the time, he'd have done anything she wanted, given her anything. Christ, he'd practically begged her to take the photos.

He snorted derisively. After he'd taken her up in the Coyote, she'd told him what they had together was nothing more than lust, but he'd refused to believe it. He'd been so convinced their relationship was the real thing, but in reality, it had been nothing but a cheap knockoff. She'd fooled him once. It wouldn't happen again.

18

"WELL, I GUESS that does it." Sedona closed the top of the cardboard box that held the last of her personal items, and ran a strip of packing tape along the seam, pressing it into place with her fingers. She looked up at Agent Denton. "Would you mind walking out to the parking lot with me? Since The Incident, I'm pretty much persona non grata around here."

Agent Denton scooped up the larger of the two boxes. "It couldn't have gone any better," he commented. "We got everything on tape, and Mike Sullivan gave us the names of the members on the Promotion Selection Board. I think it's fair to say none of them will ever get another job with the Department of Defense."

It had been three days since Sedona had confronted the members. Immediately following their "meeting," federal agents had converged on the conference room and arrested each of the men on illegal labor practices and sexual-harassment charges.

Sedona was just glad it was finally over. She didn't even regret leaving the agency. She hefted the remaining box into her arms and followed Agent Denton out of the office.

Nope, not a single regret.

She'd been given a second chance and she wasn't about to screw it up. This time, she'd find a job doing what she loved. She'd already emailed samples of her drawings to a magazine that specialized in military art. The executive editor had expressed interest in her drawings of the Coyote jets, and had indicated they were in the market for a senior illustrator.

Beyond that, the only thing she wanted was to be with the man she loved. She'd spent the past five years committed to her career, but now she'd been given a second chance and there was no way she was going to blow it.

Angel was due to fly in from Lemoore that evening. It felt like forever since she'd seen him. She'd tried calling him numerous times, but hadn't been able to get through. She told herself it was the time difference. That, and he was still providing information to the Coyote investigation team.

But there was a part of her that was hurt that he hadn't returned any of her calls, or bothered to let her know exactly when his flight was due in. With his broken ankle, he'd need somebody to pick him up at the airport and drive him home.

If not her, then who?

As she followed Agent Denton out of the office, she became aware of those who came to stand in the doorways of their offices and cubicles to watch her leave. She hadn't made any true friends during her five years with the agency, and now couldn't bring herself to look at her former coworkers. As she passed Linda, however, she thought she heard the other woman whisper, "Good job."

In the parking lot, she opened her trunk and waited while Agent Denton deposited his box inside, before sliding her own in beside it. She slammed the trunk closed, and turned to face him, shoving her hands into her pockets.

"Well, I guess I'll be seeing you around," she said, squinting at him in the bright sunlight.

"You did the right thing, Sedona."

She scuffed the ground with her toe and then shrugged. "I know. I mean, what they were doing was wrong. Still…"

"What?"

"Once the press gets wind of what happened, their careers will be over. They'll never get another job, either in government or private industry. Not to mention what it will do to their marriages."

Agent Denton didn't smile. "They brought it on themselves." He glanced at his watch. "I have to get going. One of our people will be in touch with you. Maybe I'll see you in court, okay?"

"Okay." She took his proffered hand. "Thank you for everything, Agent Denton."

"Good luck, Sedona."

She watched as he climbed into his car and drove away before glancing at her watch. It was only midmorning. Had Angel already left for the airport, or was he still at the Lemoore hotel? She pulled her cell phone out and punched in his number, frustrated when there was no answer.

She stood, undecided for a moment, unable to deny the growing sense that she was being ignored.

Or dumped.

But why? When she had left Angel at the hospital, he'd been so determined to get released, to wrap up the loose ends of the investigation and get on the next flight east to be with her. He'd kissed her thoroughly, had told her he loved her. Not once, but several times. And when she'd finally had to leave, she could tell he didn't want her to go.

She tapped her keys against the palm of her hand. If Angel wasn't going to let her know what was going on, she would have to find out on her own. She stared across the parking lot to the building where the navy test pilots maintained their own offices. She debated with herself for maybe a second before she set off in the direction of the building.

She found two of the pilots in the office, preparing their flight plans for the afternoon. One of them looked up, surprised, when she entered.

"Miss Stewart." He rose to his feet. "Can I help you?"

"Yes—" she glanced at his name badge "—Lieutenant Brodie. I'm here about Lieutenant Torres."

She paused, and he looked at her expectantly. "What about him?"

"Well, it's just that he's due to fly into Logan this afternoon, and I was supposed to meet his flight, only I lost his flight number and I can't seem to reach him. I was wondering if perhaps he contacted either you or one of the other guys with his travel plans. I'd hate to miss his flight and have him waiting at the airport for me."

The pilot looked dismayed. "Miss Stewart, I thought you knew...I mean..."

"What? Thought I knew what?"

The man made a helpless gesture. "Diablo is gone."

"What?" Fear gripped her, making her knees go weak. "What do you mean, *gone?*" She refused to believe it. Aside from his injured ankle, Angel had been fine the last time she'd seen him. The doctors had assured her he would make a full recovery.

The lieutenant glanced around desperately, clearly wishing he was anywhere else. "I mean he's been reassigned. He came back two days ago, but didn't stay. He just packed up his gear and said he was going back to the West Coast."

Sedona stared at the man, unable to believe what he was saying. "No, you must be mistaken, Angel wasn't even due to come back until today."

Lieutenant Brodie looked down at the paperwork on his desk and shuffled it, avoiding her eyes. "He came back two days ago. I thought you knew…he said he was going over to your office. He wasn't gone long, and he came back pretty pissed off." He shrugged and looked chagrined. "I figured you two had words."

"Words?" Sedona stared, bemused. "I never even *saw* him—are you sure it was two days ago? I mean, what time was it? How could I have missed him? Why didn't he wait, or try to find me?"

"I don't know, except he was pretty psyched to be back early. I think he wanted to surprise you."

And then it hit her.

If he had come back two days ago, the only possible reason he could have for leaving without contacting her and for refusing to either accept or return any of her calls, was that he'd somehow discovered her confrontation with the Membership, or how she'd used the photos of him to entrap them.

"Oh, God," she breathed. "I need to find him. Did he leave a forwarding address? Anything?"

The pilot shrugged. "Maybe, but not with me. You might want to check with his XO."

"Okay. Where do I find the XO?"

"He's located down in Newport. We only ever see him when it's time for our evaluations, or when we're due to transfer to a new assignment." The lieutenant opened a desk drawer and took out a small planner. He flipped it open and scribbled a number on a sheet of paper, tearing it off and handing it to her. "Here's his phone number. If anyone knows where Diablo is, it's him."

Sedona took the paper, feeling dazed. She walked to the parking lot, then sat in her car and stared blindly at the phone number, unable to accept that he'd come and gone without even giving her the opportunity to explain what had happened. He'd said he loved her, but apparently not enough to trust her.

Before she could chicken out and change her mind, she pulled her cell phone from her bag and punched in the XO's number.

"Commander Schiffer." The voice was deep and slightly distracted, as if the commander had other, more important things to do.

"Sir, I was told you could tell me how to reach Lieutenant Commander Angel Torres."

There was a brief silence. "I'm sorry...who is this?"

"My name is Sedona Stewart. I worked on the recent Coyote investigation with Lieutenant Commander Torres." She swallowed against the small white lie she was about to utter. "He...still owes me several flight-test reports, but I can't seem to reach him. I understand he's been reassigned to Lemoore Naval Air Station."

"Yes, actually, he has. Sedona Stewart, you said?" There was a brief pause, as if he was looking through some paperwork. "Ah, yes. I see you were the lead engineer for the engine-calibration tests during the investigation. You say he owes you several reports? I was told he had completed his reports."

"These are just some small, er, calculations that we somehow overlooked during our initial inspections."

"I understand." There was doubt in the commander's voice. "Lieutenant Torres requested reassignment to Lemoore, and considering he is currently unable to perform his duties as a flight-test pilot, the navy has agreed to assign him as an instructor at the Top Gun school."

"Oh." Sedona couldn't keep the shock out of her voice. "The decision was...very sudden, wasn't it?"

"Yes, it was. But it made sense to send Lieutenant Torres where he could do the most good. I don't yet have a duty number for him, but I do have his cell phone, which I can give you."

Damn. She didn't need his cell phone number; she already had that. She also knew he wouldn't answer if he thought it was her calling.

"Actually, Commander Schiffer, I'm going back out to Lemoore to, uh, meet with the investigation team one last time. I could always meet Lieutenant Torres there and pick up the reports I need. That is, if I knew where at Lemoore he was located."

There was a brief silence. "To the best of my knowledge, Miss Stewart, he's residing at the Bachelor Officers' Quarters until he can locate appropriate housing. He'll be working out of the Top Gun training facilities at Lemoore. I'm sorry, but that's the best I can tell you."

"Of course. Thank you very much, Commander."

"Would you like me to contact Lieutenant Torres and let him know you're coming?"

"Oh. No, thank you. I'm not exactly sure when I'll be leaving, so I'll just contact him when I get there. Thank you again for your help."

She closed her cell phone, tilted her head back against the seat and blew out her breath in frustration. It seemed there was no other option; she would be on the next available flight to Lemoore.

SEDONA STOOD BEFORE the closed door of the small apartment where Angel was staying. It was part of a complex of apartments built to quarter unmarried or unaccompanied naval officers.

She had arrived in California just hours earlier and had driven straight to Lemoore. All she'd brought with her was a change of clothes, stuffed into an oversize shoulder bag.

Was he home? What would she do if he wasn't? And what would his reaction be if he found her waiting on his doorstep like some forlorn kitten? She drew in a fortifying breath. If he didn't answer the door, she would simply go and check into a nearby hotel and return when he was home. But there was no way she was leaving without confronting him. He owed her the courtesy of telling her to her face that he was no longer interested.

Before she could change her mind, she raised her fist and knocked on the door. For one long, agonizing minute she thought he might not be in, and then the door swung open and he was standing there.

He looked disheveled and tired, with dark stubble on his jaw and lines of fatigue etched around his eyes and mouth. He wore a T-shirt and a pair of shorts, and except for the white cast on his foot, his hard-muscled, bronzed legs were bare.

In the brief instant before his expression changed, Sedona swore she saw pleasure in his dark eyes, and it gave her hope. Then his expression changed and his brows drew together. He raked her with one brief, contemptuous look before he swung away and turned back into the apartment, leaving the door open.

She followed him in.

"What are you doing here?" he growled, using one crutch to shove a duffel bag out of the way.

"I—I came because I had to," she said, glancing around the tiny room. It was bare of anything warm or personal, containing only military-issue furniture and a small television that sat on the counter separating the living area from the tiny galley kitchen. "I think you may have gotten the wrong impression about what happened in that conference room the other day." She paused, but he refused to turn and look at her. "Angel, why didn't you tell me you were coming in early? And, for God's sake, why did you leave without letting me explain?"

He swung to face her then and Sedona recoiled at the raw fury she saw on his face. "Explain what, Sedona? How you manipulated me? How you—what were the words you used—spent the entire time screwing some guy's brains out?" His hands fisted on the crutches. "If all you wanted was some stud to help you get your promotion, why'd you have to pick me? We were on a naval base, sweetheart, with squadrons of horny guys, I'm sure any one of them would have loved to play the porn star for you. In fact, Larson seemed like a prime candidate."

Sedona gasped. "Is that what you think?"

"What else am I supposed to think?" He took a step toward her, his expression harsh. "From the first night at Lemoore, you made it perfectly clear you wanted to have sex with me. I actually thought— Christ!" He scrubbed a hand over his face and turned away again. "Just get the hell out of here. I'm not interested in any more of your lies. Go on." He turned his face partially toward her, and his voice was little more than a snarl. "Get out."

Sedona flung her arms out. "So that's it? You tell me to just get out, and I do it, and that's the end?"

"What did you expect?"

"Well, jeez, I don't know." Her voice was rising and she knew she sounded more than a little hysterical, but she couldn't seem to help herself. "I expected a little more than a 'don't let the door hit you on the ass on your way out,' though. I guess I came all the way out here expecting you'd at least let me explain. Let me tell you that what you *think* you heard in that conference room wasn't real."

"It sounded pretty goddamn real to me."

"It wasn't! I swear to you, Angel, it wasn't real. When I told you about the Membership and how they were illegally promoting people—men—based on their sexual exploits, I'd already decided I wanted nothing to do with them. It wasn't until—" To her horror, her voice broke. "It wasn't until you called me a coward that I decided I needed to do something about it. I already had the photos we'd taken that morning…" Her voice trailed off, grew small. "I—I was part of a sting operation to expose them. That's all."

"And you just thought you could use compromising pictures of me to really stick it to them, is that it?"

Sedona stared at him, and the full awareness of his disappointment hit her. She could see it in his eyes, in the weary sag of his shoulders as he faced her.

"Angel, listen to me." She reached a hand toward him, but when he flinched, she jerked it back. "Okay. You're right, I did want to sleep with you, but it had nothing to do with the Membership or proving anything to those men."

A muscle in his jaw worked convulsively, but he didn't say anything, just continued to watch her. The fact that he didn't physically throw her out gave her courage.

"I wasn't lying when I told you I had a—a thing for you from the first time I saw you," she hurried on. "But my being with you had nothing to do with the Membership and their disgusting promotion requirements." She paused and looked away, unable to meet his eyes. "You see, I'd fantasized about being with you, but…" She allowed her gaze to drift back to his.

Angel's attention was riveted on her, but his voice was cool. "I'm listening."

Sedona drew in a deep breath. "But I never thought it would ever amount to anything more than that—a fantasy. The reality of being with you was like a dream come true. I was glad to finally tell you about the Membership and why Larson kept harassing me. It was a relief for you to know the truth."

Angel snorted. "You just conveniently left out the part where you planned to use our relationship to nail them, huh?"

"*No!* Of course not." Sedona laid a hand on his arm, and this time he didn't pull away. "I never wanted to hurt you, but the photos were the only way I could get the Membership to believe I wanted to be part of their club. I should have told you what I intended to do. I wish to God I had." She gave a small laugh. "Regardless of the Membership, I would have given my right arm to be with you, even though I knew it couldn't last."

Angel frowned. "Why couldn't it last?"

"Well, look at you. You're every woman's fantasy, while I'm—well, look at me." She smiled ruefully.

Angel took a step toward her. "I'm looking, *mina.*"

Sedona's breath caught at the expression in his eyes, but she determinedly forged ahead. "The entire time we were together, I knew the day would come when you'd fly off to bluer skies. I just wanted as much of you as I could get in the short time we had. I was glad we took those pictures. I was so sure that eventually, they'd be all I had of you."

"Sedona—"

"No, please. Let me finish." She stared up at him, letting her love for him show in her eyes. "When you were up in that jet, and I thought I might lose you forever, I realized how much I loved you. I still do. So if you want to end what we have together, let it be because you don't have feelings for me, but not because you think I used you."

To her utter amazement, Angel leaned his weight on his crutches and reached out to cup her face in his hands. "You think I don't have feelings for you, *mina?*" There was no laughter in his eyes. "When I heard you in that conference room, reducing our relationship to the equivalent of a quick screw in a dark alley, I couldn't believe I'd misread you so completely. I freaked."

Sedona covered his hands with her own, pressing her cheek against his palm. "I wish you had let me explain. You see, I was wearing a wire. There was a federal agent hiding in the room right across the hall, and three more waiting for those men to incriminate themselves before they could move in and arrest them."

Angel stroked a thumb over her cheek, and there was both regret and relief in his eyes. "I'm sorry, *mina*. I didn't want to hear that what we'd had was nothing but sex. You see…I fell in love with you, and I didn't think I'd have the strength or courage to see you, knowing you didn't feel the same way."

"So you left."

"Yes."

"But now you know…"

"I know I can't keep flying solo, *mina*. I need a copilot, a navigator. But, more than that, I need someone to keep me grounded."

Tears blurred Sedona's vision as she hugged him fiercely. "I love you so much, Angel. And I'm so sorry I didn't tell you about my plan to expose the Membership."

"Shh. It's okay. I should have trusted you. I shouldn't have left without at least talking with you first."

Looking up at him, she ran a hand across his stubbled cheek. "You look like hell."

Angel laughed, and this time there was real humor in his eyes. "I haven't eaten or slept since I first got on that plane to Boston. First because I couldn't wait to see you again, and then because…because I thought I'd lost you." His hands where they cupped her face tightened, and he ran a thumb over her lips.

"You haven't lost me." She searched his eyes, letting him see the truth. "In fact, I'm sort of between jobs right now, so if you know of a place where I could hang out for a while…?"

"What happened to your job?"

Sedona smiled into his eyes. "I handed in my resignation before we left for Lemoore. I knew I couldn't continue to work for the agency, but agreed to complete the inspection of the jets before I left."

"So there was never going to be any promotion for you, whether you brought back photos, or not."

"No," she agreed.

"Then, yes, I can think of a place for you to stay." He tossed away one crutch and used his free arm to pull her in close. "Right here with me. I love you, Sedona Stewart. I also know that the senior brass here at Lemoore were pretty impressed with the work you did while you were here. I'd be willing to bet they might have a job for you, if you're interested."

"Actually," she confessed shyly, "I applied for a position as senior illustrator for a military magazine."

Angel pulled back just a little and looked at her with admiration. "I'm impressed."

Sedona smiled. "I'm just taking the advice someone once gave me, and grabbing my dreams with both hands. All of my dreams." She reached up to run her fingers over his firm jaw. "I've got you now, flyboy, and I'm not about to let you go."

Angel smiled at her, a seductive slanting of his lips that caused a slow, melting warmth to spread along her veins. "You don't have to, *mina*. This flyboy has fallen, and hard."

He buried his hands in the mass of her hair and tipped her face up, and Sedona's lashes drifted closed as his lips claimed hers in a kiss that was both intensely sweet and searingly hot.

He pulled away and gazed down at her, and Sedona saw the love reflected there.

"So," she said huskily, running a hand over his hard chest. "Are you going to give me a tour of your new place, or what?"

He smiled into her eyes, his eyes full of promise. "Well, this arrangement is only until I can find a permanent place to live. A place to settle down and raise a family. The only room here you haven't seen is the bedroom. Of course, I can show that to you, if you insist."

"Oh," Sedona murmured against his lips, "I insist. I really, really insist you show me."

And he did just that.

* * * * *

SPECIAL EDITION

Life, Love and Family

NEW YORK TIMES BESTSELLING AUTHOR

DIANA PALMER

brings you a brand-new Western romance featuring characters that readers have come to love—the Brannt family from Harlequin HQN's bestselling book *WYOMING TOUGH*.

Cort Brannt, Texas rancher through and through, is about to unexpectedly get lassoed by love!

THE RANCHER

Available November 13 wherever books are sold!

Also available as a 2-in-1
THE RANCHER & HEART OF STONE

HARLEQUIN®

ROMANTIC

SUSPENSE

Get your heart racing this holiday season with double the pulse-pounding action.

Christmas Confidential

Featuring

Holiday Protector by **Marilyn Pappano**

Miri Duncan doesn't care that it's almost Christmas. She's got bigger worries on her mind. But surviving the trip to Georgia from Texas is going to be her biggest challenge. Days in a car with the man who broke her heart and helped send her to prison—private investigator Dean Montgomery.

A Chance Reunion by **Linda Conrad**

When the husband Elana Novak left behind five years ago shows up in her new California home she knows danger is coming her way. To protect the man she is quickly falling for Elana must convince private investigator Gage Chance that she is a different person. But Gage isn't about to let her walk away…even with the bad guys right on their heels.

Available December 2012 wherever books are sold!

www.Harlequin.com

HRS27801

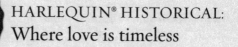

Harlequin® Desire is proud to present

ONE WINTER'S NIGHT

by New York Times *bestselling author*

Brenda Jackson

Alpha Blake tightened her coat around her. Not only would she be late for her appointment with Riley Westmoreland, but because of her flat tire they would have to change the location of the meeting and Mr. Westmoreland would be the one driving her there. This was totally embarrassing, when she had been trying to make a good impression.

She turned up the heat in her car. Even with a steady stream of hot air coming in through the car vents, she still felt cold, too cold, and wondered if she would ever get used to the Denver weather. Of course, it was too late to think about that now. It was her first winter here, and she didn't have any choice but to grin and bear it. When she'd moved, she'd felt that getting as far away from Daytona Beach as she could was essential to her peace of mind. But who in her right mind would prefer blistering-cold Denver to sunny Daytona Beach? Only a person wanting to start a new life and put a painful past behind her.

Her attention was snagged by an SUV that pulled off the road and parked in front of her. The door swung open and long denim-clad, boot-wearing legs appeared before a man stepped out of the truck. She met his gaze through the windshield and forgot to breathe. Walking toward her car was a man who was so dangerously masculine, so heart-stoppingly virile, that her brain went momentarily numb.

He was tall, and the Stetson on his head made him appear taller. But his height was secondary to the sharp

HDEXP1212

handsomeness of his features.

Her gaze slid all over him as he moved his long limbs toward her vehicle in a walk that was so agile and self-assured, she envied the confidence he exuded with every step. Her breasts suddenly peaked, and she could actually feel blood rushing through her veins.

She didn't have to guess who this man was.

He was Riley Westmoreland.

Find out if Riley and Alpha mix business with pleasure in

ONE WINTER'S NIGHT

by Brenda Jackson

Available December 2012

Only from Harlequin® Desire